of mysteries s...
Chaloner advent...
lives in Wales with her h...

Also by Susanna Gregory

The Matthew Bartholomew series

A Plague on Both Your Houses
An Unholy Alliance
A Bone of Contention
A Deadly Brew
A Wicked Deed
A Masterly Murder
An Order for Death
A Summer of Discontent
A Killer in Winter
The Hand of Justice
The Mark of a Murderer
The Tarnished Chalice
To Kill or Cure
The Devil's Disciples
A Vein of Deceit
The Killer of Pilgrims
Mystery in the Minster
Murder by the Book
The Lost Abbot
Death of a Scholar
A Poisonous Plot
A Grave Concern
The Habit of Murder

The Thomas Chaloner series

A Conspiracy of Violence
Blood on the Strand
The Butcher of Smithfield
The Westminster Poisoner
A Murder on London Bridge
The Body in the Thames
The Piccadilly Plot
Death in St James's Park
Murder on High Holborn
The Cheapside Corpse
The Chelsea Strangler
The Executioner of St Paul's

SUSANNA GREGORY

A GRAVE CONCERN

THE TWENTY-SECOND CHRONICLE OF
MATTHEW BARTHOLOMEW

sphere

SPHERE

First published in Great Britain in 2016 by Sphere
This paperback edition published in 2017 by Sphere

1 3 5 7 9 10 8 6 4 2

A CIP catalogue record for this book
is available from the British Library.

ISBN 978-0-7515-4980-5

Typeset in New Baskerville by Palimpsest Book Production Limited,
Falkirk, Stirlingshire
Printed and bound in Great Britain by Clays Ltd, St Ives plc

Papers used by Sphere are from well-managed forests
and other responsible sources.

MIX
Paper from
responsible sources
FSC® C104740

Sphere
An imprint of
Little, Brown Book Group
Carmelite House
50 Victoria Embankment
London EC4Y 0DZ

An Hachette UK Company
www.hachette.co.uk

www.littlebrown.co.uk

For Ethel May Pritchard

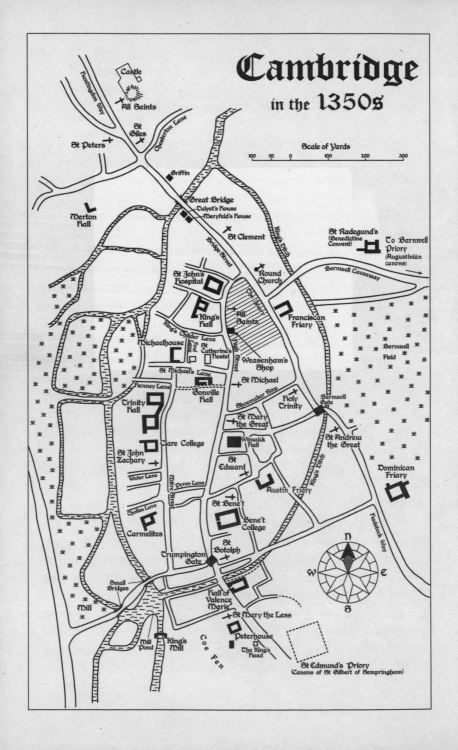

PROLOGUE

John Dallingridge did not know who had poisoned him. He only knew he would not live to be inaugurated as a Fellow in the University at Cambridge that October, something he had wanted to do ever since childhood. He sighed at the pity of it all. He would have made an excellent teacher – his students would have hung on his every word, his scholarly writings would have set the academic world afire, and his colleagues would have delighted in his mental agility.

He shifted restlessly in the bed. When he had first been afflicted by the griping pains in his innards, he had assumed that bad meat was responsible. He had been taken ill on Lammas Day after a feast at the castle, where the steward was notorious for making reckless economies. But as the days had turned into weeks and his agonies had only intensified, he began to realise that this was no innocent sickness – that someone had done him deliberate and serious harm.

The toxin was slow-acting, which gave him plenty of time to ponder the culprit's identity. Unfortunately, almost everyone he knew had been at the feast, and nearly all of them had set greedy eyes on the fortune he had accumulated – and those who were not interested in his money were jealous of his formidable intellect or his influential connections. Yet try as he might, he had failed to determine which of them had resorted to murder.

He had woken that morning knowing his end was near. His friends and family sensed it, too, and began to gather, jostling with each other to spend a few moments at his side. They murmured impassioned promises to pray for his soul, each trying to outdo the one in front. Dallingridge grimaced. They were not there out of concern for his spiritual well-being – they wanted to make sure he had not forgotten to include them in his will.

The grimace turned into a bleak smile of satisfaction, for they were all going to be disappointed. He was damned if the killer was going to benefit from the crime, and as he did not know the identity of the culprit, he had decided to disinherit everyone. Instead, every last penny of his enormous wealth would be spent on his tomb, a creation so magnificent that it would be the talk of the country. It was to be in Cambridge, because if the University he had longed to join could not have him in life, then it could house him in death.

The mason he had commissioned to build the monument was among the shuffling throng at the far end of the room, so Dallingridge beckoned him forward. His name was John Petit, a short, squat man, whose thick fingers did not look capable of producing the delicate sculptures for which he was famous.

'Are you sure you understand my exact instructions?' Dallingridge asked softly, anxious because so much depended on the mason doing as he was told. 'You will carve a good likeness of me, and set it on a canopied marble tomb-chest in Cambridge's biggest and most prestigious church, just as we discussed?'

Petit nodded reassuringly. 'It is all arranged. The scholars were more than happy to grant your request, especially once they learned the size of the donation that went with it.'

'Good.' Dallingridge closed his eyes to indicate the conversation was over, and the mason tiptoed away. Then an unpleasant thought occurred to him.

Business had been brisk for tomb-builders immediately

after the plague, as they had been inundated with requests for memorials to lost loved ones. But that was nearly ten years ago, and the backlog had been cleared. Good commissions were now few and far between, because such undertakings were expensive and only the very rich could afford them. Petit had been idly kicking his heels for the past few months, so had he acquired poison, knowing that an affluent man like Dallingridge would certainly require his services?

Dallingridge experienced a sharp stab of dismay. If so, then he had played directly into his killer's hands. Not only would the monument provide work for Petit and his apprentices, but it would furnish them with an opportunity to advertise their skills in a place that had no resident tomb-makers of its own. New work would flood in, and they would be set for years.

With mounting disquiet, he looked for Petit among the well-wishers again – it was not too late to dispense with his services and appoint another mason. But his eye lit instead on Richard Lakenham, an engraver of funerary brasses, who had been hired to make the six decorative shields that would be affixed to the tomb's sides. Lakenham was poor, so even modest commissions were important to him. Dallingridge gulped. Was Lakenham the culprit then, desperate to earn a few shillings before he and his wife starved?

Lakenham saw Dallingridge looking at him, and started to step forward, to see if he was needed, but Petit grabbed his arm and stopped him – the two men were implacable rivals and hated each other with a passion. Indignantly, Lakenham tried to break free, which resulted in an unseemly scuffle. While the other visitors watched the squabbling pair in silent disapproval, Dallingridge took the opportunity to review his shortlist of suspects for his murder, all of whom were there that day.

First, there were the folk from the castle, including its

most famous prisoner – Sir John Moleyns. Moleyns was a royal favourite, and the King had been outraged when a jury had convicted his old friend of theft, extortion and murder. Eager to win His Majesty's favour, the Sheriff treated Moleyns like an honoured guest, providing him with sumptuous accommodation, the finest food, and the freedom to roam the city as he pleased. All Moleyns had to do in return was promise not to escape. Naturally, he had been at the Lammas Day feast, so had *he* indulged his penchant for unlawful killing, just for the thrill of doing it right under the Sheriff's nose? If so, Dallingridge was sorry. He rather liked Moleyns, who was entertaining, if mercurial, company.

Moleyns was standing with his wife Egidia, a cold, grasping woman, who was resentful that her husband's 'incarceration' meant he could no longer add to the family coffers by stealing and terrorising his neighbours. Also with them was John Inge, Moleyns' lawyer, whom Dallingridge disliked intensely. Inge was sly, secretive and duplicitous, and it was common knowledge that he would do anything for money.

Dallingridge eyed the three of them thoughtfully. Since he had announced that he was dying, they had made it their business to call on him every day, purely in the hope of getting money. Moleyns had been rich, but most of his property was confiscated by the courts, so a legacy would suit him very nicely. Meanwhile, Inge and Egidia hated relying on Moleyns for the occasional hand-out, and longed to be financially independent. Could one of them have killed him, in the hope of acquiring enough cash to tide them over until the King arranged for Moleyns to be released?

In another corner was a young scholar named Will Kolvyle, and the plan had been for him and Dallingridge to enrol in the University together – two Nottingham men side by side. Unfortunately, Kolvyle was jealous of the name Dallingridge had made for himself with his sophisticated understanding of contract law, so had Kolvyle dispensed the poison, lest he should be regarded as second best when they arrived in Cambridge? Dallingridge shifted uneasily. He would not put it past the lad – Kolvyle was egotistical, callous and frighteningly ambitious.

'Lie still,' ordered Barber Cook, the *medicus* who had nursed Dallingridge since the feast. 'You will unbalance your humours if you twist around so, and then you will never recover.'

Dallingridge scowled at him, resenting the assumption that he was a fool who did not know that death was near. He would have preferred a physician to tend him, but Cook had been the first practitioner to offer his services, and Dallingridge had not been well enough to demand someone better. He studied the barber's mean, sharp face and shifty eyes. Perhaps *he* was the culprit. He had, after all, earned a fortune for his ministrations over the last few weeks, and clearly expected to be rewarded further still once his patient was dead.

It was becoming difficult for Dallingridge to see the other eager, hopeful faces, but he knew who was there – friends and family from near and far, servants, neighbours and business associates. Had even one of them come out of affection for him, or were they all hoping to gain something from his imminent demise? And with that question came the knowledge of what he must do – not build a tomb, but donate his whole fortune to the University that was to have been his home. There would be no fine monument to remind future generations of what a great man he had been, but the scholar-priests would pray for his soul, which was all that really mattered.

His mind made up, he tried to call his clerk, but his tongue was suddenly thick and heavy, so all that emerged was an incoherent gurgle. As one, the horde surged forward to gabble more meaningless platitudes, jostling for space at his bedside. He looked at them in despair before his eyes grew too dim to see. Which one had condemned him to this terrible, lingering death? He supposed he would never know.

Cambridge, October 1359

When Sir John Moleyns and his train of guards arrived in Cambridge, it was a beautiful day, and the kindly weather showed the little Fen-edge settlement at its very best. The autumn sun shone gently, and leaves were beginning to be touched with red and gold. The town's roads were little more than strips of mature and compacted rubbish, but they added a certain rustic charm that had been absent in Nottingham, while many of its churches were very handsome indeed.

By rights, the prisoner should have been delivered directly to the gaol, but Moleyns had wanted to see his new home first, and had persuaded the officer in charge to make a detour so that they arrived from the south. Sergeant Helbye had been quite happy to oblige. After all, who would not rather swap mundane duties in the castle for an afternoon of leisurely riding?

'There is St Mary the Great,' said Inge the lawyer, pointing to an enormous building near the Market Square, which thronged with scholars. He hailed from the Fens, so knew the area well. 'Also called the University Church. You may recall the name, as it is where Sir John Dallingridge asked to be buried.'

Inge had thought long and hard about his future when Moleyns had been convicted. Should he settle for a dull but safe life as a rural judge, or should he stick with his biggest client, knowing that Moleyns would eventually be pardoned, as those generous to the royal coffers always were? In the end, he had decided that his best interests lay with the devious knight, so he had followed Moleyns to 'prisons' in Windsor, Nottingham and now Cambridge.

Unfortunately, he was beginning to think he might have made a mistake. It had been three years since the trial, and there was still no sign that a reprieve was in the offing. And with no income of his own, Inge was obliged to rely on Moleyns for every last penny, which was a position no man liked to be in. But Inge was unwilling to cut his losses just yet. The move to Cambridge showed that the King had not forgotten his favourite, and Moleyns was fun company when he was in a good mood – which was why His Majesty loved him, of course.

Moleyns was looking around approvingly. 'Dallingridge was right to wax lyrical about this town, and *I* was right to request a transfer here. It will be much more comfortable than Nottingham, where the castle was draughty and its Sheriff a bore.'

At that moment, St Mary the Great's bell began to chime, a toneless clunk that made him wince. His wife, who rode at his side, started to laugh.

'Do the scholars keep a bucket in the tower?' she chortled. 'I expected a more tuneful sound from so glorious a building.'

Egidia and Moleyns had been married for nearly thirty years, and although it had been a union of convenience, both had done well out of the arrangement. She had brought him the plum manor that had won him a place at Court, and he had provided her with a steady supply of riches from his criminal schemes – at least, until his arrest had put an end to them.

'It cracked earlier this year,' explained Inge. 'But replacements have already been cast, and will be hung soon. Three of them – a gift from a wealthy benefactor.'

He pointed out more landmarks as they and their guards rode along the High Street – pretty St Catherine's Hostel, King's Hall with its stalwart walls, and the

Hospital of St John on the corner. Then they passed into Bridge Street, and caught their first glimpse of the castle.

It dominated the northern end of the town by squatting on a ridge – an unusual feature in an area that was almost uniformly flat. It was an imposing sight, a mass of grey walls and bristling towers with the mighty Great Keep rising from its middle.

'Its function is more administrative than military these days,' Inge chatted on, pleased to show off his local knowledge. 'And the most dangerous task its Sheriff performs is collecting taxes from people who do not want to pay.'

'And running a prison, presumably,' remarked Egidia.

'There are cells in the gatehouse,' acknowledged Inge, 'but those are for common felons. We will be housed in quarters that are commensurate with Moleyns' status as a close friend of the King.'

'I shall be very happy in this town,' declared Moleyns, smiling contentedly. 'I can tell. Did I mention that His Majesty has granted me even more privileges than I had in Nottingham? I shall go hunting and hawking, as well as enjoying all the usual feasts and revels that the Sheriff will have to provide. Nottingham had palled, and we all needed a change.'

'Regardless, I hope you are pardoned soon,' sighed Egidia. 'I am tired of these grim fortresses, and I want to go home to Stoke Poges.'

'Stoke Poges is not your home now,' Inge reminded her. 'It was confiscated by the courts when Moleyns was found guilty.'

'It will be returned to me the moment I am pardoned,' averred Moleyns confidently. 'Which will not be long now. The King swore not to rest until the verdict of those stupid jurors was overturned.'

'He did,' acknowledged Inge. 'But perhaps it is time for another letter reminding him of your plight. This is a pretty town, and I do not doubt that we shall enjoy ourselves here, but who would not rather be free?'

Moleyns wanted to dismount and inspect some of the interesting stalls on Bridge Street, but Helbye growled an order for the party to keep moving – taking the long way through the town was one thing, but going shopping in the shadow of the castle was another altogether. He was a grizzled veteran of many campaigns and the Sheriff's most trusted subordinate, so he was the natural choice to travel to Nottingham and bring the prisoner back. He had enjoyed the excursion immensely, despite the nagging aches in his ageing joints, and was not about to risk future jaunts by letting Moleyns defy his authority in a place where it would be noticed.

When they reached the Barbican, they met Sheriff Tulyet, who was just walking out. Helbye saluted smartly.

'Here he is, sir,' he said, jerking a callused thumb over his shoulder at Moleyns. 'One prisoner, delivered safe and sound.'

'I am a personal friend of the King,' declared Moleyns, disliking the disrespectful introduction, and aiming to let his new captor know how matters stood. 'And I expect to be treated accordingly. If you have any doubts, read the letter your man carries.'

Obligingly, Helbye handed it over. 'Apparently, it says the King wants him to have decent quarters, the best food, and the freedom to go out whenever he likes.'

'The freedom to go out *whenever I deem it safe,*' corrected Tulyet, scanning it briefly before shoving it rather carelessly into his tunic. 'But Cambridge can be very disorderly, so I do not foresee many outings, I am sorry to say.'

He did not sound sorry at all, and Moleyns struggled to keep his temper. 'You might want to reconsider that attitude,' he said sharply. 'I think—'

'See him to his cell, Helbye,' interrupted Tulyet, giving the distinct impression that he did not care two hoots what Moleyns thought. 'I will speak to him later, if I have time.'

Outraged by the implication that his arrival was inconsequential, and alarmed by the word 'cell', Moleyns dug his spurs into his mount's flanks, aiming to surge forward and give the Sheriff a piece of his mind. Unfortunately, he jabbed too hard – he had never been a very good rider – and the animal reared. He was saved from an embarrassing tumble by Tulyet himself, who jumped forward to grab the bridle.

'You had better dismount,' said the Sheriff coolly. 'We cannot have you falling off and hurting yourself. Or worse, hurting someone else.'

Moleyns was incensed by the impertinence, but Tulyet was already striding away, clearly considering the conversation over. He ground his teeth in impotent fury, outraged that he should be treated with such rank and arrogant disregard.

'We shall write to the King tomorrow,' said Inge soothingly. 'You will not suffer these indignities long, never fear.'

Moleyns nodded slowly, hot temper turning to something colder and darker.

'Tulyet will be sorry he offended me,' he said softly. 'And so will his town.'

CHAPTER 1

Cambridge, February 1360

An enormous crowd had gathered outside St Mary the Great, and everyone in it was gazing upwards. On the top of the tower, high above, the University's Chancellor was doing battle with the Devil, a desperate, frantic struggle that surged back and forth, perilously close to the edge. More than once it seemed the pair would plummet to their deaths. Or Chancellor Tynkell would: most suspected it would take rather more to eliminate Satan.

Master Ralph de Langelee of Michaelhouse and four of his Fellows were among the throng. They had been to visit friends in Peterhouse and were hurrying home when their attention had been snagged by the spectacle. All had teaching planned for that morning, but lectures had flown from their minds when they had seen what was happening on the roof.

'Whatever possessed him to tackle such a foe?' breathed Father William. He was famous for three things: a filthy Franciscan habit, scandalously bigoted opinions, and a dim-wittedness rare among those claiming to be academics. 'Even I would not dare, and *I* am a priest.'

'Let us pray he is strong enough,' whispered Clippesby, the College's Dominican. He crossed himself, then hugged the goose he was carrying. His habit of talking to animals – and claiming they talked back – naturally led most people to assume he was insane.

'This wind does not help,' added Langelee. He had been a henchman for the Archbishop of York before deciding that life as a scholar would be more fun. Like

William, he was no intellect, but he was an able administrator, and his Fellows were generally satisfied with his
rule. 'One false step, and they will both be blown off.'

Even as he spoke, a violent gust made him stagger,
then huddle more deeply into his cloak. It was bitterly
cold, with streams and ditches frozen hard, and the occasional flurry of snow dancing in the air. He turned as
Beadle Meadowman approached at a run. Beadles were
the men who kept order in the University, under the
command of the proctors. The Senior Proctor was
currently Michael, a rotund Benedictine theologian, who
was the third of Langelee's Fellows.

'We cannot open the porch door, Brother,' Meadowman
reported tersely. 'The Devil must have tampered with it,
to keep us out.'

'Then try the one in the vestry,' suggested Matthew
Bartholomew, Michaelhouse's physician and the last
Fellow in the pack. Besides teaching medicine, he was
also the University's Corpse Examiner, which meant it
was his responsibility to provide an official cause of death
for any scholar who died. He sincerely hoped that his
services would not be required for Tynkell.

'That is a good idea.' Michael sighed irritably when
Meadowman only gazed up at the tower in open-mouthed
fascination. 'Well, go on then, man!'

Meadowman shuffled away, but with such obvious reluctance that it was clear his efforts to enter the building
had not been as assiduous as he would have his Senior
Proctor believe.

'He does not want to go in, because he is afraid of
what he might encounter in there,' said Bartholomew,
watching him.

Michael scowled. 'Tynkell is fighting a *person*, Matt, not
Satan. I cannot imagine what he thinks he is doing, but
unless my beadles stop them soon, blood will be spilled.'

'It *is* the Devil.' William sounded astonished that the

monk should think otherwise. 'Look at him, Brother – dressed in black from head to toe.'

'So am I,' retorted Michael, indicating his Benedictine habit. 'But that does not mean—'

'And he has that hunched, impish look of all demons,' William went on earnestly. 'Trust me, I know. I learned these things when I was with the Inquisition in France.'

Fortunately for that country's 'heretics', William's appointment had been a short one, and he had been assigned to Cambridge when his fellow inquisitors had deemed him too extreme.

There was a collective gasp from the onlookers as the wrestling pair lurched violently to one side, dislodging a coping stone, which crashed to the ground below. Then Tynkell managed to wrap his hands around his opponent's throat. There was a cheer of encouragement from the crowd, especially when the Devil began to flail around in a frantic effort to breathe.

'Those wretched beadles are more interested in gawping than putting an end to it,' said Michael crossly, glaring at them. 'I shall have to do it myself.'

'Then hurry,' advised Bartholomew. 'Unless you want the Chancellor to commit murder in front of half the town.'

'Do not intervene!' cried William in dismay, as the monk began to stride towards the church. 'Not when Tynkell is winning. New scholars will *race* to study here once they learn that we are the kind of men who can conquer Lucifer.'

Michael did not grace the appeal with a response. He reached the church, Bartholomew at his heels, and inspected the vestry door. The beadles were more than happy to abandon their half-hearted attempts to open it, and scuttled off to join the other spectators in the High Street.

The vestry door was shut fast, but it only took a moment

13

to ascertain that a key had been used, not some diabolical device. It was still in the hole, and a jab from one of Bartholomew's surgical probes saw it drop to the floor on the other side. There was a large gap between door and flagstones, so it was easy for the physician to slip his hand beneath and retrieve it.

'I thought you had keys to this place,' he remarked, inserting it into the lock and pushing the door open. Behind him, a disappointed moan from the crowd suggested that Lucifer had just broken the Chancellor's death grip.

'I do, but I rarely carry them these days,' explained the monk, shoving past him and hurrying inside. 'There is no need, because the church is always open. It has to be – the University's recent expansion means our clerks have urgent business day and night, while the masons working on Sir John Dallingridge's tomb must be able to come and go at will.'

'Then where are they all?' asked Bartholomew, following him up the empty nave.

Michael looked around and shrugged. 'They must have left when they heard the commotion outside. Then the doors caught the wind, which slammed them so hard that they jammed.'

'Both of them?' asked Bartholomew sceptically. 'And besides, the vestry door was locked, not jammed.' He frowned when Michael pulled a bunch of keys from his scrip. 'I thought you just said you never carry those.'

'I meant the ones to the outer doors,' explained the monk. 'These are for the tower, which, as you know, houses the University Chest. There are only two sets of keys in existence, and this is one of them.'

The Chest contained all the University's money and most precious documents, so its security was taken seriously. Bartholomew was not surprised that only a limited number of people had the wherewithal to access it.

'Who has the other set?' he asked. 'Tynkell?'

'He did, but I took it away and gave it to Meadowman instead.' The monk shot his friend a rueful glance. 'I was afraid Tynkell might do something else to make a name for himself before he finally retires next summer.'

Tynkell had won the chancellorship on a technicality, but it had quickly become clear that the post was well beyond his abilities. This had suited Michael perfectly, as it allowed him to seize control behind the scenes. Loath to go down in history as the Puppet Chancellor, Tynkell had backed two schemes to see himself remembered more favourably. One was to build a Common Library – a place that would have been open to all scholars, whether rich or poor, which some masters felt set a dangerously egalitarian precedent. The other was to found a new College. Both had gone disastrously wrong, but Tynkell stubbornly refused to learn from his mistakes, and Michael lived in fear that he might try something else.

Tynkell had announced his resignation eighteen months before, but had changed his mind at the last minute, and decided to stay on. A year later, he gave notice a second time, but then had been assailed with misgivings as the leaving date had loomed. He was currently due to step down at the end of the academic year, and claimed he was looking forward to enjoying some well-earned leisure time, although no one was sure whether to believe him.

'How did he get up the tower, then?' asked Bartholomew.

'Borrowed Meadowman's, I suppose.' Michael hissed irritably when haste made him clumsy, and he could not find the right key. 'I thought I had loaded him with enough extra duties to keep him out of mischief. He should not have time for this sort of nonsense.'

Outside, there was a collective cry of annoyance, suggesting that the action on the roof had moved out of sight. Michael muttered a quick prayer of thanks when he found the right key at last. He started to thrust it into

15

the hole, then gaped in disbelief when the door swung open of its own accord.

'This is *always* kept locked,' he said angrily, gathering the voluminous folds of his habit as he prepared to tackle the spiral staircase. 'Even when one of us is working up there. Tynkell has become a real menace – I need a Chancellor I can trust, not one who runs amok.'

Knowing the monk's upwards progress would be stately, Bartholomew pushed past him and went first, climbing as fast as he dared up steps that were unlit, icy and perilously uneven. It was not easy, and he was obliged to clamber back down again when Michael fell and released a yelp of pain, although the monk flapped an impatient hand, telling him to go on without him.

The tower comprised three large chambers, set one above the other. The first contained the bells, a trio of tuneful domes suspended in a wooden frame. Bartholomew glanced in as he hurried past, noting that it was empty. The second was the Chest Room, protected by an iron-bound door with two substantial locks. He rattled it, but it was shut fast. The third was a vast empty space containing nothing but the mess left by pigeons. Then came the roof. Bartholomew opened the little door that gave access to it, and saw Tynkell slumped on the far side.

The wind buffeted the top of the tower so hard that it was difficult to stay upright, while the slates underfoot were treacherously slick with ice. As he picked his way gingerly across them, he wondered what had induced Tynkell to fight under such conditions.

'Matt!' yelled Michael, hobbling up the last few stairs. 'Wait! Where is his opponent?'

Instinct had prompted Bartholomew to go to the Chancellor's aid, and the possibility that he might be in danger himself had not crossed his mind. He looked around in alarm, but the roof was deserted.

16

'He is not here,' he called back, although Michael could see this for himself. 'He must have fallen over the edge while we were coming up the stairs.'

He reached Tynkell and shook his shoulder. There was no response. Alarmed, he felt for a life-beat, and then stared in shock when he could not find one.

'No!' he whispered in stunned disbelief. 'Tynkell . . . he is dead.'

For several moments, Bartholomew could do no more than stare in horror at the man who had been the University's public face for the last six years. Tynkell had been his patient and he had liked him. Then he dragged his eyes away and looked at Michael. The colour had drained from the monk's face, leaving it as white as snow; he clutched the doorframe for support.

'You are wrong,' he said unsteadily. 'Check again.'

Bartholomew obliged, because he was unwilling to believe the horrible truth himself, but it was not long before he sat back on his heels and shook his head. 'I am sorry, Brother.'

'But he wants to retire,' objected Michael, as if this would undo the terrible news. 'And I believe he is serious this time, because he has been making plans for his future.'

'I know,' said Bartholomew softly. 'And I am more sorry than I can say.'

Michael limped across the roof. 'How can he be dead? All he and his opponent did was grapple and shove at each other.'

'Perhaps he suffered an apoplexy.'

Michael shot him a disbelieving glance. 'Well, at least the cause of death will be easy to determine for his rival. This tower is high, and anyone who falls off . . .'

He inched towards the parapet, and clung tightly to a pinnacle as he peered over the edge. He was greeted by a sea of faces, all upturned in eager expectation.

'Who fell?' he yelled, scanning the ground below for mangled remains.

'No one,' Father William bellowed back. 'They disappeared from sight for a moment, after which Satan launched himself off the roof and flew to the Dominican Friary.'

William hated Dominicans, and was rarely logical where they were concerned.

'What *really* happened?' shouted Michael, appealing to his more sensible colleagues.

'Just what he said,' hollered Langelee. 'Lucifer spread his great big wings, and soared off in that direction.' He pointed east, which was not quite where the Black Friars' convent was located, although it was not far away.

The other spectators clamoured to say that they had also seen it, so Michael squinted in the direction indicated, but could detect nothing through eyes that streamed in the iciness of the wind. Then he went to each side of the tower in turn, and surveyed the ground and the various roofs below, but there was no evidence that anyone had landed there.

'The wind must have carried off some item of clothing,' he yelled. '*That* is what you saw flapping away – not Satan.'

'Nonsense!' countered William firmly. 'I know the Devil when I see him.'

Others roared that they did, too. Michael tried to make them see reason, but the gale was blowing harder than ever, snatching his words away before they could reach the assembled ears below. Not that anyone wanted to hear them, of course – it was far more exciting to have glimpsed the Lord of Darkness than a combatant's cloak. Michael made his way back to where the physician still crouched next to Tynkell.

'It was a *person*,' he insisted doggedly. 'And people do not fly.'

'Then where is he?' Bartholomew gestured around him. 'He is not up here; he would have been seen falling;

and he cannot have gone down the stairs, because we would have met him when we were coming up. Or is there an alcove he might have hidden in?'

'There is not. And nor did he take refuge in one of the chambers: the Chest Room is locked, and I looked in the other two on my way up. Both were empty.'

'But he *must* be in the Chest Room,' said Bartholomew, willing to accept the monk's point about the other two, because he had also seen that no one was in them. 'There is nowhere else he could have gone.'

'It is locked,' insisted Michael. 'Come – I shall prove it.'

He hobbled back down the stairs, Bartholomew trailing behind him, looking for a space where the culprit might have lurked while they had hurried past. But the walls were smooth and unbroken, and not even a sparrow could have concealed itself there.

They reached the Chest Room, where Michael unfastened its two locks to reveal a sparsely furnished chamber containing a table, two stools and the enormous coffer that gave it its name. Its walls were stone, the window a fixed frame that could not be opened, and the floor and ceiling were solid wood. Small dishes holding poison were scattered around, to ensure the University's precious records were not eaten by mice.

'You see?' said Michael. 'No one is here.'

'What about inside the Chest?' persisted Bartholomew.

Michael opened the seven great padlocks one by one, and lifted the lid. The box was packed with scrolls, books and documents, and not only was there no room for a person to hide, but someone else would have been needed on the outside to manipulate the keys.

Leaving the monk to lock up, Bartholomew descended to the bell chamber, and quickly determined that hiding there was also impossible.

The bells had originally been higher up, but when they had been augmented from one to three, the bell-hangers had decided that several tons of metal swinging around there would put too great a strain on the tower's foundations, so they had been installed just above the church's west porch. Bartholomew suffered a sharp pang of grief when he saw them: they had been bought with a benefaction from his late brother-in-law.

'Oswald died too young,' he murmured, when the monk eventually joined him. He knew he should be thinking about Tynkell's assailant, but his kinsman's untimely death remained a source of great sadness to him, and he could not help himself.

'He would have liked these bells.' Michael spoke absently, still stunned by what had happened on the roof. 'And Tynkell was proud to have had them installed under his chancellorship. But never mind that – we must find whatever flew off the roof and prove it was not Satan, or we shall never hear the end of this ridiculous tale.'

Bartholomew nodded. 'I will look for it as soon as I have carried Tynkell downstairs.'

'That will be too late – the rumour will be all over the town by then. I will detail my beadles to do it. William pointed out the direction it took, so I know where to tell them to start.'

'It is probably Tynkell's cloak. You must have noticed that he was not wearing one.'

'Pity. If it had been his opponent's, it might have allowed us to identify him.'

While Michael hurried away to brief his men, Bartholomew began the tortuous business of manoeuvring a corpse down a narrow spiral staircase. By the time he reached the Lady Chapel, he was sweating heavily, warmer than he had been since Christmas, when the cold weather had started. Then the beadles chased out the gawpers and kept guard while he conducted a formal examination of the Chancellor's body.

It was not pleasant, as Tynkell had had an unfortunate aversion to personal hygiene, and his being dead did nothing to improve matters.

Bartholomew began by checking the head for bruises or dents, but there was nothing amiss. However, when he removed Tynkell's academic tabard, he discovered a patch of blood. He pulled away the remaining garments to reveal a tiny puncture wound in the left side of Tynkell's chest, small enough to be almost invisible. It had not been made with a knife, so he supposed some kind of spike was responsible, although one that was unusually long and thin.

'It was pushed through the ribs, directly into his heart,' he told Michael, when he eventually finished and the monk came to hear his report. 'Death would have been virtually instant, and there was very little bleeding – which is why I did not notice it on the roof.'

'It makes more sense than a sudden attack of natural causes.' Michael rubbed his chin, fingers rasping against the stubble. 'So our killer stabbed Tynkell, then escaped with all the ease of Lucifer. Literally, according to at least three dozen witnesses, all of whom swear on their souls that he then flew off the tower.'

'What did they say when you showed them the cloak?'

'Nothing, because my beadles cannot find it. I suppose a pauper got to it first, and is reluctant to hand it over. I do not blame him – the weather is bitter, and such a garment might mean the difference between life and death.'

'That is unfortunate,' said Bartholomew. 'I dislike rumours about Satan – they nearly always result in trouble.'

Michael nodded agreement, then was silent for a while, staring down at the man who had worked so closely with him for the past six years. Then he reached for the blanket that Bartholomew had used to cover the body. There had always been something a little odd about Tynkell's person, which had resulted in some outrageous speculation among the students – one had even suggested that he was pregnant. Bartholomew knew what made the Chancellor different, but steadfastly refused to tell.

'No,' he said sharply, slapping Michael's hand away. 'Leave him in peace.'

'Why?' asked Michael, aggrieved. 'It cannot hurt him now, and I have manfully swallowed my curiosity all these years. Besides, it might have a bearing on his death.'

'It does not. Besides, how would you like it if pcople came to paw at *your* corpse for no reason other than prurient curiosity?'

'I have no intention of shuffling off this mortal coil,' retorted Michael loftily; he had long been of the opinion that his own death was optional. 'And certainly not before I have been made a bishop or an abbot. Which will not be much longer in the offing, of course.'

Bartholomew regarded him searchingly. The monk had always maintained that he would one day hold high rank in the Church – without the inconvenience of climbing through the stages in between, naturally – but had something happened to prompt the remark now?

'You had a letter from Bishop de Lisle yesterday,' he fished.

Michael nodded. 'He is still with the Pope in Avignon, which is a nuisance actually, because it is difficult to whisper in his ear when he lives so far away. However, I have sent him reports about the University for nigh on two decades now, and my loyal service has put him in my debt.'

'Is that why he wrote? To thank you?'

'Yes and no. He has been singing my praises to the Holy Father, and wanted me to know that an opportunity for advancement might soon come my way.'

'Not too soon, I hope,' said Bartholomew. 'We have just lost our Chancellor, and we cannot afford to lose our Senior Proctor as well.'

'Do not worry – I shall ensure that a suitable successor to Tynkell is appointed before I go anywhere. I have worked hard to build this University, and I will not leave it foundering.'

'Oh, Lord!' groaned Bartholomew, as it occurred to him that Tynkell's death would bring about changes, not all of them pleasant. 'There will have to be an election, and the last time we had one of those, there was mayhem, with scholars at each other's throats and—'

'Who said anything about an election? It would be best if I chose Tynkell's replacement, and installed him quietly. I know what is needed; our colleagues do not.'

Bartholomew knew the University's voting members would not be pleased to learn that they were about to be deprived of the right to select their own leader, but it was hardly the time or the place for a debate on the matter. He fetched the necessary accoutrements from the vestry, and began to lay Tynkell out himself, knowing it was what the Chancellor would have wanted. When he had finished, he found the parish coffin – a reusable box with sturdy clasps – lifted Tynkell into it, and fastened down the lid as tightly as he could. Then he charged two of Michael's most trustworthy beadles to guard it.

'No one looks inside, not even Michael,' he instructed, then added a lie to ensure that his orders were followed. 'Opening it would be dangerous, because there is a deadly miasma around the body.'

'We know,' said one man in distaste, holding his nose. 'We can smell it from here.'

When Bartholomew stepped into the street shortly afterwards, he was nearly blown off his feet by the force of the gale. Yet despite the mighty gusts, people still thronged around the church, reluctant to leave after the excitement. This was convenient for Michael, as it allowed him to question witnesses. Unfortunately, everyone told him the same tale: that Tynkell and the Devil had disappeared for a moment, after which Lucifer had flown away.

'You know that is impossible,' the monk was saying irritably to William Thelnetham, a Gilbertine who liked to liven up the sober habit of his Order with outrageously colourful accessories; that day, he sported yellow hose, while a pink ribbon graced the hem of his cloak.

Thelnetham had been a member of Michaelhouse, but had resigned when another foundation had made him a better offer. When the new College had come to nought, he had expected to be reinstated at his old one, and had been astonished when his colleagues had refused to accept him back. He was an excellent teacher and a skilled orator, so there was no question that he raised Michaelhouse's academic profile, but he was also acerbic and quarrelsome, and the other Fellows decided that they preferred life without him. He had been obliged to take up residence in the Gilbertine Priory instead, although he had not given up all hope that Michaelhouse would one day recant and invite him to return.

'It sounds impossible,' Thelnetham replied. 'But it is what happened – I saw it with my own eyes. And you said yourself that no one else was on the roof when you arrived.'

'What you saw take to the air was Tynkell's cloak,' argued Michael.

'Nonsense,' countered Thelnetham with considerable conviction. 'I know the difference between a gown and the Devil. Unlike you, it seems.'

'Satan does not go around stabbing folk,' said Michael, speaking just as vehemently. 'That is something *people* do.'

This remark was overheard by a Dominican named Thomas Hopeman, an unattractive individual with a low forehead and darkly glittering eyes, who promptly marched across to say his piece. He was another scholar who could not open his mouth without contradicting someone, although unlike Thelnetham, he did it without humour. He was always accompanied by a band of six or seven disciples, who were all much of an ilk – grim, unsmiling fanatics, who turned religion into something joyless and rather frightening.

'Rubbish!' he stated dogmatically. 'Lucifer has long claws that he keeps honed for the express purpose of running people through.'

His acolytes surged forward to clamour their agreement. While Michael struggled to silence them, Thelnetham took Bartholomew's arm and pulled him aside.

'What will happen now?' he asked in a gossipy whisper. 'I assume there will be an election, and Michael will put himself forward as Tynkell's successor?'

'I have no idea,' lied Bartholomew.

Thelnetham grimaced. 'He must have said something to you, Matthew. The University is growing fast at the moment, which means we cannot be without a titular head for long. Or will Michael just take the post without the bother of having himself voted in by his peers?'

'You will have to ask him.' Bartholomew tried to edge away.

'I shall then. And if he agrees to a fair and open competition, I might stand myself.'

'You will?' Bartholomew was astounded. He had not imagined it was a post that anyone would want, given that Tynkell's reign had seen it go from a position of great power to one with a hefty administrative load, an obligation to host lots of dull ceremonies, and no authority to make independent decisions. 'Why?'

'Because I love teaching, and I should like a say in the way it is managed. And when I do, substandard masters like your William can expect an end to their comfortable existences.' Thelnetham glowered to where the Franciscan was chatting to some of his brethren. 'Our students deserve better than the likes of him.'

It was difficult to argue with that. Students paid for their tuition, and it was unethical to fob them off with mediocre educators. However, it was not just William's failings in the classroom that drew Thelnetham's disapproval. When the Gilbertine had been a member of Michaelhouse, he and William had quarrelled constantly, and had loathed each other ever since.

Thelnetham flounced away at that point, so Bartholomew turned back to Michael and Hopeman. As he listened to them argue, he recalled that the Dominican was a member of Maud's Hostel. Unlike Colleges, hostels had no endowment – no pot of money that paid salaries and kept buildings in good repair – so they tended to be smaller, poorer and less stable. Maud's was the exception. It took only very wealthy students, and so was always flush with funds, although it had an unfortunate propensity to attract applicants of less than average intelligence. How lads with such short attention spans were persuaded to sit still for Hopeman's famously protracted theological expositions had always been a mystery to Bartholomew.

Then another Maud's man joined them, also keen to know what would happen now that Tynkell was dead. He was the elderly Richard Lyng, who had been Chancellor three times himself, and had been very good at it. He was a theologian of some repute, and Bartholomew had often wondered how he could bear lecturing to students who could not remember what they had been taught from one day to the next.

'No, I shall not stand myself,' replied Michael in response to Lyng's polite enquiry. 'However, organising an election takes time, so it will not happen this term and—'

'*I* could arrange one in a trice,' interrupted Hopeman. 'All you have to do is set a date, tell everyone, then count a show of hands.'

'It is rather more complex than that,' countered Michael irritably. 'The statutes—'

'The statutes are a lot of silly decrees designed to impede progress,' stated Hopeman belligerently. 'If I were Chancellor, I would scrap them.'

'Then it is fortunate for us that you are never likely to be in office,' retorted Michael coolly. He loved the minutiae of the University's rulebooks, and never tired of poring over them to extract interpretations that allowed him to get his own way.

'And we *do* need them, Hopeman,' said Lyng with a pleasant smile. 'Without our rubrics, we should have anarchy. Besides, they have served us well for a hundred and fifty years. They need a little tweaking now and again, to bring them in line with changing requirements, but they are fundamentally sound.'

'Hear, hear,' said Michael firmly.

'A hundred and fifty years?' scoffed Hopeman. 'Fool! Our University is *much* older. It was founded by King Arthur, just a year after Our Lord's glorious Resurrection.'

'I see history is not your forte,' drawled Michael, then turned back to Lyng before the Dominican could respond. 'As I was saying, it will take several weeks to arrange an election, but until then, I shall assume the mantle of Chancellor. I have—'

'Why?' interrupted Hopeman aggressively. 'You just told us that you will not stand.'

'I will not,' said Michael, struggling for patience. 'But I shall plug the breach until Tynkell's replacement is in post. Then I will step down.'

'Are you sure you can manage his duties, as well as your own?' asked Lyng worriedly. 'We have grown so rapidly over the last year that to undertake both will be a very heavy burden. As an ex-Chancellor myself, I know what I am talking about.'

'I agree,' nodded Hopeman. 'So we should hold an election immediately.'

Michael glared at him. 'It is inappropriate to discuss such matters while Tynkell is still warm,' he said curtly. 'Nothing can or will happen until he is decently laid to rest.'

'But that might take an age, Brother,' said Lyng. 'I helped him to write his will, so I know for a fact that he left funds for a tomb to be built in St Mary the Great. It will be weeks – perhaps even months – before that is ready to receive his mortal remains.'

'Oh, dear,' said Michael flatly. 'What a pity.'

But Hopeman had the bit between his teeth. 'Tynkell became irrelevant the moment he breathed his last. It is the *University* that is important now, not him. Ergo, we shall have our ballot in a few days. I shall stand myself, of course. Our *studium generale* will flourish under a devout man like me.'

His zealots murmured agreement, although Lyng was visibly alarmed by the prospect of Hopeman in charge. Foundations tended to be loyal to fellow members, so Hopeman should have been able to count on the support of anyone from Maud's. Lyng, however, was cognisant of his University's best interests.

'Then I had better put myself forward, too,' he said. 'I have plenty of experience at the post, and people will vote for me.'

He had been a popular Chancellor, who had managed to lead without being a tyrant – unlike, it had to be said, Michael – so it was entirely possible that he would be elected for a fourth term. Bartholomew was relieved that there would be at least one sensible alternative to the rabid Dominican, although Hopeman was outraged at the 'betrayal', and Michael made a moue of annoyance.

'I saw you both with Tynkell earlier today,' said the monk, pointedly turning the discussion back to the man whose shoes they aimed to fill, 'and I know he was fond of Maud's. I do not suppose he mentioned an intention to climb up to the tower roof, did he?'

'He never talked about his University duties,' replied Lyng. 'He used to, when he was first appointed, but that stopped after a couple of months. I occasionally raised the subject, but he always maintained that it was too important for idle chatter.'

'That was because he had no idea what was happening,' scoffed Hopeman. 'You never confided in him, Brother, so he was as much in the dark as the rest of us.'

'So no, he did not mention the tower,' continued Lyng, shooting the Dominican a look that warned him to moderate his tongue. 'He just said that he had a lot of work to do today, because you had left a great pile of deeds on his desk.'

'He *also* said he was looking forward to retiring, and being free of your bullying ways,' put in Hopeman spitefully. 'But I cannot stand here all day. *I* have an election to win.'

He strode away, his followers twittering excitedly at his heels.

'Are his zealots members of Maud's?' asked Michael, looking after them disapprovingly. 'They do not seem like the kind of lad you usually recruit.'

'They are deacons from the parish churches,' replied Lyng, 'whom Hopeman aims to turn into younger versions of himself. We try to dissuade him from grooming fanatics, but you know what he is like – not a man to listen to reason. But I had better go, too. He will not waste a moment before he starts campaigning, so neither should I.'

'I shall have scant time for manipulating elections if I am to perform Tynkell's duties as well as my own,' grumbled Michael, when he and Bartholomew were alone again. 'Not to mention finding his killer. Damn Hopeman! His impatience is a nuisance.'

'He will not win,' predicted Bartholomew, hiding his amusement at Michael's bald admission that he intended to cheat. 'Lyng is far more popular. So is Thelnetham.'

'Thelnetham?' echoed Michael. 'I do not want *him*,

thank you very much. He will want to ignore my advice and rule alone.'

'Then stand yourself. It is the only sure way of keeping your power.'

'But I do not want to be Chancellor! It would be wrong to put myself forward, only to leave a couple of months later.'

'A couple of *months*?' Bartholomew regarded his friend intently. 'That letter from the Bishop – what did it really say?'

Michael grimaced. 'I did not want to tell anyone yet, lest there is a hiccup, but this will force my hand. De Lisle has arranged for me to be offered a See. He told me to expect a messenger confirming the appointment in the next few days.'

Bartholomew was delighted for him. 'That is excellent news, Brother! Which diocese?'

'I do not know yet. However, I would be happier with my good fortune if I were not afraid for my University. I do not want it in the hands of a lunatic like Hopeman, while Lyng is too old, and Thelnetham has no experience. Lord! What a terrible day this is transpiring to be.'

'Especially for Tynkell,' said Bartholomew soberly.

Bartholomew was a very busy man. He had more students than he could realistically teach, plus an enormous medical practice – far larger than the town's other physicians, who tended to confine themselves to tending the wealthy elite. Thus while the monk questioned more witnesses, he hurried back to Michaelhouse, not sure whether the rest of his day would be spent teaching or seeing patients.

He arrived to discover several urgent summonses, so he left his classes a daunting number of texts to learn – a list that elicited horrified exclamations, although he genuinely failed to understand why there was a problem, when he could read twice that amount in the allocated time – collected his final-year students, and set off on his rounds.

His first patient was Isnard the bargeman, whose leg he had once been obliged to amputate after an accident with a cart. Isnard had adapted well to the loss of his limb, but the episode had not taught him to be more careful, and Bartholomew was called at least once a week to tend cuts and bruises, many sustained during nights of riotous fun in the town's less salubrious taverns.

'I toppled backwards when I was watching Chancellor Tynkell fight the Devil,' the bargeman explained, as Bartholomew and his pupils crowded into the little riverside cottage. There was a powerful reek of ale, which explained exactly why Isnard's balance had been adversely affected. 'And I sat down so hard that I hurt my back.'

'I found him shortly afterwards, and was obliged to carry him home,' added another man, emerging from the shadows. 'He could not manage by himself.'

Isnard did not always live on the right side of the law, but Bartholomew was sorry indeed to see him in company with Gundrede, a thoroughly disreputable character who could have earned a decent living from his trade as a metalsmith but preferred instead to dabble in crime. Isnard was easily led, and Bartholomew sincerely hoped that Gundrede would not drag him into trouble.

'It is a pity the battle cost Tynkell his life,' sighed Isnard. 'He was a nice man.'

'Yet there was always something a little odd about his person,' mused Gundrede. 'Between you and me, I suspect he was branded with Satan's mark, and was killed trying to stop the Devil from pulling off his tabard and exposing it.'

'What kind of mark?' asked one of the students, agog.

'Enough,' said Bartholomew sharply, as Gundrede drew breath to reply. 'The poor man is dead. Afford him some respect, if you please.'

'Did *you* see Lucifer kill him, Isnard?' asked another lad eagerly. He glanced resentfully at Bartholomew. 'We missed it, because we were stuck in the hall, reading Maimonides.'

'Reading your what?' asked Isnard, then waved an impatient hand when the student started to explain. 'Never mind. And the answer is: yes, I *did* see Satan strike. Afterwards, I watched him soar across the town, returning to his home in Hell.'

'Which lies to the east,' elaborated Gundrede darkly, before Bartholomew could tell them about the cloak, 'in the Barnwell Fields. I always said that place was desolate. I imagine he is there now, picking his way through all the boggy puddles.'

'Not if he can fly,' averred Isnard. 'He will want to avoid getting his feet wet, if he can.'

'You *saw* Tynkell killed?' asked Bartholomew, the moment he could interject a question into the discussion. 'Because no one else did. They all say that he and the Dev— his opponent disappeared from sight at the critical time.'

'I was further away, so had a different perspective,' replied Isnard grandly. 'I saw Lucifer kneel down and do something to Tynkell, after which Tynkell did not move. It looked to me as though he laid a claw on his chest and stopped his heart.'

'Did you see his face?' asked Bartholomew, although he knew to treat any 'intelligence' from the bargeman with a healthy dose of scepticism.

'He kept his hood up to conceal his wicked visage. However, I can tell you that he wore a black cloak. I could not make out much else, though. It is a long way up that tower, Doctor.'

Bartholomew was thoughtful. The tower *was* high, so no one – and especially not the drunken Isnard – could have seen what had really happened, particularly in a wind that made eyes water and that was full of flying dust. The killer had achieved what Bartholomew would have considered impossible – a murder committed in front of dozens of witnesses, not one of whom could identify him.

There followed a lively debate during which students and townsmen discussed the various ways in which a demon might end a human life. It was all nonsense, and Bartholomew let it wash over him as he examined Isnard's bruises, which, he deduced, had not come from sitting down sharply, but from the rough manner in which he had been toted home afterwards. He prescribed a soothing balm, then went to his next call. It was at the Carmelite Priory, where the talk was again about the Chancellor's spectacular and very public demise.

'Poor Tynkell,' sighed one of the friars. 'I know he wanted to leave his mark on the University before he retired, but I doubt that is what he had in mind.'

'How do you know?' asked another. 'His other schemes failed, so he was probably getting desperate. He might well have staged that display to impress us all.'

'Then it failed,' said the first grimly, 'because there is nothing impressive about being slaughtered by Satan. He should have stuck to founding libraries and Colleges.'

When he had finished with the Carmelites, Bartholomew went to a house on the Market Square, where a baker had been so engrossed in watching Tynkell's mortal battle that he had burnt his hand. Then there were three cases of lung-rot near the King's Head tavern, after which he trudged wearily homewards. He sent his students on ahead of him when he spotted Michael emerging from St Mary the Great. They did not need to be told twice, and shot away before he changed his mind, eager to warm chilled hands and feet by the fire in the hall.

'Everyone in this town is a gullible fool,' grumbled Michael. 'Even rational men claim they saw the Devil flap away over the rooftops, and no one believes it was Tynkell's cloak. How am I supposed to catch the killer when no one has anything sensible to say?'

'Investigate Tynkell himself, then,' suggested Bartholomew. 'See if he had any enemies.'

'He did – lots,' replied Michael sourly. 'As Chancellor, he embodied the University, and there are scores of townsfolk who would love to strike a blow against us. And as for his choice of friends . . . well, suffice to say that *I* would not hobnob with the men of Maud's.'

Wryly, Bartholomew wondered if Maud's had been singled out for censure because two of its members had already put themselves forward as Tynkell's successor. He was about to say so, when he saw someone standing in a nearby doorway, watching them. He could not see the fellow's face, covered as it was by a cowl, but supposed it was a cleric.

He started to walk towards him, to ask if he wanted Michael or a medical consultation, but the fellow turned and hurried away. Michael did not seem inclined to give chase, so Bartholomew did not either, and the cleric disappeared into one of the many alleys that led to the river.

Because he had liked Tynkell, and wanted his killer caught, Bartholomew accompanied Michael to the Hall of Valence Marie, the scholars of which had also witnessed the rooftop battle. Unfortunately, their testimony was no more helpful than anyone else's had been, and it was with a sense of defeat that the two Michaelhouse men began to walk home.

It was bitterly cold, although the wind had dropped, so the clouds overhead did not scud along with quite such frantic urgency. A frost was settling across the rooftops, and the ground was frozen like iron underfoot. Bartholomew had no idea of the time, but sensed it would not be long until dusk, the short winter day over all too soon.

'Your brother-in-law's tomb,' said Michael suddenly, as they passed the lane that led to the little church of St John Zachary. 'Can we go to look at it? Tynkell's executors tell me that he wants . . . *wanted* something similar, and I should like to know what he had in mind.'

'You can look, but please do not hire our mason to build it. He already has too many commissions – at least five – which means none are getting the attention they deserve. He works on Oswald for an hour, then disappears to do the same for someone else. I am beginning to think he will never finish any of them.'

'He is a builder,' shrugged Michael. 'What do you expect?'

The parish of St John Zachary had suffered heavy losses when the plague had swept through the town ten years before. Almost every resident had died, and with no congregation to pay for its upkeep, the church had fallen into disrepair. It was not until the University had bought up all the empty houses to use as hostels that the area began to thrive once more. Then Bartholomew's kinsman, Oswald Stanmore, had provided a substantial sum of money for the church's renovation, on condition that he would be buried in its chancel one day. Of course, he had not expected to need it quite so soon.

'There was a time when I thought this place would have to be demolished,' remarked Michael, as he opened the door. 'But the last few months have seen it completely transformed.'

It was true. A fine hammerbeam roof now excluded the elements, and the windows were full of pretty stained glass. The floor was paved in creamy stones, and the walls were alive with murals depicting the life of St John the Baptist.

Stanmore's tomb had pride of place, and occupied most of the south side of the chancel. The mason hired to build it was John Petit, who had come to Cambridge to erect the Dallingridge tomb in St Mary the Great. Personally, Bartholomew thought his sister should have hired someone else, as Petit was smugly aware that he was the only craftsman of his kind within a sixty-mile radius, and so tended to be both expensive and unreliable. Grand monuments were, however, currently in vogue, and Edith was determined that her beloved husband should have the best.

And even Bartholomew was forced to admit that Petit's work was outstanding. The tomb comprised a handsome chest of pink marble with a canopy, which would eventually be topped with an effigy of him lying next to his wife. However, as Edith was still very much alive, Bartholomew found this prospect deeply disconcerting, although everyone assured him that it was common practice.

As the floor beneath the chancel was filled with the bodies of plague victims, Bartholomew had advised against disturbing them, and a separate vault was being prepared nearby. This was a steep-sided pit, large enough for Stanmore and Edith to lie side by side. Petit's apprentices had dug it the first week that Edith had hired them, after which it had been lined with stone. Progress was painfully slow, however, and although the vault itself was finished, there had been problems with the granite slab that was to seal it, although Bartholomew had understood none of the explanations. As a result, Stanmore's bones continued to languish in their temporary grave in the churchyard.

Bartholomew was astonished to see Petit actually at work there that day, despite the fading light. No visible progress had been made on the tomb or the vault since he had last visited, although the masons had nonetheless managed to create a tremendous mess. He opened his mouth to remonstrate, but Petit's eyes were fixed on Michael.

'I know why you are here, Brother,' he said, smiling superiorly. 'You have come to request my services for your Chancellor. Unfortunately, I am very busy, so if you want Tynkell's tomb built in a hurry, it will cost you.'

'Then I shall tell his executors to buy one from London,' said Michael coolly.

Petit's smug grin widened. 'You can try, but the City workshops will transpire to be far more expensive in the long run – transporting large lumps of stone over such great distances does not come cheap.'

'Then we shall have a funerary brass instead,' shrugged the monk. 'Those are far more reasonably priced.'

'Brasses are rubbish,' declared Petit haughtily and with conviction. 'You do not want one of those, so let us do business. What do you have in mind for Tynkell?'

Before the monk could reply, the mason opened a bag and produced a series of exemplars – scale models of the different designs on offer. They ranged from the tastefully simple one that Edith had chosen for Stanmore, to the excruciatingly ornate monstrosity that was being created for Dallingridge. Bartholomew noted that since he had last been shown the collection, another template had been added – a sculpted canopy that would rise a good thirty feet into the air.

'Please not that,' he said, thinking it horribly vulgar.

Petit picked it up fondly. 'This is for Master Godrich of King's Hall. It will go in St Mary the Great, and he wants me to start it now, so he can enjoy looking at it while he is still alive.'

'Then he is going to be disappointed,' said Michael firmly, 'because we are not having that thing in our nave. It would spoil the symmetry of the whole building.'

'It will go in the chancel, not the nave,' said Petit indignantly. 'My work *always* sits in the holiest part of a church. I would not consider making tombs for anywhere less.'

Michael raised his eyebrows. 'The chancel is not for

the likes of Godrich – that is reserved for important scholars, such as myself. Or Chancellors, I suppose, although Tynkell did express a wish to be interred beneath the new bells.'

'Under the bells,' mused Petit, picking up a hammer and tapping desultorily at Stanmore's lid. 'That will put him in the narthex, where my handiwork will be the first thing anyone sees in ceremonial processions. Yes, I can live with that.'

Amused, Bartholomew envisioned the canopied monstrosity plonked in the west porch, where scholars and dignitaries would have to squeeze down the sides of it in order to get in. Then he remembered his responsibilities to his family and became serious again.

'You cannot start another tomb until you have finished Oswald's,' he said. 'Unless you want to annoy my sister.'

Petit blanched, as well he might, for Edith was formidable when riled, and he had been on the receiving end of more than one scolding for his lack of progress.

'It is not my fault that this is taking longer than predicted,' he whined. 'I keep losing my supplies to thieves. Take this ledger slab, for example.' He patted the tomb-chest's lid, lest they did not know what he meant. 'I had one ready cut and chamfered, but someone came along and filched it – which meant I had to start another from scratch.'

'Someone stole a great lump of marble?' asked Michael sceptically. 'Why? You are the only mason in town, and it is hardly something that anyone else will want.'

'Lakenham,' replied Petit sullenly. '*He* took it. Have you met him? He moved here at the same time as me, and set up business in direct competition. He has been doing all he can to hinder my work and annoy my patrons.'

'You mean there is a second mason for hire?' asked Michael, brightening.

'He is not a mason.' Petit's voice dripped disdain. 'He is a lattener, a mere producer of brasses.' He shuddered. 'I should not like such a thing lying over me when I die. I want something *decent.*'

'We shall bear it in mind,' said Michael. 'Now where can this lattener be found?'

'Of course, Isnard the bargeman has an eye for fine stone, too,' Petit went on, ignoring the question. 'Him and his friend Gundrede. It is possible that *they* made off with my wares.'

'Isnard is not a thief,' said Bartholomew. Michael shot him a disbelieving look, so he hastened to modify his claim. 'Not of large items, at least. He only has one leg, so lifting heavy objects is beyond— where are *you* going?'

Petit had started to pack away his tools.

'I cannot do any more work on this until the mortar is dry,' the mason explained. 'If I tried, you would not be impressed with the result.'

'What mortar?' challenged Bartholomew, who could see that the bucket used to mix the stuff had not been moved in a week.

Petit waved an airy hand. 'Mine is a painstaking craft, Doctor. Much progress has been made today, although no amateur eye will detect it. But I shall return first thing in the morning, and I will stay here all day.'

He slung his toolbag over his shoulder and marched out, leaving behind a muddle of discarded wood, dust and sundry other rubbish. Bartholomew supposed the vergers would be obliged to clean it up themselves if they wanted their chancel to be usable in the interim.

'Godrich,' mused Michael, thinking about the man who intended to have himself interred with such splendour in the town's biggest and most important church. 'Have you met him, Matt? He is a Fellow of King's Hall, and although he has only been enrolled for a few weeks, he is already making his presence felt.'

'I know the Warden is unhappy with him,' replied Bartholomew. 'Godrich is agitating for an election, so he can lead King's Hall himself. The Warden never wanted the post, but he is reluctant to yield his power to Godrich, as he thinks it may do the place harm.'

'Elections,' sighed Michael, reminded of the one that would affect him personally. 'Poor Tynkell. I cannot accept a bishopric as long as his killer is at large, so I hope you will agree to help me. After all, my entire future is at stake here.'

When put like that, Bartholomew saw he would have no choice but to oblige.

It was past five o'clock when they reached the High Street, although the town was still busy. The winter daylight hours were too short for all the business that needed to be done, so many shops stayed open well into the evening, shedding cosy golden lamplight into the dark streets outside. Bartholomew was eager to be back in Michaelhouse, wanting no more than to sit by the fire, but the monk had other ideas.

'I need you to come to Maud's with me, to question two of my suspects about Tynkell's murder. *Then* we can go home.'

'You have suspects?' asked Bartholomew, surprised.

'Of course I have suspects,' said Michael irritably. 'Namely the men who aim to profit from Tynkell's death by having themselves elected in his place.'

'Lyng and Hopeman?'

'Yes, along with Thelnetham.'

Bartholomew frowned. 'I can believe Hopeman is guilty, while Thelnetham can be ruthless, but not Lyng. He is a good man, liked by all.'

'It would not be the first time a "good man" committed murder to further his ambitions. And *is* Lyng a good man anyway? You cannot be too scrupulous if you hold high office in the University, and he was Chancellor three times.'

'Does that observation apply to the Senior Proctor, too?' asked Bartholomew wryly. Michael did not reply, so he continued. 'Lyng is too old to be the culprit, Brother. And do not say that we have encountered elderly killers in the past, because *they* did not engage in close combat on gale-swept roofs. Lyng is not robust enough for such a feat.'

'He might be,' argued Michael, 'if provided with enough of an incentive. He probably misses the esteem he enjoyed when he was Chancellor, and aims to have it back before he dies. So we shall speak to him first, then Hopeman. We can leave Thelnetham until tomorrow – assuming Lyng or Hopeman do not confess in the interim, of course.'

At that point, both scholars were obliged to step aside smartly as four horsemen cantered by, far too fast for a time when visibility was poor and the streets were full of pedestrians.

'That was Sir John Moleyns,' said Michael disapprovingly. 'He rides like a sack of grain, and should not have been given such a lively mount. A donkey would suit him better.'

Even Bartholomew, no equestrian himself, could tell that Moleyns' skill was well below par. He wondered if the prancing horse had been provided out of spite, in the hope that the knight would take an embarrassing tumble.

Moleyns was with his wife and lawyer, who accompanied him everywhere he went, while a guard had been provided in the form of Sergeant Helbye, the Sheriff's most trusted officer. As if he knew he was the subject of conversation, Moleyns turned his stallion in a clumsy half-circle and trotted back, leaving his companions to chat to some of the town's wealthy burgesses.

'Your poor Chancellor,' he said slyly. 'What a terrible affair! I was in the Market Square at the time – on my horse. My elevated position gave me an excellent view of what happened.'

'So you saw who killed him?' asked Michael, trying, unsuccessfully, to keep the hope from his voice. 'Who was it?'

Moleyns regarded him thoughtfully. 'I must reflect carefully on the matter before answering that question – I should hate to mislead you, even inadvertently. However, I am always willing to cooperate with the forces of law and order, and I am sure we shall reach a mutually acceptable agreement.'

Michael regarded him in distaste. 'In other words, you want to be paid for helping us. How much?'

Moleyns put a hand to his chest, fingers splayed in a gesture of hurt indignation. 'You misunderstand, Brother. I do not want money – I want you to remember me when you are installed in your See.'

Michael gaped at him. 'How do you know what my future holds?'

Moleyns smiled. 'I have powerful friends, who keep company with kings and bishops. You could do worse than win my good graces.'

And with that, he wheeled his horse around and attempted to gallop off, but the animal gave an angry snicker and trotted defiantly to a patch of grass by the side of the road, where it began to graze. In a pitiable attempt to make it appear as though this was what he had intended, Moleyns hailed a group of scholars from King's Hall, and began to chat. One of them was the arrogant Godrich – the man who intended to be buried in St Mary the Great with more pomp and ceremony than a monarch.

'*Does* he know who killed Tynkell?' wondered Bartholomew, watching the knight laugh and joke. 'Or is he playing games with you?'

'Who knows?' muttered Michael, irritated by the encounter. 'But he is always gallivanting around the town, which is highly irregular. What is Dick Tulyet thinking, to let a prisoner out so often?'

'I am thinking that I must obey a direct order from the King,' came a voice from behind them, cool and rather stiff.

They turned to see Sheriff Richard Tulyet, whose youthful appearance belied a bold warrior and a skilled administrator. Unlike many secular officials, he did not consider the University a threat to his authority, and he and Michael had developed an efficient working relationship. He was also a friend.

As usual, Bartholomew found himself looking around for Tulyet's son Dickon, a child with no redeeming qualities and a nasty habit of 'accidentally' battering shins with the enormous sword his doting father had most unwisely given him. Then he allowed himself to relax. Dickon was no longer learning how to be a sheriff from his sire, because Chancellor Tynkell's mother – Lady Joan of Hereford – had offered to assign him to one of her knights as a squire. The whole town had heaved a sigh of relief when Dickon had ridden away, tall and proud on his father's best horse, to become someone else's problem.

'Are you telling us that the King *told* you to let Moleyns roam free?' asked Michael in disbelief. 'But he was convicted of robbery, burglary, extortion—'

'I know,' interrupted Tulyet shortly. 'And it gives me no pleasure to let him strut about, believe me. But my hands are tied: the King did not want him imprisoned in the first place, but the evidence was compelling, so he had no choice but to accept the jury's verdict. However, he promised to make the "captivity" as pleasant as possible, and Moleyns is quick to report any grievances.'

'Why does the King stand by him?' asked Bartholomew

curiously; he had tended Moleyns in the castle several times for minor ailments, and had not taken to him at all. 'He is an amusing raconteur, but his amiability is a façade. Beneath it, he is selfish, greedy, sullen and vicious.'

'Unfortunately, the King has only met the genial joker,' replied Tulyet. 'And the man who has been generous with funds for the French wars.'

'Funds amassed by abusing his power,' remarked Michael. 'He took bribes when he was Justice of the Common Bench, then committed all manner of dishonest acts to get more.'

'Money is money as far as the King is concerned,' shrugged Tulyet. 'And his affection for Moleyns means that Cambridge folk have fluttered towards the man like moths to a flame, all hoping that he will write something nice about them in his letters to Court. Moleyns was inundated with offers of friendship from the moment he arrived.'

'You mean burgesses?' asked Bartholomew. 'The Mayor and his friends?'

'Yes, along with wealthy scholars from King's Hall, Bene't and Maud's,' replied Tulyet. 'And Michaelhouse – young Will Kolvyle is a regular. He and Moleyns laugh and gossip for hours together. I am surprised you allow it.'

Will Kolvyle was Michaelhouse's newest Fellow, a talented youth who had arrived to take up post at the beginning of the academic year. He had made no effort to endear himself to his new colleagues, all of whom thought him arrogant, irritating and wholly devoid of humour.

'We did not know,' said Michael disapprovingly. 'But I will tell Langelee, and he will put an end to it. We do not want our College associated with Moleyns.'

'Good,' said Tulyet, and sighed ruefully. 'I was appalled when I learned that Moleyns was to be foisted on me. He is a distraction I could do without.'

'Why?' asked Bartholomew. 'Are you particularly busy?'

Tulyet shot him a sour glance. 'There are taxes to be prised from folk who would rather not pay them; your University is twice the size it was a year ago; and there is a fierce feud between two rival bands of tomb-makers. So yes, I am busy.'

'We have just been listening to Petit gripe about that,' said Bartholomew. 'He thinks the others stole a ledger slab from him.'

'I know,' said Tulyet drily. 'Along with various other supplies that have recently gone missing. He mentions them every time our paths cross. It is extremely annoying.'

Michael was not very interested in a spat between craftsmen, and turned to what he considered to be a far more pressing matter.

'Were you with Moleyns when Tynkell died?'

'I was nearby – I happened to be free for an hour, so Helbye and I decided to mind him together. He and Moleyns were at your sister's cloth stall, Matt, while I was next door, taking the opportunity to remind the glovers about the tax on fur. Why?'

'Because he hinted that he knows the killer's identity, but then declined to give us a name.'

'Well, all *I* saw was a black shape flapping away to the east. But leave Moleyns to me. If he did see anything pertinent, I will prise it out of him.'

At that moment there was a clatter of hoofs – Moleyns had managed to pull his horse away from the grass and direct it back to his wife and lawyer. Once there, several scholars and townsfolk came to greet him, all nodding and bowing obsequiously. Tulyet growled something about it being time that Moleyns was back in the castle, but had not taken many steps towards his prisoner when there was a flurry of excited barks. The stallion reared and Moleyns fell off.

'*Sir* John Moleyns indeed!' sneered Michael. 'He is not

fit to bear such a title. Even you could have kept your seat then, Matt, and that is saying something.'

When Moleyns failed to stand up, Bartholomew went to see if he needed help, but so many folk had clustered around the fallen knight that it was difficult to push through them. A few carried torches, although the light they cast was unsteady, and there was a very real danger of setting someone else alight.

A person in a cloak with a prettily embroidered hem – a woman's garment – was trying to escape, and Bartholomew was shoved away rudely when they got in each other's way. While he staggered, off balance, he saw the cowled figure he had spotted earlier, but the cleric was more adept at surging through crowds than Bartholomew, and had vanished before he could be hailed. Grimly, Bartholomew resumed his journey.

'Stand back!' he shouted as he elbowed his way through the throng. 'Let him breathe.'

The spectators eased away, allowing him just enough space to crouch down and examine Moleyns. He was vaguely aware of a number of familiar faces peering at him in the gloom, including Moleyns' wife and lawyer, who had dismounted and were trying to keep their feet in the scrum.

Moleyns' eyes were closed, and he lay unmoving among the scuffling feet. It did not take Bartholomew a moment to make his diagnosis, although it was not one he had been expecting.

'Lord!' he muttered to no one in particular. 'He is dead.'

CHAPTER 2

Stars were still glittering in the black velvet of the sky when the scholars of Michaelhouse prised themselves from their beds the following day. It was still bitterly cold, and frost had settled in a hard white crust across roofs and the mud of the yard. The water in the kitchen had frozen again, despite the fire that had been left burning all night, and Agatha the laundress, who ran the domestic side of the College, could be heard cursing as she tried to break it with a poker.

As usual, the College was bursting at the seams, because Master Langelee continued to enrol far more students than was practicable in order to get their tuition fees. A run of bad luck, combined with a series of dubious investments, meant that Michaelhouse remained on the brink of financial ruin, despite several recent donations from Bartholomew's generous sister, and overloading his Fellows with pupils was an easy way for Langelee to raise much-needed cash. This had resulted in an acute shortage of space, even with all the first years sleeping in the hall.

Bartholomew had always had two chambers at his disposal, but this was a luxury the College could no longer afford. His students – at least three times as many as he should have had – were crammed into the larger one, while he slept in the room where he kept his medicines. This had originally been provided because the reek of these powerful compounds was thought to be injurious to his health, but the danger had been conveniently forgotten in the demand for berths. He did not even have it to himself, and was obliged to share with his book-bearer Cynric and Deynman the librarian.

Deynman had once been a student himself, accepted purely because his father was rich. His studies had not gone well, and everyone had breathed a sigh of relief when he had abandoned a career in medicine and had opted instead to look after Michaelhouse's small but valuable collection of books. His proud father insisted on funding the post, and as no son of *his* was going to lack creature comforts, the allowance included plenty of money for firewood.

It was a pleasant change for Bartholomew, who usually shivered all through winter, while wind howled through the gaps in his windows and froze the mould that dripped down his walls. Now, he woke each morning to a blaze that had kept the three of them agreeably toasty all night, and hot water was available for washing and shaving. Better yet, his clothes were always aired when he donned them, and were comfortably warm against his skin. Sleeping with his head under a bench and his legs bent was a small price to pay for such unaccustomed delights.

Cynric had been in Bartholomew's employ for years, and the relationship between them was more of equals than master and servant. Unfortunately, the Welshman was one of the most superstitious men in the country, so their cramped quarters were liberally adorned with bundles of herbs, amulets, charms and mysterious pouches. Those Fellows in religious Orders had asked that they be removed – or at least put somewhere more discreet – but Cynric had doggedly refused, and the witchy paraphernalia remained.

'I am sorry that Satan stabbed Chancellor Tynkell,' he said conversationally, reaching for one of his talismans and kissing it three times. 'Poor man.'

'He was killed by a person,' Bartholomew told him firmly. 'The Devil had nothing to do with it.'

'Oh, yes, he did,' argued Cynric. 'We all saw that battle on the tower, and I watched him fly away afterwards.'

'You saw the wind catch Tynkell's cloak,' explained Bartholomew. 'That is all.'

'Oh, yes?' challenged Cynric. 'Then why did Brother Michael's beadles fail to find it? I know for a fact that he had them looking all afternoon. The answer is that it was not a cloak, but Satan, who took off from the tower and soared over to the Barnwell Fields.'

'And why would he go there?' asked Bartholomew archly. 'To talk to the sheep?'

'His ways are not for us to question,' said Cynric darkly, then grew thoughtful. 'I imagine he used one of his claws to inflict the fatal wound. You did say it was not a knife.'

'Yes, but that does not mean it was a claw. It was more likely to have been a long nail or some other kind of thin spike.'

'I imagine Satan has plenty of those,' put in Deynman, who had been listening with avid interest. 'He probably carries them in his purse, along with his coins and nosecloths.'

He and Cynric began a debate about what else the Devil might keep in his scrip, so Bartholomew left them to it and walked into the yard, where his colleagues were gathering, ready to process to church for their morning devotions. While he waited, he looked around at the College that had been his home for longer than he cared to remember.

It was dominated by its hall, a handsome building with an oriel window, and a beautiful mural along one wall, which depicted Michaelhouse's scholars listening to four great thinkers: Aristotle, Aquinas, Plato and Galen. Its shutters were closed, and would remain so all day, given that none of its windows had glass, although a light gleaming underneath one showed that the students who slept in that part of it were astir.

While the scholars were at church, the servants would stack away the mattresses, and set out benches and tables for breakfast. When the meal was over, the tables would be folded away, and the hall converted into a lecture room. Langelee and his Fellows would sit in their assigned places, and struggle to keep their own class's attention over the competing racket from their colleagues.

Below the hall were the kitchens and a series of pantries, while adjacent to it was the conclave, a cosy parlour that was the undisputed domain of the Fellows, a place where they could escape from their charges and relax. At right angles to the hall were the twin accommodation wings, two storeys high and with four doors apiece. Each door led to a little vestibule with rooms on either side, and stairs leading to the upper floor. Bartholomew lived in the older, more dilapidated northern one.

'I did not sleep a wink,' grumbled Michael, coming to stand next to him. His breath plumed as he spoke. 'I could not stop thinking about Tynkell.'

'It kept me awake, too,' confessed Bartholomew. 'We saw the killer with our own eyes, as did half the town, yet we have nothing to help us identify him.'

Michael grimaced. 'He thinks he is so clever, and it makes me even more determined to catch him. Especially after what happened to Moleyns.'

Bartholomew blinked. 'Surely you are not suggesting a connection between the two? How can there be? One was a respectable scholar, the other a criminal; one was stabbed on a tower, the other fell off his horse; one died "fighting the Devil", the other chatting in the street—'

'Two well-known men and two sudden deaths in public places,' countered Michael. 'I want you to examine Moleyns properly this morning, Matt. No, do not argue – I need the truth. Then we shall combine forces with Dick Tulyet to find the culprit.'

'Linking Moleyns and Tynkell might lead you astray,' warned Bartholomew.

'Then you will just have to keep me on the right path.

We begin today, as soon as we have been to church and eaten breakfast. And do not say it is term time, and you cannot spare the time, because you have *him*.'

He nodded to Bartholomew's senior student, John Aungel, who had taken on the task of minding his master's classes when Bartholomew was busy with patients – which was greatly appreciated, as all Cambridge's *medici* were currently inundated with work arising from the continued cold snap – congested lungs, chills, injuries resulting from falls, and frost-nipped fingers, toes, ears and noses.

Aungel hurried over when he saw they were talking about him. 'I imagine you want me to teach while you find Chancellor Tynkell's killer,' he said, and beamed. 'I do not mind, sir. I know Galen's *Prognostica* backwards, and I would love to help.'

'You would?' asked Bartholomew suspiciously, wondering what mischief was brewing. Students did not volunteer for extra work out of the goodness of their hearts.

'Oh, yes! Master Langelee has offered to make me a Fellow if I prove my worth, so I am delighted that you will be otherwise engaged for a while. It will give me a chance to show off my talents.'

Bartholomew was astonished. He was so used to his pupils racing away to earn lots of money by physicking the wealthy that it had never occurred to him that one might like a career in academia. Then he realised why Langelee was so keen to acquire another *medicus*.

'Matilde,' he said heavily. 'He thinks I will resign when she returns to Cambridge, and he wants you as my replacement.'

Matilde was the love of his life, who had left Cambridge four and a half years ago in the mistaken belief that her affection for him was not reciprocated. The misunderstanding had since been set to rights, and a week earlier, a letter had arrived announcing that she was on her way back to him. But so much time had passed that he feared they could not just pick up where they had left off, and so he was unsure what to think about her imminent return, other than that it was seriously disturbing his peace of mind.

Aungel shrugged. 'He could do worse. But you *should* marry and leave the College if she asks you to wed her, sir. You have been here too long, and a change will do you good.'

'Out of the mouths of babes and those with agendas,' murmured Michael, amused, as Aungel swaggered away.

'I cannot decide what to do about Matilde,' Bartholomew confided unhappily. 'It has been a long time since we last met, and we are both different people now. It may be too late for—'

'Nonsense,' interrupted Michael. 'Not a day has passed that you have not missed her, and her recent letter made it perfectly clear that her feelings for you are unchanged.'

'Perhaps they are, but she cannot abandon me without a word, then expect to march in as though nothing has happened. If she really wanted a life with me, she would not have disappeared in the first place.'

'She went *because* she wanted a life with you – and she thought she was not going to get one. Personally, I am all admiration for her: the moment she learned that the door was still open, she set about securing enough money to keep you both from starving once you exchange your University stipend for wedded bliss.'

'Money should not matter,' persisted Bartholomew stubbornly. 'If she truly loved me, she would have come back at once. Instead, she dallied in York, meddling about with investments.'

'Sentimental claptrap! You cannot blame her for declining to live in a hovel while you squander all your earnings on medicine for the poor. You should give her a chance when she arrives, because I believe she can make you happy.'

'I am not so sure, Brother. Not now.'

'Well, at least listen to what she has to say, although I cannot see that you will have to do it very soon. It is far too cold for travel, and she will have to wait for the weather to ease. You have plenty of time before you need to make a decision.'

When Michaelhouse was first established, its founder, the rich lawyer-priest Hervey de Stanton, was determined that his scholars would not neglect their religious duties, so he had included a church in the property he bequeathed. St Michael's was a pretty building with a large chancel and a low, squat tower. It was bitterly cold inside though. Icicles dangled from the place where the ceiling leaked, and the Holy Water in the stoop had turned to Holy Ice.

The Master and his Fellows took their places in the choir stalls, with the students ranged behind them. Langelee shifted impatiently from foot to foot, clearly itching to get on with something more pressing; he hated enforced immobility. Clippesby's head was bowed in prayer, although he had a duck under either arm, and not for the first time, Bartholomew marvelled that the creatures selected for such excursions never tried to escape. William stood next to Langelee, watching with critical eyes as Suttone the Carmelite performed the ceremonies at the altar.

Portly and an indifferent scholar, Suttone was utterly convinced that the plague was poised to return, when it would claim all those who had survived it the first time. He was a theologian, and his sermons tended to reflect his nihilist convictions, which meant they could make for bleak listening. However, as he had been saying the same thing for years and none of his grim predictions had yet come to pass, people had learned to take his warnings with a good pinch of salt.

His assistant that day was Will Kolvyle, one of two scholars recruited from Nottingham. Unfortunately, the other – John Dallingridge – had died before he could take up his appointment, and was the man currently being provided with a magnificent tomb in St Mary the Great. There was a rumour that he had been poisoned, but Kolvyle assured his horrified colleagues that there was no truth to the tale, and that the hapless Dallingridge had just died of natural causes.

Bartholomew had not liked the sound of Kolvyle when he had read the lad's application, and had voted against the appointment. The other Fellows had disregarded his concerns which meant that the motion to elect Kolvyle had passed. However, they had realised their mistake the moment the young man arrived: Kolvyle considered himself to be a rising star of unusual brilliance, who would bring fame and fortune to any foundation he deigned to grace with his presence. He was selfish, arrogant and rude, and made no bones about the fact that he considered Michaelhouse well beneath him, a mere stepping stone to better things. None of his new colleagues liked him, and he was almost as unpopular at Thelnetham had been.

That morning's service was longer than usual, because it was the Feast of the Purification of the Virgin, also known as Candlemas, when candles were blessed and given to the scholars for their religious obligations throughout the following year. Cynric believed that these warded off storms, and insisted on displaying Bartholomew's supply on the windowsill, where the elements would see them and move on. For the next twelve months, there would be a mute but determined battle of wills, when Bartholomew would stack them back inside the cupboard and the book-bearer would pull them out again.

When the rite was over, Langelee led his scholars at a rapid clip out of the church and down St Michael's Lane, eager now for his breakfast. They were meant to walk in silence, but academics were talkative by nature, so it was a rule they all ignored.

'Well, Brother?' the Master asked. 'Have you charged Satan with Tynkell's murder yet?'

Michael scowled at him. 'Are you sure you can tell me nothing useful about what happened? You are a practical man – you know the culprit was a person, and that the Devil was actually a cloak.'

'I know no such thing,' averred Langelee, crossing himself. 'Especially having listened to Hopeman in the Cardinal's Cap last night. He intends to take Tynkell's place, and has promised that Satan will never set foot in Cambridge again if he is elected. I might vote for him, because we cannot have Lucifer flapping around our streets.'

'Please do not,' said Michael curtly. 'He is a zealot, and will get us suppressed. The Church dislikes rabid opinions being brayed to impressionable young minds.'

'There is that cleric again,' said Bartholomew suddenly. 'The one in the cowl.'

'Do not bother to chase him,' said Michael, although Bartholomew had no intention of doing anything so rash in a lane that was slick with ice. 'He will come to us when he is ready.'

They reached Michaelhouse to find the Sheriff waiting for them at the gate, so Michael and Bartholomew stepped out of the procession to talk to him, leaving their colleagues to hurry across the yard to the smelly warmth of the hall. Again, Bartholomew found himself looking for Dickon, and smiled when he remembered that the lad had gone.

'Moleyns,' began Tulyet without preamble. 'His death is a serious problem for me. The King will be vexed that I failed to protect the friend he placed in my custody, while Moleyns' wife Egidia threatens to sue me for negligence. Will you look at the body, Matt, and tell me exactly how he died?'

Bartholomew nodded. 'I tried to do it last night, but his lawyer – Inge, is that his name? – claimed it was outside the University's jurisdiction.'

'Did he indeed?' murmured Tulyet, eyes narrowed as he reached for his purse. 'Then here are three pennies, which means you are now officially in *my* employ, and if you discover anything untoward, Inge will be the first person I shall interrogate. The second will be Egidia, who is far more interested in suing me than grieving for her husband.'

'You *should* question them,' said Michael. 'Especially if it transpires that Moleyns has been poisoned. They were both at a feast in Nottingham, during which Dallingridge is alleged to have been fed a toxin. Kolvyle assures us that the tale is untrue, but I do not trust him.'

'He is a nasty youth,' agreed Tulyet. 'And if Moleyns is the victim of foul play, then *he* will be my third suspect. By all accounts, Dallingridge would have been successful here, and Kolvyle is not the sort of fellow to appreciate competition.'

'Petit the mason was in Nottingham then as well,' mused Michael, 'and he has done very well out of Dallingridge's death. Not only is he being paid to create his patron's princely tomb, but the project has also won him several new customers.'

'Yes, and one is my sister,' said Bartholomew sharply. 'So leave him alone until Oswald's monument is finished, if you please. The process has already dragged on far longer than it should, and it is a strain on her.'

'It has dragged on because Petit it trying to serve too many clients,' said Tulyet. 'Besides Dallingridge and Stanmore, he is also building monuments for Holty, Mortimer and Deschalers. Of course, he only accepted the last two to stop the work from going to Lakenham. He and Lakenham hate each other, as you know.'

'Godrich of King's Hall has retained Petit's services,

too,' said Michael. 'Although his monument cannot be started until I have decided where it can go – which will *not* be the chancel. Then there are Moleyns and Tynkell . . . it is a good time for tomb-makers.'

'Speaking of Tynkell,' said Tulyet, 'I hear you have no plans to take his place, Brother. I wish you would reconsider. You and I work well together, and I doubt anyone else will be as effective.'

'No,' agreed Michael. 'You will have to contend with Lyng, Thelnetham or Hopeman.'

Tulyet was appalled. '*They* are the candidates? Christ God! Hopeman will have us in flames within a week, Lyng is too old to be effective, while Thelnetham . . . well, you cannot have a Chancellor who wears pink bows on his shoes. I do not want to spend all my time quelling spats between jeering townsmen and affronted scholars.'

'Perhaps others will agree to stand,' said Michael. 'I shall have a word with a few suitable puppets . . . I mean candidates later today.'

'Good,' said Tulyet. 'But we had better see to Moleyns. Will you come now, Matt?'

'Not until he has broken his fast,' said Michael, before Bartholomew could reply. 'He cannot deal with corpses on an empty stomach, and nor can I.'

Michaelhouse was not noted for the quality of its fare, although the food on offer that morning was better than usual, because Candlemas was a Feast Day. There was pottage with pieces of real meat, although these were few and far between, followed by bread and honey. Like the processions to and from church, meals were meant to be taken in silence, so the scholars could fill their minds with religious thoughts as they ate. It was another rule the Fellows ignored, which made it difficult to enforce among the students, so it was not long before the hall was abuzz with lively conversation. Most revolved around the Chancellor.

'Poor Tynkell,' said Langelee, when he had intoned one of his ungrammatical Latin graces, and was devouring his pottage with every appearance of relish; he tended not to mind what he ate, as long as there was lots of it. 'But Hopeman says his replacement will be in post within a week, which is good – it is risky to keep such an important office vacant.'

'His replacement will not be elected until next term,' countered Michael, who had emptied his bowl before most of the others had been served, and was already holding it out for a refill. 'These matters cannot be rushed.'

'Oh, yes, they can,' argued Kolvyle, inspecting the contents of his own dish before pushing it away with a fastidious shudder. 'The statutes say that if a Chancellor dies in office, there must be an election within a month. You have no grounds to postpone, Brother.'

'Tynkell did not "die in office",' countered Michael shortly. 'He was murdered. And I shall not appoint a successor until his killer is under lock and key.'

'No, you will not *appoint* him,' said Kolvyle challengingly. 'Because he must be *elected*. And we *will* have a ballot soon, because I shall go to St Mary the Great today, and issue a demand for one to be held next Wednesday. Exactly a week from now.'

'You cannot,' said Michael irritably. 'An election can only be called by the University's senior theologian – who just happens to be me. If you have read the statutes as closely as you claim, you should know this.'

'Except *in extremis*,' argued Kolvyle with a triumphant smirk. 'And I would say that the Chancellor's murder constitutes desperate circumstances, wouldn't you? So I shall make my announcement today, and most scholars will support it.'

'Oh, I see,' said Michael, his voice heavy with understanding. 'You aim to stand yourself. Well, I am afraid that is out of the question, because you are not eligible.'

Kolvyle blinked his astonishment. 'What are you talking about? Of course I am eligible.'

'You are only a Bachelor,' said Michael sweetly. 'The Chancellor must be a Master or a Doctor.'

'I *am* a Master,' snapped Kolvyle crossly. 'I completed all the requirements, and even gave a celebratory dinner last month – one *you* attended, Brother. The only thing lacking is a certificate, which Tynkell was supposed to have signed weeks ago, but he kept forgetting. It is a formality, no more.'

Michael smiled. 'A formality that will be completed as soon as the new Chancellor is in office. Obviously, that cannot be you – you can hardly award yourself a degree.'

Kolvyle's expression was murderous, but he realised that he was making a spectacle of himself, and hastened to smother his temper. He shrugged, feigning indifference. 'Well, I am young, so there will be plenty of time for such honours in the future, unlike the rest of you. Meanwhile, I shall vote for Godrich from King's Hall. He will make a splendid Chancellor. Better than Hopeman, Lyng or Thelnetham.'

'Godrich plans to stand?' frowned Michael.

Kolvyle smirked again, pleased to be in possession of information that the monk did not have. 'He announced it last night. Did you not hear?'

'Godrich will not make a very good Chancellor,' predicted Suttone. He had dripped honey down the front of his habit, and his efforts to mop it up had left a sticky smear; a mat of breadcrumbs adhered to it. 'He will favour King's Hall at the expense of other foundations, and he is a dreadful elitist. He is not the man we want.'

'Well, *I* like him,' said Kolvyle defiantly. 'He recognises promising young talent, and I shall rise through the University's ranks more quickly with an enlightened man like him in charge.'

'No self-interest here,' murmured Bartholomew,

prodding warily at a lump in his pottage. It looked suspiciously like part of a pig's snout, complete with bristles.

'The role of Senior Proctor has grown bloated,' Kolvyle went on, 'and it is time it was reined in. Godrich said that will be the first thing he does when he wins.'

'You are rash, throwing in your lot with a rival foundation,' remarked Langelee. 'Their first allegiance is to each other, and you will find yourself out on a limb if you alienate us. And speaking of unsuitable acquaintances, I hear you were friends with Moleyns the criminal.'

Kolvyle regarded him with open dislike. 'We knew each other from Nottingham. But my personal life is none of your affair, Master, and I will thank you to mind your own business.'

The response stunned Langelee and his Fellows into a gaping silence, during which Kolvyle stood and sailed out of the hall, head held high, blithely ignoring the rule that no one was supposed to leave the table before the Master, and certainly not before the final grace.

'You chose him,' said Bartholomew, the first to find his tongue. 'I told you he would be difficult, but you refused to listen.'

'Then you should have made your point more forcefully,' snapped Langelee, eyeing him accusingly.

'You should,' agreed Michael. 'I dislike this alliance with Godrich, too – another man with delusions of grandeur, as shown by his determination to be buried in the sort of style usually reserved for bishops and nobles.'

'Godrich will make a terrible Chancellor,' said Suttone. He had tried to rinse the honey from his robe with ale, and had made a greater mess than ever. 'He is too lazy.'

'Worse, he hates women,' put in Langelee, shaking his head at such an unfathomable notion, 'and would too rigorously enforce the rule that all scholars must shun them. Celibacy is all very well for some, but what about those of us with normal appetites?'

'It would be a nuisance,' agreed Suttone, who liked the company of ladies himself, despite the religious vows he had taken. Then he brightened. 'But no one will vote for him once they know his stance on lasses. He will lose on that issue alone.'

'He will not, because he has the support of King's Hall, whose infractions he will overlook,' countered Langelee, 'while the clerics will applaud his miserable views.' He glanced at Suttone. 'Well, most of them.'

'What a choice,' muttered Michael. 'Godrich, Lyng, Thelnetham or Hopeman.'

'Lyng is a decent soul,' said Langelee, 'although I would be happier if he were not so old. He is not robust enough to withstand the rigours of office now.'

'He is not as frail as everyone seems to think,' argued Michael. 'There is a core of steel in that man, which makes me wonder to what depths he would plunge to get himself elected.'

'I do not see him engaging in tussles on rooftops while pretending to be Satan,' said Langelee doubtfully. 'Tynkell was no Hercules, but even *he* could have bested the likes of Lyng.'

Suttone cleared his throat. 'I might stand for election myself. I have always had a hankering for the post, and I am good at administration. I will not impose any unreasonable laws – the one about women can go for a start, because God would not have created ladies if He had not wanted us to enjoy them.'

Michael regarded him appraisingly, while Langelee nodded to say he fully agreed with the last part, and Bartholomew wondered if he would be able to marry Matilde and still teach.

'Would you be willing to listen to advice from a man

with experience and skill?' asked the monk keenly. 'Namely me?'

Suttone inclined his head. 'Indeed, I would welcome such counsel.'

'Well, then,' said Michael, green eyes gleaming at the prospect of a challenge. 'We shall have to see what we can do about getting you in.'

'You are both excused College duties until Suttone is safely in post,' declared Langelee promptly. 'It is high time we had a chancellor among our Fellows. However, I liked Tynkell, and his killer *must* be brought to justice. Bartholomew can help you with that, Brother.'

'I cannot,' objected Bartholomew. 'I have too many patients, and my students—'

'It is a good opportunity for me to see if Aungel can step into your shoes when you leave.' Langelee raised his hand to stop the physician from speaking again. 'I have made my decision, so do not argue. Well? What are you waiting for? Off you go.'

Disliking the way everyone assumed he would automatically hurl himself into Matilde's arms, when the truth was that he was hopelessly confused about his feelings towards her, Bartholomew trailed after Michael to meet Tulyet in St Mary the Great. On any other day, he would have suggested deliberating his romantic conundrum in the Brazen George – a tavern where Michael was always made very welcome – but the monk's face was pale with worry, and Bartholomew did not want to burden him further.

The University Church was busier than usual, partly because it was Candlemas, but also because the battle on the tower had encouraged folk to go there and see what had attracted Satan to the place. It rang with excited voices and the clatter of industry, the latter of which came from Petit and his assistants, who were setting an elaborately carved pinnacle on Dallingridge's tomb.

'You promised to work on Oswald today,' said Bartholomew, approaching them and speaking accusingly.

'His mortar is still too wet, I am afraid,' shrugged Petit. His apprentices came to stand behind him in a protective semicircle. 'It is the cold weather, you see – it slows everything down. Perhaps it will be set by tomorrow.'

Bartholomew knew exactly why Petit had elected to work in St Mary the Great that day – it was an opportunity to advertise his skills to the hordes who flocked there. The physician's suspicions were borne out when Petit grabbed Michael's arm and tugged him towards the narthex at the western end of the church. The narthex not only contained the Great West Door – the large portal that was only opened for special ceremonial processions – but was also the place where the bells were rung, as the tower was directly above it.

'Good morning, Nicholas,' said Michael amiably to the man who was preparing to haul on the ropes. Then he frowned. 'What are you doing? Mass is over.'

James Nicholas was Secretary to the Chancellor, a quiet, scholarly man who limped from a childhood illness. He had tawny hair and a pleasant smile, and was one of the more able clerks who helped to run the *studium generale*. It was not his responsibility to chime the bells, but he loved doing it, and Michael was more than happy to let him, because it meant he did not have to pay a verger to oblige.

'I shall sound them whenever I have a spare moment today,' explained Nicholas earnestly. 'It is Candlemas, and people should be reminded of it from dawn until dusk.'

He began to pull, setting first one bell swinging, and then another, until he had all three clanging in a joyful cacophony of noise, moving from rope to rope with impressive skill – most men could only manage one at a time. His face was sombre, but there was a gleam in his eye that revealed his delight in the exercise.

Meanwhile, Petit was forced to shout to make himself heard – the bells were right above their heads. Bartholomew had often wondered if this was why Nicholas loved them: it was an opportunity for a quiet, unassuming man to make a fine old din. Putting his hands over his ears, Michael retreated to the relative peace of the nave. Bartholomew and Petit went with him.

'The narthex is where Chancellor Tynkell's monument should be,' stated Petit authoritatively. 'Beneath the bells, because he was in charge of seeing them cast and hung. There is plenty of room, even with three ropes whipping about.'

'*You* cannot build another monument,' said Bartholomew shortly. 'Not until you have finished the five you have already started.'

Petit ignored him. 'I envisage a canopy with soaring arches, a tomb that will be the envy of all England, and will set a precedent for other high-ranking University men. Such as yourself, Brother. I imagine you would like something handsome, when you go.'

'If every dead official is provided that sort of monstrosity, there will be no room left in the church for the living,' remarked Bartholomew caustically. 'And Tynkell was not an ostentatious man. He would have preferred something modest.'

'Then *I* am the fellow you want,' came a voice from behind them. 'I am Richard Lakenham, and this is my apprentice Reames. We are latteners – engravers of funerary brasses. We can provide something far more suitable than the gaudy affairs created by Petit.'

Lakenham was a small, nondescript man, who looked as though he was in need of a good meal. By contrast, his pupil appeared to be very well fed, and his clothes were of far better quality than his master's. Indeed, if Bartholomew had been asked, he would have said that Reames was the one in charge, and Lakenham was the assistant.

'We will craft a nice plain chest with a pretty brass on top,' said Reames. 'You will love it, I promise.'

'We can engrave him wearing his robes of office, if you like,' added Lakenham eagerly, 'and there will be room around the edge for an inscription of your own composition.'

'They do not want your rubbish,' growled Petit, furious at the brazen attempt to steal 'his' business. 'They want something decent, something in keeping with Tynkell's elevated status. They only need to inspect the brass shields you made for Dallingridge's tomb to see that your work is vastly inferior.'

Lakenham did not deign to acknowledge the insult. He turned his back on the mason and continued to address Michael. 'Hire us, Brother. You will not regret it. Moreover, *we* do not flit from job to job like butterflies.'

'Oh, yes, you do,' snapped Petit, nettled. 'Or are you saying that it is not necessary for mortar to set or pitch to cool? No wonder all your tombs fall to pieces!'

'If they do, it is because *you* steal my supplies,' flashed Lakenham, whipping around to glare at him at last. 'You are a thief, and the sooner you are arrested, the better.'

'A third brass plate disappeared from our shed last night,' added Reames, brushing an invisible speck from his gipon. 'And we know exactly who stole it: you and your louts.'

'It is true,' said Lakenham, then jabbed a grubby finger towards Sheriff Tulyet, who was walking down the nave to join them, clearly wondering why Bartholomew had not yet made a start on Moleyns. 'And *he* will catch you eventually. He vowed only this morning that you will not keep getting the better of him, and that you will soon swing.'

'*We* are not felons,' shouted Petit, incensed. 'Accuse Isnard and Gundrede. *They* might stoop to touching the paltry contents of your vile little hut, but we would never demean—'

'This is a House of God, not a tavern,' snapped Tulyet, when he heard what was being bawled. 'If you cannot behave with the proper decorum, then leave.'

Both sides backed away, unnerved by the anger in his voice, although they had not taken many steps before they resumed their spat.

'I rue the day they arrived in my town,' growled Tulyet, watching them in rank disapproval. Then he glared at Bartholomew and Michael. 'It is your College's fault, of course. Dallingridge's death brought them here, and he was one of your Fellows.'

'Not officially,' objected Michael, 'given that he died before he could be installed. It was a pity, actually – he might have served to temper some of Kolvyle's unpleasantness.'

While he and Tulyet embarked on a detailed analysis of Kolvyle's failings, Bartholomew decided it was time that he examined Moleyns. However, he had not taken many steps towards the Lady Chapel before he was waylaid by one of Petit's apprentices. His name was Peter Lucas, and he was a hefty lad with a bad haircut.

'I know things,' he muttered, tapping a grimy finger to his temple. 'Lots of things.'

'What sort of things?' asked Bartholomew, bemused.

'You know,' said Lucas, and winked meaningfully. 'Events and people. I might tell you later, if you make it worth my while.'

He had gone before Bartholomew could ask him to elaborate.

Sir John Moleyns had been taken to St Mary the Great because it was the largest and most prestigious church in the town, and Tulyet was keen for the King to know that his friend's remains had been treated with the appropriate respect. The body was in the Lady Chapel, next to Tynkell, although it occupied a coffin far grander than the one in which the Chancellor lay, and the lid was off, so that well-wishers could pay their last respects face to face.

'Not that there have been many,' confided Tulyet. 'His "friends" dropped him like a hot coal once he was no longer in a position to do them favours at Court.'

By contrast, Tynkell had attracted a great many mourners. At that particular moment, most were Dominicans, led by little Prior Morden, who was perfectly proportioned, but the size of a small child. Bartholomew was pleased to note that the two beadles – both with scarves covering their faces – were dutifully keeping the curious at a respectful distance.

'We have been praying for his soul,' explained Morden to Bartholomew, Michael and Tulyet. 'Which is in serious danger, given what happened to his body.'

'You mean the deadly miasma that seeps from him?' asked Tulyet, wrinkling his nose in distaste, while Bartholomew wondered whether to remind them that the Chancellor had smelled like that before he had died.

'And the rest,' said Morden darkly. '*We* know why he is in a closed coffin, with all the clasps securely fastened and armed men standing guard. You are afraid that he will break out and come to haunt us.'

'No, we are not,' said Bartholomew, horrified that his attempt to protect Tynkell should have been so badly misinterpreted. 'Those are to prevent ghouls from opening the box to gawp at him. He deserves to be left in peace.'

'He will not get much of that in here,' remarked Morden, as a clatter of hammers and raised voices indicated that Petit and his people were back at work. 'But it is not necessary to conceal the truth from us, Matthew. We are priests: we know all about the Devil taking possession of corpses and using them to walk among the living.'

And with that, he flung a generous glug of holy water

towards Tynkell's casket, and led his friars out. As they went, they chanted a psalm in voices so deep that it verged on the sinister, and sent a shiver down Bartholomew's spine.

'Now look what your ridiculous insistence on secrecy has done,' said Michael irritably. 'I am sure the truth about Tynkell's . . . peculiarities cannot be more terrible than the notion that Satan aims to inhabit his body. It would be better for everyone concerned, if you were honest.'

'It is not a case of honesty,' said Bartholomew tiredly. 'It is a case of respecting his wishes. He made me promise never to tell.'

'Moleyns,' prompted Tulyet impatiently. 'Examine him now, Matt, while the Lady Chapel is fairly empty. I assume you would rather work without too large an audience?'

'I would rather work with no kind of audience,' said Bartholomew. 'So you will have to oust everyone first.'

Tulyet obliged, after which he and the beadles stood guard to ensure that Bartholomew was not disturbed at his grisly craft. Meanwhile, Michael walked to Tynkell's office in the south aisle, and experienced a sharp pang of sorrow when he saw the Chancellor's spare shoes under the table. When he closed the door behind him, he saw something else, too – Tynkell's cloak hanging on a hook at the back of it. He had glanced into the office the previous day, and was annoyed with himself for not searching it properly, because the garment was important for two reasons.

First, it told him that Tynkell had not expected to be out in the elements when he had left his office or he would have taken it with him. And second, it meant it had been the *killer's* cloak that had sailed off the roof – so it had to be found and identified as soon as possible. He waylaid a passing beadle and ordered him to continue looking, even giving the man money to make enquiries in the town's less salubrious alehouses – places no Senior Proctor could go and expect to meet cooperative witnesses.

When the beadle had gone, Michael sat in the chair that Tynkell had occupied for the past six years and sighed with genuine sorrow. The Chancellor had had his faults, but Michael had liked him, and was deeply sorry that his remaining years had been so cruelly snatched away.

He reached for the nearest pile of documents and began to sort through them, alarmed to note that matters which should have been handled weeks ago had been left unattended. They included confirming a number of degrees, one of which was Kolvyle's.

He leaned back in the chair and pondered. On reflection, the Chancellor *had* spent hours in his office with the door closed. Michael had assumed, not unreasonably, that Tynkell was busy with the extra assignments that he himself had devised – a ploy intended to prevent him from embarking on a third self aggrandising scheme. Unfortunately, the mass of neglected documents suggested he had been doing anything but University duties for the past few weeks.

Vexed that he should be left with such a muddle, Michael dealt with the more urgent matters, and was about to summon Secretary Nicholas to help with the rest when he saw the corner of a letter poking from between the pages of a book. The book was Tynkell's most cherished possession, a gift from his redoubtable mother, who had not long left the town after an extended visit.

Lady Joan of Hereford was a remarkable lady – one of few people who were a match for the hellion Dickon Tulyet – and Michael winced when he realised that he would have to tell her what had happened. He decided to delay the unhappy duty until he could also inform her that the killer had been caught. There were three reasons why this was a good idea.

First, there was a danger that she might appear with the intention of catching the culprit herself. Second, Tynkell's funeral would be a much more manageable affair without her interference. And third, she had declared several times that she would make a better Chancellor than her son, and Michael did not want her to stage a coup. She was ineligible on several counts, not least of which was her sex, but Joan was unlikely to let those stop her.

He pulled the document out. It bore Moleyns' signature, and invited Tynkell to meet him during Mass, when 'certain business' would be discussed. The tenor of the message suggested it was not the first time recipient and sender had made such an arrangement, and that they had done it in secret then, too. There was no hint of menace, so Tynkell had clearly not been coerced into an association with the felon, but Michael was puzzled, even so. What could the Chancellor of the University have had to say to such a man?

No answers came, so Michael went to the door and called for Nicholas. The Chancellor's secretary shook his head when Michael showed him the note.

'I have never seen it before. However, Moleyns *did* seek Tynkell out when he attended services here. They often stood in the nave and chatted.'

'Chatted amiably?' probed Michael.

Nicholas shrugged. 'I was never close enough to hear, but they both laughed from time to time. I did once warn Tynkell that it was unwise to keep company with such a person, especially in public, but he told me to mind my own business.'

'*Tynkell* did?' Michael was astonished. It did not sound like anything the meek Chancellor would have uttered.

'He had changed in the last few weeks,' confided Nicholas. 'I do not know why.'

'And you did not think to tell me?'

'You are always so busy, what with the University growing apace and your teaching at Michaelhouse, that I did not like to worry you. Besides, there was nothing specific, and I was afraid you would think I was wasting your time.'

'In what way had he changed? And what precipitated it?'

Nicholas's expression was pained. 'It started at about the same time that Moleyns arrived at the castle, which was October, if you recall – three months ago now. Although that is not to say that the two are connected, of course . . .'

'But?' prompted Michael when the secretary hesitated.

'But before then, Tynkell was always very polite. After, he was irritable and withdrawn. Perhaps he knew what he would soon be facing, and feared he would prove unequal to the task.'

'You mean meeting Moleyns during Mass?' asked Michael, bemused.

'I mean fighting the Devil, Brother,' whispered Nicholas, wide-eyed. 'Tynkell was not a man for combat – of any kind. And to challenge Satan . . .'

Michael regarded him balefully. 'It was not Satan, and any man with an ounce of sense should know it.'

'If you say so, Brother.'

'I *do* say so, and I would be grateful if you could help me put an end to this foolish rumour by telling people that it was the killer's cloak that they saw flying away.'

Nicholas inclined his head, although his sullenly stubborn expression told the monk that he believed he had seen the Devil, and nothing was going to persuade him otherwise. Disinclined to waste his time arguing, Michael changed the subject.

'Can you tell me anything else about these assignations with Moleyns?' he asked. 'Such as how often you saw them together.'

'Five or six times, I suppose. They talked while everyone

else concentrated on their devotions. But Moleyns met lots of people when he was out, so his encounters with Tynkell are probably irrelevant.'

Michael would make up his own mind about that. 'Now tell me about yesterday,' he instructed. 'How did Tynkell seem before he went up the tower?'

'I did not see him, Brother. The moment he arrived for work, he came in here and shut the door.'

Michael was beginning to be exasperated. 'Surely you can tell me *something* to help?'

Nicholas's expression was stricken. 'I have thought about nothing else all night – mulling over recent conversations in an effort to understand why he . . . The only thing I can tell you is that he had developed a habit of muttering about the Devil. So you see, Brother, he *did* know a confrontation was brewing.'

With the Lady Chapel empty, Bartholomew took the opportunity to open Tynkell's coffin and ensure that the body had not been disturbed. The two hairs he had placed carefully across the Chancellor's chest were still in place, telling him that Tynkell's secret remained safe. He pulled the shroud to one side to look at what had given rise to such rumour and speculation.

Some years previously, there had been a popular fashion whereby small cuts were made in a specific pattern and then rubbed with pigment. The dye remained after the wounds had healed, leaving more or less permanent marks. Bartholomew had never been tempted to decorate himself so, but Tynkell was covered in little symbols, and all were the same: a twisting serpent with a rather diabolical pair of horns.

Shortly after his election, the Chancellor had tried to remove one with a rasp, which had resulted in a nasty infection. Bartholomew had been summoned, and Tynkell had sheepishly confided how he had come by them –

after a particularly wild feast, when he had been insensible from drink, as his friends' idea of fun. His shame of the marks was such that he had elected never to wash, lest someone burst in on him and saw them. This practice had resulted in so many upset stomachs that Deynman the librarian had once drawn the conclusion that Tynkell was suffering from the kind of morning sickness that was common in early pregnancy.

Bartholomew regarded the body sadly. Poor Tynkell! But he would be in the ground soon, and everyone would forget his eccentricities.

He replaced the hairs and the lid, fastening the clasps tightly, then turned his attention to Moleyns. He began by feeling the criminal's head for suspicious bumps, then looked in his mouth and at his hands for burns that might suggest poison. There was nothing out of the ordinary, so he turned to the torso. Moleyns was still wearing the clothes in which he had died – fine ones that boasted an irritatingly large number of laces and buckles. Bartholomew fought his way through them, then stared in shock at what he found.

There was a wound in Moleyns' chest that was identical to the one in Tynkell – a small round hole. He inspected it closely, sure it had been made with the same implement – or one that was very similar. He was about to call for Tulyet when there was a commotion outside the door, and he rolled his eyes when he recognised the unpleasantly strident tones of John Cook, the town's new barber-surgeon.

Bartholomew did not like Cook, whom he considered inept and untrustworthy. The antipathy was fully reciprocated, and Cook rarely missed an opportunity to malign Bartholomew, particularly over the fact that he sometimes performed surgery. Most physicians steered well clear of such grisly work, believing it to be demeaning. Bartholomew, however, thought his patients had a right to any procedure that would make them better, and a long line of incompetent barbers meant he had learned to perform them himself.

Cook was short, sharp-eyed and bald, but had allowed the whiskers on his cheeks to grow to extraordinary length, while his chin was clean shaven. It was an odd style, particularly on a man who prided himself on his barbering skills. His clothes were of good quality, although greasy, which meant the hairs he cropped from his customers tended to stick to them, giving him the appearance of a badly cured pelt.

He hailed from Nottingham, but had accompanied the tomb-makers south, because his home town was awash with barber-surgeons, whereas Cambridge had none. He was fiercely protective of his professional rights, so it was inevitable that he and Bartholomew would clash.

'How *dare* he!' Cook was shouting. '*I* am the town's barber, not him.'

'I assure you,' drawled Tulyet, 'he is not giving Moleyns a haircut.'

'I should hope not,' snarled Cook. 'I spent ages combing those curls last night, and no one should interfere with perfection.'

Bartholomew glanced at Moleyns' coiffure, and thought if that was perfection, then he lived in a sadly flawed world. However, he was not surprised to learn that Cook was proud of what he had done: most barber-surgeons preferred to emphasise the medical part of their trade, but Cook liked to brag about his skill with hair. Moreover, he had an alarming habit of suspending surgical operations partway through, while he went to give another customer a trim.

'Let me past, Sheriff,' Cook ordered. 'Or I shall report you to the Worshipful Company of Barbers. Only a fool challenges a man who has a powerful guild at his back.'

'It is all right, Dick,' called Bartholomew, although he

seriously doubted that such an august organisation would race to defend the likes of Cook. 'I have finished.'

Tulyet stepped aside and Cook thrust past him. The barber was followed by Inge and Egidia, both patently uneasy, which led Bartholomew to wonder if they knew more than was innocent about what had happened to Moleyns.

Seeing the Lady Chapel open, others crowded in on their heels. They included a gaggle of University clerks, some scholars from King's Hall, three Gilbertines and several members of Maud's Hostel, none of whom had a legitimate reason for being there. Michael trailed in at the end, with Secretary Nicholas and two beadles. Absently, Bartholomew noted that four of the five men who wanted to be Chancellor were among the press – Lyng, Hopeman, Godrich and Thelnetham. He was glad Suttone had the good taste not to come a-gawping.

'You have ruffled his locks,' declared Cook indignantly. 'And why? For *anatomy*!'

He hissed the last word, giving it a decidedly sinister timbre, which had the onlookers crossing themselves against evil and exchanging uneasy glances.

'Inspecting a corpse is hardly anatomy,' argued Tulyet coolly. 'It is a—'

'Oh, yes, it is,' countered Hopeman. 'And it is the Devil's work. I shall put an end to such practices when I am Chancellor.'

'You will never be elected,' scoffed Godrich. He was a tall, aloof man in a fur-lined cloak, with protuberant eyes and bad skin. He made no pretence at scholarship, and had made it clear from the first that the University was an irritating but necessary step towards a career in the royal household. 'We need a leader with important connections, not a religious fanatic.'

'Gentlemen, please!' cried Lyng, distressed. 'No quarrels here, I beg you. It is inappropriate.'

'Then let us go outside,' suggested Thelnetham. 'We shall hold a public debate, and see then who is the strongest candidate.'

None of the others moved to accept the challenge, perhaps because they knew they were no match for Thelnetham's razor intellect and quick tongue. Then Egidia stepped forward.

'Well?' she demanded haughtily. 'What killed my husband? I imagine it is something that can be attributed to the poor level of care he suffered at the castle.'

'He was stabbed,' replied Bartholomew, aiming to see what a bald statement of fact would shake loose. Unfortunately, the only ones who seemed shocked by the announcement were Michael and Tulyet. 'You can see the mark here quite clearly.'

'You claim *that* as a death wound?' asked Inge in disbelief, as everyone craned forward to look. 'Surely it is far too small?'

'Cook will prove the truth, by inserting a surgical probe into it,' said Bartholomew. 'Then you will all see that the killer's weapon penetrated his victim's heart.'

'I do not hold with desecrating the dead,' declared Cook, taking a brush and beginning to rearrange the corpse's hair. It was macabre and Bartholomew found himself unable to watch, although he knew it was actually less gruesome than what he had just proposed.

'Wait a moment, Matt,' said Michael, finding his voice at last. 'Are you saying we have *two* murders to explore?'

Bartholomew nodded. 'And the similarities between them suggests that both were killed by the same weapon, probably wielded by the same person. You were right to see a connection between them.'

'Lord!' breathed Tulyet, stunned. 'We were there when Moleyns died. He was dispatched right under our noses!'

'Not just ours,' said Michael soberly. 'Lots of people

surged towards him when he fell off his horse. And Tynkell was killed in full view of half the town.'

Lyng crossed himself. 'So the Devil strikes a second time. Poor Moleyns!'

'Poor Moleyns indeed,' agreed Godrich. 'Of course, a lot of tomb-builders clustered around him when he fell. And who benefits when a rich man breathes his last?'

'No, the culprit is Satan,' stated Hopeman matter-of-factly. 'And he will claim other victims until a priest – a friar, like myself – is elected to the chancellorship.'

There was a clamour of agreement from his supporters, but Godrich cut across them.

'No vulgar commoner will ever be Chancellor. How could he, when his duties include representing our University to kings and bishops?'

Hopeman and his deacons reacted with furious indignation, and their ringing voices echoed through the church. It was some time before the racket subsided, and Bartholomew saw that Michael had let it run on purpose, in the hope that temper would result in careless admissions. Unfortunately, no one had made that mistake.

'I am a priest, too,' said Lyng, when he could make himself heard. 'I can face down demons just as well as any Dominican.'

'But I am a *canon*,' stated Thelnetham loftily. 'A cut above mere mendicants. If a religious man is needed as Chancellor, then I am the best choice.'

Gradually, perhaps realising that squabbling over the corpse of the man they intended to replace was unedifying, the four contenders took their leave, although none went very far. They stopped in the nave, where a second row broke out. Most of the onlookers had followed, although a few lingered in the Lady Chapel, to see what would happen next with Moleyns.

'You assume that John was stabbed in the street,' said

Egidia to Bartholomew, as Cook continued to ply his comb. 'But maybe it happened earlier, while he was in the castle – a place where he should have been safe, as I am sure the King will agree.'

'Impossible,' replied Bartholomew promptly, much to Tulyet's obvious relief. 'The wound would have been almost instantly fatal.'

Egidia shot him a very unpleasant look.

'We all saw him fall off his horse,' said Tulyet. 'So did he fall because he was stabbed, or was he attacked once he was on the ground?'

'The latter,' replied Bartholomew. 'Because the culprit would have had to reach up to stab him on his horse, which we would have noticed.'

'Then perhaps someone shot him,' suggested Tulyet. 'From a distance.'

'If that were the case, the projectile would still be in him,' argued Bartholomew. 'No, this happened when he was on the ground. I am sure of it.'

'You do not know what you are talking about,' sneered Cook. 'Because wounds are *my* business, not yours. And in my expert opinion, Moleyns fell on something sharp. Ergo, his death is not murder, but an accident – one the Sheriff should have prevented.'

He smiled ingratiatingly at Egidia, and received a nod of appreciation in return.

'So Moleyns speared himself on a spike that just happens to be identical to the one that killed Tynkell a few hours earlier?' asked Bartholomew sceptically. 'Do you really think that is likely?'

Cook scowled. 'You scholars are obsessed with logic, yet we barbers see "impossible" happenings on a daily basis. No one should accept the word of a physician on this matter.'

'Well, we do,' said Tulyet shortly. 'Matt is the University's Corpse Examiner, and has been giving us his opinion on suspicious deaths for years. We trust him implicitly. You, on the other hand . . .'

He eyed Cook with such obvious contempt that the barber bristled, and to avoid another unseemly row, Michael showed Inge and Egidia the note he had found in Tynkell's office.

'He and my husband liked to discuss weaponry,' explained Egidia with a careless shrug. 'They often met here on the pretext of attending Mass. Well, why not? It was convenient for them both, and these rites can often be very dull. They needed something to keep them entertained.'

'Weaponry?' echoed Tulyet sharply, before Michael could remark that the University's Chancellor was not a man to be bored with his religious duties. 'Are you telling me that Tynkell was going to provide my prisoner with arms?'

'Of course not,' said Inge impatiently. 'Tynkell was interested in siege engines, and planned to write a treatise on them when he retired. Moleyns had seen them in action, and was willing to give him eye-witness accounts.'

'Tynkell *was* fascinated by war machines,' acknowledged Bartholomew. 'He often talked about them to me.'

'Then why meet Moleyns furtively?' asked Michael doubtfully. 'He could have gone to the castle for these sessions.'

'Perhaps he found the place objectionable,' suggested Egidia, looking at Tulyet out of the corner of her eye. 'And who can blame him?'

'I never saw Moleyns with Tynkell, here or anywhere else,' said Tulyet, 'but I will ask Helbye. He usually escorted Moleyns on his excursions, and will know what he did. If there was anything untoward in this association, he will find it.'

CHAPTER 3

The men who wanted to be Chancellor were still quarrelling when Bartholomew, Michael and Tulyet left the Lady Chapel, although Lyng flung up his hands in resignation before walking out, claiming he wanted no part of such an unbecoming spectacle. Scholars from the hostels nodded approval, while others came to shake his hand when he reached the street.

'He is popular,' mused Michael. 'Suttone will have to *ooze* charm to defeat him, so let us hope he is equal to the task. After all, there is only so much I can do to facilitate his election without eyebrows being raised.'

Tulyet laughed. 'Watch your words, Brother. It sounds as though you intend to cheat.'

Michael did not smile back. 'I cannot work with Lyng.'

'Why not? He seems a decent soul, albeit far too old.'

'Because he will refuse my advice, on the grounds that he thinks he knows everything already. But times have changed since he was last in power and—'

'There is that cowled man again,' interrupted Bartholomew irritably. 'I wish he would just come to talk to us. I dislike the sense of being watched all the time.'

'Could he be the killer?' asked Tulyet sharply, preparing to give chase if so. 'Monitoring you to assess whether you are closing in on him?'

'The killer will be eager to stay as far away from us as possible,' replied Michael with conviction. 'We must bide our time with this shadow. He will approach us when the time is right.'

Bartholomew wanted to argue, but a sudden hammering drew their attention to the Great West Door, where Kolvyle was nailing up a notice. He was with scholars from King's Hall, who were patting him on the back.

'His demand for an election,' predicted Michael sourly. 'Well, he shall have one, although his favourite Godrich will not win. I shall write a statute to keep upstarts like Kolvyle in their place when all this is over. I dislike youthful arrogance.'

'So Suttone will be Tynkell's successor?' asked Tulyet. He reflected for a moment. 'He is better than the others, I suppose. Godrich is only interested in furthering his own career, Hopeman is a reckless zealot, Thelnetham dresses wrongly, and you have just said that Lyng would not be suitable.'

Bartholomew was not sure the Carmelite would be much better. He liked Suttone, who was a good man on the whole, but he would be another Tynkell, a meek nonentity ruled by Michael. Except that Michael would be in his See, and thus not in a position to guide him, so what would happen to the University then? Would chaos reign, because a strong Chancellor was needed to govern a lot of opinionated, unpredictable and vociferous academics?

'I cannot believe the audacity of this killer,' Michael was saying to Tulyet, dragging Bartholomew's thoughts away from University politics. 'Moleyns' murder was especially bold.'

'Yes and no,' said Tulyet. 'It was dark and the torches did more to confuse than illuminate, so it was difficult to see anything well. I would argue it was a very good time to choose.'

'I saw a woman in a cloak with an embroidered hem,' said Bartholomew suddenly, as Tulyet's words jolted his own memory of the flickering confusion that had ensued after Moleyns' fall. 'She was shouldering her way out of the press, which was odd when everyone else was craning forward.'

'What else did you notice about her?' asked Tulyet keenly.

'Her hood was up, so I did not see her face. But it was cold, so everyone else's was up as well, including my own. There was nothing suspicious about that.'

'Could it have been Egidia?' pressed Tulyet. 'She does not seem overly distressed by her bereavement, and I did say that I would look to her, should any harm befall her husband. She will certainly benefit from his death, because not only will she inherit all his worldly goods, but she is now free to live wherever she wants.'

'She was free before,' said Michael, frowning. 'She was not forced to keep him company in prison – she chose to do it.'

'Because he held all their money – or what remained of their wealth after the courts had seized most of his assets,' explained Tulyet. 'Had she gone to live alone, she would have been as poor as a church mouse. She begged him any number of times for an allowance, but he always refused. She resented it bitterly, and so did Inge, who was also obliged to rely on Moleyns' largesse. Such as it was.'

'Inge has no funds of his own?' asked Bartholomew.

'He did, but they have long gone – he expected Moleyns to be released within a few weeks, and never imagined the ordeal would drag on for years. He could have left and struck out alone, but then what? He had sold himself to Moleyns, body and soul, so his only option was to hold fast and hope that Moleyns would one day be in a position to reward his loyalty.'

'Now Egidia can reward it,' remarked Michael. 'I assume she is Moleyns' sole heir?'

'She is,' nodded Tulyet. 'She has already laid claim to the store of money he kept in his room, which was no mean sum, and I am sure Inge will help her spend it. I have the sense that they are rather more than just lawyer and client, which makes them both prime suspects for his murder in my book.'

'But they were in the Market Square when Tynkell died,' said Bartholomew. 'With you. And we have decided that Moleyns and Tynkell were claimed by the same hand.'

'*Moleyns* was with me,' corrected Tulyet. 'Egidia and Inge had gone to St Mary the Great to look at the tombs.'

'Why would they do that?' asked Michael suspiciously. 'So they would know what to commission when Moleyns needed one?'

'Perhaps. Regardless, it means they have no alibi for Tynkell's death, and they were certainly nearby when Moleyns was killed.' Tulyet turned back to Bartholomew. 'So I repeat: could the cloaked woman you saw have been Egidia?'

'Yes, I suppose. However, when I pronounced Moleyns dead, she was standing right next to me. It seems unlikely that she would fight her way out of the press, then battle back in again.'

'Was she wearing this distinctive cloak?' asked Tulyet, and when Bartholomew shook his head, he raised his hands in a shrug. 'Then maybe it was bloodstained, obliging her to get rid of it before someone noticed. Then she hurried back to play the distraught widow.'

'It is possible,' acknowledged Bartholomew, although he doubted Moleyns' wound had produced much gore. He would have noticed, even in the unsteady light of the bobbing torches.

'Who else was in the crowd?' asked Michael. 'I am afraid my thoughts were on Tynkell, so I was not really paying attention.'

'All the tomb-makers, plus Isnard and Gundrede,' replied Tulyet promptly. 'I was watching them, because I was afraid they might start a fight over these stolen supplies.'

'Isnard has nothing to do with that,' said Bartholomew

sharply. 'Why would he? He can hardly sell such items here.'

Tulyet regarded him pityingly. 'He is a bargeman, Matt, which means he can transport goods anywhere he likes, and there is a huge market for illicit brass and stone in London. However, I might have given him the benefit of the doubt, if he had not developed this odd friendship with the felonious Gundrede.'

'Who else did you see in the crowd?' asked Bartholomew, unwilling to admit that the Sheriff might have a point.

'Godrich, Hopeman and Lyng,' said Tulyet. 'The first two quarrelling, while Lyng tried to act as peacemaker – a spat I noticed, because I was afraid your other scholars would join in and start a brawl.'

'Suttone was not there, because he was teaching in Michaelhouse, and two dozen students will testify to that fact,' said Michael. 'But what about Thelnetham?'

'Not that I noticed. I spotted Kolvyle, though. He was one of the first to surge forward when Moleyns fell.'

'Lord! I hope *he* is not the culprit,' exclaimed Michael. 'A killer in the College might damage Suttone's election campaign.'

'Barber Cook was also very quick on the scene,' Tulyet went on. 'I would not mind at all if he is the villain – I cannot abide the fellow. Of course, he does give a lovely shave . . .'

'I would not let him near *me* with a sharp knife,' said Bartholomew shortly.

'That is probably wise in your case,' remarked Tulyet. 'He loathes physicians.'

'So are these all our suspects?' asked Michael. 'Inge and Egidia; the warring tomb-builders; Isnard and Gundrede; Hopeman, Lyng, Godrich and Kolvyle; and Barber Cook?'

'If only!' sighed Tulyet. 'A host of others raced to Moleyns' side as well – the Mayor and his burgesses; scholars from

84

King's Hall, Maud's and several other University foundations; the woman in the embroidered cloak . . .'

'What about motives?' asked Bartholomew. 'What links Tynkell to Moleyns, other than their odd meetings in St Mary the Great?'

'That is easily answered,' said Michael. 'Tynkell was killed either to make way for a new Chancellor or to strike a blow against the University. And Moleyns intimated that he knew the culprit, so he was dispatched to prevent him from blabbing.'

'Which means that the killer was close enough to hear what Moleyns told us,' said Bartholomew, 'and launched a plan to stab him within a few moments. Is that likely?'

Michael and Tulyet had no answer.

'Someone will have seen something,' said Michael eventually. 'No matter how careful he was. So I will question scholars, while you speak to townsmen, Dick. However, before we start, I should like another word with the grieving widow.'

'Not here,' advised Tulyet. 'She will accuse you of heartlessness. Come to the castle at noon.'

The cold weather meant that Bartholomew had yet more summonses from ailing patients, so he used the intervening time to visit the most urgent cases. He trudged around the town with his older students in tow – other than Aungel, who had offered to read to the younger ones – treating a variety of colds, coughs and lung complaints. He visited his regulars first, then went to the first of three new customers. It was a butcher who had been tended by Cook a week before. Unfortunately, the barber had made such a hash of sewing up the man's injured thumb that the only option left was to amputate.

'It is important that all wounds are thoroughly cleaned before they are stitched,' he informed his students, noting their pale, horrified faces and hoping they would learn from Cook's negligence, even if it would do the patient scant good. 'Leaving wood shavings inside them, as happened here, will always result in trouble.'

The next client had a broken leg, which Cook had failed to immobilise properly, and it took Bartholomew and two of his strongest lads – a burly pair named Islaye and Mallet – to reset it. The third was dying, because a wound that could have been treated with a simple salve had been reopened and drained so many times that her blood was now poisoned.

'It was not a serious cut,' whispered Islaye, when they had done all they could to make her comfortable and had left her to the parish priest. He was a sensitive lad, who was too easily distressed by the plight of others to make a good physician. 'It should not have killed her.'

'No,' agreed Bartholomew. 'So remember that all injuries must be treated with equal care. Minor does not equal inconsequential.'

'*I* shall not deal with them at all,' declared Mallet, who did not have a compassionate bone in his body, and made no secret of the fact that he had chosen medicine for its financial rewards. 'I shall leave it to the surgeons. After all, it is their job, and Cook told me that the Worshipful Company of Barbers prosecutes anyone who trespasses in their domain.'

'You may have no choice,' warned Bartholomew. 'Or will you watch a patient bleed to death while you wait for another practitioner to appear?'

'Yes,' replied Mallet, quite seriously. 'If the alternative is being sued.'

'Well, I shall dive in with needle and thread,' declared Islaye stoutly. 'And if that irks Cook, then so be it. When I am qualified, I shall not let a barber anywhere near my patients.'

'Many are competent men,' cautioned Bartholomew, although it had been a long time since he had met any.

'Do not judge them all by . . . by what you have seen today.'

'Yet Cook does give a beautiful shave,' said Mallet, running an appreciative hand over his jaw. 'And the lasses do love a smooth chin. You should visit him before your woman arrives, sir. It is certain to have her tumbling into your bed.'

'Do not let Cook near your throat with a knife!' cried Islaye, while Bartholomew gaped his astonishment at Mallet's presumption; his students did not used to be so disrespectful. Or was he just getting old and prickly? 'He hates you. I heard him say so to Moleyns and Tynkell.'

Bartholomew stared at him, indignation forgotten. 'All three were together?'

Islaye nodded. 'In St Mary the Great. Sergeant Helbye was there, too, but Egidia was railing at him over something, and he did not notice – he usually shoved folk away if they got too close. He takes his duties as watchdog very seriously.'

So Cook had been part of the curious assignations that had taken place in the University Church, thought Bartholomew. Could *he* be the killer? He had been to hand when Moleyns fell off his horse, while his antipathy towards the University gave him a motive for dispatching Tynkell. And who better than a surgeon to kill with such clinical precision? Or was Bartholomew allowing dislike to interfere with his reason?

He sent his students back to College, and was about to collect Michael from St Mary the Great when he saw Langelee with Petit. Curious, he followed them into St Michael's Church, where he found them looking at the slab of black marble that lay over the final resting place of an unpopular former Master named Thomas Wilson. It was in the chancel, but was too large for the space allotted to it, which meant it was vulnerable to collisions. Recently, a corner had been knocked off.

'Kolvyle,' explained Langelee grimly. 'He claims he hurt himself when he bashed into it and is considering legal action against us, so I thought we had better get rid of the evidence.'

'Perhaps we can sue *him*,' said Bartholomew. 'You do not break stone by brushing against it, so he must have hit it with something.'

'That is what I told him, but he insists it was just his hip.'

'It is only a matter of time before it happens again,' warned Petit, running his finger along the jagged edge. 'So I recommend you arrange for it to be mended immediately.'

'But not by you,' said Bartholomew coolly. 'Not while Oswald's tomb is—'

'This represents a serious hazard,' interrupted Petit sternly. 'It would be criminally negligent to leave it in this state. It is what happens when you hire inferior craftsmen, of course. Even my rawest apprentice knows the importance of making monuments to measure.'

Langelee raised a hand to quell Bartholomew's objections when the mason named a fee and he agreed. 'It is not my fault, Bartholomew. Blame Kolvyle.'

'But how will we pay for it?' demanded Bartholomew, watching Petit swagger away triumphantly. 'There is no income from our pier, and we no longer own the dyeworks.'

The pier had been badly damaged by fire, while the dyeworks had been sold to fund emergency repairs to the conclave roof. Losing the income from the pier had been especially painful, as it had been a lucrative venture. Replacing the charred timber would cost a fortune – one Michaelhouse did not have – and was unlikely to happen in the foreseeable future.

'We will find a way,' sighed Langelee. 'We must, because if we leave the slab as it is, Kolvyle will certainly lodge a claim for compensation. And do not glare at me, Bartholomew. If you had argued more forcefully against his appointment, we would not be in this position now.'

Bartholomew regarded him archly. 'So it is my fault he is here, even though the rest of you were the ones who insisted on appointing him?'

'Of course. You had obviously guessed what he would be like, while we were in blissful ignorance. You should have warned us.'

Disgusted, Bartholomew went to St Mary the Great, and found Michael in the Chancellor's office. He opened his mouth to release a stream of invective against Langelee, Kolvyle and tomb-makers in general, but shut it when he saw that a furious dressing-down was in progress.

'How could you allow this to happen?' Michael was yelling, while Secretary Nicholas stood in front of him, hanging his head. 'Surely you noticed these documents piling up?'

'He refused to let me in,' said Nicholas, miserable and defensive in equal measure. 'I thought it was because you had given him confidential duties, so I did not question him. Besides, I was already overwhelmed with work – he delegated, you know – and I dared not risk getting lumbered with more.'

'Delegated?' demanded Michael suspiciously.

Nicholas nodded. 'For example, he took the credit for conferring all those licences to study last week, but it was I who drafted them all out.'

'Really? He told me that he had done them himself.'

'I know, but I let it pass, because I assumed he had been working on other important University business. After all, what else could he have been doing in here with the door so firmly closed?'

'Tynkell is transpiring to be rather a mystery,' confided Michael, as he and Bartholomew left the church and began to walk to the castle. 'He misled his secretary, shut himself in his office, neglected his duties, and met Moleyns under the pretext of attending his devotions. I hope he was not doing anything untoward.'

'Is there any reason to suppose he might?'

'Other than the lies, the suspicious behaviour, and the fact that he had dabbled in murky waters twice before – once when trying to build a new College, and once when trying to inflict a Common Library on us?' asked Michael caustically. 'No, no reason at all.'

They walked in silence up the High Street, then turned towards the Great Bridge – a grand name for the wooden structure that always seemed to be on the brink of collapse, and that had been the scene of more than one distressing mishap. Before they reached it, however, Michael ducked into St Clement's Church.

'There is a monumental brass in here,' he explained. 'And I want to see whether it is nicer than a sculpted effigy before I decide which to let Tynkell have.'

'It is your decision? I thought he had already chosen, and his executors would implement his wishes. And you are not one of them.'

'We are talking about St Mary the Great, Matt. It is a splendid building, and it is my moral duty to ensure that it stays that way. After all, we do not want it to look like London Blackfriars, which has so many tombs that you can scarcely move for the wretched things.'

Sir John Knyt had been a member of the now defunct Guild of Saints, a charity dedicated to helping the poor. He had been much loved in the town, so the Mayor had arranged for a tomb to be built by public subscription. Enough had been raised to fund a neat marble chest topped by an engraving – of an armour-clad Knyt lying with his feet on a lion, although Lakenham, who had made it, had never seen such a beast, so it looked like a fluffy dragon.

By chance, the lattener was there that day, polishing his handiwork with a cloth. His wife Cristine was with him, and when she saw Michael, she stormed towards him angrily. She was twice the size of her husband – taller by a head and twice as fat – which made her a formidable sight.

'Your town is full of thieves,' she snarled. 'You should do something about it.'

'Her cloak was stolen,' explained Lakenham. 'And she is vexed about it.'

'Of course I am vexed!' exploded Cristine. 'What am I supposed to wear when I go out? I am no wealthy scholar, who can afford to buy another. My husband earns too little for that sort of luxury, so I am now condemned to shiver until summer comes.'

'Her cloak was filched yesterday morning, and a brass plate went last night,' sighed Lakenham before Michael could respond. 'It was my biggest one, and I was hoping to use it for Chancellor Tynkell or Sir John Molcyns. If I win one of the commissions, of course.'

'Well?' demanded Cristine of Michael. 'What are you going to do about it?'

'I am afraid it is the Sheriff's concern, not mine,' replied Michael. 'He is—'

'My cloak was stolen from St Mary the Great,' interrupted Cristine. 'The *University* Church. I took it off to have a go on the bells, you see – Secretary Nicholas let me ring them in exchange for an apple – but when I went to pick it up, it had gone.'

'Then I shall inform my beadles,' replied Michael, and added pointedly, 'Although hunting it down must take second place to their enquiries about the Chancellor's murder.'

'Are you here to discuss his tomb then?' asked Lakenham eagerly. 'I hope you are not considering a sculpted effigy. A brass is much nicer.'

At that moment, the vicar arrived. Richard Milde was a friendly, amiable man with a lisp and a soft voice, a combination that rendered his sermons all but unintelligible. Fortunately, he kept them short, so his congregation did not mind.

'I do not envy you your task, Brother,' he said. 'I cannot imagine how you will charge the Devil with Tynkell's murder. However, I saw Moleyns take his tumble, and I can assure you that Satan was not responsible for that. I would have *sensed* him, you see.'

'Right,' said Michael flatly. 'So who did kill Moleyns?'

Milde considered the question carefully. 'Well, his wife and lawyer were leaning over his inert form at one point. Have you considered them as suspects?'

'Oh, yes.'

The vicar turned to Lakenham and Cristine. 'You were there as well. Did you see anything that might help?'

'We only came later,' said Lakenham quickly. 'And we saw nothing.'

Milde frowned. 'Really? I was sure you were . . . but no matter. It was dark, and my eyes are not what they were.'

'Quite,' agreed Lakenham. 'And it is easy to be mistaken. But about this brass for Tynkell, Brother. Here are some sketches I made last night, and if you choose one, I will devote every waking moment to it. Unlike Petit, who will put you at the back of a very long queue.'

It was some time before Michael could extricate himself from the eager lattener. He was thoughtful as they left the church.

'We shall certainly keep Lakenham and Cristine on our list of suspects,' he said. 'Even if he baulks at murder, she will not. And their motive is obvious: they are desperate for the work. Godrich was right to remark that the death of a wealthy man is good news for tomb-makers.'

* * *

The castle stood on a ridge above the town, reached by a short but stiff climb. It had started life as a simple motte raised by the Normans shortly after the Conquest, but had been expanded since, and was now a significant fortress. It comprised a curtain wall that surrounded a very large bailey, punctuated by towers and the Great Keep. There were also barracks, a chapel, storerooms, a huge kitchen, stables and an armoury.

Sergeant Helbye was in the bailey, supervising drill. He had been one of Bartholomew's first ever patients, and he had not been young then. Now he moved as though his joints hurt, and there was a weariness in his eyes that had not been there before. The physician wondered how long it would be before he was forced to retire, although Helbye, who claimed his ancestors had been warriors since the time of William the Conqueror, was determined to avoid such an ignominious fate.

Tulyet's office was a sparse, functional space on the first floor of the Great Keep. A bench was available for visitors, although it was not a very long one. When Bartholomew and Michael arrived, Egidia and Inge were already sitting on it, which meant that they were obliged to stand.

'What, again?' groaned Egidia, when Michael asked her to tell him what had happened the previous evening. 'I have repeated it at least a dozen times already.'

'And you might have to repeat it a dozen more,' said Michael coolly, 'if it helps us catch the villain who dispatched your husband in full sight of his lawyer and loving wife.'

Egidia looked sharply at him. 'I hope you are not suggesting that Inge or I were responsible. We had no reason to harm John, and his death leaves us prostrate with grief.'

They did not look particularly distressed, leaving Bartholomew to reflect that Tulyet and Vicar Milde might be right to suggest them as suspects for the murder. Of course, that would mean Cook was innocent, which would be a pity. Unless the three of them had colluded, of course – they had been acquainted in Nottingham, and might be bosom friends for all Bartholomew knew.

'How well do you know Cook?' he asked, deciding to find out, although the question was something of a non sequitur to the others, who had no way of knowing the direction his thoughts had taken.

'As well as any man knows the fellow who shaves him,' replied Inge cautiously. 'We were acquainted in Nottingham, and I use his services here, because he is the only barber-surgeon in town. Why?'

'He wrote to tell us that Cambridge was a charming place,' said Egidia, before Bartholomew could reply. 'But he lied. It is vile, and it will be more wretched still once we win compensation for our grievous loss. We will be awarded so much money that it will take you years to pay it off.'

'I recommend you wait for the result of our official enquiry before making that sort of threat,' warned Michael sharply, while Bartholomew noted that the association between Cook, Egidia and Inge must be tighter than they were willing to admit, if the barber had taken the time and trouble to send them missives. 'Or we might claim compensation from you – for slander. Now tell us what happened yesterday.'

'We went to the Market Square to buy cloth,' replied Inge, although Egidia bristled at the reprimand. 'From Edith Stanmore. But Moleyns took so long over it that Egidia and I went to St Mary the Great to admire Dallingridge's tomb instead.'

'Why?' asked Michael suspiciously.

'Because it is a fine spectacle, with its soaring pinnacles and the elegant brasses along its sides,' replied Inge smoothly. 'And we both appreciate good art.'

'We hurried outside when we heard the commotion on the tower,' Egidia went on, 'but the best vantage points were gone, so all we saw was the occasional bobbing head or arm.'

'How well did you know Tynkell?'

'Not at all,' replied Egidia promptly. 'I never met him.'

'Nor I,' averred Inge. 'There has been no need to deal with scholars, not when so many townsfolk have hastened to make our acquaintance.'

'You *do* have dealings with scholars,' countered Tulyet crossly. 'The Fellows of King's Hall and the Dominicans were always popping in and out. Then Lyng and Kolvyle were regular visitors, along with the vicars of St Clement's, St John Zachary and—'

'They came to see Moleyns,' interrupted Inge with a bland smile. 'Not us. Besides, Tynkell was never among them.'

'Then what about in St Mary the Great?' pressed Michael. 'Did Tynkell meet you there?'

'He may have spoken to John,' replied Egidia, although a slight pause indicated that she had considered her answer carefully before speaking. 'But never to us.'

'So what did you do when the spectacle on the roof was over?'

'We collected our horses and rejoined Moleyns in the market,' replied Inge. 'And as he had seen no cloth that he wanted, Mistress Stanmore invited us to her warehouse in Milne Street, where there is more of a selection.'

'We were there a long time, so she offered us home-baked cakes,' continued Egidia. 'When we had eaten our fill, we started to ride back to the castle . . .'

'We took the High Street route, because it was less icy than the side roads,' said Inge. 'Helbye was with us, and you were behind, Sheriff.'

'Yes – *behind*,' spat Egidia, glaring at Tulyet. 'If you had been at his side, where you belonged, John would still be alive.'

'We stopped frequently to exchange greetings with friends and acquaintances,' Inge went on when Tulyet declined to respond. 'He spoke to you two, if I recall aright.'

'Yes, he did,' nodded Michael. 'To hint that he might know who killed Tynkell.'

Inge and Egidia exchanged a glance that was impossible to interpret.

'Really?' asked Inge warily. 'He said nothing about it to us.'

'Who else did he greet?'

Inge waved an expansive hand. 'Lots of folk – most had seen the Chancellor slain by Satan, and it is difficult to return to one's duties after such an event, so a good many people were out and about. For example, Moleyns chatted to the men of King's Hall, while Egidia and I spoke to the Mayor and his burgesses.'

'We had all just made our farewells, and were moving forward again, when a dog ran across the road, which made John's horse rear.' Egidia scowled at Tulyet again. 'He should never have been given such a lively beast.'

'I did not *give* it to him,' snapped Tulyet, nettled at last. 'My best destriers are not for jaunts to the Market Square. But he told me that was the horse he wanted, and he stamped his foot and sulked like a spoilt child until he got his way.'

Egidia sniffed. 'You should have resisted. Anyway, he fell off after the dog barked, and pandemonium ensued. Dozens of people came to cluster around us – too many to list. We dismounted, and gave our horses to Helbye, lest someone was trampled, but there was such a crush that it was difficult to reach poor John's side. It took us an age.'

'As we said in the church, Moleyns was killed with a

96

long, thin spike,' said Michael. 'I assume you have no objection to us looking through your possessions – purely for elimination purposes, of course?'

Inge smiled serenely. 'I am afraid they are currently being moved to the Griffin – you can hardly expect us to stay in the castle now that Moleyns is dead – but you may see them this evening, after we have unpacked.'

When any such item would have been removed, thought Bartholomew, disgusted.

'Moleyns was accused of murder thirty years ago,' said Tulyet, changing the subject abruptly. 'How was his victim dispatched, exactly?'

'*Thirty* years ago?' echoed Michael. 'I thought it was more recent – three or four.'

'He faced charges of unlawful killing more than once, Brother,' explained Tulyet, and turned back to Egidia and Inge. 'Is that not so?'

'He was acquitted of the earlier charge,' replied Egidia sharply. 'So your question is irrelevant.'

'He was acquitted because he chose the jury himself.' Tulyet tapped a pile of documents, which caused Inge and Egidia to exchange another uneasy glance. 'I made enquiries about his past when I learned he was to be my guest, to ascertain what kind of man I would be hosting. The verdict of that first trial remains contentious.'

'Nonsense,' said Egidia. 'That particular accusation was a lot of rubbish, and twelve good men agreed with me, which is why they found him innocent. Besides, Peter Poges was a fool, and no one missed him.'

'Peter Poges was her uncle,' said Tulyet to Michael and Bartholomew. 'Lord of the manor of Stoke Poges in Buckinghamshire. After his death, his estates passed to Egidia, where they not only gave Moleyns a centre of power, but brought him to the attention of the King. Without them, Moleyns would have remained a landless nobody.'

'This is untrue!' snapped Inge. 'You—'

'So how *did* Poges die?' interrupted Tulyet, rounding on him. 'Was he stabbed with a long metal spike?'

'No,' replied Inge stiffly. 'He was poisoned.'

'Just like Dallingridge then,' mused Tulyet. 'How very interesting.'

'Dallingridge was *not* poisoned,' barked Inge crossly. 'He died of natural causes. Ask anyone.'

'I asked the Sheriff of Nottingham,' said Tulyet, patting the documents again. 'He tells me that Dallingridge was fed a toxic substance on Lammas Day. Ergo, Dallingridge and Peter Poges died in an identical manner. And you two and Moleyns were present on both occasions.'

'Have you never heard of coincidences?' demanded Inge scathingly.

'Yes,' acknowledged Tulyet. 'But I do not believe in them.'

The sun had been shining when Bartholomew and Michael had entered the castle, but it was hidden behind a bank of clouds when they stepped into the bailey. The dull light matched Bartholomew's sombre mood, and he wondered how they would ever learn what had happened to Tynkell and Moleyns, when the killer had left them so little in the way of clues.

'We *will* catch him,' said Michael with grim determination, as Tulyet escorted them to the gate. 'We must, because I cannot accept a bishopric as long as Tynkell's murderer is on the loose, while Dick needs a culprit to present to the King.'

'Then perhaps we had better speak to Petit's apprentice – Lucas,' said Bartholomew. 'He claims to have information to sell.'

'I will do it,' offered Tulyet. 'Straight away, lest he suffers the same fate as Moleyns.'

'We should speak to Helbye, too,' said Michael, nodding to where the sergeant was still overseeing the soldiers' training. 'He was riding next to Moleyns when he fell, after all.'

'Poor Will,' said Tulyet sadly. 'He is mortified – feels he has let me down.'

'Well, he has,' said Michael bluntly. 'Because Egidia is right: Moleyns should not have died when he was being guarded.'

'We cannot stop dogs from barking or bad horsemen from taking tumbles.' Tulyet was defensive of the man who had served him for so many years. 'Do not be too hard on him.'

He led the way to where Helbye was using a young soldier – Robin, a nephew of Agatha the laundress – to demonstrate the move he wanted practised. The elderly warrior favoured his right knee, while a hand to a hip suggested a problem there, too, and Bartholomew suspected he could not have managed a 'crosswise thrust' if his life depended on it.

'It all happened so fast,' Helbye began wretchedly, when Michael asked him to recount what had happened. 'I was close behind Moleyns – very close, as he had no business being on Satan, given that he was such a terrible rider—'

'Stephen,' corrected Tulyet crisply. 'The horse's name is *Stephen*.'

'Well, he answers to Satan, which better suits his evil nature.' Helbye turned back to Michael. 'Suddenly, a dog raced out of St Michael's Lane, and tore right in front of him. Satan reared, which would not have bothered a decent horseman, but Moleyns . . .'

'Was Stephen the only beast that bucked?' asked Michael.

'The others shied, but the rest of us had them under control, even Egidia. Then, once Moleyns was on the ground, lots of people surged forward, some to help, others to jeer.'

'Jeer?' queried Michael. 'I thought people were keen to win his favour.'

'The wealthy were – those who wanted him to write nice things about them to the King. However, to normal folk he was just a felon who should not have been allowed out of his cell. They disapproved of the freedom he enjoyed, while those whose crimes are not nearly so serious are locked up in the dungeons.'

'And who can blame them?' muttered Tulyet. 'I was irked about it myself, and would have refused to do it if I had not received direct orders from the King.'

'So what did *you* do, Helbye?' asked Bartholomew. 'Dismount and race to his rescue?'

'No – all four horses were skittish, so I went to tether them on the other side of the road.' Helbye's face was a picture of misery. 'I thought I was doing the right thing – taking them to a safe distance, so they would not hurt anyone. Or themselves. Satan in particular cost a fortune.'

'What then?' asked Michael.

'The crowd had pressed around Moleyns very tightly, and although I did my best to push through quickly, people kept shoving me back. But it never occurred to me that he was in danger and—'

'Who was in this throng?'

Helbye recited much the same list as everyone else, although he included two new names: Father Aidan, the Principal of Maud's Hostel, and Weasenham, the University's stationer and the biggest gossip in the county.

Michael groaned at the mention of the latter. 'I am sure *he* will have plenty to say, and all of it will be pure speculation.'

'There were women, too,' Helbye went on. 'For example, that fat Cristine Lakenham, and a lass in the cloak with the fancy hem, who elbowed me rather hard . . .'

'This dog,' mused Bartholomew. 'Did it run across the lane of its own volition or was it released on purpose?'

Helbye frowned. 'Now that you mention it, the animal *was* chasing something – as if someone was playing a game of fetch with it. A child, probably.'

'Or an adult, who knew that Moleyns would fall if Stephen was startled,' suggested Bartholomew. 'And who also knew that an accident on the High Street would attract a jostling crowd, thus providing him with an opportunity to jab a spike into his victim's chest. What kind of dog was it?'

'A mongrel,' replied Helbye, then added perfectly seriously, 'Ask Clippesby about it. He probably knows the animal well, and it will have told him anything important.'

It was dusk by the time Bartholomew and Michael had finished at the castle. The physician glanced across the winter-bare fields to the east as they crossed the Great Bridge. The darkening countryside was brown and bleak, the trees stark skeletons against a lowering sky, and he was not surprised that some folk believed that the Devil had taken up residence there.

'Egidia is right: Dick does bear some responsibility for Moleyns' death,' mused Michael. 'He let his prisoner ride a horse that was well beyond his abilities, and he provided a guard who is past his prime. And he knows it.'

'Then let us hope the King does not know it as well. It would be a great pity – for the University and the town – if he was dismissed. So we had better set about finding the culprit, for everyone's sake. Who are your prime suspects?'

Michael considered. 'Well, Inge and Egidia obviously. They were to hand when Moleyns died, and they were in St Mary the Great when Tynkell was on the tower. I cannot imagine why they should want Tynkell dead, but it seems he changed these last few weeks, so if we discover what he was doing in his office with the door closed, we might have our answer.'

'But why stab their victims when poison would be so much easier?'

'That is a good question, given that Peter Poges and Dallingridge may also have ingested toxic substances, and both have connections to that pair. Of course, Egidia and Inge are not my only suspects for the murders here. Lakenham and Cristine were not being entirely honest with us earlier. Then there are those who aim to be Chancellor – Godrich, Hopeman, Lyng and Thelnetham.'

'No one has mentioned seeing Thelnetham in the crowd that gathered around Moleyns.'

'No, but most folk wore hoods, so that means nothing. Then, I am sorry to say, there is Kolvyle, who thought he would be eligible to fill Tynkell's shoes and who knew Moleyns from Nottingham. He is certainly the kind of man to solicit the good opinion of a royal favourite, and then dispatch him to suit himself.'

'I think the culprit is Cook. He was among those who raced to "help" when Moleyns fell.'

'And his motive?'

'Perhaps Moleyns criticised his barbering skills.' Bartholomew hurried on when the monk looked sceptical. 'He also tried to make us think that Moleyns stabbed himself by accident, and he met slyly with Moleyns and Tynkell in St Mary the Great.'

Michael raised his eyebrows. 'Does this accusation stem from the fact that he is a dire *medicus*, and you aim to prevent him from harming more of his patients by seeing him hanged?'

Bartholomew eyed him balefully. 'I accuse him because I believe he might be guilty. He probably has a fine collection of thin spikes in his surgical toolkit.'

'But what about Tynkell? Why would Cook take against him?'

'Because he hates scholars. *All* scholars.'

'I see,' said Michael, and changed the subject before

they wasted time on an argument neither would win. 'What do you make of the dog?'

'We should find out if Cook owns one.' Bartholomew saw Michael's irritable look and shrugged. 'The story is true. I heard it bark, and I saw it dart across the road.'

'It cannot be coincidence – the dog upsetting the horse, while the killer just happened to be waiting with a deadly spike. Yet he must have moved fast, to set the creature loose, and then dash in to stab Moleyns. Would he have had time?'

'There is nothing to say that Moleyns was dispatched the moment he hit the ground. He may have been too shocked to get up immediately, or was prevented from rising by the sheer press of people.' Bartholomew stopped walking suddenly. 'There is that cowled man *again*! I am getting tired of him trailing after us all the time. It is disconcerting.'

Ignoring Michael's injunction to pay no heed, Bartholomew shot across the street, aiming to lay hold of the shadow and have some answers. The figure started in alarm, then dived into the nearest shop, which happened to be the stationer's. This was a spacious building, always busy, because academics gathered there not just to purchase what they needed for their studies, but to chat with friends, and to browse its extensive collection of books and scrolls.

Bartholomew flung open the door and looked around wildly, aware that his dramatic entry had startled everyone within into silence. All were looking at him. Most were wearing dark cloaks and there were cowls galore. Then he heard a door slam at the back, so he hared towards it. It had been jammed shut, and by the time he had wrenched it open, his quarry was gone. Disgusted, he traipsed back to the main room to find Michael the centre of attention.

'Of course I know who will win the election,' the monk

was declaring, 'Suttone, because he is the best man. You will all vote for him if you want your University to flourish.'

'I shall support Godrich,' said Geoffrey Dodenho from King's Hall, a scholar who was not nearly as intelligent as he thought he was. 'He is wealthy, well connected, and will attract plenty of rich benefactors.'

Godrich was next to him, all haughty superiority, an attitude that immediately antagonised a number of hostel men, including Secretary Nicholas, who limped forward to have his say.

'But Thelnetham has by far the sharpest brain,' he said earnestly. 'And if we want to attract bright young minds, we must have a celebrated scholar in post, or they will all go to Oxford instead. I am Chancellor's secretary, so I know better than most what is required.'

'In other words, Thelnetham has offered to let you keep your position if he wins,' sneered Godrich. 'It is not the future of the University that concerns you, but your own.'

'My friars and I will support Hopeman,' said little Prior Morden, cutting across Nicholas's offended denials. 'We do not want another puppet of the Senior Proctor, but a man who can make his own decisions. Subject to the approval of his Order, of course.'

'Yes, the next Chancellor must be a priest,' nodded Father Aidan of Maud's, a man whose missing front teeth gave him a piratical appearance that belied his timorous nature. 'But an independent one, not a Dominican or a Carmelite. He must also hail from the hostels, who will, after all, represent the bulk of our scholars. Ergo, Lyng is the only man for the job.'

'Well, I am voting for Suttone,' declared Doctor Rougham of Gonville Hall, one of Bartholomew's medical colleagues. 'Purely for his sensible views on women. It is time we moved with the times, and abandoned these outmoded notions of celibacy. I applaud his enlightened attitude.'

Bartholomew was sure he did, given that he was a regular visitor to Yolande de Blaston, the town's most popular prostitute.

'Maud's cannot be an easy place to live,' said Weasenham the stationer. The gleeful glint in his eye suggested he would make hay with Rougham's candid opinions later. 'Most foundations have one candidate for election, but yours has two – Lyng and Hopeman.'

'We shall vote for Lyng,' declared Aidan shortly. 'Hopeman has his own following.'

'You mean his fanatics,' corrected Weasenham, 'who say he is the only man capable of besting Satan. They tell me that Tynkell tried, but was unequal to the task, so the Devil killed him – before flying off to dine in the Dominican Priory.'

'Watch what you say,' warned Morden, before Michael could tell them about the killer's cloak. 'You know perfectly well that Lucifer flew over the top of us, and went to sup with the Benedictines at St Edmundsbury.'

'Now, now,' chided Michael mildly, although anger flashed in his eyes. 'No slandering of rival Orders, please. It is ungentlemanly.'

'Perhaps other contenders will step forward,' mused Weasenham. 'I imagine there are plenty who think they can do better than the five currently on offer.'

'The statutes stipulate a timetable for these events,' said Nicholas, 'and the deadline for nominations was noon today. No new names can be accepted now.'

'Then God help the University,' declared Weasenham.

'On the contrary, we have the man we need,' said Kolvyle, glaring at him. 'Namely Godrich, who is a skilled administrator, a fine warrior, and knows the King. I agree with your reservations about the others, though – Hopeman is too radical, Lyng too meek, and Suttone and Thelnetham have connections to Michaelhouse.'

Michael's eyes narrowed. 'You have connections there

yourself, lest you had forgotten. You are our Junior Fellow.'

'Yes – and it has taught me that Suttone would be rubbish,' flashed Kolvyle.

There was a startled silence, as it was rare to hear anyone publicly disparage fellow members of the foundation that housed him and paid his stipend. However, while Michael was livid at the gross breach of etiquette, he knew better than to challenge Kolvyle in front of an audience. Instead, he confined himself to patting him on the head like an errant child, a gesture that drew chuckles from the onlookers and a furious scowl from the recipient. Then someone else entered the fray: Thelnetham, whose cloak was fastened with a large purple-jewelled brooch of a type rarely seen on a man, let alone a cleric.

'I am proud to have been a member of Michaelhouse,' he said quietly. 'It is a fine place, and I deeply regret the misunderstanding that led me to resign. I would return there in an instant, should I be asked. However, in the meantime, I believe *I* will make a worthy Chancellor. For a start, I have published more academic treatises than any other candidate.'

'But you are not a warrior,' said Kolvyle in disdain. 'Nor do you have links to royalty.'

Thelnetham smiled. 'I sincerely doubt I shall be required to defend the University with a sword. And as for royal connections, I shall acquire those once I am in post. There is nothing to say they need be of long duration. Indeed, perhaps it is preferable to have none, as old alliances might be dangerous or inappropriate.'

'That is a good point,' nodded Secretary Nicholas. 'It is common knowledge that Godrich has enemies at Court – and his enemies will become ours, if he is Chancellor.'

'Thelnetham speaks well,' murmured Michael to Bartholomew, as Nicholas's remark occasioned a furious denial from Godrich. 'But no one will elect a man who wears women's jewellery and minces about like a—'

'What are you two whispering about?' came a voice from behind. It was Weasenham, his eyes alight with the prospect of gossip.

'Murder,' lied Michael. 'Do you have any intelligence to impart?'

Weasenham's eyes gleamed brighter still. 'Well, I was nearby when Moleyns fell. Unfortunately, I could not get a place at the front of the throng, because his wife and friend were in the way.'

'They told us it took some time to reach him,' said Michael. 'They had to dismount first, then fight their way through people like you – idle gawpers.'

'Then they are lying,' said Weasenham, unfazed by the rebuke. 'However, they did not kill him. That honour goes to Satan, who claimed Tynkell's life, too. Everyone saw the fight on the roof, while Moleyns rode him down the High Street.'

'Stephen,' said Michael coldly. 'The horse that Moleyns rode is named *Stephen*.'

'That is not what the soldiers say,' countered Weasenham with malicious satisfaction, before turning on his heel and stalking away to regale his customers with his dubious theories.

CHAPTER 4

The sun was shining the following day, although its light was pale and thin, with no warmth in it. Even so, it lifted Bartholomew's spirits, and he found himself humming as he strode around the town, visiting patients. The man whose thumb he had amputated was doing better than he expected, while the lad with the reset leg was comfortable and cheerful.

When he had finished his rounds, he delivered a lecture on Galen's *Prognostica* in Michaelhouse, then asked Aungel to read the next instalment of Maimonides' views on breathing disorders to his first years, while he tested the remaining classes on their grasp of humoral theory. He joined his colleagues in the hall for the noonday meal, after which Aungel offered to supervise a writing assignment, so that the physician could help Michael.

The first item on their agenda was to visit Edith Stanmore, given that one murder victim had been buying cloth from her while the other had fought for his life on the tower. Bartholomew knew where she would be at such an hour – at her husband's tomb. They arrived to discover it a flurry of activity: Petit was there with three of his apprentices.

'Wonders will never cease,' breathed Bartholomew. 'I know Petit said he would work on Oswald today, but he has never kept his promises before.'

'The Worshipful Company of Masons probably forbids it,' drawled Michael. 'Along with staying at one job for more than three hours in any given day.'

'It probably also insists that all its members have at

least four commissions on the go at any one time, and that while work must never be finished on schedule, bills should always be presented early.'

Michael laughed. 'But one of those apprentices is Lucas. Dick will have interrogated him by now, but I say we also buy whatever intelligence he has to offer. He may be more forthcoming with us than the Sheriff.'

He and Bartholomew walked to the little aisle near the chancel, where Edith was watching the craftsmen build a hoist to lift the heavy granite slab that would eventually seal Oswald's stone-lined vault. Bartholomew was glad the burial chamber would soon be closed, because every time he saw it, he was reminded that his beloved sister would lie inside it one day.

He and she were unmistakably siblings, although she had aged since the death of her husband. Her once-raven locks were streaked with grey, and there was a sadness in her dark eyes that worried him, although she smiled when she saw him and Michael.

'There has been a miracle,' she said serenely. 'Petit claimed the mortar was too wet to allow work on Oswald's monument today, but it set spontaneously when I marched into St Mary the Great and made a speech about craftsmen reneging on their vows.'

'Your tirade had nothing to do with it,' countered Petit stiffly. 'I told you I would return here at the earliest opportunity, and I did. I *am* a man of my word.'

'I am glad to hear it,' said Edith, 'because if you let me down one more time, I shall cancel the effigy, and have a brass instead. Indeed, I went so far as to discuss the matter with Lakenham, who is here to erect a memorial to poor John Cew.'

She nodded to the other side of the chancel, where the lattener was attaching a metal plate to the wall, although one so small as to be virtually invisible. Bartholomew understood why Cew's colleagues were reluctant to provide anything too conspicuous: the hapless King's Hall Fellow had once possessed a formidable intellect, but then he had lost his reason, which had been acutely embarrassing to a foundation that put so much store by outward appearances.

'*I* would not have accepted such a lowly commission,' scoffed Petit, watching Lakenham stir the pitch that would glue the memorial in place. He raised his voice, to ensure his rival heard. 'But Lakenham is so poor that he will accept any old job. Stanmore's tomb will have to be carefully guarded from now on, lest bits of it disappear.'

'I have my own supplies, thank you,' retorted Lakenham. 'And do not accuse *me* of stealing Dallingridge's feet last night. I went nowhere near them.'

Bartholomew blinked. 'Dallingridge's feet?'

'It is cheaper to carve effigies in sections, rather than using a single piece of stone,' explained Lakenham sneeringly. 'And niggardly masons are always looking for ways to cut corners.'

'To save our clients money,' corrected Petit sharply.

'It is common practice these days,' put in one of his apprentices, a lanky, freckle-faced lad named Peres. 'Me and Lucas worked hard on those feet, and we finished them yesterday. They were beautiful, too – we had them resting on a greyhound.'

'But someone came along in the night and stole them from our workshop,' said Lucas, glaring at Lakenham.

Bartholomew was bemused. 'Why would a thief take such a thing?'

Petit regarded him pityingly. 'So he can sell them to some unscrupulous mason in London, who will then adapt them to fit another tomb, and pass off our work as his own. The sly b—'

'This is why brasses are superior to sculptures, Brother,' interrupted Lakenham smugly. 'Feet, noses, hands, feet and even heads are very vulnerable on effigies.'

'But brasses can be prised off in their entirety and spirited away,' countered Petit.

'Not my brasses,' argued Lakenham. 'I use pitch *and* pins to anchor them down.'

'So you say,' jeered Petit, and shot the lattener a look of utter contempt before turning his back on him to smile ingratiatingly at Michael. 'I have taken the liberty of designing exemplars for Tynkell and Moleyns. Would you like to see them?'

'Exemplars cannot be put together overnight,' said Lakenham to Michael, his expression vengeful. 'Which means he knew in advance that those two men would die. So question *him* about the murders, Brother, because that is suspicious.'

Petit hauled a burin – a chisel with a wooden handle and a sharp metal point – from his belt and fingered it menacingly. 'You have a poisonous tongue, Lakenham, and you will be wanting a funerary brass for yourself, unless you stop wagging it.'

'You see, Brother?' said Lakenham archly. 'That was almost a confession.'

'I want to know where you *all* were when Tynkell died,' said Michael.

'*He* was in St Mary the Great,' said Lakenham, stabbing an accusing finger at his rival. 'Perfectly placed to slip up the tower and pretend to be Satan while he killed Tynkell.'

'Nonsense! We all ran outside when we heard the commotion,' said Petit, although he licked his lips nervously and his men exchanged furtive glances. 'When the excitement was over, we came here to work.' Then he went on an offensive of his own. 'And how would *you* know where we were, Lakenham, unless you were nearby?'

The lattener was ready for this. 'Because the beadles told me,' he replied smugly. 'I, however, was in St Clement's Church with my wife.'

'That is not what you said yesterday,' pounced Bartholomew. 'Cristine claimed her cloak was stolen from St Mary the Great – she had taken it off to ring the bells.'

'You see?' crowed Petit. 'Lakenham is a liar! *He* stabbed Tynkell and Moleyns, because he hopes to build their tombs.'

Lakenham became flustered. 'Perhaps we did slip into St Mary the Great for a few moments, but I am not a killer. Not a thief either. Come and look in my shed – you will find no carved feet there. Petit's workshop, however, will be stuffed full of my brasses, nails and—'

'That tool,' interrupted Bartholomew, pointing to Petit's burin. 'May I see it?'

'Why?' demanded Petit suspiciously, hiding it behind his back.

Michael fixed the mason with an icy glare until he handed it over, which he did with obvious reluctance. The tool was intended for fine work, and possessed a long, slender point. Bartholomew pressed it into some damp clay, where it made a tiny circular hole.

'The murder weapon?' asked Michael.

'Possibly,' replied Bartholomew. 'Or something similar.'

Petit was pale with alarm. 'But lots of craftsmen have these! Indeed, Lakenham has several that are longer and thinner, which he uses for engraving. You cannot accuse me of—'

'You were in the High Street when Moleyns was killed,' interrupted Michael. He included the grinning lattener in his proctorly glower. 'You both were – among the crowd that clustered around him after his fall.'

'Yes, but I was busy minding my wife,' said Lakenham, his smirk vanishing like mist in the sun. 'Making sure she was not unduly jostled.'

From what Bartholomew had seen of Cristine, she was perfectly capable of looking after herself. Indeed, he imagined that if any protecting needed to be done, she would be far better at it than her diminutive spouse.

'And I could get nowhere near Moleyns,' added Petit. 'There were too many people.'

Michael continued to ask questions, but neither craftsman could be persuaded to say more, and nor could their apprentices, and in the end he let them go. Lakenham scuttled away in relief, while Petit and his lads resumed their work on the winch. They did so in silence, clearly unsettled by the monk's ruthless interrogation.

When Michael had finished frightening the tomb-makers, he and Bartholomew went to find Edith, who had been unable to listen to the discussion for fear that Petit would be arrested, and her husband's tomb would be subject to even further delays. They found her in the little Lady Chapel, lighting candles for Stanmore's soul.

'Moleyns told us that he was buying cloth from you when Tynkell died,' said Michael. 'And that he saw more of the fight than the rest of us, because he was on horse-back.'

Edith smiled wanly. 'He dared not dismount lest he was unable to get back on again – Satan is a feisty beast. However, I doubt he saw enough to identify Tynkell's killer. His elevated position might have let him see a little more than me, but not *that* much.'

'Then why did he give us the impression that he did?' asked Bartholomew.

Edith's expression was wry. 'You obviously did not know him very well. He liked to be the centre of attention, and was willing to do or say anything to get it.'

'So he was lying?'

'Yes, if he claimed he saw the killer's face. And if you do not believe me, then borrow Satan from the castle, and sit on him in the Market Square yourself.'

'I believe you,' said Michael. 'Especially as Dick Tulyet

113

thinks much the same. What about Inge and Egidia? Where were they?'

'They stormed off when Moleyns announced that he was buying cloth for himself only – that if they wanted new cloaks, they would have to purchase the material themselves. They marched towards St Mary the Great, but I was more interested in making a sale to Moleyns, so I cannot tell you whether or not they went inside.'

Michael's eyes narrowed. 'They told us the reason they left was because they were bored with him taking so long to make his decision.'

'Lies,' said Edith firmly. 'They were perfectly happy with his dithering when they thought they might be getting something out of it. Do you think they had a hand in Moleyns' death? It would not surprise me.'

'Would it not?' probed Michael keenly. 'Why?'

'Because both are ruthless and greedy, and I know for a fact they were beginning to fear that his royal pardon might never arrive – that they might be doomed to spend the rest of their lives living as prisoners with him. Egidia told me so herself. And do not say they could just leave him. It was too late – they had hitched themselves too tightly to his wagon.'

'Then they must be glad their ordeal is over,' said Michael, 'despite their protestations to the contrary. And if Egidia has inherited all his worldly goods . . .'

'His store of money,' corrected Bartholomew. 'Which will not last long now that they are obliged to pay for their bed and board, instead of living free at the castle.'

'His "store of money" was probably larger than you think,' said Edith. 'Because he had a unique way of ensuring that it was regularly replenished.'

'He did?' asked Michael curiously. 'How?'

'He stole,' replied Edith, pursing her lips in disapproval. 'For example, the Mayor's purse disappeared a month ago, and he is sure Moleyns took it. The coward! He dared not say anything when Moleyns was alive, but now he is dead . . .'

'He was afraid of him?' asked Bartholomew.

'Afraid of what Moleyns might tell the King – he was a royal favourite, remember, which meant that everyone was keen to stay in his good books. But now he can no longer write anything mean, all manner of unsavoury tales will emerge about the man. You mark my words.'

Lucas the apprentice had gone to fetch water from the well by the time Bartholomew and Michael had finished talking to Edith, so they loitered in the graveyard, aiming to waylay him discreetly when he returned. While they waited, they discussed what they had learned, although both conceded that it was rather less than they had hoped. Then Lucas appeared, staggering under the weight of two large buckets.

'Talking is dangerous, so you will have to make it worth my while,' he stated without preamble, glancing around uneasily. 'How much are you offering?'

'That depends on what you tell us,' replied Michael. 'Do you know who killed Tynkell and Moleyns? For that information, I might be persuaded to part with threepence.'

Lucas's eyes gleamed greedily. 'Very well then. Meet me here at midnight – alone.'

He started to walk away, but Michael grabbed his arm. 'You will speak to us now or not at all.'

Lucas scowled as he tried to free himself. 'Then it will be not at all. Did you not hear me? Talking is dangerous.'

'*Not* talking is dangerous,' countered Bartholomew. 'Because the Sheriff will—'

'So it was you who put him on to me, was it?' spat Lucas. 'I might have known! Well, I told *him* nothing – I do not deal with officers of the law. And the price is now sixpence. Come at midnight. Or not. It is all the same to me.'

He wrenched his arm out of the monk's grasp and went on his way. Irked, Bartholomew started to follow, but Michael stopped him.

'Leave him, Matt. Could you not see the fear behind that bluster? We will get nothing from him unless we meet him on his own terms, so we shall have to wait. After all, we do not want to earn *him* a burin in the heart for spilling his secrets.'

'A spike,' corrected Bartholomew. 'We do not know it was a burin. But Lucas will be safe once he gives us the name of the killer – he cannot be hurt if the culprit is arrested.'

'If it were that simple, he would have told us the name and grabbed the money at once,' said Michael. 'Which makes me suspect that his intelligence may not be as precise as we hope.'

As they left the churchyard, they met the parish priest. His name was Roger Frisby, and he was patently unsuited to a career in the Church. He was brusque, drank too much, liked irreligious jokes, and was unsympathetic if his flock came to him with problems. He looked more like a brawler than a man of God, with thick fists and a flattened nose. He was kin to Secretary Nicholas, although there was little similarity between the quiet, scholarly clerk and the hard-living vicar.

'I wish these tomb-builders would hurry up and finish,' he grumbled. 'Petit swore that I would barely notice his presence, and that any inconvenience would only last a few weeks, but it has been months and I am sick of it. The dust alone is enough to drive a man to claret.'

'I understand you visited Moleyns at the castle,' said Michael, tactfully not mentioning that it took far less than a bit of dirt to steer Frisby towards the wineskin. 'Why?'

'Because he knew how to enjoy life,' replied Frisby with a sudden grin. 'And I admire that in a man. There

116

is too much sobriety in this town, and it was fun to carouse with a fellow who was not afraid to hold back. We showed that prim Tulyet a party or two!'

'Often?' asked Bartholomew.

'Not as often as I would have liked. But Moleyns was over sixty years old, and once or twice he had to cancel our revels or excuse himself and leave early, claiming weariness. I was nearby when he fell off his horse, and could not believe it when you declared him dead.'

'Tell us what you saw,' instructed Michael.

Frisby closed his eyes as he searched his memory. 'A dog started it all. Someone lobbed a bone, and the thing tore across the road to get it.'

'A bone?' probed Michael. 'You mean the dog was deliberately encouraged to dart out?'

'Now you have made it sound sinister,' said Frisby, folding his brawny arms. 'Whereas all I am saying is that a bone arced across the road with a dog in pursuit. I suspect someone was just trying to get the animal to go away – you know what a nuisance these strays can be.'

'Did you see who threw it?' asked Bartholomew.

'It was too dark, and I only noticed the bone because it landed by my foot. It was a lamb shank, if that is any help. I wish I could tell you more, but that is all I know.'

As the afternoon wore on, the day turned colder, and Bartholomew began to long for his little room with its welcoming fire. However, he did not object when Principal Haye of White Hostel invited him and Michael to dine – it was an opportunity to question more witnesses about the deaths of Tynkell and Moleyns, not to mention the fact that White was famous for the high quality of its victuals.

'Yes, I visited Moleyns in the castle,' said Haye, in response to Michael's question. 'Because he promised to put in a good word for us at Court.'

'You mean for nobles to send their sons to you?' asked Bartholomew.

'Yes, and reminding them that donations to our coffers are always gratefully received. However, he never bothered, and I am sure *he* was the rogue who stole my purse. I dared not mention it when he was alive, lest he avenged himself with a spiteful letter to the King, but now he is dead . . .'

'Curious,' mused Michael. 'The Mayor thinks Moleyns filched *his* purse, too.'

'And there will be others.' Haye passed the platter of roasted meat. 'Moleyns was a light-fingered rogue, and His Majesty should have been more careful in his choice of friends.'

Bartholomew and Michael were pleasantly replete when they left. Night had fallen, and the monk declared himself too tired for listening to more useless testimonies, so they headed home. They were almost at Michaelhouse when the physician glimpsed a flicker of movement out of the corner of his eye, and knew without looking that it was the spy in the cowl.

'I should visit Isnard before turning in,' he said, loudly enough for his words to carry. 'To see if he needs more salve for his bruises.'

Without waiting for a reply, he strode towards the river. He turned the corner, then doubled back and peered up the lane. He saw Michael waiting for the gate to be opened, while the spy watched from behind a buttress. Keeping to the darkest shadows, Bartholomew edged towards them, tiptoeing at first, then breaking into a run as he came closer. The figure started in alarm at the sudden clatter of footfalls.

'Matt, no!' cried Michael.

But Bartholomew was sick of being followed, and gave a whoop of triumph as he laid hold of his quarry. At the same time, Walter the porter opened the gate, and when he saw a Fellow wrestling with a stranger, he hurtled forward to help. The spy was ridiculously easy to overpower, after which it was a simple matter to bundle him into the porter's lodge for questioning. The commotion drew a screech of alarm from Walter's pet peacock, which was relaxing by the fire with a jug of ale.

'I told you not to let him drink,' said Bartholomew to Walter, while the spy brushed himself down and Michael stood in silent disapproval in the doorway. 'It is bad for him.'

'Yes, but he loves ale,' said Walter defensively. 'Besides, if I deprive him, he only goes to the kitchen and helps himself. I do not want him there – not when Agatha keeps threatening to wring his neck.'

'Your College's peacock is a drunkard, Michael?' drawled the spy. 'Singular.'

'He is not a drunkard,' objected Walter, offended. 'He just likes an occasional tipple.'

But Bartholomew was more interested in the fact that the spy had addressed Michael by name. 'You two know each other?'

The question was answered when the spy unfastened his cloak to reveal the Benedictine habit underneath. It was made of the finest cloth, which suggested he was no ordinary monk – as did his supercilious demeanour. Meanwhile, Michael was glaring at Bartholomew. Sensing trouble, Walter prudently made himself scarce, taking his tipsy bird with him.

'I told you he would approach us when the time was right, Matt,' Michael said irritably. 'You really should have let him be.'

The spy's eyes narrowed. 'You *knew* I was following you? How? I kept to the shadows.'

Michael smiled superiorly. 'You had not been in Cambridge an hour before your presence was reported to me. Of course I knew you were dogging my every move.'

'Then why let me continue with the pretence?' demanded the spy crossly.

'I assumed you had your reasons, and far be it from me to question them.' Michael turned to Bartholomew. 'Allow me to introduce Richard de Whittlesey. You may remember him – he was once Master of Peterhouse, but left to become the Bishop of Rochester's envoy.'

'Before my time,' said Bartholomew curtly. Whittlesey was not the only one who was annoyed with Michael for failing to be open with him.

'Those were happy days,' sighed Whittlesey wistfully. 'And although I have done well since leaving the University, I still hanker for the intellectual sparring that only scholars can provide. I debated theology with Bishop Sheppey, of course, but it was not the same.'

'So why did you come back?' asked Bartholomew. 'If it is to stand for Chancellor, you are too late – the closing date for applications has passed.'

Whittlesey laughed. 'I have better things to do than struggling to impose order on a lot of opinionated academics. No, I came to bring Michael news. Some good and some bad.'

Michael frowned. '*Bad* news? Not about my family, I hope?'

'Yes, in a way. Bishop Sheppey is dead, God rest his sainted soul.' Tears shimmered in Whittlesey's eyes before he blinked them away. 'He died after a long illness, which he endured with courage and patience. He was a fine man, and I am honoured to have been his friend.'

'A fine man indeed,' agreed Michael quietly. 'A Benedictine, like us. I first met him as a youth, when I heard him preach at Paul's Cross in London. I had already decided to take holy orders, but he was the one who convinced me to become a Black Monk.'

'He was proud of his sermons,' said Whittlesey with a sad smile. 'I wrote some of them down, and will publish them for him later this year. He was fond of you, Brother, and that is the good news – he has nominated you as his successor.'

Michael reacted with such a serene lack of surprise that Bartholomew wondered if the monk had been entirely honest about what had been in the letter from Avignon. 'Then he has made a good choice, and it is fitting that Rochester will pass to another Benedictine. Continuity is important.'

'Of course, your appointment still needs to be confirmed by the Holy Father,' warned Whittlesey. 'The King and the Archbishop have endorsed it, though.'

Michael waved an airy hand. 'Formalities – the Pope will accede to Sheppey's wishes. Yet I am surprised you came yourself. Do you not have messengers for this sort of task?'

'The Archbishop sent me. He wanted to be sure that you were all Sheppey – and your patron, the Bishop of Ely – had promised. Which you are, of course. The University is five times the size it was a decade ago, and has grown stronger and more stable under your guidance.'

Michael inclined his head graciously. 'So when do we travel to Rochester?'

'Would tomorrow be convenient?'

Michael regarded him askance. 'It would not! I cannot leave Cambridge for at least another month – I have a murdered Chancellor to avenge and an election to manage.'

'Unfortunately, time is a luxury you do not have,' said Whittlesey soberly. 'The absolute latest we can go is next Thursday – the day after the election. Hopefully, it will be enough to allow you to usher in the candidate of your choice and catch the killer. But if you have not nabbed him by then, you will just have to entrust that task to your successor.'

'Why the rush?' asked Bartholomew suspiciously.

'Because Michael has competition: the Bishop of Bangor is desperate for a better See, and he is expected to reach Rochester by Monday week. He may arrange to have himself installed if Michael is elsewhere, and then it will be difficult to oust him.'

'He aims to steal my mitre?' cried Michael in alarm. 'We shall see about that! He—'

He stopped speaking when Cynric burst in. The book-bearer was panting hard.

'There you are, Brother,' he gasped. 'Petit's apprentice Lucas is dead, and the Sheriff wants you in St John Zachary at once.'

'Lucas? Dead?' breathed Michael, stunned, while Bartholomew gaped his shock. 'How? Not murdered?'

Cynric shrugged apologetically. 'All I can tell you is that the Sheriff wants you to hurry. You can ask for details when you get there.'

'But we were going to meet Lucas later,' cried Michael, horrified. 'He has information about the murders.'

'Then you should have prised the intelligence from him at once,' said Whittlesey, although the monk did not need to be told. 'You might have had the case solved by now.'

'I did not want to put him in danger,' explained Michael, then turned to Bartholomew, his troubled expression reflecting the physician's own guilt-racked conscience. 'I hope he is not dead because the killer saw us talking to him. Petit and his boys were inside the church, although Lakenham had left . . .'

'Anyone might have been watching,' said Bartholomew, and looked pointedly at Whittlesey. He did not care that the man was a bishop's envoy or that he was an old acquaintance of Michael's. Whittlesey had behaved peculiarly, as far as he was concerned, and his instincts were to distrust him. 'Present company *not* excepted.'

'Not me,' said Whittlesey carelessly. 'I was busy with other matters at the time.'

'What other matters?' demanded Bartholomew, thinking the question begged to be asked.

'It was personal,' said Whittlesey shortly, before going to sit by Walter's fire. He settled himself comfortably and helped himself to the peacock's ale. 'Go and do your duty, Michael. I shall wait here until you return. Then we shall talk.'

'Is he a friend?' asked Bartholomew, as he and Michael hurried towards St John Zachary. 'Because I cannot say I took to him.'

'He is an acquired taste,' acknowledged Michael. 'But no, he is not a friend, although I have always admired his intellect and ambition. He will go far in the Church and in our Order.'

Bartholomew was sure he would, although he was less certain that it would be a good thing for either organisation.

They arrived at St John Zachary, where Bartholomew was dismayed to learn that Lucas's body lay at the bottom of his brother-in-law's vault. With Tulyet's help, he hastened to haul it out, lest Edith heard about the desecration and came to see for herself. Once Lucas had been retrieved, it did not take Bartholomew long to ascertain how he had died.

'Stabbed in the back.' He pointed to a trail of bloody spatters that ended with a discarded chisel. 'With that, I imagine.'

At that point, there was a commotion at the back of the church, which heralded the arrival of Petit and his remaining apprentices. They stormed to the chancel en masse, demanding to know what had happened. Tulyet told them tersely.

'He volunteered to stay late,' wailed Petit, and jabbed an accusing forefinger at Bartholomew. 'He and his sister are always urging us to work faster, so I agreed, thinking to appease them. Poor Lucas! He was such a diligent boy.'

'It was not diligence that kept him out tonight,' said Michael bluntly. 'It was money – he was going to meet us at the witching hour, and sell us the name of the person who killed Tynkell and Moleyns.'

'But he did not know it!' cried Petit. 'If he had, he would have told me. I was like a father to him.'

'That chisel,' said Bartholomew, nodding towards it. 'Is it yours?'

Petit gaped at it. 'It is Lucas's, which means the culprit used the poor boy's own tool to dispatch him.' He turned accusingly to Tulyet. 'This is your fault. You should have been out hunting this vile murderer, not listening to Lakenham whine about stolen brasses. If you had done your duty, a third innocent life would not have been lost.'

'*Is* Lucas the killer's third victim, Matt?' asked Michael in a low voice, as the mason continued to rail at Tulyet, his apprentices clamouring their agreement at his side.

'I do not believe so,' Bartholomew whispered back. 'First, Moleyns and Tynkell were stabbed cleanly, whereas Lucas has five separate and very messy punctures – this killer did not know what he was doing. Second, they were stabbed in the front, but Lucas was attacked from behind. Third, they were murdered publicly, while this was an assault on a lone man in the dark. And finally, Moleyns and Tynkell were dispatched with a thin spike—'

'A burin,' interrupted Michael, looking pointedly at the masons.

'*Possibly* a burin,' corrected Bartholomew. 'Whereas a chisel was used on Lucas.'

Petit chose that moment to stop haranguing the Sheriff and hurl himself across Lucas's body in a dramatic expression of grief. The freckled Peres hurried to comfort him, although Petit's distraught sobs abated when Bartholomew,

Michael and Tulyet retreated to the far side of the chancel to talk, and there was no audience.

'I agree,' said Tulyet, when Bartholomew had outlined his conclusions. 'This is not the work of the rogue who dispatched Moleyns and Tynkell with such surgical precision. We have two killers here, not one.'

'Perhaps this death is an escalation of the feud between latteners and masons,' suggested Michael. 'The stakes are high, with a chancellor *and* a favourite of the King needing tombs. We had better see if Lakenham has an alibi for Lucas's murder – he has access to this church at the moment, because he is making a memorial brass for Cew.'

'It would be a tidy solution,' said Tulyet. 'The only problem being that Lakenham *does* have an alibi – he was with me when Lucas died. We were discussing his stolen supplies.'

'Then perhaps he hired someone else to do it,' suggested Michael.

'Does he have that sort of money?' asked Bartholomew doubtfully. 'He has won no major commissions since Knyt – Cew's little plate cannot have earned him much.'

'Then maybe Cristine did it,' suggested Tulyet. 'She is a powerful and determined lady, quick to take offence. Of course, we should not discount Petit as a culprit either. I am unconvinced by his showy display of grief, and he is certainly callous enough to sacrifice one of his own lads to compromise a rival.'

'I agree,' said Michael, looking to where the mason had abandoned Lucas's body now that no one was watching, and was ordering Peres to rinse off the chisel.

'And nor can we forget Isnard and Gundrede,' added Tulyet. 'They also have a hearty dislike of these tomb-builders.'

'Who found Lucas?' asked Michael, cutting across Bartholomew's immediate defence of the bargeman. 'Frisby?'

'I did,' replied Tulyet. 'Frisby is in his house, drunk.'

'What were you doing here in the dark?' asked Michael curiously.

'Looking for Lucas. He refused to speak to me earlier, so I came to press him again. He was still warm to the touch, and I wish to God I had arrived a few moments sooner. Then we might have had answers, and he would still be alive.'

'His murder comes under your jurisdiction,' said Michael, 'so you investigate him, while I concentrate on Tynkell and Moleyns. It will be the most efficient use of our time.'

But Tulyet shook his head. 'I will take Lucas, you can have Tynkell, and we will *share* Moleyns. I cannot delegate the murder of a prisoner, Brother. The King would not approve.'

'Very well,' said Michael. 'But we must meet regularly, to compare notes.'

Tulyet smiled. 'The University and the town working together to thwart criminals. Are you sure you would not rather be a chancellor than a bishop, Brother? Cambridge needs you.'

'It does,' agreed Michael immodestly. 'But so does Rochester.'

CHAPTER 5

As it was not every day that a member of Michaelhouse was offered a bishopric, the Fellows celebrated with considerable vigour that night, merrymaking with an abandon rarely seen in the College. As a consequence, there were sore heads aplenty the following day, and the students, who had been kept awake by the racket, spoke in deliberately loud voices, in a concerted attempt to make their teachers wince. It was disappointingly easy with all the Fellows, except two.

Bartholomew rarely drank to excess, lest he was summoned by a patient. He knew other *medici* did not allow such considerations to limit their pleasures, but he hated the notion of failing someone for the sake of a few cups of wine. He had still enjoyed himself enormously, but was quite happy to sip watered ale and smile at the antics of the others. Meanwhile, Kolvyle had sat in sulky silence all night, plainly jealous of the monk's good fortune. His colleagues treated his pouting envy with the contempt it deserved by ignoring it.

'There was something wrong with that wine last night,' whispered Michael, as he joined his colleagues in the yard to process to Mass. He looked very much the worse for wear, with a pasty face and bloodshot eyes. 'It has given me a headache.'

'And I have a sour stomach,' agreed Langelee. 'Return the barrel and demand a refund.'

'I would, but there is none left to prove our point,' said Michael. 'I imagine the students finished it after we went to bed. After all, the seven of us cannot have emptied it alone.'

'The *five* of you,' corrected Bartholomew. 'And you did.'

'I think we had better let Kolvyle take our classes this morning,' said Langelee, hand to his middle. 'I am not well enough to teach, and if you are suffering similar symptoms . . .'

'That is a good idea,' said Suttone weakly. His portly features were grey-green above a vomit-flecked habit. It was rumpled, too, suggesting he had slept in it, and had risen too late to change. 'I feel dreadful.'

'I suppose I can oblige,' said Kolvyle grudgingly. He was freshly shaven, his hair was brushed, and he was wearing clean clothes. Just the sight of him made his older colleagues feel worn, jaded and very shabby. 'After all, we do not want the students to complain. None of you are decent teachers on a good day, so after a night of intemperate hedonism . . .'

'I am much respected in the lecture hall,' objected Suttone, albeit feebly. 'Indeed, I promised my lads a discourse on *reductio ad absurdum* today, which is no easy topic. Of course, I cannot recall what I planned to say, exactly . . .'

'Your thesis was that Ethel the chicken must weigh something, or she would spend all her time floating in the air,' supplied Clippesby, who held the bird in question in his arms. His eyes were glazed, and he wore the silly grin that indicated he was still drunk. 'You will base your argument on the fact that denial of the assertion will have a ridiculous result. In other words, it will demonstrate this very common form of logical argument.'

'I know what *reductio ad absurdum* means, Clippesby,' said Suttone irritably. 'But was that really the example I intended to use? Lord! I had better find another, or my lads will think I have lost my reason.'

'They will,' agreed Kolvyle spitefully. 'Clearly, it would be better if you all left this morning's work to me. *I* will not let our pupils down.'

He flounced away, startling Langelee and his Fellows by opening the gate and walking to church by himself. Allowing the Master to lead the way was not a written rule, but it was a custom everyone followed, and all were astonished that Kolvyle should have chosen to flout it.

'I hope we did not do anything embarrassing last night,' said Suttone uneasily. 'Especially in front of him. I recall very little after the Master stood on the table and recited that poem about the nuns and the dragon, and it would be a pity if our night of levity damaged my chances of being Chancellor. Kolvyle is the kind of man to gossip about any . . . indiscretions.'

'It *was* quite a night,' grinned William, who looked much as he usually did, given that he was not a clean man to start with, so any new spillages were difficult to detect. 'I cannot recall the last time we enjoyed ourselves so.'

'We had much to celebrate,' smiled Michael. 'My See and Suttone's chancellorship.'

'Suttone may not win,' warned Bartholomew. 'Lyng has the support of the hostels, and that is where most votes lie. It will not be easy to defeat him.'

'I thought the same, but Michael says he has a plan.' Suttone beamed suddenly. 'I shall like being Chancellor even more if he is not here to push me around. I am doubly delighted that he is leaving.'

Michael's expression darkened. 'I most certainly *will* tell you what to do! I shall be watching your every move like a hawk.'

'How?' asked Bartholomew curiously. 'You will be in Rochester.'

'I have my ways,' replied Michael mysteriously. 'But do not worry about Lyng, Suttone. No killer will ever hold the post of Chancellor.'

'Killer?' echoed Langelee, startled. 'You mean it was *Lyng* who made an end of Tynkell and Moleyns? Lord!

He seems such a decent fellow, and I have always liked him.'

'Most people do, which is why he felt free to commit murder,' said Michael airily. 'He thinks he is the last man we will accuse, just because he is charming and elderly.'

'So you have solved the case?' asked Bartholomew, pleased. 'You did not mention it last night, but I am glad it is over. I shall teach my lads Maimonides' *Tractus contra passionem asthmatis* today. They will prefer that to some tedious monologue from Kolvyle.'

'I have not *solved* it exactly,' hedged Michael, 'but Lyng is my chief suspect. However, I shall need you to help me to gather the necessary evidence, so Maimonides will have to wait.'

Bartholomew regarded him through narrowed eyes. 'Do you really think Lyng is the culprit, or have you picked on him because he is Suttone's most serious rival?'

'A little of both,' admitted Michael. 'But he does have the strongest motive for killing Tynkell – namely dispatching the present incumbent, so that he could be Chancellor once more. It makes sense – he is old, and Tynkell kept delaying his departure.'

'And that is your scheme to secure me the post?' asked Suttone worriedly. 'Accusing Lyng of murder? Is that not unethical?'

'Not if he is guilty,' replied Michael glibly. 'And if he is innocent . . . well, he will just have to weather the storm as best he can.'

The scholars attended Mass in St Michael's, although it was not easy to concentrate on their devotions, because Petit arrived and began to prise the damaged lid from Wilson's tomb. He and his apprentices obviously thought they were being unobtrusive, but there were a lot of loud whispers, much clattering of tools, and they failed to understand the concept of tiptoeing, so their footsteps clattered loudly enough to render some of the rite inaudible.

'I *know* I promised to work on Stanmore today,' the mason said stiffly, when the ceremony was over and Bartholomew went to have words with him. 'But you cannot expect us to enter the building where Lucas was so vilely killed. At least, not for the foreseeable future.'

'It was a terrible shock, see,' added the freckled Peres, sticking out his chin challengingly. 'So we have decided to concentrate on our other masterpieces for a while.'

'If you abandon Oswald again, I shall follow my sister's lead, and make speeches about unreliable craftsmen,' warned Bartholomew. 'So think very carefully before doing anything rash.'

Petit shot him a foul look as he left, while young Peres shoved past the physician roughly enough to make him stagger. Then the lad was almost knocked from his own feet when he found himself in Langelee's path, and the Master did some jostling of his own.

'I *had* to hire them,' said Langelee defensively, as Bartholomew regarded him with silent reproach. 'Petit is the only monumental mason within a sixty-mile radius. Or do you *want* Kolvyle to win a claim of compensation against us?'

Bartholomew scowled at him, and they processed home in silence. No one ate much at breakfast, some because their stomachs were still too delicate, and the rest because what was on offer was virtually inedible – the servants had also raised a goblet to Michael's future success. Agatha the laundress was decidedly fragile, while Cynric had yet to get out of bed.

'Your lads will enjoy Kolvyle's lecture, Bartholomew,' said Langelee, after he had recited a shockingly short final grace, and the students had filed out. 'He will speak on Gratian's *Decretum*, which is always fun. Or so he tells me.'

'Not as much fun as Maimonides,' said Bartholomew firmly. 'And do not suggest letting Aungel teach *Passionem asthmatis*, because he does not know it well enough. Michael's beadles can find the evidence he needs to convict Lyng, but my duties lie here.'

'Lyng is not the killer,' said Langelee in a low voice. 'I understand why Michael thinks so, but he is wrong – Lyng is not bold enough. It is far more likely to be Hopeman. However, Michael cannot leave Cambridge until the case is solved, and our College needs the glory his promotion will bring. Thus you *must* help him, to ensure he catches the right man.'

'I do not think—'

'It is common knowledge that the Bishop of Bangor has been waiting for Sheppey to die so he can grab Rochester. Thus Michael must get there as soon as possible, which he cannot do until Tynkell's murder is properly solved. *That* is your duty, Bartholomew, not passionate asthma. Moreover, he cannot arrange for Suttone to be elected if he is busy hunting killers.'

Bartholomew supposed the Master was right. He capitulated with a grudging nod, and Langelee expressed his thanks with a vigorous clap on the back that made his teeth rattle. Then the bell rang to announce the start of the day's teaching, and the students trooped into the hall to hear what Kolvyle had to say about the principles of canon law. Bartholomew was sorry for them, sure that even the lawyers among them would be more interested in Maimonides' views on lung diseases.

As usual, Kolvyle was in no hurry to begin his work, preferring instead to let the suspense build before gracing the audience with his presence. He was still in his room, and Michael indicated that Bartholomew was to accompany him there.

'Partly to make sure he does not dally too long – my Premonstratensians are restless today,' he said as they walked, 'but also to ask what he saw when Moleyns died.'

Although the most junior Fellow was usually allocated the meanest room, Kolvyle had made such a fuss that even Langelee had been incapable of withstanding the litany of complaints. As a consequence, he occupied quarters that were far nicer than anyone else's – they were not only larger and in better repair, but also beautifully decorated.

Bartholomew and Michael arrived at them to discover that Kolvyle already had a visitor in the form of Suttone, who looked plump, soft and dissolute next to his bright and youthful colleague.

'But it will do me harm if a member of my own College openly supports another candidate,' he was objecting. 'You cannot declare for Godrich.'

'I already have,' said Kolvyle smugly. 'You are too old for the post anyway. There should be a rule that no one over twenty-five should be allowed to stand, because it is time our University was in the hands of younger, more dynamic officers.'

'Do not underestimate experience,' argued Suttone. 'It is—'

'What experience?' Kolvyle shot back snidely. 'You do not have any, and your campaign is based on two things: scaring everyone by saying the plague is about to return, and then trying to make them feel better about it by offering to lift the ban on women. You silly old fool!'

'We created a monster by letting him have his own way every time he stamps a sulky foot,' murmured Bartholomew to Michael. 'It would not surprise me to learn that he killed Tynkell, and is piqued because he will not be the one to benefit from it.'

'If so, he will suffer the consequences,' vowed Michael. 'Member of my College or not.'

He marched into the room, but Kolvyle was gathering notes for his lecture, and pretended not to notice. Suttone tried again to reason with him, then threw up his hands in defeat when Kolvyle began to sing, drowning him out.

'You talk to him, Brother,' he spat as he left. 'He is incapable of listening.'

'I do not listen, because Suttone has nothing to say,' declared Kolvyle when the Carmelite had gone. 'His jaw flaps, but only rubbish emerges.'

'I saw you near Moleyns when he took his tumble,' said Bartholomew, coming straight to the point so he would not have to spend a moment longer than necessary in such objectionable company. 'Will you tell us exactly what happened?'

Kolvyle shrugged. 'A dog barked, Satan bucked, and Moleyns hit the ground. I hurried to help him – he was swearing, so he was definitely alive – but then there was a stampede, and I dislike being jostled by inferiors, so I withdrew.'

'Which particular inferiors were these?' asked Michael. 'Godrich? I know for a fact that he was there, too, because I saw him.'

Kolvyle regarded him with open dislike. 'He is not a man for rubbing shoulders with commoners either – he followed me away. However, Lyng did not. He is probably the killer, desperate to do something meaningful before he dies of old age. Or Hopeman, perhaps, driven by his low intellect. Or a tomb-maker, for the delight of building another grave.'

'In other words, you have no idea,' said Michael, unimpressed.

Kolvyle smiled, an expression of such smug arrogance that Bartholomew was seized with the sudden and most uncharacteristic desire to slap it off him. 'Oh, I have plenty of theories, all sure to be better than anything *you* might have devised. However, to solve the case, you need to identify exactly how the two victims are connected.'

'Clearly,' agreed Michael with admirable patience. 'And do you have the answer?'

'Of course,' replied Kolvyle, and turned back to his notes.

'So what is it?' pressed Michael, while Bartholomew clenched his fists behind his back and was all admiration for the monk's self-control.

'There was a special service in St Mary the Great last week, to pray against a return of the plague. Suttone insisted on holding it, if you recall.'

'Yes,' said Michael. 'I attended it myself. Was Moleyns there, too? I did not notice.'

'He was,' replied Kolvyle. 'And he spent a lot of time chatting to Lyng. Afterwards, Lyng went straight to our Chancellor, whispered in his ear, then returned to Moleyns. Obviously, Moleyns and Tynkell had business together, and Lyng was their go between.'

'We know Tynkell and Moleyns met,' said Bartholomew. 'Tynkell was interested in siege warfare, and Moleyns was willing to give him eye-witness accounts. Moleyns sent him messages, inviting him to meet in St Mary the Great.'

Kolvyle released a shrill bray of laughter. 'You believe that? What an ass you are, Bartholomew! Of course they were not discussing weapons!' He turned back to Michael. 'So there is your connection, Brother, although you should not have needed me to draw it to your attention. Now all you need to do is find out what they discussed.'

'Do you know?' asked Michael.

Kolvyle hesitated, but then shook his head, although it was plain he wished it were otherwise, so he could gloat a little more about his superior knowledge.

'What about Cook?' asked Bartholomew, fighting down his irritation by pondering whether the barber or Kolvyle was more disagreeable. 'Did he join this discussion?'

'He might have done. He was always hanging around Moleyns, because he knew him from Nottingham, and liked to consider himself the friend of a friend of the King.'

'Ah, yes, Nottingham,' said Michael. 'The place where Dallingridge was poisoned. I wonder who could have done such a terrible thing.'

'He *claimed* he was poisoned,' said Kolvyle contemptuously. 'But there was nothing to prove it, as I have told you before.'

'That is not what Nottingham's Sheriff thinks,' said Michael. 'He is—'

'Nottingham's Sheriff!' sneered Kolvyle. 'That man is an idiot of the first order. Now, if you will excuse me, I have work to do.'

He elbowed Bartholomew and Michael out of his room and locked the door behind him. He was the only College member who took such precautions, and Bartholomew had always considered it an affront. Then, head held high, the youngster swaggered across the yard.

'I will look the other way while you thump him, Brother,' offered Bartholomew.

'Do not tempt me, Matt.'

Unfortunately, several patients needed Bartholomew, and as he refused to delegate their care to his students, the monk went alone to St Mary the Great to hear his beadles' reports, hoping one had learned something to help him catch the killer. He had ordered them to trawl the taverns the previous night, and had allocated a generous sum from the University Chest to buy any information on offer. He arrived at the church to find Whittlesey waiting for him, too.

'Thank you for your offer to house me in Michaelhouse for the duration of my stay here,' the envoy said. 'But I have been lodging in King's Hall since I arrived, and

Godrich will be offended if I moved now. I am sure you understand.'

'As you wish,' said Michael, simultaneously relieved that Michaelhouse's poverty would not be exposed to a man he wanted to impress, but hurt that his hospitality should be rejected. 'Godrich is a friend of yours then? How did you meet?'

'We are kin – both cousins to the Archbishop of Canterbury.' Whittlesey hesitated for a moment, but then forged on. 'My familial ties to the country's leading cleric proved very useful for Bishop Sheppey. Moreover, I learned a lot about Church politics during my years in his service – the sort of experience that could be of considerable value to his successor . . .'

Michael smiled. 'Forgive me, Whittlesey. I did not invite you to serve as my envoy, because I assumed it was a given. I am sure we can do a great deal for each other.'

Whittlesey smiled back, pleased. 'In that case, I should like to watch you at work again – openly this time. I must make myself familiar with your ways quickly, because we shall both be busy once we reach Rochester. Do not mind me – you will not know I am here.'

Michael seriously doubted that, and was acutely aware of his beadles casting uneasy glances in the envoy's direction as they delivered their reports. He understood why: there was something unsettling about the silent, black presence in the shadows, especially as Whittlesey liked to keep his cowl up, to protect the back of his neck from draughts. It was, the monk thought, rather like having Death looming over his shoulder.

'So none of you learned anything to help me catch Tynkell's killer?' he asked when his men had finished speaking, struggling to keep the disappointment from his voice. 'Despite spending four shillings on ale?'

'Sorry, Brother,' replied Meadowman, their leader and

his favourite. 'All we can say is that the culprit is more likely to be a scholar than a townsman.'

'And why is that, pray?' asked Michael warily.

'Because no one has stepped forward to take credit for the deed, which a guilty townsman would definitely do, for the glory it would win him among his peers. Most *real* folk are delighted that the University has lost its leading scholar.'

'And if the culprit is not a scholar, then it is the Devil,' added another. 'After all, he did fly away after he stabbed the Chancellor.'

Michael's eyes narrowed. 'Is this why you have failed to locate the cloak – you are all of the asinine belief that it was Satan you saw fluttering off the roof?'

'It *was* Satan,' the beadle assured him earnestly, while his cronies clamoured their agreement, 'so the "cloak" will never be found, because it does not exist.'

'Of course, the tomb-makers are also on our list of suspects,' said Meadowman before the Senior Proctor could argue. 'I know they are not scholars, but they cannot be classed as townsfolk either, because they have not been here long enough.'

Michael dismissed them in disgust, then attended Tynkell's burial, a small, private ceremony for friends – a public requiem would be held later. Even so, there was an impressive turnout, and Secretary Nicholas was not the only one who wept when the body was lowered into the ground. Afterwards, heavy of heart, Michael settled down to some administration, aware of Whittlesey shuffling restlessly behind him as time ticked past and there was nothing interesting to see. Eventually, Nicholas arrived, red-eyed, but back in control of himself once more.

'Here is the official notice for the Great West Door,' he said, waving it to dry the ink. 'Authorising the election for noon next Wednesday. Lyng will be disappointed, of course. He would rather it were sooner – before Hopeman and Godrich can besmirch him.'

'Does he have anything they can besmirch him with?' asked Michael keenly.

'I doubt it, but they could find ways to defame a saint. A lot is at stake here, Brother, and all five candidates are determined to win.'

'You support Thelnetham, I recall.'

'Yes, but *not* because he promised to let me keep my job – Weasenham just said that for spite. It is because he will make the best Chancellor. He is intelligent, astute, dynamic, tough, a gifted teacher and a brilliant orator. The other candidates pale by comparison.'

Michael leaned back in his chair. 'But they all have powerful backers: Lyng has the hostels, Godrich has King's Hall, Hopeman has the Dominicans, and Suttone has me. Thelnetham has no one.'

'He has his own order – the Gilbertines.'

'Yes, but they only amount to two dozen voting members, and they have never been very influential in the University.'

Nicholas smiled. 'True, but he also has the support of *intelligent* men – clever scholars who can see beyond simple and arbitrary allegiances. They may be a minority, but they are eloquent and persuasive. Do not underestimate them or him.'

'Unfortunately for Thelnetham,' said Michael, 'I suspect even that may not be enough.'

With Meadowman walking in front, bearing the declaration like a holy relic, Michael and Nicholas, with Whittlesey trailing behind, processed to the narthex. While they were there, Nicholas took the opportunity to ring the bells, hauling on each rope in turn until he had all three clanging in a joyful cacophony. He grinned his delight at the exercise, although the noise was deafening, drowning out the sound of Meadowman nailing the proclamation to the Great West Door and the remarks of those who gathered to read it.

The bells'clamour caused other scholars to come and see what was happening, so it was not long before there was quite a crowd. It included Hopeman, Godrich, Thelnetham and Suttone, although there was no sign of Lyng. Michael wondered why the old man had elected to stay away when it was an ideal opportunity to win more votes.

'The bells will remain silent until a new Chancellor is elected,' declared Michael, the moment he could make himself heard again. A sigh of relief rippled through the onlookers, although Nicholas's face fell. 'Then all scholars will know that the interregnum has ended.'

Vicar Frisby was grinning his amusement. 'Five days without bells will be agony for you, Nicholas. You had better come for a drink, to take your mind off it.'

'It is too long to be without a proper leader,' objected Hopeman, and glared at Michael. 'I know why you want the delay, of course – to give your creature Suttone more time to rally support.'

'I am no one's creature,' objected Suttone indignantly. 'Nor do I need to cheat. Why would I, when I have the support of the Senior Proctor and the Carmelites?'

'And the votes of lustful rogues who aim to ravage Cambridge's women,' Hopeman snapped back. 'You pander to the lowest kind of scum – the kind I shall not tolerate when I am in charge.'

There was a chorus of jeers at this pronouncement, and Michael was pleased that the Carmelite's attack on celibacy was making him popular. The statute in question could never be revoked, of course – the town would not tolerate having open season declared on its women, and relations between it and the University would become so strained as to be untenable. The rule, no matter how inconvenient, was there to stay, although that was not something he would reveal just yet, naturally.

'Anyone who does not support me supports Satan,' brayed Hopeman. 'I have the Lord on my side, and He will rain down his wrath on all those who oppose me.'

Godrich gazed theatrically upwards. 'I see nothing but clear skies, Father. You must have misunderstood Him. And I am glad the election will not be until next week, because it gives us all time to make a proper, informed decision.'

'And him a chance to buy more votes,' murmured Nicholas in Michael's ear.

'Lyng will win,' called Father Aidan from Maud's. 'How can he not, when every hostel is behind him?'

'Lyng?' sneered Godrich, and gestured around him. 'A man who is nowhere to be seen on this most momentous of occasions. Where is he? In bed, resting his ancient bones?'

'Perhaps he is unwell,' suggested Thelnetham, whose cloak was again pinned by the gaudy purple brooch, but this time he had added red hose and a pink hat to the ensemble. 'The excitement of such an occasion must be considerable for a man of his advanced years.'

Michael took all four candidates aside and asked again for their thoughts on what had happened to Tynkell and Moleyns. All except Thelnetham admitted to being near the felon when he had died, and to watching Tynkell frolic on the roof with the Devil, but no one had seen the killer's face.

'I was in the Gilbertine Priory,' said Thelnetham. 'With Nicholas and several of my brethren, should you require alibis. So I missed all the fun.'

'I hardly think murder constitutes *fun*,' admonished Michael.

Thelnetham inclined his head. 'Forgive me, Brother; it was a poor choice of words. By the time the tale reached my convent, both men were dead. However, I did see a rider gallop down the Trumpington road at a furious lick shortly after Moleyns is said to have perished. He was bundled up in his cloak, so all I can tell you is that he rode a brown horse. However . . .'

'Yes?'

'Stoke Poges. Have you heard of it?'

Michael nodded. 'It was Moleyns' manor, which he inherited through Egidia when her uncle Peter Poges was murdered.'

'I passed through it last summer,' said Thelnetham. 'The village has a motif – a pilgrim's staff – which I remember because it is similar to the crutch that is the symbol of my Order. Well, I thought I saw one embossed on this rider's saddle.'

'How, if the horse was going as fast as you claim?' scoffed Godrich.

'I saw it when the rider stopped at the Trumpington Gate to pay the toll,' explained Thelnetham patiently. 'Once through, he took off like lightning.'

Michael frowned. 'Are you saying that this horseman came from Stoke Poges?'

'No, Brother. I merely report that his saddle was marked with an emblem that matched the one that Stoke Poges uses. I do not know what – or even *if* – it is significant. That is for you to determine.'

While Michael questioned him further, Hopeman and Suttone went to canvass among those who milled around the door. Godrich cornered Whittlesey and began to whisper to him, although he left when Michael approached, rather too furtively for the monk's liking.

'What were you two muttering about, Whittlesey?' he demanded.

'The election,' replied the envoy smoothly. 'I hope he wins. Lyng might be popular, but he holds old-fashioned views. Meanwhile, Hopeman is a lunatic, Suttone a bumbling nonentity who aims to promote licentiousness, and Thelnetham is eccentric.'

'And Godrich offers what, exactly? Other than an arrogance that will alienate everyone?'

'Wealthy friends, who will provide vital funding. My kinsman will be good for the University, Brother. Give him a chance to prove it.'

While Michael was busy with University affairs, Bartholomew visited a patient near the Dominican Priory, then began to walk to the parish of All Saints-next-the-Castle for three cases of lung-rot. He met Isnard and Gundrede on the way – the pair had just been released from the castle after spending a night in Tulyet's custody, where they had been quizzed relentlessly about Lucas's murder.

'But we did not kill him,' declared Isnard, all righteous indignation. 'How dare the Sheriff accuse us! We did not steal the tomb-builders' supplies either.'

'He had to let us go in the end,' smirked Gundrede, 'because he had no good excuse to keep us, although it grieved him to admit it. However, me and Isnard were in the King's Head when Lucas was stabbed, and it is not our fault that no one there remembers.'

Bartholomew watched them go unhappily. The King's Head was brazenly opposed to the forces of law and order, and the landlord and his regulars would think nothing of fibbing to defend fellow patrons. However, they did not condone murder, and the fact that they declined to provide Isnard and Gundrede with alibis was worrisome. And if the bargeman and his friend were lying about where they had been, then what *had* they been doing?

He visited the first two patients with lung-rot, and was about to enter the home of the third when he spotted Lakenham, Cristine and their elegantly clad apprentice, Reames. Like Isnard and Gundrede, they were also coming home from the castle: Tulyet had been busy.

'He wanted to know if we had arranged to have Lucas

killed,' said Cristine, although Bartholomew had not asked. 'He knows we did not do it ourselves, because we were with him at the time. However, he did not detain us for long this morning.'

'Because she gave him a piece of her mind for thinking such a vile thing,' said Lakenham, reaching up to slip an affectionate arm around her mountainous shoulders. 'She also told him, in no uncertain terms, that it was not us who pinched the lead off Gonville Hall's chapel roof yesterday.'

Reames shoved his hands out of sight quickly, although not before Bartholomew had seen that they were filthy, which was odd, given the care that he obviously took with the rest of his appearance. Did that mean he *had* stolen the lead? The metal did, after all, leave tell-tale marks on those who touched it. Or was there an innocent explanation for the stains?

'We work hard,' said Reames shortly, when he saw where the physician was looking. 'And hard work means dirty hands. What of it?'

He had turned and flounced away before Bartholomew could inform him that this answer was unsatisfactory. Bartholomew started to follow, but a child came to tug at his sleeve, pleading with him to tend her ailing grandmother. By the time he had finished with the old woman, the latteners were nowhere to be seen. He tended his third case of lung-rot, then walked to his last scheduled customer of the day. This was in the castle, where one of Tulyet's men had been injured during training. He was conducted to the barracks by Robin, Agatha's nephew.

'Yevele says I cut him during sword drill,' the lad grumbled as they went. 'But it is a lie. I wish the Sheriff had not taken him on. Do you remember coming to tend his frost-nipped nose last week? Well, he let that happen on purpose, purely to get out of guard duty.'

Bartholomew had suspected as much at the time. It

had been an unusually cold night, but even so, Yevele's claim that his nose had frozen while walking from one side of the bailey to the other was patently untrue.

'I do not need you, physician,' growled Yevele ungraciously, when Bartholomew approached his bed. Robin rolled his eyes and left. 'Barber Cook sewed me up nicely, and gave me a free haircut into the bargain. He does a special offer every Friday, see – a free trim with every medical procedure.'

Surprisingly, Cook had managed a reasonable job on the wound, although the stitches were ugly, and would leave a scar. Bartholomew suspected Yevele would not mind – the soldiers at the castle were proud of their 'badges of honour', and the bigger they were, the better they liked them.

'I do not know why you called me,' said Bartholomew to Tulyet and Helbye, who were waiting outside for him when he emerged. 'Not when Cook has already been.'

'Because of Mother Salter,' explained Tulyet. 'Dead of a scratch at the hands of that butcher. I would have refused to let him in, but he had been and gone before I could stop him.'

'Cook is all right,' said Sergeant Helbye, who was grey-faced with fatigue and moved as if he was in pain. 'And he does give a lovely trim. He even made Norys look presentable.'

He nodded towards the soldier in question, a surly lout who would always look like a ruffian, no matter how many sessions he had with a barber. Then Helbye mumbled something about going to check on Yevele, and Bartholomew felt a surge of compassion for the old warrior when he saw how hard he was trying not to limp.

'He and I questioned Isnard and Gundrede nearly all night,' said Tulyet. 'Then we tackled the tomb-makers, but none of them confessed to Lucas's murder. We wasted our time.'

'You do realise that Helbye is no longer young?' said Bartholomew quietly. 'You might be able to forgo your sleep, but it is more of a strain for him.'

'Nonsense! He is as strong as an ox. Besides, he is my right-hand man, and I do not know how I would manage without him.'

'You might have to, unless you treat him more gently.'

Tulyet grimaced. 'He would be mortified if I suggested light duties. But do not fret, Matt – he will feel better when winter turns to spring.'

Bartholomew doubted it, but was disinclined to argue. 'Did you ask Egidia and Inge about the discrepancy between their version of events and Weasenham's – whether they reached Moleyns sooner or later, once he had fallen off his horse?'

'I did, but they are sticking to their tale and will not be budged. Perhaps Helbye is not the only one who is too old for this line of work – I am sure I could have terrified a confession from the culprit five years ago. Perhaps I should take a leaf from Michael's book, and have myself promoted.'

Cambridge would be a very different place, thought Bartholomew unhappily, without its Sheriff and its Senior Proctor, and he was not sure he would like it. Perhaps he should leave, too, and begin a new life somewhere with the woman he had once loved so deeply.

CHAPTER 6

Friday afternoons were dreaded by the whole town, because it was when the Michaelhouse Choir met. The choir comprised a large number of spectacularly untalented individuals who had joined solely for the free bread and ale that were dispensed after rehearsals. They compensated for their lack of skill with volume, and prided themselves on being heard over considerable distances. Michael was their conductor, and was fiercely proud of them, although Bartholomew failed to understand why, given that the monk was a talented musician, with standards.

'At least it drove Whittlesey away,' said Michael, when the rehearsal was over and all Cambridge heaved a sigh of relief that there would not be another for seven blissful days. 'He asked to shadow me, to learn how I operate. I thought I would not mind, but I do – I cannot be myself with him looming over my shoulder. But a few notes from my tenors sent him running.'

Bartholomew was not surprised, but refrained from saying so, as Michael seemed frayed and downhearted – which was odd, as he usually enjoyed choir practice.

'What is wrong, Brother?' he asked gently.

'My singers have heard that I am leaving,' explained the monk wretchedly. 'And they looked at me with such reproach . . . But what do they expect? I cannot stay here for ever, and they must realise that I have ambitions.'

'The choir is important to them. For most, it is the only decent meal they have all week.'

'Do not make it worse, Matt,' groaned Michael. 'I feel bad enough as it is.'

Each alone with his thoughts, they walked to Maud's Hostel, where Michael wanted to ask Lyng about the curious encounter that Kolvyle had described – where the elderly priest had scurried between Moleyns and Tynkell in St Mary the Great.

As Maud's catered to wealthy students, it occupied a very handsome mansion. Its teachers were not obliged to room with students, its furnishings were luxurious, and the food and drink were of the very highest quality. Its Principal, Father Aidan, came to greet the visitors, accompanied by Richard Deynman, brother of the Michaelhouse librarian. Both Deynmans were of an ilk – good-natured, ebullient and deeply stupid.

'I am glad you are here, Brother,' said Aidan worriedly. 'Because Lyng went out last night at about eight o'clock, and none of us have seen him since.'

'And you wait until now to tell me?' cried Michael in alarm. 'What are you thinking?'

'That we do not want to damage his chances in the election,' snapped Aidan. 'You heard what his rivals sniggered when he was not there to see the notice nailed to the Great West Door – they mocked him, and accused him of resting his ancient bones.'

'Did he tell you where he was going?' asked Bartholomew.

Aidan shook his head. 'But we assumed it was something to do with winning a few more votes. He is very excited about the prospect of being Chancellor again.'

'Which he will be, of course,' put in Richard brightly, 'because all the hostels want him, and they comprise most of the University.'

'Not *all* of them,' said Michael coolly. 'A good many have expressed a preference for Suttone. But never mind this now. Has Lyng stayed out all night before?'

'Never,' replied Aidan, 'which is why we are concerned. He was not back when I extinguished the lamps at ten o'clock last night, but I assumed he was busy electioneering.

However, when I went to see why he was late to breakfast today, I saw his bed has not been slept in.'

'Have you spoken to his friends in other foundations?' asked Bartholomew. 'Perhaps he decided to stay with one of them overnight, rather than walk home in the dark.'

'Now there is an idea!' exclaimed Richard. 'I shall do it at once. Being old, he probably just fell asleep somewhere, and is happily napping in another hostel.'

'If he is, I suggest he withdraws, Aidan,' said Michael after the lad had sped away. 'We cannot have a Chancellor who dozes off on other people's property.'

'Oh, I am sure you would love that,' said Aidan bitterly. 'But do not think it will help Suttone – scholars who would have voted for Lyng will just transfer their allegiance to Hopeman, on the grounds that he is another priest.'

'Suttone is a priest,' Michael pointed out.

'Yes, but one who aims to challenge the rules of celibacy, and who terrifies everyone by telling them that the plague is poised to return. He is also a member of a College, whereas Hopeman is a hostel man.'

'*Your* hostel,' remarked Michael. 'How fortunate for you that Maud's is offering two candidates for election.'

'I would much rather have Lyng,' said Aidan stiffly. 'So let us hope he returns unharmed.'

Michael inclined his head. 'Tell me when Richard finds him. I shall also ask my beadles to keep their eyes peeled. In the meantime, perhaps you will answer some questions. First, I want to know how well Lyng knew Moleyns and Tynkell.'

Aidan gave a tight smile. 'He knew Tynkell very well. They were good friends, and Tynkell often sought his advice about University affairs.'

'Did he indeed?' murmured Michael.

Aidan looked away. 'But as for Moleyns . . . well, I cannot say I am sorry he is dead. He was a felon, and it vexed me to see him strutting freely about our town. Lyng did not like it either.'

'Then why did he whisper to him during services in St Mary the Great?'

'You are mistaken, Brother. Lyng would never have interrupted his devotions to chat to a criminal. He despised Moleyns, and said so several times.'

'Did he explain why?'

'Is it not obvious? Moleyns was a thief and a murderer. Did you not hear about the man he killed in order to inherit Stoke Poges – his wife's uncle? He was acquitted only because he was allowed to choose his own jury, a travesty of justice that shames our legal system.'

'Did Lyng also feel strongly about this?'

Aidan pursed his lips. 'What you are really asking is: did Lyng kill Moleyns on a point of principle? Well, the answer is no. Lyng is a gentle man.'

'Will you show us his room? There may be something in it that will tell us where he has gone.'

'There will not,' predicted Aidan. 'Besides, I cannot let just anyone rummage through my masters' chambers. It would be a violation of their rights.'

'I am not "just anyone",' objected Michael. 'I am the Senior Proctor, investigating the murder of our Chancellor *and* a friend of the King – which Moleyns was, no matter what you think of him. Now, unless you want me to tell His Majesty that Maud's was uncooperative . . .'

'Follow me,' said Aidan quickly, and led the way up the stairs.

The upper floors were as opulently appointed as the ones below, and Lyng had been allocated a wood-panelled chamber overlooking the yard. It smelled of lavender and sage, and was scrupulously clean, although north-facing and so gloomy. Above the bed was a row of books that would have any theologian drooling with envy, while the table was well supplied with ink, pens and parchment.

An unopened letter had pride of place. Michael picked it up and raised questioning eyebrows.

'It arrived yesterday morning, but he said he would open it later,' explained Aidan.

'Who is it from?'

'I have no idea – the seal is not one I recognise.' Aidan blushed when he realised that this remark revealed that he had inspected it rather more closely than was polite.

'The parchment is expensive,' noted Michael. 'Another wealthy scholar, perhaps?'

'It is possible. Put it back, Brother. Not even the Senior Proctor can open private correspondence without good cause.'

Reluctantly, Michael did as he was told.

Once outside, Michael decided that he was hungry, so they headed for his favourite tavern. Such places were off limits to scholars, but he saw no reason why this should apply to the Senior Proctor, and was such a regular visitor to the Brazen George that Landlord Lister had set aside a chamber at the rear of the premises for his exclusive use. It was a pleasant room that overlooked the garden, although the shutters were closed. Dusk was approaching, and the temperature was dropping fast.

'We shall have snow soon,' said Lister conversationally, as he fussed around his guests. 'I feel it in my bones.'

'Perhaps it will arrive on Wednesday,' said Michael hopefully. 'And will force scholars to stay indoors and leave appointing chancellors to those who know best. Namely me.'

He ordered one of his gargantuan repasts of meat and bread, then sent a potboy to invite Tulyet to join him. He had scant new information to share, but felt it was important to liaise with the Sheriff as often as possible.

'Who should we believe about Lyng's relationship with Moleyns, Matt?' he asked while they waited for Tulyet to arrive. 'Kolvyle or Aidan? Because they both cannot be right.'

'Actually, they could. Perhaps Moleyns *forced* Lyng to carry messages to Tynkell, which would mean that Kolvyle was telling the truth. And as Lyng would resent being pushed around by a felon, he might well have told Aidan that he disliked Moleyns.'

Michael regarded him askance. 'And why would a respectable priest allow himself to be browbeaten by Moleyns?'

Bartholomew shrugged. 'It is something we will have to find out.'

Michael was thoughtful. 'Yet your thesis does make sense. It means that Lyng dispatched Tynkell because he wanted to be Chancellor, and he killed Moleyns to rid himself of a bully. I know you are reluctant to see a cold-hearted killer in that seemingly gentle old man, but even you must admit that his relationship with Moleyns is suspicious.'

At that moment, the door opened and Tulyet walked in, although his expression of eager anticipation faded when Michael indicated that he had nothing of significance to report. He slumped on a bench and wearily rubbed his face with his hands.

'Reames is dead,' he said. 'Do you know the lad I mean? The lattener's apprentice, who always dressed like a courtier.'

Bartholomew blinked. 'But I saw him not long ago, walking home from the castle with Lakenham and Cristine. You had been interrogating them about Lucas's murder – which they could not have committed themselves, because they were with you at the time.'

'I should have kept them in the castle for their own protection – Petit believes they are responsible for Lucas's death, and I should have anticipated a revenge attack. Petit was in St Mary the Great when Reames was

152

dispatched, and has alibis to prove it, although the same cannot be said of all his apprentices.'

'Wait a minute,' said Michael, holding up a plump hand. 'Are you saying that Reames was *murdered*? We have a *fourth* suspicious death to investigate?'

'I am afraid so. Yet I do not believe his life was claimed by the rogue who killed Moleyns and Tynkell. He was attacked from behind, and his brains were bashed out with a rock – a frenzied attack, rather than a cool spike in the heart.'

'Matt will inspect his corpse anyway,' determined Michael.

Tulyet nodded his thanks, then sighed morosely. 'It was a bad day for the town when these warring tomb-builders arrived. I shall monitor them constantly from now on, and the next time one commits a crime, we shall have him.'

'Good,' said Michael. 'My beadles will help.'

At that point, Lister began to bring food to the table, and the Sheriff gaped his astonishment as platter after platter of meat and bread were set down.

'Was my entire garrison included in the invitation to dine here, Brother?'

'It is just a morsel,' declared Michael, fastening a piece of linen around his neck to protect his habit from greasy splatters. 'We all have healthy appetites, after all.'

Tulyet declined to comment, but listened with interest as the monk told him what Kolvyle had said about Lyng relaying messages between Tynkell and Moleyns during the Mass in which the Almighty had been begged to spare Cambridge from a second wave of the plague.

'I attended that service,' he said. 'Lyng *did* hobble up to Moleyns and begin whispering, although I did not see him go to Tynkell.'

'I was there, too, but noticed nothing amiss,' said Michael. 'Incidentally, I need to talk to Egidia and Inge about a rider on a brown horse with a pilgrim-staff embossed on his saddle – Thelnetham says that he galloped away shortly after Moleyns' murder. Perhaps they did not commit murder with their own hands, but hired a trusted retainer from Stoke Poges to do it.'

Delighted by the prospect of a lead, Tulyet surged to his feet. 'We shall do it now.'

'Yes,' said Michael, not moving. 'The moment we have finished eating.'

Years of dining in College, where fast eaters tended to be better fed than those who took their time, meant it was not long before Michael had reduced the meal in the Brazen George to empty plates and a pile of gnawed bones. Then the three of them went to St Clement's Church, where Reames' body had been taken, but Bartholomew was able to tell them nothing they did not already know. The attack had been a vicious one, and the killer had delivered far more blows to the apprentice's skull than had been necessary to end his life. There were no other injuries.

'You are right about one thing, Dick,' mused Michael, who had kept his eyes fixed on Reames' torso to avoid looking at the ruin of his head. 'He did dress like a courtier.'

'Which is odd,' said Bartholomew, 'considering that Lakenham is so poor that he cannot afford to buy Cristine a new cloak.'

Tulyet shrugged. 'Perhaps Reames hailed from an affluent family, who gave him an allowance. But are you *sure* there is nothing to help us catch his killer, Matt? Whoever did this is abnormally violent, so the sooner he is locked up, the better.'

Bartholomew shook his head, and was about to accompany Michael and Tulyet to visit Egidia and Inge when Cynric appeared, hot, tired and gasping for breath, because he had been frantically hunting the physician for some time.

'Isnard,' he rasped. 'He needs you and says it is urgent.'

As the bargeman had been hale and hearty not long before, Bartholomew ran to his cottage in alarm, fearing that he had engaged in a violent confrontation with the tomb-makers, and had suffered some terrible injury, like Reames and Lucas.

'Come in, Doctor,' Isnard called jovially when Bartholomew arrived. 'The fire is lit, the ale is hot, and good company awaits.'

The house was crammed with people, although it was difficult to tell precisely how many, because night had fallen, and Isnard only had one small lamp, which had been turned low.

'Are you hurt?' Bartholomew asked, a little testily, because he had risked life and limb by racing through streets that were slick with ice. 'Or ill?'

'No, I have information to impart,' replied Isnard grandly. 'I would have called Brother Michael, as it concerns him really. But I did not think he would come.'

'He would not,' agreed Gundrede. 'Not after what happened at singing practice.'

Isnard was a long-term member of the Michaelhouse Choir, and had adopted a very proprietary attitude towards it. As his eyes became accustomed to the gloom, Bartholomew saw that most of the people in the room were basses, along with a smattering of tenors and a few women who should not have been permitted to join an all-male chorus. They went in disguise, and although Michael was perfectly capable of identifying false beards and horsehair moustaches, he never had the heart to turn them away.

'It was his own fault,' said the bargeman stiffly. 'He should not be leaving us. I can lead the music, of course, but who will bring the food?'

'I shall miss him, too.' Bartholomew spoke gently, because Isnard's eyes had filled with tears. 'But he has been waiting for this opportunity for years. Would you keep him from it?'

'Of course we would!' cried Isnard, distressed. 'We *need* him. And what happened earlier was just a mark of our affection. It was not our fault that he ended up covered in feathers.'

Bartholomew thought it best not to ask.

'So we decided to tell you our news instead,' said Gundrede. 'And you can pass it on. Our first nugget is about Thelnetham the Gilbertine.'

'He used to be at Michaelhouse,' said Isnard, as if he thought Bartholomew might have forgotten. 'And he is always *very* rude about our singing. However, we do not speak out of malice, but so that Brother Michael will know what sort of man he is.'

Bartholomew did not want to hear it. The choir members were very touchy about criticism, and Thelnetham had always been one of their more vocal detractors. He started to tell them to keep their gossip to themselves, but Gundrede overrode him.

'He eats slugs,' he declared. 'He hunts for them under cover of darkness.'

Bartholomew was so taken aback that for several moments he could think of nothing to say. 'How do you know?' he asked eventually.

'Because we have seen him,' replied Isnard. 'And do not say he was just looking for something he had lost, because *I* saw him near the Trumpington road, *Gundrede* noticed him by the Great Bridge and *Marjory* spotted him by St Clement's.'

'I did,' said Marjory, a woman of indeterminate age who sold dubious remedies and charms from her little house in the Jewry, and made no bones about the fact

156

that she considered Christianity to be a very inferior religion when compared to her own.

'Besides, if he had been searching for mislaid objects, he would have done it in daylight,' Gundrede went on. 'He was eating slugs, and that is all there is to it. And if Michael will not take any notice of what we say, then we shall make it public ourselves.'

'Please do not,' begged Bartholomew, suspecting the trio had not been sober when they had drawn these particular conclusions. The fastidious Thelnetham was the last man on Earth to have anything to do with slugs, but his detractors would capitalise on the tale anyway, and it might destroy his chances of being elected, which was hardly fair. 'Michael will look into it.'

'Good,' said Isnard. 'But he must do it soon.'

'You can tell him we are not thieves either,' said Gundrede sourly. 'He thinks I made off with the lead on Gonville's chapel, just because I used to be a metalsmith. However, I rarely bother with that sort of work these days, so he can keep his nasty opinions to himself.'

'And *I* do not ferry stolen goods about on my barges,' declared Isnard. 'Besides, those tomb-makers are probably lying about what they claim has been stolen. But sit down and have a drink, Doctor. You look tired, and we have some lovely French claret— Ouch!'

Gundrede had kicked him under the table, and it did not take a genius to guess why: the cask had been imported illegally, almost certainly on one of Isnard's boats. Bartholomew began to back out, unwilling to consume contraband wine lest Tulyet or one of his men chose that particular evening to pay Isnard a visit.

'I have to see Edith,' he said, blurting the first excuse that entered his head. 'To ask her about progress on Oswald's tomb.'

'She should have hired a mason from London to do it,' said Gundrede, his voice thick with disapproval. 'That Petit is a worthless rogue, and Lakenham is no better.'

Bartholomew took another step towards the door, but Isnard moved to stop him. 'We have more to tell you yet, Doctor. And if you want something to occupy your hands while we talk, we can provide you with plenty of interesting ailments. Marjory has a rash, for a start.'

'Here,' said Marjory, baring her arm with a flourish. Bartholomew had treated it before, but it had taken a new and intriguing turn since he had last seen it. He sat.

'Moleyns,' hissed Isnard. 'We have information about him, too. None of us saw who killed him, as we have said before, but—'

'Wait!' cried Gundrede. 'We need assurances first.' He turned to Bartholomew. 'You must promise that Sheriff Tulyet will never know who told you. We could be hanged.'

'He *cannot* betray us,' declared Isnard confidently. 'He is bound by oaths of discretion. Cynric told me so, when I asked him to find out what odd affliction made Chancellor Tynkell so different from the rest of us. He says physicians can never reveal their patients' secrets.'

'About your ailments,' clarified Bartholomew quickly. 'Not about anything else.'

'Well, you are tending an ailment now,' said Marjory, indicating her arm. 'So we are covered. And someone must pass what we know to the appropriate authorities.'

'Moleyns got out of the castle at night,' blurted Isnard, before Bartholomew could demur. 'And he wandered around the town . . . doing business. Tell him, Gundrede.'

The metalsmith obliged. 'Moleyns charmed his "friends" – those who fluttered around him in the hope that he would write something nice about them to the King – into confiding where they kept their money. Then he hired us . . . I mean he hired *burglars* to get it for him.'

Bartholomew was thoughtful. He knew for a fact that being imprisoned had not stopped Moleyns from stealing, because Principal Haye and the Mayor had both lost purses to his sticky fingers. And Moleyns had enjoyed a lavish lifestyle in the castle, even though most of his estates had been confiscated. He recalled the felon as he had been when he had needed the services of a physician – smug, sly and deceitful, certainly the kind of man to beguile the gullible into telling him about their precious hoards.

'So he escaped from the castle and came to tell you which houses to burgle?' he asked, wanting to be sure he had understood them correctly.

'Told *accomplices* which houses to burgle,' corrected Gundrede, while all around there were a lot of earnestly nodding heads.

'So it *is* you . . . I mean Moleyns, who has been stealing the tomb-makers' supplies?'

'No,' snapped Gundrede angrily. 'I just told you – we had nothing to do with that. Moleyns was interested in *money* – coins, which could be spent on food, wine and clothes. He was not in a position to filch heavy items for resale in distant cities.'

'Quite,' agreed Isnard. 'However, the point of all this is that Moleyns' death marks the end of a lucrative arrangement, and we are very sorry about it. Which means that no townsman killed him, so you should look to a scholar as the culprit.'

'Were any University men involved in this . . . operation?' asked Bartholomew.

'Not that we are aware,' replied Isnard. 'Although we were not party to his every move. No one was, not even his wife and lawyer.'

'Master Lyng might have been in league with him, though,' mused Marjory. 'When Moleyns fell off his horse, Lyng was the first to reach him, and I saw them whispering.

I was too far away to hear what was being said, but Lyng nodded.'

'Nodded how?' asked Bartholomew, wondering if the felon had muttered something to provoke a fatal attack. 'Angrily? Amiably? Urgently?'

'It was too dark to tell, and then other folk surged forward and hid them from view. Lyng did not stay long, though – he was gone before you managed to fight to the front, Doctor.'

'They *might* have been discussing Moleyns' next exploit, I suppose,' conceded Isnard, 'although that would have been risky in front of so many flapping ears.'

'Tynkell, Moleyns and Lyng,' sighed Marjory. 'They certainly had secrets!'

'Do you know what they were?' asked Bartholomew hopefully.

Marjory shrugged and looked away, giving the impression that she did, but was unwilling to say in front of an audience. He supposed he would have to corner her when she was alone.

'So *how* did Moleyns leave the castle?' he asked, tactfully changing the subject. 'Dick Tulyet does not usually let prisoners stroll in and out as they please.'

'It has a sally port,' explained Gundrede. 'And guards who like wine. It was a simple matter to unlock a few doors while the Sheriff and his more trustworthy officers slept.'

The notion that Moleyns had been breaking the law under the Sheriff's nose had unnerved Bartholomew, but he dared not tell Tulyet about it himself: the Sheriff would demand to know the source of such alarming intelligence, and he was not very good at lying. He decided to visit his sister, in the hope that her calm company would allow his thoughts to settle, after which he might be able to devise a way to pass on the information without getting anyone executed.

She lived in a handsome mansion on Milne Street, from which she ran her dead husband's cloth business. It was a profitable venture, although less so than when Stanmore had been alive. There were two reasons for this. First, because Edith preferred *her* transactions to be legitimate; and second, because she had taken it upon herself to champion Cambridge's fallen women. She had employed them to work in her dyeworks at one point, which had brought her a whole raft of trouble; then she had arranged for them to produce ready-made academic tabards. Although considerably cheaper than bespoke ones, they did not sell very well, because many scholars disliked wearing garments that had been put together by prostitutes.

Milne Street was an important thoroughfare in its own right. It boasted not only several large merchants' houses, but two Colleges, the Carmelite Friary and the Church of St John Zachary. One College – Trinity Hall – was in the process of building itself a massive new dormitory, and workmen could still be seen swarming industriously over the complex web of scaffolding that encased it. Each held a lantern, so the whole structure was alive with purposefully bobbing lights.

The dormitory was causing a good deal of resentment in the town, because it stuck much further out into the road than had been agreed at the planning stage. But Trinity Hall desperately needed the space, and stubbornly ignored the complaints of those who objected to a huge building sprawled halfway across a public highway.

Bartholomew entered Edith's house, breathing in deeply of the comfortingly familiar aroma of spices, beeswax and wood-smoke. His sister was in her solar, a pleasantly airy room with embroidered cushions, a huge fire in the hearth, and tapestries on the wall.

'I am going to dismiss Petit if he does not work on Oswald's tomb tomorrow,' she declared. 'I want it finished *now*, not in a decade. But you look troubled, Matt. What is wrong?'

Bartholomew was not about to tell her the truth, because she would guess in an instant who had gossiped to him about Moleyns. 'I do not like hunting killers,' he said instead.

Edith smiled. 'Then take comfort in the fact that it will be the last time. Michael will go to Rochester to become a bishop, and you will marry Matilde. The University will have to find someone else to solve its crimes.'

Bartholomew experienced a familiar sinking feeling in the pit of his stomach when he recalled the decision he would soon have to make. Surely it should not be this difficult? And why did his heart not sing when he thought about Matilde, as it had in the past? Did it mean his love for her had grown cold? Or was it just the prospect of a major life change that so terrified him?

'I am not sure about Matilde,' he said unhappily.

'Why not?' asked Edith gently. 'It is what you have wanted for years.'

'Quite – for years. It has been too long, and we may not like what the other has become.'

'Oh, she will like you,' predicted Edith confidently. 'And you need someone to make you smile, so do not dismiss her out of pride or fear. As Oswald always said, if something is worth having, it is worth the wait. Except tombs, of course. They need to be finished when they were promised.'

When Bartholomew left Edith's house, he was still not ready to tell Tulyet about Moleyns. His spirits were low, as they often were on evenings when it was dark and cold, and the houses he passed were shut up tight against the weather. Lights spilled from a few, which served to make him feel excluded, and he quickened his pace, keen to be home. He passed St John Zachary, which looked pretty with candles shining through its stained-glass windows, and on impulse he went inside, feeling a sudden urge to pray for Oswald's soul.

He opened the door and heard voices within – the dissipated Vicar Frisby was talking to Thelnetham and Nicholas. The Gilbertine had added a length of puce silk, which he wore like a scarf, to his array of colourful accessories. The shade contrasted pleasingly with his purple brooch, and Bartholomew found himself thinking that Matilde would appreciate his sense of style. Or perhaps she would disapprove, given that canons were supposed to resist such vanities, and she was a devout woman. The fact that he was uncertain told him yet again that he no longer knew her as he once had.

'I am canvassing for votes,' said Thelnetham. 'Frisby has just promised to support me.'

'On my kinsman's recommendation,' said Frisby, giving the little secretary an affectionate pat on the back that almost sent him flying. 'I trust his judgement.'

'Good,' said Nicholas, hobbling on his lame leg to regain his balance. 'Because only a fool would opt for anyone else. Even Suttone, I am sorry to say. He is a nice man, but his views on women . . . well! We cannot have a lecher as Chancellor.'

'Did you hear the speech I gave in St Andrew's Church today, Matthew?' asked Thelnetham with one of the superior smiles that Bartholomew found so irritating. 'It received a standing ovation. My rivals cannot match me for eloquence, and that is all there is to it.'

'Lyng can,' said Nicholas, earning himself a hurt scowl. 'But he seems to have left town, which is stupid, as no one will want a Chancellor who disappears at critical junctures.'

'Will you back me, Matthew?' asked Thelnetham. 'We were friends at Michaelhouse, and I always considered you the best of all its members.'

'Thank you,' said Bartholomew, although 'friends' was not how he would have described their relationship – there had been some serious antagonism, nearly all of it arising from the Gilbertine's barbed tongue. 'But I cannot vote against another Fellow.'

'*I* was a Fellow,' said Thelnetham reproachfully. 'And if Langelee had reinstated me, as I requested, then I would have been Michael's pet candidate. Not Suttone.'

'I suppose so,' said Bartholomew, although he was sure that Michael would never have chosen Thelnetham, on the grounds that the Gilbertine was too intelligent to manipulate.

Thelnetham dropped his hectoring manner and became sincere. 'I honestly believe that I can do some good, and I would like the opportunity to try. You know how seriously I take scholarship. I am the only one who will put it first – and it *is* why we are all here, after all.'

'True,' conceded Bartholomew. 'But—'

'Our University is more important than blinkered allegiances,' interrupted Thelnetham earnestly. 'And if I win, I will give Suttone a post to salvage his wounded pride.' He laughed suddenly. 'Official Plague Monitor, perhaps, given that he is so obsessed with it.'

'I have been Chancellor's secretary for six years,' said Nicholas quietly. 'So I am better qualified than most to judge what is needed. And it is not Suttone.'

'I am a lawyer, too,' Thelnetham went on. 'Which means I can handle complex legal matters. Suttone is a theologian, who has never run a College, let alone a University.'

They spoke convincingly, but Bartholomew's hands were tied – College loyalty ran too deep in him, and Suttone was a better friend than Thelnetham would ever be. He settled for dispensing some helpful advice instead. He nodded to Thelnetham's scarf.

'That will lose you votes – it makes you appear rebellious and unsteady. And a manly stride, rather than a dainty mince, will give an impression of strength and purpose.'

Thelnetham sighed. 'Nicholas says the same. I had hoped to run an honest campaign, where people see me as I am, but I suppose I had better yield to popular prejudice. It is a pity – I bought some lovely cerise hose this morning and was looking forward to showing them off.'

Frisby, who was taking a surreptitious swig from his wineskin, almost choked. 'You do not want to be wearing pink stockings, man! People will think bad things.'

Bartholomew left them discussing it, and went to stand by Stanmore's tomb, whispering the prayers that he hoped would shorten his kinsman's sojourn in Purgatory. Then he left the church, eager now for the conclave fire. However, he had not taken many steps along Milne Street before he ran into Hopeman and his followers, who had been visiting the hostels along Water Lane. They clustered around him rather menacingly.

'That sinful Lyng dares not show his face,' Hopeman crowed. He held a lantern, which cast eerie shadows on his dark features and made him look sinister. 'He knows he is no match for me. And Godrich is Satan's spawn – I shall exorcise him if I see him out tonight.'

'We carry the necessary equipment with us at all times,' elaborated a disciple, hefting a sack that bulged. 'We can be ready to combat Lucifer in a trice.'

'The Devil would not have flown away if he had tackled *me* on the tower,' declared Hopeman. 'I would have vanquished him once and for all. And if you care anything for the safety of your soul, you will elect me next week.'

He did not wait for a reply, clearly thinking that no more needed to be said, and turned to rap on the door to White Hostel. He pounded with such vigour that he dislodged several icicles from the roof, causing his men to scatter in alarm. He stood firm though.

'I am God's chosen,' he informed them loftily. 'Nothing can harm me.'

Bartholomew hoped for his sake that he was right.

The physician was glad to reach Michaelhouse. He walked across the yard, feet crunching on frost, and glanced up at a sky that was splattered with stars, some brighter than he had ever seen them. He arrived at the conclave to find all the other Fellows there, some reading, the rest talking quietly. Kolvyle sat apart from them, as if he considered himself too good for their company. When Clippesby tried to draw him into an innocuous conversation about the College cat, the younger man stood abruptly, snapping shut the book he had been perusing.

'I do not have time for idle chatter,' he declared shortly. 'Especially with lunatics.'

'The cat is not a lunatic,' objected Clippesby, stroking her silken head.

The other Fellows laughed, which drew a petulant scowl from Kolvyle and a look of hurt confusion from Clippesby. The cat purred and settled herself more comfortably on the Dominican's knees. Kolvyle collided roughly with Bartholomew as their paths converged, but the physician had anticipated such a manoeuvre and was ready, so it was Kolvyle who staggered. The others laughed again, and Kolvyle stamped out furiously, slamming the door behind him.

Bartholomew poured himself some mulled ale and went to sit next to Suttone. There were crumbs down the front of the Carmelite's habit, and he had not bothered to shave that day, so Bartholomew found himself comparing Suttone rather unfavourably to the cultivated Thelnetham. Or even to Hopeman, who was not relaxing by a fire, but busily working to secure himself more votes. If Suttone did win, he thought, it would be because

166

Michael had engineered a victory, not because of the Carmelite's own efforts.

When Michael came to join them, Bartholomew saw the solution to his conundrum regarding Isnard was at hand, and berated himself for not thinking of it sooner: *Michael* could tell Tulyet what the bargeman had confided. The moment Suttone went to pour himself more wine, leaving the two of them alone, Bartholomew took a deep breath and began to repeat what he had heard, phrasing his report with infinite care, so as not to reveal his source.

'Isnard,' deduced the monk when he had finished. Appalled, Bartholomew started to deny it, but Michael raised his hand. 'Do not worry – his secret is safe with me. I suspect he would have preferred to tell me himself, but there was an incident at choir practice . . .'

'One involving feathers, I understand.' Several still adhered to the monk's habit.

'They gave me a lovely cushion, a gift to encourage me to stay. Unfortunately, it exploded when I sat on it – which I would not have minded if they had at least *tried* not to laugh.'

'Has Lyng come home yet?' asked Bartholomew, changing the subject before he laughed, too. 'It would be useful to know what Moleyns whispered to him as he lay on the ground.'

'I visited Maud's less than an hour ago, but he is still missing. Perhaps he has fled the town, knowing we are closing in on him.'

'Fled where? This has been his home for more than forty years. Yet it is difficult to see him as the culprit. My money is still on Cook, who is ruthless, greedy and devious.'

'Then Cook must be a villain indeed, as it is not often that you denounce anyone so vigorously. But you fared better than me with fact-gathering – I learned nothing at all from Egidia and Inge. When I mentioned that Weasenham's testimony contradicts theirs, they simply told me that he was mistaken, and they deny knowing anything about a horseman with the Stoke Poges insignia on his saddle.'

'Their claims will be irrelevant if Lyng transpires to be guilty.'

'True.' Michael picked a feather from his lap and sighed sadly. 'Leaving my choir will not be easy. I do not suppose you would take my place as conductor, would you?'

'Me?' blurted Bartholomew, startled. 'But I cannot sing.'

Michael's expression was wry. 'That will not be a problem. And you play the lute, so you could lead the practice, while Matilde organises the victuals. She is good at that sort of thing.'

The remark reawakened the unease Bartholomew had experienced when talking to Edith, and it was with a troubled mind that he later retired to bed. Unusually, he found the fire in his room too hot, and he was kept awake by Deynman's snoring. When he did finally sleep, his dreams teemed with disturbing images, although he could recall none of them when Walter came to shake him awake a few hours later.

'Thelnetham is here,' he whispered. 'A body has been found by the King's Ditch, and he says it is Lyng's.'

CHAPTER 7

The King's Ditch arced around the eastern side of the town, and was used as a sewer and a convenient repository for rubbish. Unfortunately, it was too sluggish to carry its malodorous contents far, with the result that it comprised a reeking, festering ribbon of slime that posed a serious risk to health. Although its name suggested connections to royalty, all self-respecting monarchs would have vigorously denied any association with such a revolting feature.

Master Lyng had been found on its north bank, near the Hall of Valence Marie. To the south lay Peterhouse, the Gilbertine Priory and the King's Head tavern, a townsmen-only establishment that was famous for fighting, and was a favourite haunt of Isnard and most of the Michaelhouse Choir.

Lyng's body had been neatly positioned, his hands folded across his middle. His robes were carefully straightened, and someone had made a pillow of his hat and tucked it under his head. He was cold, and his clothes were dusted with rime, which told Bartholomew that he had lain undisturbed for some time.

The discovery had attracted onlookers, despite the unsociable hour – scholars from the nearby Colleges, canons from the priory, and a gaggle of patrons from the inn, all being held back by a cordon of beadles. Several, including Isnard and Gundrede, carried pitch torches, although the sky was lightening in the east and dawn was not far off.

'Murder,' reported Bartholomew tersely, indicating the now-familiar puncture wound. 'A lump on the back of

Lyng's head suggests that he was stunned first, then stabbed as he lay helpless. He did not arrange himself like this, so his killer must have done it.'

'Meaning what?' demanded Michael. 'That the culprit is sorry, and thinks that treating the body with respect will make amends?'

Bartholomew shrugged. 'Only he can answer that.'

Michael crouched next to the corpse, so they could speak without being overheard by the growing throng of spectators. 'I am deeply sorry to see Lyng like this – a three-time Chancellor deserves to end his days peacefully.'

'He was a good man,' agreed Bartholomew sadly. 'We were wrong to include him on our list of suspects.'

Michael nodded. 'And his death is a severe blow to our enquiries. Now we cannot ask him what Moleyns whispered before he died, or about the messages that he ferried between Tynkell and Moleyns in St Mary the Great. And as all three are dead, I suspect that both matters were important.'

'Unless he was killed because he was the man most likely to win the election,' suggested Bartholomew, and nodded to where Thelnetham, Godrich and Hopeman were watching with wary faces. 'In which case, the culprit is one of them. Or Suttone, I suppose – the only candidate who has not come to gawp.'

'Which is a point in his favour, as far as I am concerned,' retorted Michael, then added wryly, 'Although I suspect the real reason is because he is still abed. So when did Lyng die? Give me a *precise* time, so we can begin exploring alibis.'

'You know that is impossible.' Bartholomew gestured to the bridge above their heads. 'He is invisible from the road, so he might have lain here since he was first reported missing.'

'Which was Thursday night.' Michael stood and called to the crowd. 'Who found him?'

Thelnetham raised his hand, and the beadles let him past. The flickering torchlight showed that he had taken Bartholomew's advice to heart, because his habit was devoid of vibrant accessories, other than the brooch that fastened his cloak. He also stood more erect and seemed to be more manly – until he glanced at the body, at which point he whipped out a silken cloth and pressed it to his eyes in an effete gesture of distress.

'I was walking along this bank when I tripped over him,' he began. 'It gave me a scare, I can tell you! I climbed back up to the road, and raced straight to Michaelhouse—'

'You were walking *here?*' asked Michael, glancing around in distaste. 'In the dark?'

'I could not sleep after nocturns, so I decided to visit the clerks in St Mary the Great – some work all night, as you know, because the University's recent expansion is generating so much extra work. I want their votes.'

'I see,' said Michael. 'However, that does not explain why you chose to make your way there via the edge of the King's Ditch. And do not say you glimpsed Lyng while crossing the bridge, because he cannot be seen from the road.'

Thelnetham lowered his voice and spoke a little crossly. 'If you must know, I was with a companion. But that is my business, and I would sooner not turn my personal life into the subject of prurient gossip. I am sure you understand.'

'What companion?' demanded Michael, although he allowed the Gilbertine to propel him away from the gathering crowd. No one would have been able hear their discussion, given that they had kept their voices low, but there was always a danger that someone could lip-read. Bartholomew followed.

'Him.' Thelnetham nodded towards Secretary Nicholas, who was looking simultaneously defensive and furtive.

'Obviously, we cannot meet in my priory or his hostel, so we have taken to using other places. Here, near St Clement's Church, under the Great Bridge. All are usually deserted, so we can . . . do what we like.'

'Which does not include eating slugs, presumably,' muttered Bartholomew. He shook his head when Thelnetham regarded him questioningly. 'You were seen. Find somewhere else.'

'Yes, do,' agreed Michael with a shudder. 'It cannot be pleasant to lurk down here, especially for a man of refined tastes like yourself.'

'No,' sighed Thelnetham ruefully. 'Unfortunately, the nicer refuges are always occupied by others. You have no idea how hard it is to find somewhere private in this hectic little town.'

'Did you come here yesterday?' asked Bartholomew, hoping to narrow down the time that Lyng had been dead.

'No – we have been too busy. The last time we met was on Wednesday, but that was near the Great Bridge, not here.'

'Did you move Lyng? Or tidy his robes?'

'I probably jostled him when I stumbled over his corpse. But the moment we realised that he was . . . well, we both backed away as fast as we could. I hurried to Michaelhouse, while Nicholas went to tell Lyng's colleagues at Maud's. He told them to bring a bier, students to carry it, and the necessary equipment for anointing a body, but they should be here soon.'

Michael gestured to his beadles, telling them to let Nicholas through.

'It is not what you think, Brother,' the secretary began in a frightened gabble. 'We were looking for lost coins, to donate to the University Chest and—'

'It is all right, Nicholas,' said Thelnetham softly. 'They know my habits from living with me at Michaelhouse. They do not judge us.'

'Then I hope they will be discreet,' gulped Nicholas, not much comforted. 'Our friendship is *private*.'

'It will not stay so,' warned Michael. 'People will wonder what you were doing down here together – and the tale *will* out if Thelnetham persists in standing for election, because he will be in the public eye. It will be better for you both if he withdraws.'

The Gilbertine smiled thinly. 'I shall say the wind caught my hat, so I came to get it. No one need know that Nicholas was with me.'

'But it would be a lie,' said Michael. 'From a man who aims to lead our University.'

'I told you it was a mistake to trust him, Thelnetham,' said Nicholas bitterly. 'We should have sent him an anonymous message, as I suggested. Then no one would be trying to blackmail you.'

Thelnetham's face was pale in the flickering torchlight. 'I will *not* step down – it would be feeble to bow to pressure, and I am no weakling. Very well, then, Brother. Bray my secrets to the world if you must. I shall take the resulting censure in my stride.'

'I am neither a gossip nor an extortionist,' objected Michael huffily, although Bartholomew was not so sure about the second, given that he was so determined to see Suttone in power. 'I will keep your trust. However, Weasenham is among the spectators, so do not be surprised if the truth – or some approximation of it – seeps out.'

Thelnetham inclined his head. 'Thank you for the warning.'

'Yet it is convenient for you that Lyng is dead,' Michael went on. 'He was by far the most popular candidate.'

'Perhaps,' acknowledged Thelnetham. 'But I am quite capable of fighting with my tongue, and have no need to resort to physical violence. However, the same cannot be said of Godrich and Hopeman, so I suggest you look to them first.'

'And Thelnetham has not been alone since Lyng disappeared anyway,' added Nicholas. 'He has either been out campaigning with me, or in his priory with his brethren. Between them and me, every moment of his time can be accounted for.'

'You should speak to Suttone, too,' said Thelnetham. 'Just because he is your favourite does not mean that he is innocent. After all, why is he not here? All the other hopefuls are keen to learn what is happening in the University they aim to govern, so why does he keep his distance?'

When the Maud's men arrived with the bier, Bartholomew helped them lift Lyng on it, after which they carried him to their church. The onlookers followed in silence, all cloaked and hooded against the bite of an icy winter morning. When they reached Holy Trinity, Father Aidan opened the door for the body and its bearers, then closed it firmly behind them, leaving the spectators to mill aimlessly in the graveyard, unwilling to disperse lest they missed something interesting. Hopeman was quick to take advantage, and began to speak in a self-important bellow, much to the annoyance of Godrich.

'It is inappropriate to electioneer on an occasion such as this,' he informed Michael imperiously. 'So do your duty, and shut him up.'

Michael had actually drawn breath to silence Hopeman, but no one told the Senior Proctor how to do his job, and he resented the presumption extremely. He closed his mouth with a snap.

'When will our University accept that it needs a righteous priest at its helm?' Hopeman was bawling. 'Satan has claimed Lyng's life, showing us that *he* was not pious enough, but Godrich, Thelnetham and Suttone are worse.'

'You zealot!' sneered Godrich, abandoning the moral

high ground when he saw that staying quiet would put him at a disadvantage. 'God will not want a low-bred fellow like you as Chancellor. You would set the religious Orders at each other's throats within a week.'

'Yes – there *will* be factions,' ranted Hopeman, eyes blazing. 'Two: those who stand with me to fight evil, and those who delight in it. I do not need to ask which one you will be on.'

Godrich responded with a stream of insults that had the Dominican bristling his fury. Their followers responded in kind, and soon there were forty men haranguing each other. Thelnetham urged them to moderate their language, but no one listened, and he retreated sharply when Godrich began berating him as well.

'You should have listened to Godrich, and ordered that lunatic priest home,' said Whittlesey, coming to murmur in Michael's ear. 'It would have averted an unedifying scene.'

'There would have been no "unedifying scene" if Godrich had maintained a dignified silence,' Michael shot back.

'But a good leader would have quelled this spat before it started,' argued Whittlesey. 'Your decision to let Hopeman rail was a poor one.'

'On the contrary,' said Michael stiffly, 'it is allowing our scholars to see both men in their true light, thus enabling them to make a more informed choice. In other words, it has reinforced Hopeman's reputation as a truculent radical, and exposed Godrich as a man who does not know when to hold his tongue.'

'And I suppose that makes Suttone more appealing?' asked Whittlesey drily.

Michael smiled serenely. 'I would say it does. However, you are right: this unseemly behaviour has gone on quite long enough.'

175

He waded into the mêlée just as words were turning to shoves, although it transpired to be much more difficult to restore peace than it had been to break it. Moreover, the raised voices had attracted additional spectators, including the kind of townsfolk who always appeared when the University was at loggerheads with itself, ready to join in any brawl.

'Enough!' roared Michael eventually, a stentorian bellow of which any member of his choir would have been proud. He scowled first at Godrich, then at Hopeman, and both had the sense to stay quiet. 'Now tell me where have you been since eight o'clock on Thursday evening?'

A hush fell over the whole churchyard as people craned forward to listen to the replies.

'I cannot possibly list all the places I have visited,' declared Hopeman haughtily. 'That was . . .' He did some calculations on thick, grubby fingers; Godrich smirked his disdain that the Dominican should be unable to work it out in his head. 'More than thirty-four hours ago. However, I was never alone. My followers were with me every moment.'

'Even during the night?' asked Michael sceptically.

'Yes,' replied Hopeman firmly. 'Even then.'

'Except when he was in private conversation with God,' put in one of the deacons helpfully. 'Which was quite often, given that he is a favoured Son of Christ.'

'But I keep my holy audiences short,' said Hopeman hastily, and the disciple received a look that was none too friendly. 'I assure you, Brother, I have had no time to kill anyone.'

'And you, Godrich?' asked Michael.

'I do not have to answer that,' retorted Godrich, but something in Michael's face caused him to reconsider the wisdom of this response, because he added sullenly, 'I spent most of it visiting convents and Colleges, outlining my vision of the University's future.'

'And the rest of the time?' asked Michael.

Godrich raised his voice, to ensure that everyone could hear. 'I have decided to buy books for some of our poorer foundations, so their masters have been flocking to King's Hall to make their cases to me – day *and* night. And when I was not dispensing my largesse to our less fortunate colleagues, I was with Whittlesey.'

'It is true, Brother,' said Whittlesey with a smile. 'I was with my cousin every moment that I was not with you.'

Michael turned to another matter. 'How well did you know Moleyns?'

'Not at all,' replied Whittlesey pleasantly, although the question had actually been directed at Godrich. 'Other than by reputation, of course.'

'Nor did I,' put in Hopeman. 'I do not count felons among *my* acquaintances.'

'That is curious,' said Godrich slyly, 'because I saw you with him at the castle – twice. Or are you going to tell us that you went there to save his soul?'

'I did, as a matter of fact,' said Hopeman, flushing angrily. 'But it was too steeped in sin for rescue, even by me. However, *you* were his friend – you went to Stoke Poges like an errand boy, spying there, to see what was happening on his behalf.'

'What is this?' demanded Michael, eyes narrowing as he regarded the King's Hall man intently. 'You did favours for Moleyns?'

Godrich shrugged carelessly, although his eyes revealed his dismay. 'I happened to be passing, so I looked in on the place for him. However, it was Lyng who should have done it, not me. Tell him why, Thelnetham.'

While Godrich and Hopeman were being grilled by Michael, the Gilbertine had been standing quietly to one side with Nicholas. He started in surprise when Godrich whipped around to address him, and stepped forward reluctantly.

'Not here, Godrich,' he said softly. 'Not when Lyng lies dead in the—'

'He is past caring,' interrupted Godrich, a callous remark that had a number of listeners exchanging glances of disapproval. 'Now tell the Senior Proctor what you know.'

'Lyng hailed from the village next to Stoke Poges,' replied Thelnetham, although he spoke with obvious reluctance. 'Last term, he regaled me with an account of the delights of Buckinghamshire for an entire evening.'

'Why did you not mention it before?' demanded Michael. 'You must see it is important.'

'Is it?' asked Godrich slyly. 'Why? Did you suspect Lyng of being the killer then?'

'Of course not,' lied Michael. 'But these coincidences matter. I should have been told.'

'How can they matter?' asked Nicholas, defensive of his friend. 'All Moleyns' estates – including Stoke Poges – were confiscated when he was convicted.'

'Yes, but the King promised to restore them to him,' argued Michael. 'And Moleyns certainly considered himself Lord of the Manor still.' He scowled at the Gilbertine. 'What about Tynkell? Will I later learn that *he* had connections to Stoke Poges as well?'

'He hailed from Hertfordshire,' replied Thelnetham. 'Miles away. However, he was working on a scheme to get Stoke Poges' chapel for the University, so he must have visited it at some point. After all, how else would he have known that it was worth having?'

'He did *what*?' exploded Michael. 'He never mentioned it to me.'

'Perhaps he was afraid you would stop him,' shrugged Thelnetham, 'which he would not have wanted, as it represented his last chance to make his mark on the University.'

'I *would* have stopped him,' declared Michael vehemently.

'We cannot accept property from a place with links to a convicted felon! What would our other benefactors think?'

'Thank God that Tynkell is dead,' brayed Godrich. 'He was a fool with his reckless ideas. After all, look what happened when he tried to foist a new College on us.'

'And a Common Library,' put in Principal Haye of White Hostel. 'A venture doomed to failure from the start. Poor Tynkell! We shall have to ensure he is not forgotten by building him a nice tomb instead.'

Hopeman was more interested in exploiting the revelations about Stoke Poges. 'Moleyns' old manor is a popular place. Godrich, Lyng and Tynkell all visited it. Oh, and so did Thelnetham, of course. In the summer. He told me so himself.'

Michael turned to the Gilbertine, only to find he was no longer there.

'He has gone to attend terce,' explained Nicholas. '*He* will not forsake his sacred offices, even if others put their devotions second to gossiping in graveyards.'

Several listeners nodded approvingly, although others resented the censure, and as a ploy to gain votes, the remark had probably lost Thelnetham more support than it had won. As the Gilbertine was unavailable, Hopeman resumed his attack on Godrich.

'*He* was Moleyns' bosom friend,' he declared, stabbing an accusing finger. 'And I have always said that one can judge a man by the company he keeps.'

No one spoke, but all eyes went to the grim-faced fanatics who were ranged behind him.

'Are you disparaging Moleyns, Hopeman?' asked Godrich sweetly. 'Then I must tell the King. Moleyns was a favourite of his, and I am sure he will be interested to know what you—'

'I cannot waste time here when there is *holy* work to be done,' interrupted Hopeman, sensing he was on uncertain ground, and so opting to exit on his own terms. 'Come, brothers. Let us be about our saintly business.'

He and his deacons marched away, chanting a psalm. Their voices were loud, and it was still early, so a number of lamps went on in the houses they passed. Bartholomew winced, sure there would be complaints about the racket later.

The rest of the morning was taken up with trying to ascertain exactly what had happened to the hapless Lyng. A more detailed examination of his body revealed brown dust on his heels – it matched the road's, suggesting that he had been attacked in the open and dragged out of sight afterwards. Michael and Bartholomew started their investigation in the Hall of Valence Marie, the buildings of which were closest to the scene of the crime.

'And you noticed nothing amiss?' asked Michael of its Master, John Tinmew. 'No quarrel in the street, or mysterious shadows along the King's Ditch?'

'Of course not, or we would have told you,' replied Tinmew. 'Yet I cannot say I am sorry that Lyng is dead. He was not as kindly as he wanted everyone to think, and was too fond of the hostels for my liking. Now he is out of the running, Godrich will be Chancellor.'

'Will he indeed?' murmured Michael. 'What makes you think so?'

'He has the backing of all the Colleges except Michaelhouse, and Lyng's death means the hostels will switch their support to him – because of his free-book campaign.'

'Do you really want a Chancellor who has bought the post?' asked Michael in distaste.

'Why not, if he can afford it?' shrugged Tinmew.

'Why do you prefer Godrich to the other candidates?' asked Bartholomew curiously.

'Because Hopeman is a fanatic, while there must be

some reason why Michaelhouse refused to reinstate Thelnetham after he resigned. He probably has a dark secret, which means he is not the sort of man we want.'

'Then vote for Suttone,' urged Michael. 'He is neither a fanatic nor a man with nasty secrets. Moreover, like you, he is a College man – and one who lives in a foundation that is home to the Senior Proctor into the bargain.'

But Tinmew shook his head. 'While I applaud his modern views on women, I cannot vote for someone who thinks we will all be dead of the plague in a few months. It means he is unlikely to develop any meaningful forward-looking policies.'

Next, Michael visited Peterhouse, while Bartholomew went to the King's Head. Scholars entered this particular tavern at their peril, but most of its patrons were his patients, so while he was not welcomed with open arms, he was at least allowed inside. Unfortunately, everyone claimed that the first they had known about a body on the banks of the King's Ditch was a horrified screech from Thelnetham.

'Slugs,' explained Gundrede. 'We just assumed that one had bitten him back.'

'Normally, it would have been me who found Lyng,' added Isnard, 'because I go past that spot every Saturday morning, delivering coal to the Austins. But I did something else today.'

'What?' asked Bartholomew, thinking the question simply begged to be put, but Isnard turned furtive and refused to reply.

'Ask the tomb-makers if *they* killed Lyng,' suggested Gundrede helpfully. 'After all, they were conspicuous by their absence today – everyone else came to see what was going on.'

'It was still early,' said Bartholomew. 'Most folk were still in bed.'

'Then no wonder they take so long to do their work,' said Isnard contemptuously. 'I had been up for *hours* by then, and . . .'

He trailed off when Gundrede shot him a warning glance. Bartholomew did not want to hear more, lest he learned something he would be obliged to report, so he left the tavern and went to see if Michael had finished in Peterhouse. The monk had, and was standing outside it, talking to Tulyet and Helbye.

'Lyng was last seen alive on Thursday evening,' Michael was saying, 'and while Matt thinks he was probably killed soon afterwards, he cannot prove it. Not surprisingly, no one is able to provide alibis for the whole time.'

'Thelnetham can,' said Bartholomew. 'In the form of Nicholas or his fellow Gilbertines.'

'So can Egidia and Inge,' said Helbye. 'The Sheriff ordered a watch put on them when they went to stay in the Griffin, so they have been under surveillance since Thursday afternoon. *And* we started monitoring the tomb-makers after Reames lost his brains yesterday.'

'If you mean the kind of surveillance that you deployed on Moleyns, I am disinclined to trust it,' said Michael coolly. 'We have witnesses who say he slipped out of the castle to commit crimes all over the town, and if *he* could corrupt your guards, then others can, too. I had planned to visit you this morning, to ask you about it, but you have saved me the trek.'

'What nonsense is this?' demanded Tulyet. 'Moleyns did nothing of the sort, I assure you.'

'He was wealthy,' said Michael. 'And your soldiers are poorly paid—'

'No!' snapped Helbye, although there was alarm in his eyes. 'Our men would never put money before their duties.'

'Who told you this tale, Brother?' asked Tulyet coolly. 'A scholar?'

'I cannot say,' replied Michael, while Bartholomew suddenly found a hole in his sleeve to examine, which allowed him to avoid Tulyet's eyes. 'However, it is true, because I mentioned it to my beadles, and several say they saw Moleyns out without an escort after dark. They assumed it was with your blessing, and were astonished when I told them that was unlikely.'

Tulyet turned so furiously on Helbye that the sergeant took an involuntary step backwards. 'Tell me this is untrue.'

'Of course it is untrue!' cried Helbye. 'You know how carefully we watched Moleyns. He never went out unless you or I was with him.'

'My beadles saw him at night,' said Michael. 'So I suspect he waited until you were tucked up safely in your beds, then used his purse on less scrupulous individuals.'

Tulyet was appalled. 'Christ's blood! What if he had taken it into his head to escape? The King would have had me executed!'

'No!' insisted Helbye stoutly. 'None of this is true. Your beadles are mistaken, Brother. I watched Moleyns every waking moment. I swear I did.'

Tulyet rubbed his eyes. 'Yes, you are above reproach, Will. However, the same cannot be said for all the villains under our command.'

'Moleyns preyed on the "friends" who visited him in the castle,' Michael continued, 'after he had cajoled them into revealing where they kept their money. He did not steal all of it, of course, as that would have raised eyebrows. But he took enough to keep him in ready cash.'

'He *was* always flush with funds,' acknowledged Tulyet. 'I often asked him how, given that most of his property had been confiscated, and he always told me that Inge got it for him. Yet he was frequently heavy-eyed in the mornings, but would never explain why . . .'

'Vicar Frisby loved carousing into the small hours with

him,' recalled Bartholomew, 'but sometimes, Moleyns cancelled the revels or claimed he was too tired. I suspect these "early nights" coincided with his rambles outside the castle walls.'

Tulyet sagged against a wall as the evidence mounted. 'When he first arrived, we crossed swords – he tried to bully me and I resisted. He vowed then that he would make me sorry. Well, it seems he has succeeded, because I shall never live this down.'

'Could Egidia and Inge have been involved as well?' asked Michael.

'Unlikely.' It was Helbye who answered, his cheeks burning with shame. 'They had separate rooms – at Moleyns' insistence. He said it was because he snored, and he did not want to bother them . . .'

'But it was to prevent them from seeing what he was doing,' finished Tulyet heavily. 'God damn the man!'

'So let us recap what we know about the relationships between our three victims,' said Michael, feeling the recriminations had gone on quite long enough, and it was time to change the focus of the discussion. 'Moleyns and Lyng hailed from neighbouring villages; Moleyns whispered something to Lyng shortly before his death; Lyng and Tynkell were friends and fellow scholars; Moleyns sent invitations for Tynkell to meet him in St Mary the Great . . .'

'And Lyng carried messages between them,' finished Bartholomew. 'Cook was there, too – not with Lyng, but while the other two chatted. We should speak to him about it.'

'I had better do it – he is unlikely to cooperate with you.' Tulyet turned to Michael. 'Do you think Moleyns used Lyng and Tynkell to help him steal?'

'I cannot see them burgling the town's worthies,' replied the monk evenly, while Bartholomew kept his eyes on the hole in his jerkin again. 'However, Nicholas said Tynkell changed after Moleyns arrived, and took to shutting himself in his office. Perhaps he was being black-mailed . . .'

'Yet Kolvyle told me that their discussion was amiable,' said Tulyet. 'Which would not have been the case, if one had been forcing the other to act against his will.'

Michael frowned, annoyed that the youth had confided something to the Sheriff that he had not mentioned to the Senior Proctor; he already knew it from Nicholas, but that was hardly the point.

'Inge claimed they discussed siege engines,' he mused, 'although Kolvyle disagreed . . .'

'So do I,' said Tulyet firmly. 'Moleyns might have been a knight, but he was no warrior, and if Tynkell had wanted to find out about weapons, he would have asked me.' He rubbed his eyes again. 'You two had better explore these peculiar ties between our three victims, while I find out how Moleyns contrived to escape. And when I do, heads will roll.'

Michael and Bartholomew went on their way, but had not gone far before Whittlesey appeared, asking if he might observe them at work. There was something about the suave Benedictine that Bartholomew did not like at all, and he was about to suggest that Michael used the envoy as a helpmeet instead, when Whittlesey stumbled over a pothole. He yelped, and hobbled away to perch on a nearby trough, rubbing his knee and wincing.

'I hurt myself falling down the stairs on Thursday night,' he explained. 'Barber Cook stitched it up, but it still hurts like the Devil.'

'Cook?' echoed Michael in distaste. 'Why would you demean yourself by hiring him?'

'Because he offered me a free haircut at the same time,' explained Whittlesey, 'and my tonsure needed attention. Besides, Godrich summoned him almost before

I had picked myself up. My cousin is very solicitous of me, and is never far away. It would not surprise me to learn that he is watching over me now in fact.'

Michael glanced around irritably, disliking the notion that he was being monitored by unseen eyes. 'Matt will ease the pain in your leg, Whittlesey. He has a rare talent with knees.'

'Good,' said Whittlesey, and snapped imperious fingers. 'Come, Bartholomew, we shall use the Cardinal's Cap. It is far too cold to sit around out here.'

He began to limp towards it before Bartholomew could respond. The physician was sorely tempted to ignore such an impolite order, leaving the arrogant Benedictine to wait inside in vain, but Michael chose that moment to waylay Master Heltisle of Bene't College, another person Bartholomew disliked, and Whittlesey was the lesser of two evils. He entered the inn, and found the envoy sitting on a bench by the window.

'You did this tumbling down some stairs?' he asked, examining the damaged joint.

'Yes, and it was most embarrassing. I fear some King's Hall men thought I was drunk.'

'And were you?'

'No,' said Whittlesey indignantly. 'Here is a shilling for your pains – conditional on you posing no more impertinent questions.'

It was an enormous sum, and would replenish nicely Bartholomew's dwindling stock of remedies for lung-rot. He nodded acceptance of the terms, then called for hot water and bathed the wound before removing Cook's tight little stitches – the gash was long, but shallow, and did not need them. He smeared it with a healing balm, then covered it with a clean dressing.

'That is the third time you have washed your hands since we came in,' remarked the envoy when Bartholomew had finished. 'And Cook tells me that you are in the habit of boiling bandages over the kitchen fire. It strikes me that these are peculiar practices. Overly finicky.'

'Perhaps,' shrugged Bartholomew. 'But they seem to prevent festering. Of course, I do not understand why . . .'

'Then perhaps you should spend more time reading,' suggested Whittlesey. 'The answer will be somewhere in the vast body of literature available to diligent practitioners. However, you have eased my pain, so I shall not complain too loudly about your academic shortcomings.'

'Good,' said Bartholomew coolly. 'Come back to see me in a—'

He faltered when the door burst open and Cook stormed in. Kolvyle was at his heels, and the younger scholar's face was bright with malice.

'You see?' Kolvyle said. 'I told you he was in here with one of your patients.'

'This is an outrage!' howled Cook, shoving Bartholomew away with considerable force. 'You are a physician, not a surgeon. You have no right to tend *my* clients' wounds.'

'I asked him to do it,' said Whittlesey, standing quickly and raising his hand to prevent Cook from pushing Bartholomew again. 'He did not volunteer. And I am glad of it, as it happens, because I am much more comfortable now. You could learn a lot from him.'

It was not a diplomatic remark, and served to send Cook into even greater paroxysms of fury. His voice rose to a shriek, and spittle flew from his mouth. Worse, he began wagging his finger, a gesture that Bartholomew had always found intensely annoying.

'Stick to urine flasks and astrological charts,' he screeched, and the offending digit came so close to Bartholomew's face that it was in danger of poking out an eye. 'The next time you trespass in my domain, the Worshipful Company of Barbers will crush you like a snail.'

'Do not bother suing him though,' put in Kolvyle

poisonously. 'He does not have any money, because he spends it all on the poor. That is why they go to him for treatment. You would be a rich man, Cook, if it were not for his misguided generosity.'

Incensed, Cook lurched forward and grabbed the front of Bartholomew's tabard. 'You arrogant bastard! Poach my business again and I will break your—'

He did not finish, because Bartholomew thrust him away, hard enough to send him crashing into a table, where he suffered a painfully cracked elbow. More livid than ever, Cook surged forward a second time, finger at the ready. Bartholomew could not help himself. When it wagged in his face, he grabbed it and squeezed as hard as he could.

'They come to me because they do not want to die,' he said, in a quiet voice that nevertheless held considerable menace. Cook's eyes widened in alarm. 'And the next time I see evidence of your incompetence, I will tell the Sheriff to prosecute you. Is that clear?'

He held the finger a little longer, then released it abruptly. Cook gazed at him with open hatred, and Bartholomew supposed he should have controlled his temper. He did not want a feud with a fellow practitioner, and was sorry that he and the barber had failed to find a way to work together. However, he was tired of standing by while Cook butchered his patients, and his threat had not been an idle one.

'You will not win,' hissed Cook. 'I will kill you first.'

'Such hot words,' said Whittlesey reproachfully. 'It is hardly becoming. Come, both of you. Shake hands, and agree to be friends.'

'Never!' declared Cook hotly, while Kolvyle smirked at his side. 'I would sooner cut off my right arm than make peace with him. But his days are numbered and—'

'Why were you in St Mary the Great with Tynkell and Moleyns?' interrupted Bartholomew, going on an offensive of his own and ignoring the voice in his head that told him to leave such questions to Tulyet. 'The Chancellor was my patient, so do not say you were consulting them on a matter of medicine.'

'That is none of your affair.'

'Then tell me where you were on Thursday night,' ordered Bartholomew, more than ever convinced that a sly jab in the heart would not be beneath the loathsome barber.

'I was with customers. Lots of them, so do not think to accuse me of killing Lyng, because I have plenty of alibis.'

But worthless ones, thought Bartholomew, if Cook had been traipsing from house to house. After all, how long would it take to hit an elderly priest over the head, stab him, and drag the body out of sight?

'You will probably die from his ministrations, and it will serve you right,' Cook snarled at Whittlesey, before spinning on his heel and stalking out.

Kolvyle watched him go with spiteful satisfaction, so Bartholomew rounded on him.

'Why did you bring him here? What have you achieved?'

'I have exposed a physician who treads on the toes of barber-surgeons,' replied Kolvyle haughtily. 'It is time you chose between medicine and scholarship, Bartholomew, as it is obvious that you cannot do both.'

Bartholomew did not rise to the bait, but only because Whittlesey was there, and he did not want witnesses when he gave Kolvyle the benefit of a few home truths.

'I shall bear it in mind,' he said mildly. 'So tell me: how well did *you* know Lyng, Tynkell and Moleyns?'

'Oh, I see,' sneered Kolvyle. 'You aim to accuse *me* of being the killer now. Well, I am sorry to disappoint you, Bartholomew, but I am innocent. I cannot prove where I was every moment since Thursday night, but neither can anyone else. Including you.'

'Moleyns, Cook, the tomb-builders,' listed Bartholomew. 'You were friends with all of them in Nottingham, and you have continued the association since – criminals, charlatans and men engaged in a bitter rivalry. You—'

'My private life is none of your concern,' interrupted Kolvyle indignantly. 'And the tomb-makers are not my friends, thank you very much. I do not associate with commoners.' Then he whipped around to address Whittlesey. 'And speaking of Nottingham, *you* were there, too. I always thought it odd that you happened to be passing just when Dallingridge was poisoned.'

'He *was* poisoned?' pounced Bartholomew, although he was astonished to learn that the Benedictine had been in Nottingham during that fateful time – and that he should be in Cambridge now. 'You always claim he died of natural causes. Have your changed your mind?'

Kolvyle's face was as black as thunder. 'Do not make an enemy of me, Bartholomew. You will not win, and you will end up being more sorry than you can possibly imagine.'

'I have never liked him,' confided Whittlesey, when the youngster had gone. 'He might have a brilliant mind, but his character leaves much to be desired. I hope he cuts a niche for himself in academia, because I should not like him to join the Church.'

'*Were* you in Nottingham when Dallingridge first became ill?' asked Bartholomew. He would not mind at all if Whittlesey transpired to be the culprit, although it would not be as satisfying as seeing Cook accused, of course.

Whittlesey shook his head. 'I arrived a few days later, with my cousin Godrich. And we *did* just happen to be passing, no matter what that vituperative little brat claims.'

When Bartholomew returned to Michael, having cunningly dispensed with Whittlesey's company by advising him to rest his leg, the monk was with Father Aidan. The Principal's face was wet with tears, which had attracted a circle of interested onlookers. Sobbing, he was telling Michael that he could not talk in the street, but that he might be able to manage a short conversation in Maud's after he had downed a restorative cup of wine. Any number of people heard the remark, and there was much malicious sniggering. As it was so cold, hoods shielded faces, but Bartholomew was fairly sure Cook and Kolvyle were responsible for some of it. Richard Deynman came to put a comforting arm around Aidan's shoulders.

'I shall want that letter,' warned Michael. 'The unopened one from Lyng's room.'

'Softly, Brother,' murmured Bartholomew, disliking the way so many spectators were brazenly hanging on their every word.

Michael lowered his voice as he continued to address Aidan. 'It might contain a vital clue. Unless you have opened it already?'

'Of course not!' declared Richard, before his Principal could reply for himself. 'Maud's men do not read other people's personal correspondence. We leave that for less scrupulous individuals. Like senior proctors.'

There was more chortling among the listeners, which Michael ignored. He indicated that Aidan should return to Maud's at once, where they could talk without an audience, and fell into step behind him. Bartholomew went, too, at the same time telling the monk what had happened in the Cardinal's Cap. Michael, however, was more interested in how Moleyns had contrived to escape from the castle.

'Because of Helbye,' he said. 'The man has become a liability. Of course, it was the journey to Nottingham to collect Moleyns that did it – it was too hard a jaunt for a man his age, and it has prompted a fatal decline.'

'Yet I understand why Dick is reluctant to replace him,'

191

said Bartholomew. 'Helbye has been his right-hand man for longer than he cares to remember, just as Cynric has been mine, and Meadowman is yours. That sort of trust takes years to build.'

'Except that Dick's was betrayed. Not deliberately – I am sure Helbye would sooner die – but the plain fact is that he was let down.'

Bartholomew was about to return to the more interesting subject of Cook, when there was a flicker of movement in the trees at the end of St Bene't's churchyard. It was a strange place for anyone to be, so he stopped to look.

'I saw it, too,' said Michael. He pointed suddenly. 'There! By the wall.'

Bartholomew opened the churchyard gate, which precipitated an immediate flurry of activity. Several figures materialised from behind the graves and ran to a cart, which they began shoving as fast as the frozen ground would allow. It was not quick enough, and Bartholomew soon caught up with them, although when he saw so many chisels and mallets brandished, he wished he had not bothered.

'Put those down,' ordered Michael sternly from behind him. 'How dare you menace members of the University. Do you not know that I can fine you for belligerent behaviour?'

'Oh, it is you,' said Petit with a sickly grin, indicating that his apprentices were to lower their 'weapons'. 'We thought it was Isnard and his cronies. Or worse, that rogue Lakenham. He would love to catch us out here with this.'

Bemused, Bartholomew lifted the blanket that covered the cart and peered underneath. Lying there were several flat metal plates.

'Brasses!' he exclaimed. 'Are they Lakenham's?'

'No, they are not,' snapped Petit crossly. 'They are mine.'

'But you are a mason – you work with stone, not metal.

192

Are these the materials that Lakenham thinks have been stolen from him?'

'No, they are the supplies I ordered from London,' replied Petit curtly. He sighed irritably when Bartholomew raised sceptical eyebrows. 'All right, all right, I will explain. Normally, when a client wants a bit of brass on his tomb, I subcontract a lattener to do the work. However, in Cambridge, that means hiring Lakenham—'

'And we would sooner die than do him a favour,' put in the freckle-faced Peres. 'So we have decided to make the brasses ourselves instead.'

'But Lakenham will make a dreadful fuss if he finds out,' Petit went on. 'For trespassing on his professional domain. So we are obliged to keep them hidden until it is too late for him to do anything about it.'

'Not to mention the fact that he will try to pinch them,' added Peres. 'As he has pinched so much else. Now, if you do not mind, we need to hide them before he sees.'

Petit nodded to his apprentices, and together they hastened to trundle their haul away, hoods drawn up to hide their faces. They looked so manifestly suspicious that Bartholomew was sure the Sheriff's men would stop them if their paths crossed, regardless of whether or not they were doing anything illegal.

'Will you tell Dick, Brother?' asked Bartholomew, when they had gone. 'I am sure he will be interested.'

Michael nodded. 'Moreover, that little encounter has just placed Petit and his boys at the top of my list of murder suspects. Perhaps Lyng caught them doing something similar, so they stabbed him to keep him quiet. They also knew Moleyns from Nottingham, and may have killed Tynkell in the hope of winning the commission for his tomb.'

'Cook remains my first choice,' said Bartholomew. 'He was in Nottingham as well, where he was Dallingridge's *medicus*. He probably poisoned him to win a wealthy patient.'

Michael blinked. 'Lord, Matt. That is a wild leap in logic, even for you.'

'Not so – Dallingridge lingered for weeks, so Cook would have earned a fortune from tending him. Then here, Cook tried to convince us that Moleyns was not murdered; he was to hand when both Moleyns and Tynkell died; he cannot prove his whereabouts for Lyng's death; and he met Tynkell and Moleyns slyly in St Mary the Great. He is our killer. I am sure of it.'

'We shall bear it in mind,' said Michael, although he failed to look convinced. 'However, our list is a lengthy one, because it also includes Egidia and Inge, Kolvyle—'

'Oh, yes – Kolvyle is certainly on it,' agreed Bartholomew. 'Especially now that I have experienced first-hand the depth of his malice.'

'Then there are the men who want to be Chancellor: Godrich, Thelnetham and Hopeman.'

'Not Suttone?' Bartholomew felt treacherous for asking.

'Do not be ridiculous, Matt. He is a member of Michaelhouse.'

'So was Thelnetham.'

'True, but Suttone was not ousted from it for being disagreeable.'

Bartholomew supposed that was true. 'We should include Whittlesey as well.'

Michael frowned. 'Whittlesey? Why on Earth would you accuse him?'

'Because I have just learned that *he* was in Nottingham when Dallingridge was poisoned as well, and—'

'No, he was not,' interrupted Michael. 'He arrived a few days later.'

'So he claims,' said Bartholomew. 'But can we believe him?' He hurried on before Michael could answer. 'Then people started to die the moment he came here, and I had the sense that he was lying to me about how he cut his leg. Perhaps solving these crimes is a test for you – to see whether you are good enough to step into Sheppey's shoes.'

'That would be rather an extreme way to find out,' said Michael, wide-eyed. 'And I cannot believe it of him. However, we shall keep him on our list, if it pleases you. Why not? We can no more eliminate him than any of the others.'

They reached Maud's Hostel to find Richard waiting to let them in. He escorted them to Aidan's quarters, where the Principal was downing a very large cup of wine to steady his nerves.

'I cannot believe it,' he said hoarsely. 'Poor Lyng . . .'

'Are you sure he did not tell you where he was going on Thursday?' asked Michael. 'Now he has been murdered, you will appreciate that the question is important.'

'It was important when he was missing,' countered Aidan bitterly. 'Learning his plans now cannot help him.'

'No,' said Michael quietly. 'But it might help us catch his killer.'

'You want the case solved, so you can flounce off to Rochester and begin your new life,' said Aidan accusingly. 'While the rest of us remain here, steeped in grief.'

'He wants it solved to prevent the killer from striking again,' said Bartholomew gently. 'And so that Lyng and the others will have the justice they deserve.'

'The tomb-builders will be in for a disappointment, though,' Aidan went on, ignoring him, 'because Lyng did not want a monument. He specifically asked to be buried in the churchyard with a simple wooden cross. He was a modest man, whose only ambition was to serve a fourth term as Chancellor.'

'Shall we discuss his last known movements now, Brother?' asked Richard brightly. 'I have painstakingly visited all his favourite haunts, so I know exactly where he went and what he did on Thursday. Shall I tell you?'

'Go on, then,' said Michael warily. If Richard was anything like his brother, the testimony would have to be taken with a very large pinch of salt.

'Well, after breakfast he visited St Austin's and Bede's hostels to ask for their votes. Then he went to the Market Square, to make speeches with the other candidates.'

'The event was acrimonious, and it distressed him,' recalled Aidan. 'He said it made the four of them look like squabbling schoolboys, so he came back here to lie down and recover.'

Richard nodded. 'When he felt better, he got up and visited Copped Hall and Physwick, before coming home for dinner.'

'He ate a whole pig's heart,' put in Aidan. 'It was his favourite. I was a little peeved, actually, as I should have liked a slice myself, but he did not offer. Thank God I did not make a fuss! It was his last meal, and I might have ruined it for him.'

'Then he went out yet again,' Richard continued. 'It was roughly eight o'clock – very late – and I accompanied him as far as the High Street, where I turned towards Michaelhouse to visit my brother.'

'Did he speak to anyone along the way?' asked Michael.

'Oh, yes, lots of people. First, there was that sinister Benedictine who works for the Bishop of Rochester. They muttered together for ages while I waited.'

'Whittlesey?' asked Michael uneasily. 'Did you hear what they discussed?'

'No, because they were whispering.' Richard looked sheepish. 'I did try to eavesdrop, but they saw me and moved away. After, Lyng and I walked on a few paces until we were stopped by Cook, who told him that he needed a haircut. That horrid Michaelhouse lad was with him – the one who thinks the rest of us are stupid, and that only *he* is good enough to be a scholar.'

'Kolvyle might have an outstanding mind, but a lesson

in humility would not go amiss,' agreed Aidan. 'He told me the other day that Maud's should be suppressed, on the grounds that we are an embarrassment to the University. It was rude.'

'You should have boxed his ears,' said Michael. 'If he insults you again, you have my permission to do it. And when he complains, I shall fine him for being an irritating little brat.'

Aidan smiled for the first time. 'I might hold you to that, Brother.'

Michael turned back to Richard. 'Who else did Lyng greet?'

'Suttone, Thelnetham, Moleyns' wife, Godrich, the Mayor, and some of the tomb-builders, although I cannot tell you which ones, because it was too dark to tell. But I know it was them because they were muttering about casement-and-bowtell edge moulding.'

'So virtually all our suspects saw Lyng out and about after nightfall,' mused Michael. He turned to Aidan. 'But I had better read this letter now. Let us hope it contains something helpful.'

'I shall fetch it for you,' offered Richard, and thundered up the stairs before Michael could inform him that he would rather go himself – and take the opportunity for another rummage through Lyng's belongings at the same time. There was silence, followed by a shriek.

Bartholomew exchanged a glance of mystification with Michael, then hurried upstairs to find out what was happening. He flung open the door to Lyng's room just in time to see a black shape slither across the floor and start to climb through a window. Unfortunately, all the other shutters were closed to exclude the inclement weather, making it too dim to see properly. Richard was a blubbering heap in the corner.

'The Devil!' he wept. 'It is Satan himself!'

Bartholomew was sure it was not, especially as there

was a very human curse when the invader's cloak caught on a nail. He darted after him but 'Satan' freed himself quickly and began scrambling down the ivy-coated wall outside. Bartholomew leaned out after him, and managed to snag enough of his hood to stop him from going any further, but not enough to haul him back up again.

'I came in, and Lucifer was standing in the middle of the room,' wailed Deynman, as Michael and Aidan hurried in to find out what was happening. 'Which it why it is so cold in here – an icy blast from Hell.'

'Hell is hot,' said Michael authoritatively. 'Your "icy blast" came from the open window.'

'What was Satan doing?' breathed Aidan, while Bartholomew struggled to get a better grip on his quarry.

'Nothing,' gulped Richard. 'But I saw the red gleam of his terrible eyes – in a face that was invisible under its hood.'

'You could see his eyes but not his face?' demanded Michael sceptically. He hurried to the window, reaching it just as Bartholomew's tenuous hold on the hood snapped loose, allowing the culprit to continue his escape unimpeded. 'After him, Matt!'

'You do it,' retorted Bartholomew. It was a long way down, and the ivy was covered in frost and icicles.

'With my heavy bones? Are you mad? Quickly now, or he will escape.'

'Then go down to the yard and cut him off,' ordered Bartholomew, unwilling to take all the risks while everyone else just stood and watched.

He clambered over the sill, and took hold of a branch, wincing at the cold, slick feel of it on his fingers. Then he began to descend, although rather more gingerly than 'Satan' had done. His caution was not misplaced: the invader's frantic flight had loosened the plant's hold on the wall, and it began to peel away. Alarmed, Bartholomew tried to move faster, aware of his quarry swearing pithily below as bits of ice and vegetation began to shower down on him.

Then, with a swishing hiss, the whole thing tore free, sending Bartholomew and the invader tumbling to the yard below, although their fall was cushioned by leaves and branches. The ivy kept coming after they had landed, though, and Bartholomew found himself submerged in foliage. By the time he had fought free of its prickly embrace, 'Satan' had gone.

'Did *you* do all this damage, Matt?' came Michael's voice from somewhere on the other side of the green mountain. 'Heavens! I am glad I did not listen to you and attempt it myself. I might have been hurt.'

'The Devil *flew* away,' shouted Richard, who had recovered from his gibbering fright and was standing with Aidan at the window. 'If he had tried to clamber down the branches, like Doctor Bartholomew did, he would also be entangled in the leaves. But he has gone!'

'Just as he soared away after Tynkell was stabbed,' gulped Aidan. 'We are fortunate he did not kill you, too, Bartholomew.'

'That was a *person*,' said Michael firmly. 'Not Lucifer. And he stole Lyng's letter, because it is no longer in his room. It was the killer, of course, making off with the clue that would have exposed him.'

'Yes, and *you* told him you were coming for it,' said Bartholomew in a low voice. 'You announced your intentions in the graveyard, and lots of people heard. Most were hooded, so I cannot tell you who they were, but I am sure Cook and Kolvyle were among them.'

'So were Godrich and Hopeman,' said Michael. 'It is a wretched shame that Richard raced upstairs before we could stop him. If you or I had gone, the villain would now be in custody.'

CHAPTER 8

As Bartholomew was keen to ensure that his students were on track with the reading he had set, he and Michael returned to Michaelhouse, where the monk took the opportunity to give Langelee an update on their findings. Suttone listened, too, on the grounds that he should know what was happening in the University he would soon be running. He nodded sagely, but when Michael asked for his opinion as to the culprit's identity, he mumbled an excuse and shuffled off to the kitchens in search of food.

'Are you sure he is up to the task?' asked Langelee worriedly. 'Obviously, I would love to see a Michaelhouse man in charge. But Suttone . . . well, he has his failings.'

'Kolvyle has been saying the same,' sighed Michael. 'So will you keep the brat here until the election is over? His disloyalty is doing Suttone great harm, and I shall devise a pretext to expel him when I have a spare moment. Perhaps I can banish him to Oxford. That will teach him not to cross me.'

'I know how to occupy him today,' said Langelee. 'He can give the Saturday Sermon.'

He referred to a tradition that he had started, where the Fellows took it in turns to lecture on a light-hearted subject of his choosing, after which there was a debate. Michael laughed.

'Excellent! He takes himself far too seriously, and Matt's lads will heckle him if he tries to regale them with some tedious monologue on law. It will show him that he is fallible.'

He had arranged to meet Tulyet in the Brazen George

again, so he and Bartholomew hurried there as soon as the physician was satisfied that his pupils were not falling behind with their work. They arrived to find the Sheriff waiting, having ordered a very modest meal. There was one salted herring and a hard-boiled egg each, along with a dish of pickled onions to share.

'We caught Petit lugging brasses about on a cart not long ago,' said Michael, taking one look at the spread, and indicating that the landlord was to bring something more suitable. 'I assume they belong to Lakenham, although Petit denied it, of course.'

Tulyet nodded. 'Helbye cornered him by the Trumpington Gate, and brought him to the castle to explain himself. I was delighted – I thought we had our thief at last. Unfortunately, the metal *is* his – he has receipts to prove it.'

'Then the thief must be Lakenham,' said Bartholomew.

Tulyet shook his head. 'The latest crime is to his detriment – the brass he made for Cew has been stolen. It disappeared at roughly the same time that Petit was with me, which suggests that neither is the guilty party. And there is the fact that they are under surveillance – if they had stolen Cew's plate, we would have noticed. Which leaves Isnard and Gundrede.'

'You were watching *all* the masons and *all* the latteners?' asked Bartholomew sceptically. 'Apprentices, as well as masters?'

'Well, no,' acknowledged Tulyet. 'But I am inclined to drop them in favour of Isnard and Gundrede because Isnard and Gundrede have left the town.'

'Left it to go where?' asked Michael.

'No one knows, which is suspicious in itself. However, I saw Isnard's barge slipping down the river at first light this morning. I was too far away to stop it, but it was very low in the water, and I suspect it was loaded down with contraband.'

'Wine, probably,' said Michael. 'We know he smuggles claret on occasion.'

'It looked too heavy for that – more like the kind of weight that would come from ledger slabs, brasses, Dallingridge's feet and the lead from Gonville's chapel. Obviously, the rogues will ferry it through the Fens, then around the coast to London.'

Michael frowned. 'But who will want second-hand tomb parts? Or is there a large population of dead Cews in the city?'

'The back of the plate will be blank,' explained Tulyet. 'So a lattener will just flip it over and engrave his own design on the other side. Or scratch out Cew's name, and etch someone else's over the top of it. It is a lucrative business, and such a load will fetch a fortune.'

'Well, we will soon know if Isnard and Gundrede are the culprits,' said Michael. 'Because they will start throwing their profits around, and we will hear about it. Neither is the kind of man to be discreet about any ill-gotten gains.'

Bartholomew sincerely hoped they were wrong.

'We had better review what we have learned,' said Michael, rubbing his hands eagerly as Lister began to replace Tulyet's meagre repast with plates of meat and bread. 'And I mean facts, not conjecture and supposition. First, Tynkell. I thought he was working on University business when he shut himself in his room, but it transpires that he was doing something else altogether. I have been unable to ascertain what. So far, at least.'

'Moleyns sent him invitations to meet in St Mary the Great.' Bartholomew took up the tale. 'We do not know why, but it was probably nothing to do with siege engines. Then he went up the tower and fought a person who then managed to escape, even though there was nowhere to hide.'

'Either Tynkell or his killer used Meadowman's keys to get up there,' Michael went on. 'But they were back in their hiding place shortly after his death, which means the killer must have returned them.'

'Unless Tynkell unlocked the tower and replaced them *before* going upstairs,' said Tulyet. 'It is an odd thing to do, but little about these murders makes sense.'

'Moleyns died next,' continued Michael. 'A dog was set racing after a bone, which caused his horse to unseat him. He chose Satan himself, so we cannot blame anyone else for giving him a mount that was beyond his skills. The culprit merely took advantage of the fact – as he did the mêlée when half the town clustered around the fallen Moleyns. No one saw him kill his victim.'

'I believe *someone* did,' said Tulyet. 'The woman in the cloak with the fancy hem, who saw what happened and fled for her life. Unfortunately, I have still not managed to identify her.'

'Moleyns was also engaged in untoward activities – namely sneaking out of the castle at night to steal.' Michael shrugged when Tulyet winced. 'It is the King's fault for giving him such outrageous freedoms. Moleyns should have been kept locked in a cell, like the felon he was.'

'I doubt that argument will win me much sympathy at Court,' muttered Tulyet.

'Moleyns met Tynkell – and Cook – in St Mary the Great,' said Bartholomew. 'Where Lyng carried messages between them.'

'Inge and Egidia deny all knowledge of Moleyns' nocturnal forays,' said Tulyet. 'They also insist that they could not get close to Moleyns immediately after he fell, although Weasenham and Kolvyle claim otherwise. Inge and Egidia are liars, and we should believe nothing they say.'

'And finally, there is Lyng,' said Michael. 'Who probably aimed to spend Thursday evening winning votes, but was ambushed near the King's Ditch. The killer arranged his body neatly, and left it in a place where it was unlikely to be discovered very soon.'

'Lyng received a letter,' mused Bartholomew. 'And someone took a huge risk to retrieve it, so it must have been important.'

'It was my fault that he succeeded,' said Michael bitterly. 'I should not have announced to all and sundry that I was going to Maud's to collect it. Lord! It makes my skin crawl to think that the villain was there, monitoring my every word.'

'You must have noticed someone paying you special attention,' said Tulyet. '*Think*, both of you. Who was listening when you brayed your plans?'

'I did not *bray* them,' objected Michael testily. 'I spoke in my normal voice. Even so, it is unfortunate that Matt did not hush me sooner.'

'Cook was there,' said Bartholomew to Tulyet, more interested in talking about suspects than apportioning blame. 'Along with Kolvyle.'

Michael rolled his eyes. 'And four dozen others, all of whom had his – or her – hood pulled up to ward off the chill. But *you* saw the rogue on the ivy, Matt. Surely you noticed something that will allow us to identify him?'

'The room was too dim to let me see more than a shape, and once he was outside, he was hidden by leaves.' Bartholomew spread the fingers on his right hand and stared at them. 'I even had hold of him for a moment, but he managed to pull away from me.'

'Could it have been one of the tomb-makers?' pressed Tulyet, rather keenly. 'After all, Moleyns, Tynkell and Lyng were killed with a burin.'

'With something *akin* to a burin,' corrected Bartholomew. 'Or perhaps a surgical instrument – of the kind that that Cook will own.'

'I spoke to Cook about his encounters in St Mary the

Great with our victims,' said Tulyet. 'He claims they met there by chance.'

'Then he is lying, and you should interrogate him again,' said Bartholomew, ignoring the fact that his own attempt to prise the truth from the barber had been no more successful.

'There is another connection between the victims, besides the manner of their deaths and their meetings,' said Michael. 'Namely Stoke Poges: Moleyns once owned it, Lyng hailed from the next village, Tynkell wanted its chapel for the University, and a rider with its insignia was seen galloping away shortly after Moleyns' murder.'

'Then I shall invite Inge and Egidia to the castle, and we shall discuss the matter again,' said Tulyet, 'but do not hold your breath. Inge is a lawyer with experience of criminal courts, so getting a confession from him will be nigh on impossible. And do not suggest cornering Egidia alone – I tried that, but she refused to speak to me until someone had fetched him.'

'What about the deaths of Lucas and Reames?' asked Bartholomew, moving to another subject. 'How are those enquiries going?'

'Poorly,' replied Tulyet glumly. 'Incidentally, we should not forget Dallingridge in all this. I am sure he was murdered, and his death precipitated something dark and wicked, with Moleyns like a spider at its centre. My chief suspects are Egidia, Inge and all the tomb-makers, who were in Nottingham at the time.'

'So was Cook,' said Bartholomew, promptly and with great satisfaction. 'Along with Kolvyle and Whittlesey.'

'Well, you are both wrong,' declared Michael, 'because the culprit is Godrich. Whittlesey let slip that *he* was in the vicinity of Nottingham on the day that Dallingridge was poisoned, although I can think of no good reason for him being there.'

'Have you asked him?' queried Tulyet.

'Of course, but he told me to mind my own business, which was no way to convince me that he has nothing to hide. He is dangerously ambitious, and will do anything to achieve his goals. The same is true of Kolvyle, who is second on my list, with Hopeman a close third.'

'Hopeman was never in Nottingham,' said Bartholomew.

'How do you know?' retorted Michael. 'It was in the summer vacation, when lots of scholars were away. He was one of them – I checked.'

'What about Thelnetham and Suttone?' asked Tulyet. 'Were they away, too?'

'Yes,' admitted Michael. 'But Suttone is too fat to fly off roofs and scramble down walls, while Thelnetham has alibis for the deaths of Tynkell and Moleyns in the form of Nicholas and his Gilbertine brethren. Moreover, Thelnetham would not have "found" Lyng's body if he was responsible for killing him. He would have left it for someone else to discover.'

'True,' acknowledged Bartholomew. 'It led to awkward questions – ones that may have lost him votes.'

'Yet Godrich told us that Thelnetham visited Stoke Poges in the summer,' Tulyet pointed out. 'Perhaps he also has secret connections to Moleyns.'

'Not necessarily,' said Michael. 'There is a Gilbertine cell nearby, so he had a perfectly legitimate reason for passing through the place.'

'Right,' said Tulyet, standing abruptly. 'I will speak to Egidia, Inge and the tomb-makers again, then resume my hunt for the woman in the embroidered cloak. I will also try to learn more about Stoke Poges. Perhaps one of my knights knows something. What will you do?'

'Concentrate on Godrich, Hopeman and Kolvyle,' replied Michael. 'And re-question as many witnesses as will talk to me.'

'I need to visit patients,' said Bartholomew. 'But I will listen for rumours, and I will challenge Cook if I see him. And Whittlesey, who we need to ask about the discussion he held with Lyng on Thursday night – the one witnessed by Richard.'

'No!' exclaimed Michael and Tulyet in unison; Michael continued. 'Whittlesey is too influential a man to irritate, while your dislike of Cook will not allow you to be objective. Leave them to us, if you please.'

Unfortunately, Bartholomew's customers were of scant help in providing useful nuggets of information. The general consensus was that the Devil was responsible for all the murders, and that anyone who tried to investigate would be wasting his time. The theory was propounded particularly strongly by Marjory Starre, who had summoned Bartholomew to tend her rash. He was glad to see her, as it happened, because he wanted to explore what she had said in Isnard's house – about a clandestine connection between Moleyns, Tynkell and Lyng.

'I understand you met Satan in Maud's Hostel,' she said conversationally, as she opened her door and ushered him inside. 'You are lucky he likes you, or he might have resented being chased down the ivy like a common felon.'

Bartholomew blinked. 'I hardly think—'

'But he let it peel from the wall in such a way that you would not be hurt,' she declared with conviction. 'He appreciates everything you do for us, see.'

'Please do not say that to anyone else,' begged Bartholomew. 'I will be dismissed from the University if my colleagues think I am one of the Devil's favourites.'

'Yes, most scholars *are* narrow-minded fools,' she said sympathetically. 'It will be our little secret then. Of course, Lucifer does not like the University.' She spoke as though this was something he had confided personally. 'It has too many priests for his taste.'

'I am sure it does,' muttered Bartholomew, and hastily moved to a safer subject. 'You mentioned the last time we met that Moleyns, Lyng and Tynkell were associated in some way. Will you tell me how?'

'Why, through Satan, of course,' replied Marjory; she sounded surprised that he should need to ask. 'All three solicited his help on occasion, but they must have angered him in some way, so he decided to make an end of them.'

Bartholomew cursed himself for a fool. He should have known better than to expect sensible intelligence from a woman who made no bones about the fact that she was a witch.

'Moleyns, perhaps,' he said, 'but not the other two. Lyng was a priest, for a start.'

'Yes, but we never hold that against anyone,' she replied graciously. 'Yet I see you do not believe me, so ask yourself this: why was Master Tynkell covered in those marks?'

'What marks?' Bartholomew kept his attention on her rash, lest she read the truth in his face.

'The ones inked all over his body. You know what I am talking about, Doctor, so do not play the innocent with me.'

He looked up accusingly. 'Did you open his coffin?'

'Of course not – there are beadles minding it.' From that response, he assumed that she would have done, had it been left unattended, and was glad he had taken precautions against such liberties. 'I saw them on another occasion.'

'How? He went to considerable trouble to keep them hidden.'

'He was not always ashamed of them.' Marjory pulled up her skirts to reveal a pale white calf, and he was startled to see a horned serpent drawn there. 'I have one, but he had lots. We put them on ourselves as a mark of respect to darker powers. Of course, I have a cross on the other leg, as a sop to Jesus. It is reckless to put all your eggs in one basket, after all.'

It was an uncomfortable discussion for a man who spent

a lot of time in church, but Bartholomew felt obliged to persist anyway – the secret Tynkell had worked so hard to keep would likely be spread about the town if Marjory's claim went unchallenged, so it was his duty to see it nipped in the bud. 'Tynkell's symbols were inked on him while he was drunk – by friends, who did it as a joke.'

She raised an eyebrow. 'Is that what he told you? Pah! These take hours to make, and the process is painful. No one could slumber through all of it, not even a man in his cups. He lied to you, Doctor, because the truth is that he *wanted* them there.'

'Then it was a youthful mistake and he recanted,' said Bartholomew firmly. 'Which explains his determination to hide the things. Besides, Lyng and Moleyns had no such marks. I would have noticed when I examined their bodies.'

'Did you inspect the soles of their feet? No? Then of course you did not see them! Go and look at Master Lyng if you do not believe me, although if you want to view Sir John Moleyns, you will have to dig him up, because he was buried today.'

Bartholomew rubbed a hand through his hair. 'But Lyng was a priest,' he said again.

'A priest who was terrified of the plague,' she said quietly, 'when many folk learned that God and His saints could not be trusted to save them. Master Lyng wanted to survive, so he enlisted the help of another power. I could name dozens of people who did the same. Most returned to the Church when the danger was over. Master Lyng was one of them.'

'You cannot claim that Tynkell weakened during the plague, though – that was only a decade ago, and his marks are much older.'

'He was a devout Christian most of the time, but he came to me when he needed extra help. The plague was one such time, and the last election for the chancellorship was another.'

'Lord!' muttered Bartholomew, not liking to imagine what the town would make of the claim that it was Lucifer who had picked the University's last leader.

'Yes,' said Marjory serenely. 'But which one?'

Bartholomew's thoughts were reeling. So, was a shared interest in witchery – whether current or past – why Tynkell, Lyng and Moleyns met in St Mary the Great? And if so, was it significant that Cook was there, too? He asked, but Marjory's expression turned haughty.

'I never discuss the living – only the dead, to whom it no longer matters. However, your brother-in-law said the Devil could have *his* soul if Edith were spared. Satan was so touched that he allowed them both to live. Look on his tomb if you do not believe me. Round the back, you will see a horned serpent. It will protect him in the after-life, should God forget.'

Bartholomew was so unsettled by Marjory's revelations that he was not sure where to go first – to look at Lyng or to inspect Stanmore's tomb. In the end, he opted for Lyng, where it took but a moment to see that she had been telling the truth. He scrubbed at his face with shaking fingers. So was she right about Stanmore, too? His brother-in-law had certainly dabbled in such matters on occasion, and might well have bargained with the Devil for Edith's life, given that she had meant the world to him.

With a heavy tread, he turned towards St John Zachary. He saw Cook on the way, and received a furious glare. As the barber had just emerged from the home of Siffreda Sago, an old friend, Bartholomew felt obliged to knock on her door, to make sure she was still alive.

'We are not ill,' Siffreda said cheerfully, waving him inside. Her house was not very clean, and smelled of rotting cheese. 'He came to cut our hair. He has a two-for-one offer this week, you see. But he visited my mother yesterday and gave her a potion – this cold weather plays havoc with her lungs – and she has not been very well ever since. Would you look at her?'

Supposing Stanmore's tomb could wait, Bartholomew allowed himself to be conducted to a hovel north of the castle, where he learned with relief that Cook's medicine comprised nothing more sinister than nettles and arrow-root. However, the old woman needed an expectorant that worked, so he sent to the apothecary for a syrup of hyssop and horehound instead. When he had finished, he emerged to find a small crowd waiting for him.

'Barber Cook said you were too busy to bother with us any more,' explained one crone tearfully. 'And that we must hire him instead. So we are glad you found a few moments to visit Mother Sago, because she got worse when he took over her care.'

Bartholomew felt his temper rise – not only that Cook should dare tell his patients lies about him, but that they should be fobbed off with worthless remedies into the bargain. He prescribed better ones for the people who pressed eagerly around him, assured them that he would never abandon them to the likes of Cook, and began to stalk back down the hill, aflame with righteous indigna-tion. Unfortunately, Cook happened to be coming up it. The barber stood still for a moment, then darted down the nearest lane. Bartholomew caught him with ease.

'Stay away from my patients,' Bartholomew snarled furiously, grabbing his arm and swinging him around. 'You might have killed one with—'

He only just managed to jump back when Cook swiped at him with a dagger. He stumbled, and suddenly he was pinned against the wall with Cook's blade at his throat. Too late, he realised that he had been deliberately lured there – to a deserted place, where no one would see what was happening. The knife began to bite.

'I am tired of your arrogance,' Cook hissed. 'How dare you challenge my authority!'

More angry than afraid, Bartholomew fumbled for a knife of his own, but could not reach his bag. He tried to twist to one side, and when that did not work, he kneed Cook in the groin. The barber grunted with pain, but the grip did not loosen. Bartholomew was just gathering strength for a struggle that would see him free, when Cook was suddenly hauled backwards.

'Enough!' barked Sergeant Helbye, when Cook lunged forward with murder in his eyes. 'I do not know what is going on here, but you will scarper if you have any sense.'

'He started it,' hissed Cook between gritted teeth. 'I am lucky to be alive.'

Helbye glared at the barber until he slouched away, then turned crossly to Bartholomew.

'I know you scholars love a scrap, but please try to control yourself. We cannot afford to lose the town's only barber-surgeon.'

'He has been foisting useless remedies on my patients,' explained Bartholomew, loath for the sergeant to see him as a brawler.

'Perhaps he has, but fighting is no way to make him stop.' Helbye's stern expression softened. 'I appreciate that you long for the battlefield, Doctor. Cynric is always telling us about your prowess at Poitiers, and I like a skirmish myself. But the Sheriff will not approve of you breaking the King's Peace, so no more of it, eh?'

Bartholomew winced. When Matilde had left, he had embarked on a determined hunt to find her, and bad timing had put him and Cynric in the place where King Edward's troops were preparing to take on a much larger French force. He had been pressed into service, and had comported himself adequately, although it had been in tending the injured afterwards that he had made a real difference. Cynric loved describing the clash, and his accounts had now reached the stage where he and Bartholomew had defeated the French all but single-handed.

But Helbye was right – Bartholomew was a *medicus*, and chasing colleagues down dark lanes was unworthy of him. He nodded his thanks for the rescue, and went on his way.

There was a scything wind to accompany the plummeting temperatures that afternoon, and Bartholomew walked briskly towards St John Zachary. He met Petit on the way. The mason had his apprentices at his heels, and was beaming happily.

'I have just won the commission for Tynkell,' he announced gleefully. 'He will be buried under the bells in St Mary the Great – in the narthex – although I shall have to make his tomb very narrow, or it will be in the way of the ceremonial processions that stream past it. Still, that is no problem for a man of my talents.'

'Edith will dismiss you, if you start Tynkell without finishing Oswald,' warned Bartholomew. 'And she will sue you for breach of contract.'

Petit regarded him coolly. 'We were on our way to work in St John Zachary now, as a matter of fact. In the interests of good customer relations, we have agreed to overlook our distress at being in the place where poor Lucas was murdered. Is that not so, lads?'

There was a growl of agreement, after which he put his nose in the air and strode away, his boys at his heels. Bartholomew followed them into the High Street, where he was met by a curious sight. The men who wanted to be Chancellor had taken up station at strategic points along it, to demonstrate their oratory skills to those scholars who were walking home from the day's general lectures.

Hopeman had chosen the corner with Bridge Street, and was by far the loudest. He brayed about Satan, while his besotted deacons cheered his every word. Most Regent masters – those eligible to vote – were giving them a wide berth, and only those with radical opinions of their own stopped to listen.

Thelnetham was next, and had attracted a huge group of scholars, all of whom were laughing fit to burst – the Gilbertine had the enviable talent of being able to entertain and instruct at the same time, which was why he was so popular with students. Bartholomew noted that Thelnetham had dispensed with his trademark accessories, although hc had not been able to lose the mince, which was still very much in evidence as he flounced back and forth. Secretary Nicholas limped among the listeners, asking politely for their votes.

'He is very clever,' said Master Braunch of Trinity Hall, wiping tears of mirth from his eyes. 'But there is more to being Chancellor than making us chuckle – namely having the kind of royal contacts that Godrich possesses in abundance.'

'*And* Thelnetham needs to brush up on his geometry,' said Tinmew of the Hall of Valence Marie. 'A chancellor should be well-versed in the *quadrivium,* as well as law and theology.'

'I suppose a knowledge of angles and lines might come in useful for some ceremonial occasions,' acknowledged Braunch cautiously. 'Although I would not say it is an *essential* skill.'

From that response, Bartholomew assumed that Braunch was no geometrician himself, although he thought Tinmew's pretext for not supporting Thelnetham was unreasonable. The Gilbertine was an excellent scholar, far better than the other candidates, so condemning him for having a poor grasp of one specialist subject was hardly fair.

Godrich was outside King's Hall, where he could reinforce the fact that he had the University's biggest and most powerful College at his back – literally as well as figuratively. His discourse was arrogant and disjointed, but it did not matter, because he made up for his lack of eloquence by distributing free wine to his audience. Whittlesey was one of those who was passing a jug around.

'Godrich will make an excellent leader,' the envoy said, coming to offer Bartholomew a sip of claret. 'There is no other choice as far as I can see.'

'Are you sure about that?' asked Bartholomew, as Godrich began a sneering discourse about the shabby tabards worn by hostel men, either ignorant or uncaring of the fact that most could barely afford rent and food.

Whittlesey smiled wryly. 'He will learn tact in time.'

'Yes, but by then his offensive opinions might have torn the University apart.'

'He is more than capable of quashing riots,' shrugged Whittlesey. 'He is a skilled warrior, after all.'

Bartholomew regarded him with distaste, and although Michael and Tulyet had ordered him to leave the envoy for them to interrogate, he could not help himself. 'I understand that you talked to Lyng on the night he disappeared.'

Whittlesey raised laconic eyebrows. 'As did many other folk. Why do you want to know? To assess whether our conversation gave rise to me shoving a burin in his heart?'

'A burin?' pounced Bartholomew. 'Why mention one of those?'

'Because Michael told me it was the implement used to kill Lyng, Tynkell and Moleyns,' replied the Benedictine smoothly. 'But to answer your question, Lyng and I discussed the weather, like any self-respecting Englishmen.'

'Then why did you whisper?'

Whittlesey smiled. 'Because we were out in the street, and some residents had already retired to bed. Or would you rather we had bawled our opinions and earned complaints?'

Bartholomew was beginning to realise that Michael and Tulyet had been right to suggest he leave the slippery-tongued envoy to them. He nodded to the jug. 'Is it not beneath your dignity to serve wine to paupers and hostel men, especially when you should be sitting down, resting your knee?'

'Yes, but Godrich asked me to do it. He is keen to keep me close at the moment – for the prestige of having a man of my elevated status among his supporters, I suppose. He is kin, so I am under an obligation to please him.'

Bartholomew could see he would learn nothing more, so he went on his way, where he saw Suttone outside St Michael's Church, addressing a group that comprised nothing but Michaelhouse students. Bartholomew suspected that Langelee had sent them, so the Carmelite did not end up pontificating to himself. Suttone's discourse was rambling and uninspired, although he smiled with genuine sweetness, and was by far the nicest of the remaining candidates.

'You spout arrant nonsense, man,' came a scornful voice. 'Thomas Aquinas did *not* say that human souls are made of vegetable matter – he said that we are different from plants because we have rational and immortal spirits.'

It was Kolvyle, his voice loud and combative. As one, the students turned to scowl at him.

'Aquinas said it if Master Suttone claims he did,' shouted Mallet. 'And it is *you* who spouts nonsense – you do not even know who heads the tables in the camp-ball league. I have never heard such a miserable Saturday Sermon in all my life.'

There was a growl of agreement from the others, leading Bartholomew to surmise that the Master had deliberately picked a subject the youthful Fellow knew nothing about. Camp-ball, a rough game that involved kicking, punching and biting, was Langelee's favourite pastime, and he often treated the College to analyses of statistics and fixtures, so the students were generally very well versed in them.

'I wanted to speak about the canonical aspects of Apostolic Poverty,' said Kolvyle sourly. 'It would have been much more edifying, but Langelee—'

'We do not discuss that sort of thing on Saturdays,' interrupted Aungel, his voice dripping contempt. 'You should know that – you have been a member of Michaelhouse long enough.'

'He is too close to their own age to command their respect.' Bartholomew turned to see Michael behind him. 'That is why they challenge him so brazenly.'

'He does not have their respect, because he has not earned it,' countered Bartholomew. 'He does not know how, and thinks that flaunting his intellect is enough. But I thought Langelee was going to keep him inside today.'

The words were no sooner out of his mouth, when the Master himself appeared. Langelee stalked up to Kolvyle and grabbed his arm.

'I told you to help Deynman in the library,' he hissed. 'So what are you doing out here?'

Kolvyle tried, unsuccessfully, to free himself. 'I am not wasting my precious afternoon in company with a dunce like him,' he declared pettishly. 'I refuse.'

Langelee's smile was predatory. 'Do you? Good! Your defiance means I can fine you a shilling. Now, unless you want it doubled, I suggest you do as I say.'

Kolvyle opened his mouth to argue, but the Master's expression was dangerous, and he wisely closed it again. Langelee snapped his fingers, and Mallet and Aungel came to escort the errant Fellow back to the College. Kolvyle went with ill grace.

'My apologies,' called Langelee to Suttone. 'He will not annoy you again. Now what were you saying about Thomas Aquinas's soul being made of cabbage? Pray continue.'

Bartholomew arrived at St John Zachary to find Frisby just finishing Mass. The vicar tottered to the porch, where he greeted his parishioners by the wrong names, and asked after kinsmen they did not have. Many lingered to chat to each other in the churchyard outside, and Tulyet moved discreetly among them, asking questions about the murders. He broke off when he saw Bartholomew, and came to talk to him.

'I have identified the guard who let Moleyns out at night,' he said in a low voice. 'I got the bastard because of you – and a frost-nipped nose.'

Bartholomew ran through a mental list of all those he had treated for that particular complaint. There had been any number, but only one at the castle: the surly, ungrateful soldier, who had later been injured while sparring with Agatha's nephew.

'Yevele? He was the traitor?'

Tulyet nodded. 'You said at the time that his nose was unlikely to have been frozen when walking from one side of the bailey to the other, as he claimed. Well, you were right: it happened while he was lurking by the sally port, waiting to let Moleyns in and out.'

'I assumed he had left his nose exposed on purpose, in the expectation that you would give him inside duties instead. Night patrols must be miserable when the weather is so cold.'

'I should have seen through his lies.' Tulyet was disgusted with himself. 'He arrived in the summer, begging for work, and I should have refused, given that I disliked him on sight. But Helbye thought he could make something of him, and it seemed unkind not to give the lad a chance . . .'

'Did he tell you anything else?'

'Unfortunately, he sensed I was closing in on him, and bolted to the Fens. Helbye is organising a posse to hunt him down as we speak.'

Bartholomew glanced up at the dull winter sky and shivered. Dusk was not far off, and it would not be pleasant out in the open once night fell. He left Tulyet and entered the church, where Petit and his boys were busy working on the tracery around the tomb's lofty canopy. Despite the distracting racket, Bartholomew bowed his head and whispered a prayer that Marjory was wrong. She was not – the little horned serpent was carved on a corner, near the base.

'What is that?' he asked of the labouring craftsmen, pointing at it.

Petit came to look. 'Peres must have put it there – he was working on it last. I suppose he has chosen it as his masons' mark. Why? Do you not like it? I can get him to pick another.'

'Where is he?' It had not escaped Bartholomew's notice that Petit had named the one apprentice who was missing, and thus not in a position to confirm or deny the claim.

'I sent him to buy a new chisel. But what is—'

'Have you seen this mark before?' interrupted Bartholomew, aiming to find out if any of the craftsmen had a penchant for witchy symbols.

All shook their heads. 'But I agree that it is not quite appropriate for church-work,' said Petit. 'I shall tell him to file it off when he comes back, and replace it with something less . . . demonic.'

They returned to the canopy, leaving Bartholomew to stare at the little snake and think sadly about the many people whose faith had wavered in those dark and desperate times, when the plague had claimed the lives of one in three, and no one knew who would sicken next.

At that moment, the door opened and Lakenham entered with his enormous wife. They walked to the place where Cew's plate had been affixed, and he ran disconsolate fingers over the empty indent, as if he thought it might reappear if he stroked it long enough.

'I worked hard on that piece,' he said tearfully, when Bartholomew passed him on his way out. 'It may not have been very big, but I gave it my all, and it was beautiful. Tynkell's executors would have agreed, but it was

219

stolen before they could see it – which is why they gave that commission to Petit instead.'

'It is not fair,' growled Cristine. 'Petit should not be allowed to have so many jobs on the go at the same time. None will ever be finished, you know.'

'I thought we might win Lyng though,' sighed Lakenham. 'Given that he was a modest man with simple tastes. But we have just learned that he did not want any kind of monument at all. Perhaps he considered himself too sinful to lie in a church for all eternity.'

Or perhaps he had not wanted to lie in a place that other deities would consider off limits, thought Bartholomew unhappily, recalling the mark on the old priest's foot.

'There is still Moleyns,' he said encouragingly. 'Petit does not have him yet.'

'But he will,' predicted Cristine glumly. 'Because he moves in higher circles than us. For example, he was invited to dine in King's Hall a few weeks ago, which is where he persuaded Godrich to invest in the sculpted effigy that will go in the chancel of St Mary the Great.'

'And Godrich will spend even more money on the thing if he is elected Chancellor,' sighed Lakenham. 'It makes me sick! I could have done so much with such an assignment, whereas Petit will just churn out one of his usual scabby pieces.'

'Yet perhaps we should not hanker too fiercely after the Moleyns commission,' said Cristine. 'He was a criminal, and we have standards.' She glanced at Bartholomew. 'We saw him sneaking around the town in the dark when he should have been locked up. Twice, in fact.'

'Then tell the Sheriff,' suggested Bartholomew. 'It is something he will want to know.'

'We would rather not,' said Lakenham. 'He has a nasty habit of accusing us of theft every time our paths cross.'

'And murder,' added Cristine indignantly. 'He thinks

we killed Lucas, although we never did. Worse, he has made scant effort to find out who brained poor Reames. He was the only apprentice we had, and I cannot imagine how we will manage without him.'

Very easily, thought Bartholomew, if they failed to secure themselves new work. 'Did he hail from a wealthy family? His fine clothes suggested he did. Perhaps they will want a brass to honour his memory.'

'He was an orphan,' said Lakenham glumly. 'And the money left over from his inheritance will not buy him a funerary plate. It might have done, had he invested it with a goldsmith, but he insisted on squandering most of it on pretty tunics. Foolish boy!'

Bartholomew suddenly became aware that Petit was watching him, and as he had no wish to be interrogated about what had been said, he chose a route out of the church that would avoid the mason's clutches. It took him past Stanmore's vault. The hoist was finished, and beneath it sat the great granite slab that would be lifted into place once the bones were brought from the church-yard. Bartholomew was glad. Even if Petit took an age to complete the effigy, at least Oswald would soon lie in his final resting place.

Then he frowned. Was that blood on the lip of the hole? He went to look more closely, then started in shock when he saw Peres lying at the bottom with a knife protruding from his chest.

CHAPTER 9

It was not long before the little church thronged with people. Some carried lamps, as darkness had fallen outside. Petit huddled with his apprentices, wailing that he had been deprived of another beloved pupil, while Lakenham and Cristine stood side by side, watching their rivals with expressions that were difficult to read in the gloom. Then Vicar Frisby arrived.

'A second murder in this most holy of places,' he slurred, squinting at the body through bloodshot eyes, and almost toppling into the vault when he leaned over too far. 'Poor Stanmore! He must be wondering how many more interlopers will inhabit his grave before he gets the chance to use it himself.'

'Frisby has a point, Matt,' murmured Tulyet, as he helped Bartholomew to pull Peres up and lay him on the floor. 'You should arrange for Stanmore to be interred before someone else ends up down there.'

'You can do it next week,' sobbed Petit, overhearing. 'The granite slab will be ready to seal it up by Wednesday. Or perhaps Friday.'

'I shall have to resanctify the whole church now,' interjected Frisby crossly. 'Or is that the Bishop's prerogative? But he is in Avignon with the Pope, and might be gone for months, so how shall I earn a living in the interim? Hah! I know. Michael can do it. He is almost a prelate.'

'Did you notice anything amiss when you came to say Mass earlier?' asked Tulyet, obviously unimpressed that the vicar was more concerned with his own circumstances than the victim's.

'If I had, I would not have conducted the rite,' said

Frisby, intending piety but achieving only dissipation. 'It is my belief that Masses should never be performed with corpses in the vicinity. Except Requiem Masses, I suppose, when it is unavoidable.'

'When did *you* last see Peres?' asked Tulyet of the mason and his remaining lads.

'I sent him to buy a chisel,' replied Petit tearfully. 'Four or five hours ago now. I wondered what was taking him so long, but I never imagined he would be . . .'

'Four or five hours?' Tulyet turned back to Frisby. 'Were you in here the whole time?'

'No, I was in my house for most of it, praying.'

A titter of amusement rippled through his parishioners at the notion that their worldly priest would engage in anything remotely pious.

'So who was in the church when you arrived?' pressed Tulyet.

'No one,' replied Frisby. 'I began setting out my accoutrements, and the congregation trickled in, but they all stood in the nave. I do not let them into the sacred confines of the chancel while the Host is up here. It involves wine, you know, and they might try to take it.'

'What about the rest of you?' said Tulyet, addressing the assembled masses. 'Did you notice anything unusual when you came in?'

No one had. Meanwhile, Petit knelt next to Peres and began to go through his clothes.

'What are you doing?' asked Bartholomew in distaste.

'Looking for the new chisel,' replied the mason, then held up three coins. 'But here is the money I gave him for it, which means he was killed *before* he reached the market. He must have come to check Stanmore's vault first, and was ambushed here.'

'That makes sense,' nodded Tulyet. 'No one saw the killer, because he had been and gone before the Mass started. What about the knife? Does anyone recognise it?'

There were a lot of shaken heads, which was no surprise, given that it was cheap and unremarkable – the kind that could be bought anywhere for a few coins.

'Well, Lakenham?' asked Petit, unsteadily, still kneeling next to the body. 'Are you satisfied? Another of my boys dead at your hands.'

'Not ours,' said Lakenham firmly. 'We were in St Clement's all day, as Vicar Milde will attest. And you never liked Peres anyway, so you probably dispatched him yourself.'

'How, when I was in St Mary the Great with a dozen witnesses to prove it?' demanded Petit angrily, surging to his feet. 'But I know your game, Lakenham – you murdered Peres in the hope that my distress will lead me to refuse the Tynkell commission. Well, it will not work.'

The argument swayed back and forth, and Tulyet let it run in the hope that temper would lead to incriminatory slips. Bartholomew crouched down to examine Peres more closely. Like Lucas, it had not been a clean kill, and several vicious jabs had been inflicted before the fatal blow. He was about to cover him up when he noticed something caught in one of the boy's fingernails. It was a thread of an unusual shade of aqua.

'From his attacker?' asked Tulyet, peering at it.

Bartholomew nodded. 'I think so – his nail is torn, which suggests he snatched at his assailant in an effort to ward him off.'

'I have never seen anyone wearing an item of clothing this colour. However, it is distinctive, and I shall start my search for it in the tomb-makers' homes. When we have the garment, we shall have our killer.'

'You will have Peres' killer,' corrected Bartholomew. 'And perhaps Lucas's and Reames'. But not Moleyns', Tynkell's and Lyng's. That culprit is altogether more efficient.'

* * *

As Edith sold cloth, Bartholomew decided to ask her if she recognised the thread. He arrived at her house to find her sitting at a table surrounded by documents, which she was struggling to read by lamplight. She was delighted by the interruption, as she had never liked record-keeping. He sat by the fire and accepted a large piece of almond cake. Then he showed her the aqua fibre, and was disappointed when she shook her head.

'It did not come from here,' she said. 'And I do not mean just our warehouses – I mean Cambridge. It was dyed somewhere else.'

'You mean our killer is a visitor?' asked Bartholomew keenly.

'Or someone who lives here, but who bought it on a journey. Or had it sent.'

Bartholomew's brief surge of hope for an easy solution faded. 'Damn!'

They sat in silence for a while, enjoying the comfortable crackle of the fire and the scent of burning pine cones. Then Edith stood and fetched something from the table. It was an exemplar of a funerary brass.

'Lakenham made it for me. He says I should dismiss the masons, and put this on top of Oswald's tomb-chest instead of the carving that Petit is supposed to make. What do you think?'

He took it from her. It had been crafted with loving care, and the engraving caught perfectly the clothier's flowing robes and practical hat. Bartholomew was impressed.

'I think it is more tasteful than an effigy, and will be finished a lot sooner.'

'Then I shall inform Petit that his services are no longer required. He only has himself to blame – I have berated him countless times for not turning up when he promised, and so have you. I suspect others will follow my example, because everyone is fed up with his unreliability.'

'Then let us hope they do not all hire Lakenham, or we shall be back where we started.'

Edith smiled, then began to chat about her day. Bartholomew let the flow of words wash over him, his thoughts returning to Peres. Was the apprentice's murder connected to the serpent he had carved on Stanmore's tomb? Or was it just part of the rivalry between latteners and masons? Then something Edith was saying brought his attention back to her with a snap.

'What?'

'I *said* I was cross when I saw that Marjory Starre and her cronies had arranged for that nasty little snake to be etched into Oswald's grave. I know his faith wavered on occasion, but he was *not* one of them. I told her to get it removed immediately.'

Bartholomew stared at her. 'Do you think she asked Peres to do it? Is that why he went to St John Zachary instead of the market?'

'Well, he was a regular visitor to her house – for potions to remove his freckles, according to her, although they clearly did not work, so you have to wonder why he kept going back.'

'So he was a Satan-lover?'

'Or just deeply superstitious. It is not unusual, Matt – a blend of the Church and witchery is more common than you might think. After all, just look at Cynric. Would you call him a Satan-lover?'

'No, but he does not go around carving horned snakes on other people's tombs.'

'As far as you know,' said Edith drily.

'Who else adheres to these beliefs? Did Lyng, Tynkell or Moleyns?'

Edith shrugged. 'Well, if they did, it would explain why they all chatted so disrespectfully during Mass, and why Moleyns sometimes used it as an opportunity to steal his friends' purses. I told you about Widow Knyt, did I not? She found herself minus three shillings when Moleyns "accidentally" bumped into her in St Clement's Church.'

'What else can you tell me about witchery?'

'Nothing, Matt, but ask Cynric. He knows far more about these matters than I do.'

Bartholomew had the opportunity to speak to his book-bearer when he left Edith's house, because Cynric had been looking for him, and was waiting with a summons from a patient.

'Lots of folk visit Marjory for charms,' said Cynric, falling into step at his side. He kept one hand on the hilt of his long Welsh dagger, because the streets were never very safe after dark. 'It is common sense to hedge your bets, especially as Master Suttone says the plague will be back this summer. Only fools do not bother with precautions.'

'Did Tynkell and Lyng visit Marjory?' asked Bartholomew.

'Not that I saw, but she has a back door for customers who do not want to be seen. She is very discreet.'

'What about Moleyns?'

'I spotted him there several times, usually in the small hours of the morning. I assumed he was out with the Sheriff's blessing – he strutted about so confidently that it did not occur to me that he had escaped. Which is why no one ever reported him, of course.'

'Who else frequented her house? Barber Cook?'

'Yes – Cook buys her amulets to protect him from nasty diseases, which is wise for a man in his profession. You have some, too. I put them in your bag.'

'Lord!' muttered Bartholomew, not liking to imagine what his colleagues would say if they found them. He made a mental note to empty it out later, and burn them.

Cynric began to list all the people he had seen purchasing Marjory's wares, a roll that went on and on, but that comprised mostly townsfolk. Scholars, it seemed, were either more careful about being noticed, or were happy with the Church. Except one.

'Godrich?' echoed Bartholomew. 'Are you sure?'

'Of course. I cannot bear that man – he is too arrogant by half, and is deeply unpopular with his servants. He bought a spell to make sure he won the election, but I told Marjory to sell him one that does not work.'

Bartholomew rubbed his eyes, and wondered if she and Satan would take credit for selecting the next successful candidate, as well as the last one.

He and Cynric continued along Milne Street, aiming for the house at the end, where his patients – Robert and Yolande de Blaston and their sixteen children – lived. Unfortunately, there was a problem en route.

'Thieves,' said Master Braunch of Trinity Hall angrily, when Bartholomew demanded to know why the road was completely blocked by rubble that stood more than the height of two men. 'They stole the scaffolding from our new dormitory, which caused one entire end to collapse. Surely you heard it tumble? It made a tremendous din.'

'I did,' put in Cynric. 'But I assumed it was Chancellor Tynkell, trying to escape from his grave in St Mary the Great's churchyard.'

'Was anyone hurt?' asked Bartholomew, before the book-bearer could pursue that particular line of conversation any further.

Braunch crossed himself. 'No, thank God. But the wind has picked up, as you can no doubt feel, which helped to bring it down.'

'It cannot have been very well constructed then,' said Bartholomew, 'if a few gusts could knock it over.'

He thought, but did not say, that the collapse was a blessing in disguise. The building was huge, and would house a very large number of scholars. If it had fallen when it had been occupied, the carnage would have been terrible.'

Braunch shot him a baleful look. 'No, it was not, and it is the tomb-makers' fault. Benefactors are now more interested in commissioning grand memorials for themselves than making donations to worthy causes, so we are forced to cut corners in an effort to defray costs. Are you in a hurry, by the way? If so, you can scramble over the top.'

'I will give you a leg up, boy,' offered Cynric. 'But do not ask me to come over with you.'

It was patently unsafe to attempt such a feat, so Bartholomew declined, although it meant a considerable detour, even though he could see the Blastons' roof from where he stood. Cynric escorted him there, then disappeared on business of his own.

Yolande de Blaston supplemented her husband's income by selling her favours to the town's worthies. Edith had tried to reform her by providing employment as a seamstress, but sewing was not nearly as much fun, and Yolande had not plied a needle for long before returning to what she knew best.

'Good,' she said briskly, as she ushered Bartholomew inside her house. 'You have come to tend my bunion, Alfred's bad stomach, Tom's sore wrist, Robert's chilblains, Hugh's stiff knee and the baby's wind.'

'Oh,' said Bartholomew, daunted. 'Is that all?'

'No,' replied Yolande. 'But you can do the rest next time.'

He sat at the table and made a start, enjoying the lively chatter that swirled around him. The Blastons were among his favourite patients, and he loved the noisy chaos of their home. But then the discussion turned to the murders.

'Tynkell, Moleyns and Lyng were Satan's beloved,'

stated Blaston matter-of-factly. 'And Tynkell was not *fighting* him on the tower, but having a friendly romp – for fun.'

'I disagree,' said Yolande. 'Tynkell was not a man who enjoyed physical activity.' She spoke with confidence, as well she might, given that he had been one of her regulars. 'And I will hear nothing bad about Lyng. He gave us money for bread when times were hard last year. It was good of him.'

'But he had a vicious temper,' gossiped Blaston. 'I overheard a terrible row when I went to mend a table in Maud's Hostel. He was beside himself, and said some vile things.'

'When was this?' asked Bartholomew, surprised. He had never seen the elderly priest lose his equanimity. 'Recently?'

Blaston nodded. 'Thursday – the evening he went out and never came back.'

Bartholomew regarded him hopefully. 'What had upset him?'

'I could not hear everything, because he and whoever had annoyed him were upstairs, but the words "black villain" were howled, and so was "Satan". My first thought was that he was arguing with the Devil, but then I heard Lyng slap him. Well, no one belts Lucifer, so I was forced to concede that it was a person who had earned his ire. Hopeman, probably.'

Bartholomew blinked. 'And Lyng *hit* him? Are you sure it was not the other way around?'

'Quite sure, because I heard Lyng say "Take that, you black villain". I might have laughed, but I did not want him to hear and come to clout me as well.'

Bartholomew's mind was racing. 'What makes you think it was Hopeman?'

'Three reasons. First, he is a *Black* Friar. Second, he loves to rant about Satan. And third, he is a member of

Maud's, so was likely to be there. However, I did not see him, so I cannot be certain. They were in Lyng's room, you see, and I was in the kitchen.'

'Aidan should have mentioned this to Michael,' said Bartholomew crossly.

'He does not know – everyone but those two was out.' Blaston grinned. 'The punch hurt though, because Hopeman howled like a girl, and called Lyng a bully. Lyng! A bully!'

'So did Hopeman kill him for that slap?' asked Yolande, agog. 'Because he has learned from his experiences with Tynkell and Moleyns that he will never be caught?'

It was certainly possible, thought Bartholomew.

Bartholomew left the Blaston house, deep in thought. He could not imagine Lyng hitting anyone, yet Blaston had no reason to lie. Moreover, the Master of Valence Marie had expressed reservations about Lyng's character, while the mark on the elderly priest's foot suggested that there was rather more to him than simple appearances had suggested.

So *was* Hopeman the recipient of the slap? Bartholomew was inclined to think he was, for the same reasons that Blaston had given: because the conversation had revolved around his favourite topic; because "black villain" was an insult Lyng might well have levelled against a Dominican; and because both lived in Maud's. There was also the fact that Hopeman was argumentative, and could needle a saint into a quarrel.

Bartholomew was so engrossed in his thoughts that he did not see Thelnetham until they collided. The Gilbertine yelped, then bent to peer disgustedly at the mud on his habit.

'Watch where you are going, Matthew,' he said irritably. 'Or do you want me to lose the election by virtue of campaigning in a filthy robe?'

'It is only a smear.' Bartholomew smiled, to make amends. 'You spoke well earlier.'

'Thank you,' said Thelnetham. 'But I did not stop you to fish for compliments, no matter how deserving. I have been listening to rumours, and I heard a few things that might help you and Michael catch the villain who murdered our colleagues. The first is that Lyng and Tynkell were not devoted sons of the Church.'

'Yes,' sighed Bartholomew. 'I know.'

'Oh,' said Thelnetham, deflated. 'Do you? You do not seem very shocked.'

'Of course I am shocked,' said Bartholomew quickly, lest it was put about that he condoned such activities. 'But apparently, it is not as rare as we might think.'

'Neither is murder, apparently, but that does not make it acceptable.'

'No,' acknowledged Bartholomew. 'How did you find out?'

'Nicholas had the tale from one of his fellow clerks. Apparently, Tynkell had a diabolical mark on his wrist, while Moleyns and Lyng had them on their feet. They were seen proudly showing them off to each other in St Mary the Great.'

'Which clerk?' asked Bartholomew, knowing that Michael would want to question him.

'Nicholas refused to say, because it was told in confidence. Perhaps Michael will have better luck in prising a name from him, although do not hold your breath. Nicholas is not a man for betrayal.'

'No,' said Bartholomew. 'But—'

'Did you hear that terrible roar earlier? It was Satan, calling for his dead followers to rise from their graves and follow him. Fortunately, all have been buried deep, so they cannot oblige, although woe betide anyone who disturbs them with a spade.'

Bartholomew regarded him askance. 'What nonsense!

I am surprised at you, Thelnetham. I thought you were a man guided by reason.'

'I am, but not everything in this world can be understood by human minds, not even clever ones like ours. And if you want proof, then consider the mysteries of our own faith. Transubstantiation, for example. You would not imagine that it is possible for wine to become in substance the Blood of Christ, but it happens every time Mass is celebrated.'

'I suppose it does,' acknowledged Bartholomew.

Thelnetham pursed his lips. 'Of course, witchery is not all that connected Lyng, Tynkell and Moleyns.'

'You refer to Moleyns' manor,' predicted Bartholomew, 'which you visited last summer.'

'I passed *through* it last summer,' corrected Thelnetham. 'I did not stay there. My prior sent me on business to a Gilbertine cell nearby, but floods forced me to leave the main road and take a detour. In other words, it was chance that took me to Stoke Poges, not design.'

'You never did explain how you learned about Tynkell and the Stoke Poges' chapel. Did he tell you himself? Or confide in Nicholas?'

'No.' Thelnetham hesitated briefly before continuing. 'I met a young man when I stopped to water my horse there, and we . . . understood each other. I mentioned that our Sheriff is always looking for recruits who do not mind hard work . . .'

Bartholomew could well imagine the scene. Thelnetham sensing a kindred spirit, and encouraging him to migrate to a town where such liaisons were more readily accepted. 'And he acted on your advice?'

Thelnetham nodded. 'We have been friends ever since. It was he who told me about Tynkell and the chapel. He also mentioned that the village's motif is a pilgrim staff – the symbol I saw on that rider's saddle.'

Bartholomew regarded him uneasily. 'I do not suppose

this man was Yevele – the soldier who let Moleyns out at night? It makes sense that Moleyns would use a lad from his own manor for such business.'

Thelnetham grimaced. 'Yes, which means I bear some responsibility for what happened. Of course, I had no idea that Moleyns had blackmailed him until today . . .'

'Moleyns *blackmailed* him?'

'By threatening to expose his peccadillos. Moleyns said he just wanted to go out the once, but then he demanded a second excursion and a third, and poor Yevele was locked in a cycle of deceit. After Moleyns' death, he came to me in such terror that I gave him money to run away.'

'Are you sure that was wise? Dick Tulyet will be livid.'

'Of course it was not wise, Matthew, but it was the right thing to do. Yevele should not suffer because Moleyns was a rogue who preyed on the vulnerable.'

'Did Yevele tell you anything else?'

'Just that Moleyns murdered Egidia's uncle – Peter Poges – to get his hands on the manor, and that he was a villain who was corrupt to the core. Perhaps that roar was the Devil coming for *him*, because he is certainly the kind of man Satan would want in Hell.'

'What you heard was Trinity Hall's new dormitory tumbling down.'

'So you say,' muttered Thelnetham, crossing himself.

CHAPTER 10

The next day was Sunday, when there was a longer service in church, followed by a marginally nicer breakfast than that served during the rest of the week. Formal teaching was forbidden, but the University's masters knew better than to release hundreds of lively young men into the town with nothing to do, so some form of entertainment was always arranged. In Michaelhouse, it revolved around games, the reading of humorous tracts or mock disputations. The Fellows took turns to organise something, and that week Langelee ordered Kolvyle to oblige.

'I doubt he will best what you did last Sunday,' murmured Michael to Bartholomew. 'My theologians are still talking about *tenundum liberalis quam prandendum*. They tell me they have never laughed so much in all their lives.'

The debate had been about whether it was better to eat more at breakfast than at dinner, and Michael had been one of the disputants. The monk had been unable to bring himself to say that he might consume less at either, and the seriousness with which he took the question had amused the whole College. Afterwards, there had been ball games in the orchard for those with energy to burn, or a quiz on Aesop's fables for those of a more sedentary nature.

'Kolvyle does not have a comic bone in his body,' said Langelee. 'Perhaps it is because he knows nothing about camp-ball, which is a sure sign of an undeveloped mind.'

They processed to the church, where they were startled to discover that the lid to Wilson's tomb was gone, leaving behind an open chest containing a lot of rubbish left by the original mason. Scratches on the flagstones showed where the slab had been lugged to the door.

'Perhaps Petit took it away,' suggested William, as they all clustered around to look.

'He has not, because we agreed that he would work on it in situ,' said Langelee worriedly, 'to save on costs. Lord! I hope it has not been stolen.'

Michael's expression was grim. 'I imagine it has – and we cannot afford to replace it.'

'I heard that Isnard and Gundrede arrived home last night,' said Kolvyle slyly. 'Perhaps you should ask them if they took it.'

'I know how to investigate a crime, thank you,' said Michael sharply.

'Do you?' sneered Kolvyle. 'That is not how it seems to me. We have six unsolved murders, while robbers continue to make off with whatever they please. You are doing nothing about any of it. At least, nothing that is effective.'

He took his place in the chancel before Michael could respond, then stood with his head bowed, although Bartholomew was sure he could not be praying after such a spiteful tirade.

'I admire your patience, Brother,' growled William. 'I would box his ears if he spoke to me like that. Indeed, I am considering boxing them anyway, just for being an irritating—'

'I shall deal with him in my own way,' interrupted Michael shortly. '*Without* recourse to violence. He will not emerge the victor, never fear.'

It was Suttone's turn to officiate at the altar, but his performance was unusually lacklustre, and the students began to shuffle and fuss restlessly. He finished eventually, and Langelee led his scholars back to the College. The Fellows sat in silence for once, each sunk in his own concerns, although the students were lively, eagerly anticipating the entertainment that would soon begin. Bartholomew suspected they were going to be sadly disappointed.

Langelee intoned a final grace, and everyone left the hall for the servants to clear up. The Fellows – other than Kolvyle and Clippesby – stood together in the yard, chatting about their plans for the day. Langelee was due to play camp-ball that afternoon, and was looking forward to fighting his friends in the name of sport, while William planned to visit the Franciscan Friary. Both promised to use the occasions to secure Suttone more votes.

'I spent most of yesterday evening visiting hostels,' said Suttone. 'It was callous, I know, given that it was where Lyng was popular, but Godrich, Thelnetham and Hopeman started the moment they learned he was dead. At least I had the decency to wait for a few hours.'

'Do not allow scruples to hold you back,' advised William sternly. 'You must be as ruthless as your opponents, if you aim to win.'

'*More* ruthless,' corrected Langelee. 'I can give you plenty of tips in that direction, if you like. For example, Godrich is currently in the lead, so how about a rumour to disparage him? We can say he slept with the Queen when he was last at Court.'

'Did he?' asked Suttone wistfully. 'I do not blame him. She is a beautiful lady.'

Langelee reflected thoughtfully. 'I suppose that might raise him in the estimation of some. Perhaps we should say that he has formed an unnatural affection for his horse then.'

'No,' said Michael firmly. 'I cannot condone that sort of tactic. At least, not yet – we may have to review the situation come Wednesday.'

'Actually, we are doing quite well in the polls,' said

William. 'Especially after I went to the Austin Friary, and told them to vote for Suttone. They agreed – all twenty-seven of them.'

'Thank you, Father,' said Suttone, pleased.

'I told them that you were the only candidate who would know what to do in a second wave of the plague,' William went on. 'Unfortunately, I think I might have frightened them.'

'We must do anything – *anything* – to secure a victory,' said Langelee. 'So I shall visit a few fellow heads of house this morning. Godrich will be a disaster for them, because he will favour King's Hall, whereas Suttone will be impartial. At least, that is what I shall tell them.'

At that moment, Clippesby hurried up with Ethel, the College's lead hen, under one arm. 'You told Kolvyle to organise today's entertainment, Master,' he said, rather accusingly. 'But his idea of fun is to invite Hopeman to tell us why he should be Chancellor. May I be excused? Ethel says he is too obsessed with Satan to be pleasant company, and I agree.'

Suttone gaped at him. 'Hopeman plans to give an election speech in *my* College?'

Clippesby nodded. 'Along with Godrich and Thelnetham, so the event will be acrimonious as they all attack each other's stances. Ethel dislikes discord, and we would both rather spend the day with her flock.'

'Yes, go,' said Langelee, aware that letting visitors see a Fellow with a chicken on his lap was unlikely to do much for Michaelhouse's reputation as a foundation for serious learning. 'But not to the henhouse. Visit your friary, and persuade Morden to vote for Suttone.'

'I have already tried, but he will not go against a member of his own Order. Indeed, he is pressuring me to vote for Hopeman, too. But I shall stand by Suttone. He is the better man.'

'Even a slug is a better man than Hopeman,' growled

William. 'You should hear his nasty views on Apostolic Poverty.'

'You will,' predicted Clippesby, backing away. 'At noon, when he is due to arrive.'

'This is unacceptable,' wailed Suttone. 'I know it will make no difference to the election – Michaelhouse will vote for me no matter what the other candidates say here today – but that is beside the point.'

'Why did they agree to come?' asked Bartholomew, bemused. 'They know where our allegiance lies.'

'I imagine Kolvyle devised some spurious logic to convince them that it is in their best interests,' replied Michael, scowling. 'And we cannot turn them away, because it will look as though we think Suttone is unequal to the challenge of besting them. I am afraid Kolvyle has presented us with a *fait accompli.*'

'The slippery little toad,' spat Langelee. 'I am beginning to think the only way to muzzle him is to lock him in the cellar. One more stunt like this, and I shall do it.'

'Do it now,' begged Suttone. 'Before he loses me the election.'

'Not yet,' said Langelee. 'We shall have to let him put in an appearance at this debate, or the other candidates will assume that we were obliged to muzzle him because we cannot keep him in order. However, the moment it is over . . .'

'Three days,' said Michael. 'Then Suttone will be Chancellor, and we can all turn our attention to solving the nuisance that Kolvyle has become. It is not long to wait.'

'It feels like an eternity to me,' grumbled Suttone.

'Here is Kolvyle now,' said Langelee. He beckoned the youngster over, and launched into a lecture about College etiquette – which did not include Junior Fellows inviting outsiders to speak to the students without the Master's prior permission.

Kolvyle shrugged insolently. 'Our boys *should* see how poorly Suttone compares to Godrich. They have a right to know what sort of man Michaelhouse thinks should be in charge of the University.'

'There will be nothing wrong with my performance,' objected Suttone, stung.

Kolvyle looked him up and down, taking in the stained habit, plump face still dappled with crumbs from breakfast, and cloak that was rumpled from spending the night in a heap on the floor. Then he put his head in the air and stalked away without a word.

'Three days,' repeated Michael. 'Then that little snake will be gone. I swear it.'

'Good,' said Suttone, and turned to Bartholomew. 'I saw him talking to Edith late last night. She looked very cross, so you might want to make sure he did nothing to upset her. He despises us all, and would think nothing of striking at us through those we love.'

Alarmed, Bartholomew went to visit Edith as soon as his students had been settled in the hall with Kolvyle, whose idea of light entertainment until the would-be chancellors arrived was to read aloud from a variety of legal tomes. If William had not agreed to stand guard at the door, Bartholomew's classes would have been out, and there would have been nothing Kolvyle could have done to stop them.

Michael accompanied Bartholomew, because Edith's Sunday breakfasts were famous for their quality, and Agatha's egg-mash had not quite hit the spot that morning. It was another clear day, although bitterly cold, and the ruts in the road had frozen so hard that they made for treacherous walking. The yellowish quality of the light suggested there might be snow before too long.

They reached Milne Street to find Trinity Hall's rubble still lying across the road, although a narrow corridor had been cleared through the middle of it. The pathway was not wide enough for carts, but there was room for two pedestrians to pass each other – unless one of them happened to be Michael. The monk battled his way through, then grimaced when the first people they met on the other side were Godrich, Whittlesey and some King's Hall cronies.

'Tell Suttone to withdraw before he suffers an embarrassing defeat, Brother,' Godrich said gloatingly. 'Because Trinity Hall has just changed its mind about supporting him. It is astonishing how loyalty can be bought with the promise of funds for clearing up this mess.'

'Very honourable,' said Michael icily. 'Your family must be proud of you.'

Godrich shrugged. 'They understand expediency.'

'And does this expediency extend to dispatching your rivals?'

Godrich's manner went from smug to angry in the wink of an eye. 'You cannot prove I had anything to do with Lyng's death, and you will be sorry if you use it to stop me from winning.'

'Yet you do not deny the accusation,' mused Michael.

'Of course I deny it!' cried Godrich. 'You twist my words.'

'Easy,' said Whittlesey, coming to place a warning hand on his cousin's shoulder. 'You will gain nothing by challenging the Senior Proctor. Besides, he knows you are innocent of these crimes.'

'Do I indeed?' murmured Michael. 'That is interesting to hear.'

'I will be Chancellor in three days,' said Godrich, reining in his temper with difficulty. 'And the first thing I shall do is appoint a *new* Senior Proctor. The University will be very different in the future.'

'You think you can oust me?' asked Michael, amused by the notion.

'It will not be necessary to oust you – you will go to Rochester of your own accord. Your successor will be Geoffrey Dodenho.'

Dodenho stepped forward to bow, and Bartholomew struggled to mask his dismay. The King's Hall man was decent enough, but wholly unsuitable for such a demanding post. Godrich shot Michael a gloating sneer, and led his friends away, although Whittlesey lingered.

'Godrich is tenacious, dedicated and energetic,' he said quietly. 'He rose before dawn to begin visiting hostels with a view to securing their support. Can Suttone say the same?'

'He was in church, dedicating his time to God, not his own interests,' retorted Michael, overlooking the fact that the Carmelite had then returned to College and consumed a leisurely breakfast. 'And Godrich is not the sort of person we want in charge.'

Whittlesey frowned. 'Of course he is. I have just listed his virtues and—'

'He is my chief suspect for killing Tynkell, Lyng and Moleyns,' interrupted Michael. 'So you might want to distance yourself from him while you can. It will do your own career no good to be associated with a murderer.'

Whittlesey gaped at him. 'Godrich is no murderer! I would stake my life on it.'

'You *are* staking your life on it,' retorted Michael, 'because who knows who will be next for a burin in the heart? Besides, it is not your place to meddle in University affairs.'

Whittlesey gave him a pitying smile. 'Do you honestly believe that? Powerful men are impressed by what you have achieved here, and they do not want your work undone. My remit was not only to tell you of your good fortune and bring you safely to Rochester, but also to ensure that your departure does not leave a dangerous void.'

'Then do not foist Godrich on us. Suttone will be a much more—'

'Suttone will not be as malleable as you think,' warned Whittlesey. He forced a smile. 'But let us not quarrel. You will see I am right in time.'

He patted the monk on the shoulder, and hurried after his cousin.

'What powerful people is he talking about?' asked Bartholomew, also resenting the envoy's interference. 'Courtiers? I do not think it matters what they think.'

'He means the bishops, who have a vested interest in both universities, because it is where their priests are trained.'

They continued on their way, and were just passing St John Zachary when the door opened and Egidia flounced out, Inge at her side. Frisby was behind her, grinning in delight, while Tulyet brought up the rear, his face as black as thunder.

'A toast!' Frisby declared, producing a wineskin. His flushed face and bright eyes suggested that he had probably done this several times already. 'To our agreement.'

'What agreement?' asked Michael warily.

'The one that says Sir John Moleyns will have his tomb here, in *my* church,' replied Frisby happily. 'Because of his name.'

'John,' explained Egidia, lest the scholars had not made the connection. 'St Mary the Great is getting rather full, what with Dallingridge, Godrich *and* Chancellor Tynkell destined to bag great swathes of space there, so Inge and I looked to see what else was available.'

'I dislike the mess masons make, of course,' slurred Frisby. 'But the King himself is likely to visit his dear friend Moleyns, so it will be worth the inconvenience. His Majesty will reward me handsomely if I oversee the provision of a suitable monument.'

'No doubt,' said Tulyet between gritted teeth. 'But *I* am not paying for it.'

'Oh, yes, you are,' countered Egidia sharply. 'You failed to protect him from killers, so it is the least you can do.'

'I have not forgotten the horseman who galloped away moments after his death,' said Michael. 'The one whose saddle bore the Stoke Poges insignia. Are you *sure* he was not carrying messages from you to the villagers, informing them about a change of circumstances?'

'Yes, we are sure,' said Inge tightly. 'As we told you the first time you asked.'

'Because he rode out so soon after the murder that I am left wondering if he knew it was going to happen,' Michael continued. 'And—'

'That is ridiculous,' interrupted Inge sharply. 'And now, you must excuse us, because we have important business to attend.'

'You will not catch them out, Brother,' said Tulyet, watching them strut away. 'Believe me, I have tried. Inge is far too slippery and Egidia is guided by him. If you really think they are the culprits, we must find another way to trap them.'

'Like finding the woman in the embroidered cloak and asking her to identify the culprit,' said Michael pointedly.

Tulyet inclined his head. 'I shall make a concerted effort to track her down today. Incidentally, I hear you lost a tomb lid last night, just as Isnard and Gundrede returned from the Fens. Curious, eh?'

Edith was at home when Bartholomew and Michael arrived, readying her household for Mass in St John Zachary, and all was noisy chaos. The younger apprentices stood in a chattering line to have their faces and hands inspected for cleanliness, while the servants were hurrying to finish their chores before it was time to leave. Bartholomew went to the solar to wait until she was free, which suited Michael very well, as it was where breakfast had been laid.

'What did Kolvyle say to you last night?' asked Bartholomew, when Edith came to see what they wanted. He spoke quickly, to distract her from the fact that Michael had made rather significant inroads into her household's victuals. 'Suttone thought he might have upset you.'

'He *did* upset me,' said Edith shortly. 'He told me that your College has hired Petit to fix Wilson's tomb, which will slow down progress on Oswald. He says it shows that you love Michaelhouse more than you love me.'

'It was Langelee who hired Petit,' said Michael, while Bartholomew marvelled that the young scholar should be so vindictive. 'Matt had nothing to do with it.'

'I know that,' said Edith impatiently. 'And I told Kolvyle exactly what I think of sneaky youths who bray lies about my brother. He will not come *here* trying to make trouble again, the loathsome little worm!'

'And you need not worry about Wilson interfering with Oswald anyway,' said Bartholomew. 'Because his ledger slab was stolen last night. You did not take it, did you?'

Edith laughed. 'I think it might be a little too heavy for me to tote around. However, it does not matter anyway, because I dismissed Petit this morning. I have hired Lakenham instead, and Oswald will have a nice brass in place of an effigy.'

Her steward called up the stairs at that moment, to say that everyone was ready to leave. Bartholomew and Michael followed her to the yard, where she gave her household one last inspection to ensure that all was in order, then led the way out on to the street.

'Go with her, Matt,' instructed Michael. 'The tomb-makers attend St John Zachary, so try to find out which of them stole Wilson's lid. We cannot afford another, so it is vital that we get it back.'

'You do not believe Isnard took it, then?' asked Bartholomew, not sure how he was expected to solve a theft when the Senior Proctor and Sheriff had tried and failed.

'He would never act against Michaelhouse – he loves the choir too much. Of course, he is bitter about the fact that I shall soon be unavailable to lead it, and he listens to that rogue Gundrede far too much for his own good . . .'

'Where will you be while I am doing your work?' asked Bartholomew. He was unwilling to accept that Isnard would steal from their church, even if Michael was wavering.

'King's Hall. I plan to bribe a porter to let me search Godrich's room.'

Obediently, Bartholomew hurried to St John Zachary, where Frisby was thundering wine-scented greetings to his parishioners. Inside, he saw Lakenham and Cristine inspecting Stanmore's tomb in readiness for beginning work on it the following day, so he went to speak to them first. However, he had only just stepped into the chancel when he found himself surrounded by Petit and his apprentices.

'No one cancels my commissions,' the mason hissed angrily. 'So tell your sister to take me back, or Stanmore will not be in his tomb alone for long – *you* will join him there.'

'It is your own fault,' said Bartholomew, more irritated than unnerved by the threat. 'You should have kept your promises.'

'I *did* keep them,' snarled Petit. 'But laymen do not understand how long these things take. And it is stupid to dismiss me now, just when the end is in sight.'

Bartholomew was sure it was nothing of the kind. 'The decision has been made,' he said coolly. 'So that is that.'

'Well, she is not getting her deposit back,' flashed Petit.

'Wilson's ledger slab,' said Bartholomew, watching the masons intently as he embarked on what he suspected would be a futile set of questions. 'It has been stolen, but it can never be resold, because every church in the country knows that particular piece of stone. It is unique.'

It was a lie, but two of the apprentices exchanged an uneasy glance, while he thought there was a flicker of alarm in Petit's eyes. Of course, furtive reactions were not evidence of guilt, and more than that was needed to see them charged with its theft. With a final glower, Petit led his lads away, but they had barely left the chancel before Lakenham and Cristine came to stand at Bartholomew's side.

'Did they accuse *us* of stealing your stone?' demanded Cristine angrily. 'Because we never did. We have been nowhere near St Michael's. However, we lost two big boxes of brass nails, three hammers and a bucket of pitch last night. We are sure *they* took them.'

'It is easy to target us now that Reames is dead, you see,' explained Lakenham. 'He used to sleep in our supplies shed – which is why they killed him, of course.'

Bartholomew was inclined to believe them over the belligerent Petit. Or was he wrong to base his suspicions on the fact that he liked the latteners more than the masons? He asked more questions but learned nothing of relevance, and turned to leave. Then he jumped in shock when he saw Edith's steward standing in the shadows, so still and silent that he might have been an effigy himself. The man abandoned his hiding place when he saw he had been spotted.

'Edith sent me over when she saw Petit corner you,' he explained. 'But the hero of Poitiers needed no help from me.'

'Look after her,' said Bartholomew softly. 'I do not trust Petit.'

'He will come nowhere near her, never fear.' A determined gleam lit the steward's eyes. 'We will get her deposit back and all.'

When Bartholomew left the church, he walked to the river for no reason other than a desire to stand quietly and think for a while. The lane he chose happened to be the one that led to Michaelhouse's pier, which had been a busy dock just a few weeks earlier. Now all that remained was a mess of charred timbers. He was surprised to see a boat moored to one of its scorched bollards – a boat containing Isnard and Gundrede.

'What are you doing?' he called. 'You know you should not be there.'

The structure had been deemed unsafe by the town's worthies, and river traffic was forbidden to use it. However, it was by far the best place to unload goods bound for the Market Square, so some bargemen surreptitiously flouted the ban. Bartholomew supposed he should have guessed that Isnard, with his cavalier disregard both for authority and his own safety, would be one of them.

'Just looking, Doctor,' the bargeman replied airily, beginning to cast off. 'That blaze made quite a mess of this poor quay. When will you be getting it mended?'

Never, thought Bartholomew glumly, unless a wealthy benefactor could be persuaded to pay for it. However, Michaelhouse's Fellows were not in the habit of making their financial difficulties public, so he asked a question instead.

'Have you heard that part of Wilson's tomb was stolen from our church?'

'A vile act of desecration,' declared Isnard, while Gundrede busied himself with the ropes and refused to look at the physician. 'I hope the Sheriff catches the rogue responsible.'

With a cheerful wave, he poled the boat away, meaning

that Bartholomew either had to drop the matter or bawl his next question at the top of his voice. He watched the little craft skim away, wondering what the pair had been doing at the wharf in the first place.

Michael's illicit visit to Godrich's quarters had yielded two discoveries of interest. First, a scroll itemising all the bribes that had been promised in exchange for votes – so many he was sure that Godrich could not possibly make good on them all. Unfortunately, the disappointed parties would already have voted him into power by the time they realised that he had no intention of honouring the pledges he had made.

The second was a letter from Dallingridge, written shortly before his death. It stated unequivocally that he *had* been fed a toxin, and a list of suspects was appended. It comprised many people Michael did not know, but a number he did, including Kolvyle, Egidia, Inge, the tomb-makers and Barber Cook. Whittlesey's name was also there, and Godrich was instructed to ignore any claim the envoy might make about being nowhere near Nottingham on Lammas Day. Dallingridge was sure Whittlesey was lying, and Godrich should ask himself why the envoy should feel the need for such brazen untruths.

Michael was not sure why Dallingridge should have chosen to confide in Godrich, of all people, but the answer came at the very end of the missive: Dallingridge had asked Godrich to draft out his will, on the grounds that he was neither kin nor a close friend, and therefore could not expect a legacy. However, judging by the way the letter had been screwed up into a tight ball – the monk had found it under the bed, where it had evidently rolled after being tossed away in a rage – Michael suspected that Godrich *had* entertained hopes of a reward, and had been vexed when he had learned that he was not going to get one.

Godrich therefore could not be eliminated from Michael's list of suspects for the murders in Cambridge. Or for Dallingridge's death in Nottingham, for that matter.

The monk was back in Michaelhouse by noon, ready to ask Godrich about the letter when he arrived to address the students. The other Fellows joined him in the yard, although Kolvyle lingered in his room, primping. Suttone came from the kitchens. He had been at the wine, perhaps for courage, so his cheeks were flushed, while his best habit had suffered a mishap in the laundry and was too tight around his middle. His boots were muddy, and the book he held in an attempt to appear erudite was one on arithmetic, which everyone knew he would not have read. Bartholomew itched to take him aside and brush him down, disliking the slovenly spectacle he presented.

Thelnetham was the first to arrive, smart, clean and businesslike in a pristine robe. He was ushered in with genuine pleasure by Walter – the Gilbertine had been quietly generous to the College staff, and had often slipped them gifts of money and food. He looked around fondly.

'You have repaired the conclave roof, I see,' he said amiably. 'It must be nice to sit there of an evening, and not feel the patter of rain on your heads.'

'It is,' agreed William stiffly. He loathed Thelnetham, and hated seeing him in the College again. 'And Stanmore bequeathed a sum of money for fuel, so we have fires most nights.'

'It sounds positively luxurious,' drawled Thelnetham. 'What about the food? Has that improved, or is Agatha still in charge?'

'Lower your voice, man,' hissed Langelee. 'She might hear, and then you will never be Chancellor, because you will be dismembered.'

Thelnetham shuddered. 'True, and living in terror of her is one thing about Michaelhouse that I have definitely *not* missed.'

'She will be vexed if you defeat me in this election,' warned Suttone, a sly move that had Langelee and William nodding their approval. 'She likes the idea of a Michaelhouse man in charge.'

'I shall bear it in mind,' replied Thelnetham. He turned to Michael. 'I know you think you will continue to rule the University through Suttone when you are in Rochester, but such an arrangement will be a disaster. We need a Chancellor who can make pronouncements instantly, not one who needs to wait for an exchange of letters.'

Michael laughed. 'The University has never made a rapid decision in its life, and if you aim to indulge in that sort of madness, you should withdraw before you do us any harm.'

'Besides, you underestimate me,' said Suttone, hurt. 'I *can* run the University alone.'

'Of course you can,' sneered Thelnetham, with such sarcastic contempt that everyone was reminded of why he had been so difficult to like. Then he turned his back on Suttone and addressed Michael again. 'Have you caught the killer yet?'

'No,' replied Michael coolly. 'But I have a number of leads.'

'Good,' said Thelnetham, although Bartholomew suspected the monk was lying, purely because he could not bring himself to admit that he was stumped. 'It is not comfortable knowing that there is someone walking around who likes to shove knives into people.'

'Not knives – a burin,' said Michael.

'You mean one of those pointed things used for engraving?' asked Thelnetham. 'Then surely the case should be easy to solve? There cannot be many people who own such items.'

'You would be surprised,' sighed Michael. 'They feature in the toolboxes of most craftsmen, and even Deynman the librarian has one – he uses it to clean the locks on his books.'

Thelnetham was thoughtful. 'Then I imagine horsemen have them, too, for prising stones from hoofs, which is what I saw Godrich doing yesterday. He was using a long metal spike.'

'Really?' asked Michael keenly. 'Now that is most interesting.'

A short while later, the gate was flung open and Godrich strode in. He had not knocked, and he did not wait for Walter to conduct him across the yard, which precipitated a murmur of resentment from his hosts. He had brought Whittlesey with him, who shrugged apologetically behind his back – he appreciated College etiquette, even if his kinsman did not.

'Dallingridge,' said Michael, irked by the impertinence and so launching an attack. 'Tell me about your association with him.'

'What association?' asked Godrich contemptuously. 'There was none.'

'Oh, yes, there was,' countered Michael. 'He wrote you letters and you drafted out his will.' He assumed a haughty expression when he received a sharp glance of suspicion. 'I have spies in many places, so please do not lie to me. I will always know.'

Godrich sighed angrily. 'I had forgotten about the will – it was an insignificant incident that took place months ago. And perhaps he did write me a note burbling about poison and suspects for his murder. However, I did not take it seriously, as he was clearly out of his wits. Why do you—'

'Were you in Nottingham on Lammas Day?' demanded Michael, including Whittlesey in the question.

'No,' replied Godrich shortly. 'I was in Derby, running an errand for King's Hall.'

'And I was on diocesan business in Leicester,' said Whittlesey mildly. 'As I have told you before. I am sure our Benedictine brethren will confirm it, should you wish to offend your new envoy by declining to believe him.'

'Of course I believe him,' said Michael flatly, and renewed his assault on Godrich before Whittlesey could remark that it did not sound as if he did. He changed the subject abruptly in an effort to disconcert. 'Show me the tool you use for tending your horse's hoofs.'

Godrich blinked his bemusement. 'What tool? And why should I—'

'I am conducting a murder investigation here,' interrupted Michael sharply. 'I shall arrest you if you refuse to cooperate.'

'No one is refusing,' said Whittlesey quickly. 'Let him see it, Godrich. Clearly, he aims to eliminate you as a suspect, and this will help.'

Godrich scowled, but he opened the pouch at his side and pulled out a short nail.

'You had a different one yesterday,' said Thelnetham. 'It was longer and thinner.'

The look Godrich gave him would have intimidated the boldest of souls, although Thelnetham held it without flinching. With ill grace, Godrich produced a spike that was as long as his hand, topped off with a wooden handle. Bartholomew inspected it carefully, ignoring the impatient sighs of those waiting for his verdict.

'It might be the murder weapon,' he said eventually. 'It is the right size and shape. But I cannot be certain. However, there is dried blood here—'

'Horse blood,' said Godrich, snatching it back. 'And you cannot prove otherwise.'

'You might want to be careful, Michael,' advised

Whittlesey softly, as Godrich stalked away. 'It is unwise to accuse powerful scholars of murder.'

'I accused him of nothing,' countered Michael. 'I merely asked to inspect his burin.'

'It is not a burin – it is a hoof-pick.' Whittlesey lowered his voice even further. 'I mean what I say, Brother. I should hate to see you fall before you are consecrated, simply for the want of a little discretion. I speak as a friend – which I hope we are, despite the reservations you evidently still hold about my whereabouts on Lammas Day.'

'Dallingridge's reservations,' said Michael. 'Expressed in a letter to Godrich.'

Whittlesey raised his hands in a shrug. 'From what I hear, the poor man was raving in his final days. You would be wise to ignore anything he might have written.'

Michael inclined his head, then glared at Bartholomew once his fellow monk had hurried across the yard to prevent Godrich from entering the hall without the Master's invitation.

'It was our chance to arrest the killer, and you let it slip away,' he hissed accusingly. 'You *know* that was the burin that killed Tynkell, but you refused to say so.'

'I know nothing of the kind,' countered Bartholomew crossly. 'And you would not thank me if I gave a verdict to please you, and it later transpired that Godrich was innocent.'

'He tried to conceal the weapon,' said Michael between gritted teeth. 'That was suspicious. *And* there was blood on it. That should have been enough.'

'I agree with Matthew, Brother,' said Thelnetham with quiet reason. 'It is better to wait for something less ambiguous.'

He might have added more, but the gate opened a third time, and Hopeman stepped through. His deacons were behind him, and there was an unseemly scuffle when Walter refused to let them pass.

'Hey, you!' bellowed Hopeman, stabbing a furious fore-finger at Langelee. 'Either allow my disciples to accompany me, or I am leaving.'

'Leave,' shrugged Langelee. 'It makes no difference to me. Come, Suttone. Let us go and show everyone who is the superior candidate.'

Suttone looked anything but superior as he trailed after his Master, leaving Bartholomew to wonder if Thelnetham was right to question the Carmelite's ability to rule. Anger suffused Hopeman's face at the dismissive treatment, and he surged forward to grab Langelee's arm.

'I am God's agent on Earth,' he boomed. 'You will afford me the respect I deserve.'

'I *did* afford you the respect you deserve,' retorted Langelee, freeing his arm firmly. 'What I did not afford you was the respect you *think* you deserve.'

The students were expecting entertainment to rival the fun they had enjoyed the previous week, so their faces fell when Suttone, Thelnetham, Godrich and Hopeman – the latter sans disciples – strode towards the dais. It would be a good test of the candidates' strength of character, thought Bartholomew, if they could keep his lively lads in order – he could already see them exchanging the kind of glances that suggested mischief was in the offing. But he had reckoned without Aungel.

'No!' hissed the senior student fiercely. 'You will *not* risk our reputation by misbehaving in front of guests from other foundations.' Bartholomew was pleasantly pleased by his responsible stance, until Aungel added, 'I am supposed to be in charge of you, and any loutish antics might hurt my chances of a Fellowship.'

Bartholomew studied the four men while they waited for Langelee to call the audience to order. Hopeman stood with his hands on his hips, his dark gaze sweeping disdainfully across the assembly. Godrich leaned nonchalantly against the wall, inspecting his fingernails in an attitude of calculated boredom. Thelnetham looked smug, clearly of the opinion that this was an encounter he would win. And Suttone was visibly daunted by the ordeal that was about to commence, an unease that intensified when Thelnetham whispered something in his ear. Bartholomew grimaced: undermining the confidence of a nervous rival was cruel, and should have been beneath a man of Thelnetham's stature.

'This "entertainment" will not hold the students' interest for long,' murmured Langelee to Kolvyle. 'So I hope you are ready to step in with an alternative when they grow restless.'

'You would doubtless prefer to see them racing about on a camp-ball field, punching the stuffing out of each other,' scoffed Kolvyle. 'I cannot imagine why you were ever installed as Master. You are a lout, with the intellectual agility of a gnat.'

Langelee was so astonished by the insult that he could do no more than gape as Kolvyle strutted to the front of the hall. By rights, it should have been the Master himself who opened the proceedings, but Kolvyle had hopped on to the dais while Langelee was still standing in mute disbelief. An immediate hush descended on the gathering.

'The impudent bastard!' breathed Langelee, finding his voice at last. 'I will trounce—'

'Not in front of visitors,' whispered Michael sharply. 'Wait until they have left.'

'He has gone too far this time,' hissed Langelee furiously. 'He will apologise or pack his bags.'

'Which is exactly how he wants you to react,' warned Michael. 'And when he has needled you into a confrontation, during which you will say or do something rash, he will use it to make a bid for the mastership. We

256

prevented him from standing as Chancellor, so he has decided to go for the next best thing.'

'Well it will not work,' determined Langelee, fists clenched. 'He is the last man I want as my successor. Not that I have any plans to resign just yet.'

'Good,' said Michael. 'Then do not let him manipulate you.'

Kolvyle did not speak immediately, but let the anticipation mount. When he did start, his voice oozed arrogance and conceit, and resentment rose from the students in waves.

'As commensurate with a foundation that aims to promote education, learning and research,' he began pompously, 'I have organised a superior form of diversion today – something more significant than silly debates or boisterous games. Namely the choice of our next Chancellor.'

'That is very good of you,' called Deynman the librarian, never one to be daunted by a sense of occasion. 'But we are not eligible to vote. Only the Fellows are, so it does not matter if we are impressed or not, because we cannot elect them anyway.'

Kolvyle smiled stiffly. 'Yes, but the outcome affects you all, and it is my contention that you have the right to make your opinions known. You can do this by lobbying your masters – to *make* them choose the candidate *you* want.'

'We want Suttone,' called Aungel dutifully. 'Because he is a Michaelhouse man.'

'Yes, he is,' agreed Kolvyle, turning to look the nervous Carmelite up and down. 'But will he best serve your interests? You are not yet in a position to know, because you have not heard what the other candidates have to say. That will be rectified today, and once the other foundations have seen what we have done, they will follow our example.'

Hopeman looked uneasy, Thelnetham was impassive, while Godrich fingered the heavy purse at his side with a meaningful smile. Suttone was ashen-faced though, desperately racking his brains for policies that would encourage his supporters to stay loyal.

'Students are entitled to a voice,' Kolvyle went on. 'And I aim to ensure that it is heard. You have been at the mercy of the Fellows for far too long, but a new age is dawning, when younger men, like myself, will lead the University to a more enlightened future.'

'You make our Regent masters sound like old men,' called Deynman. 'They are not. Well, Suttone has grey hair, I suppose, but you should see Master Langelee racing around the camp-ball field, while Doctor Bartholomew could not tend so many patients if he was ancient.'

'Grey hair signifies experience and wisdom,' said Suttone sharply, offended. 'The chancellorship is not a post that should be occupied by some selfishly ambitious greenhorn.'

'Quite,' agreed Thelnetham. 'He should have been a member of the University for at least three years, so he knows its strengths and weaknesses.'

'Rubbish,' countered Godrich, who was also a relative newcomer and so did not fulfil this particular condition. 'The only thing that is important is an ability to secure large donations.'

'The only thing that is important is combatting evil,' countered Hopeman hotly. 'Money will be irrelevant if our University is suppressed because Satan is in charge.'

Thelnetham opened his mouth to join the debate, but Kolvyle took command again.

'Suttone will speak first,' he said, 'because this is his College. I shall decide on the order for the others when he has finished. Right. Off you go.'

The order came so abruptly that the hapless Carmelite was left gaping stupidly while he rallied his thoughts.

Then he began a wretched, rambling discourse that had his rivals grinning superiorly. Except Thelnetham, who had the grace to wince on his behalf.

'Well, there you have it,' drawled Kolvyle, when Suttone eventually stuttered to a halt. 'You next, Hopeman.'

'I speak at *God's* command, not yours,' declared Hopeman. 'I will not play your games.'

Kolvyle addressed his audience. 'It is generally claimed that Hopeman is a zealot with untenable views on theology. If he is happy with that summary of his abilities, we shall move to our next speaker.'

'Lord, he is sly!' murmured Michael grudgingly. 'How can Hopeman remain silent now?'

The Dominican could not, and launched into a diatribe that was unnerving both in its intensity and the distasteful prejudice of its opinions. It was accompanied by a lot of finger wagging, and it was not long before William could bear it no longer.

'You are a fool, Hopeman,' he boomed, using the voice he reserved for his own feisty orations. 'And the Devil must be delighted to have gained such a faithful servant.'

'No interruptions!' snapped Kolvyle, before the Dominican could respond. 'I shall invite comments from the audience afterwards, but they cannot be abusive, and they must contain at least a modicum of intelligent analysis. However, I think we have heard enough from Hopeman. Godrich? Would you care to respond to the issues our Dominican has raised?'

'I would not debase myself by acknowledging them,' declared Godrich loftily. 'But I have plenty to say about how the statutes might be adapted to suit our current needs. They were drafted more than a century ago, and it is time they were modernised.'

'That man is a damned fool!' hissed Michael angrily. 'The statutes are what keep our University together – sensible rules devised by rational men.'

'Women,' began Godrich, immediately snagging the students' attention. 'They are forbidden to us, but I shall change that stricture when I am in power. Being scholars does not make us priests, and it is ridiculous to force us to live celibate lives.'

This raised a cheer from Bartholomew's lads, although Michael's monastics maintained a disapproving silence.

'But that was *my* idea,' cried Suttone, dismayed. 'I forgot to mention it in my speech just now, but *I* was the one who first suggested—'

'You had your turn, Suttone,' interrupted Kolvyle sharply. 'So shut up and allow Godrich the same respect he afforded you by listening to him in silence.'

He indicated that Godrich should resume, nodding encouragingly. The King's Hall man spoke well, and Suttone shrivelled further with every word. Bartholomew felt for him, especially as Godrich was a noted hater of women, and had started his campaign by mocking Suttone's recommendation that the rules regarding them be relaxed.

'There,' said Kolvyle, when Godrich had finished. 'Are there any questions before we end this session and move on to the next stage?'

'I have one,' said Thelnetham mildly. 'Have you forgotten me?'

Kolvyle regarded him disparagingly. 'You want to speak, do you? Very well, but make it brief. We cannot waste time.'

It was rude, as well as patently unfair, but the Gilbertine rose to the challenge, and laughter soon reverberated around the hall. Kolvyle's face was stony, while the other candidates were openly envious at the applause that marked the end of Thelnetham's speech – a short one, because the Gilbertine also knew when to stop. Then Bartholomew felt someone tugging at his sleeve. It was Clippesby, red-faced, sweaty and breathless.

'I went to my friary, as Langelee ordered,' he whispered. 'And I got talking to a couple of cockerels. It seems that Hopeman had a very fierce argument with Lyng on Thursday night, after which Lyng stalked off towards the Trumpington road.'

Michael frowned. 'Are you telling us that Hopeman killed Lyng?'

'No, Brother,' replied Clippesby. 'I am telling you that they quarrelled the night he died. The cockerels did not witness this fight themselves, though – Almoner Byri did, and they overheard him telling Prior Morden about it. Apparently, it was a very savage row, and threats were made . . .'

'What threats?' demanded Michael.

'Hopeman said that he would sooner kill Lyng than let him be Chancellor – he genuinely believes that God guides his wild opinions, you see. The cockerels are afraid that Hopeman realised Lyng was the most popular candidate, and decided to eliminate him . . .'

'Well, then,' said Michael, 'we had better visit Byri and have this tale from the horse's mouth before tackling Hopeman with it.'

'The horses were not there,' said Clippesby seriously. 'Just the cockerels. But wear your warmest cloaks. The wind is getting up again, and it is bitterly cold. Ethel says there will be snow soon.'

'I will come with you, Brother,' said Bartholomew. He nodded towards the dais. 'I do not think I can stand any more of this.'

CHAPTER 11

A Dominican Priory had been founded in Cambridge not long after that Order had first arrived in the country, and its founders had chosen a site east of the town, rather than in the centre, like the Carmelites, Austins and Franciscans. This meant it had been free to expand unfettered by constraints of space, and so was enormous. It was centred around its beautiful church, which rivalled St Mary the Great in size and splendour. Other buildings included a refectory and dormitories for its sixty or so priests, and a range of sheds, pantries, storerooms and stables.

The lay-brother who answered the gate invited them to wait by the fire in his lodge while he went to announce their arrival to Prior Morden. His kindness came with a caveat, though.

'And no stealing my bread and cheese, Brother. I know exactly how much there is, and will notice if any is missing.'

'He seems to have a very odd impression of me,' said Michael when the man had gone. 'Does he really imagine that I wander around the town scoffing whatever I happen to find?'

Eventually, they were conducted across the garden to the Prior's House, an elegant edifice that had been built that summer, and that was larger than many hostels. It had a tiled roof, and its walls were stone. Michael had developed a mischievous habit of entering the old one by flinging open the door hard enough to startle its occupant – a practice that nearly always resulted in damage to the wall. However, Morden had evidently taken this into account when he had designed his new parlour, so Michael thrust open the door with his customary vigour, only to have it snap back at him, landing him a painful crack on the nose.

'Do come in, Brother,' said Morden, struggling to keep a straight face.

He was in company with Almoner Byri, a plump man with white hair, who leaned against the wall while tears of mirth rolled down his plump cheeks. Bartholomew saw the door had been fitted with a thin strip of metal, which meant it would always spring back at the opener – and the harder it was pushed, the more violently it would return. The Dominicans were famous for their love of practical jokes.

'This is dangerous,' he said disapprovingly. 'You could hurt someone.'

'They *have* hurt someone,' said Michael nasally. 'I feel as though I have been punched, and the Senior Proctor can levy fines for that sort of thing.'

'It is only a bit of fun,' said Morden. He was sitting on a stool behind his desk, which had been piled high with cushions; his little legs swung in the empty space below them. 'Where is your sense of humour?'

'There is nothing amusing about visitors' noses being mashed into the back of their skulls,' growled Michael. 'I have cautioned you about these pranks before.'

'You are as bad as Hopeman,' said Morden, rolling his eyes. 'He is all grim business and no play, too. However, we only deployed that device when we heard you were here, Brother. My walls are new, and I do not want them dented by one of your forceful arrivals.'

'Here is some wine to make you feel better,' said Byri. He saw the monk's eyes narrow, so took a sip himself. 'Best quality claret. This is not another jest, I promise.'

Michael took the proffered goblet with ill grace, and plonked himself down on a bench. He should have known better, and squawked in shock when it tipped violently. Quick as lightning, Bartholomew grabbed the end that flew into the air, and preserved the monk's dignity by sitting on it himself. Morden and Byri were openly disappointed.

'I am here on a serious matter,' said Michael sternly. 'Murder. It is not an occasion for merriment, so I suggest you desist with these foolish antics before you annoy me.'

Morden became serious. 'My apologies, Brother. We are very sorry about Tynkell and Lyng. Both were good men, and Lyng would have made an excellent Chancellor.'

'Yet you support Hopeman,' Michael pointed out, 'who will not.'

'Yes, because he is a Dominican,' explained Morden. 'We cannot vote for Thelnetham or Suttone, because one is a Gilbertine and the other a Carmelite, while Godrich will not do at all.'

'Why not?' probed Michael.

Morden indicated that Byri should reply.

'He has been bribing hostels to vote for him,' obliged the almoner, although he spoke reluctantly; he was not a man for gossip. 'But he was overheard saying that he cannot possibly honour all the pledges he has made, and will renege on most the moment he is in post.'

'Then there is his friendship with Moleyns,' added Morden. 'I assume you know what happened in Stoke Poges all those years ago, when Moleyns was charged with the murder of Egidia's uncle, but was acquitted?'

Michael nodded. 'He chose the jury himself.'

'Yes, and one of its members was Godrich.' Byri frowned when he saw Michael's surprise. 'No one told you?'

'No,' said Michael stiffly. 'How did you find out?'

'The village priest is a Dominican, and I met him at a conclave recently. He said that Godrich bragged about telling the other jurors how to vote. Godrich was sent there from Court, you see, to make sure that a man who was generous to the royal coffers was not convicted.'

'Then it was a pity for Moleyns that Godrich was not available for his next trial as well,' murmured Morden acidly. 'I imagine he was horrified when he was pronounced guilty of all those terrible deeds – theft, cattle rustling, harbouring felons . . .'

'You should have mentioned this sooner, Byri,' said Michael aggrieved. 'How am I supposed to solve these murders when people withhold vital information?'

'I assumed that Godrich would tell you himself,' replied Byri defensively. 'On the grounds that keeping it quiet makes it look as though he has something to hide.'

'Yes,' agreed Michael caustically. 'It does, doesn't it.'

'Do you think Godrich is the killer?' Morden answered the question himself. 'It would make sense: he stabbed Tynkell to force an election, Moleyns to prevent unsavoury details about his past from emerging, and Lyng to rid himself of his most dangerous rival.'

'Are there any other "unsavoury details" that I might not know?' asked Michael crossly.

Byri raised his hands in a shrug. 'Not that I am aware. However, Godrich would not have done that sort of favour for Moleyns and then forgotten all about it. Moleyns will have expressed his gratitude to him in some significant way, you can be sure of that.'

Michael thought so, too. 'But we are here on another matter, as it happens. Tell us about the argument you overheard between Hopeman and Lyng.'

Byri gaped at him. 'How on Earth do you know about that? The only person I have told is Prior Morden, and he has been in here with me ever since, going through our accounts.'

'The Senior Proctor has very long ears,' replied Michael smugly.

'Or his spies do,' muttered Byri. 'Very well, then. It was on Thursday night, well after nine. I had been away on priory business, and I stopped at St Botolph's Church to give thanks for my safe return. When I came out, Hopeman and Lyng were in the graveyard. I suppose I should have made myself known, but I was very tired and Hopeman can be . . . wordy.'

'You did not want him to keep you from your rest with a diatribe,' surmised Michael. 'So you skulked in the dark, waiting for him to leave.'

'It sounds sly when put like that,' objected Byri. 'Whereas I merely decided that it would be more comfortable to have his news the next day, rather than there and then, out in the cold.'

'So what did you hear, exactly?'

'They were talking about the chancellorship, amiably at first. Then Lyng told Hopeman to stand down and support him instead. He said he was going to win anyway, and Hopeman could save himself a lot of embarrassment by withdrawing before the votes were counted.'

Bartholomew frowned. 'Lyng said that? I thought he was a modest man.'

'So did I, which just goes to show that you never know anyone as well as you think.'

Bartholomew recalled the argument in Maud's Hostel, where Blaston the carpenter had overheard a quarrel that had involved physical violence. Perhaps Byri was right.

'Needless to say, Hopeman was incensed,' the almoner went on. 'He began to rant and screech, and said some terrible things, including . . .'

'Yes?' pressed Michael. He grimaced when Byri glanced at his prior. 'I need the truth about this encounter, Byri. If Hopeman is the killer, he needs to be stopped. I know he is a Dominican, and you are reluctant to betray him, but think of his victims.'

'Michael is right, Byri,' said Morden quietly. 'You have a duty to tell the truth.'

'Very well,' sighed the almoner. 'Hopeman said he

would kill Lyng if he interfered with God's plans. Lyng retorted that Hopeman might be the one to die, but they were both seriously angry by this point, and men often say things in temper that they do not really mean.'

'And temper often exposes their true intentions,' countered Michael, and stood so abruptly that Bartholomew was tipped off the other end of the bench, although no one laughed. 'We shall return to Michaelhouse and see what Hopeman has to say about this matter.'

'He is not the killer,' said Morden, although his voice lacked conviction. 'He may be a zealot, but he would never break one of the Ten Commandments.'

'If he had nothing to hide, he would have mentioned this encounter when I questioned him about Lyng's disappearance,' said Michael. 'But he told me that he had not seen Lyng since noon. Which means he *does* break the Commandments – by bearing false witness.'

'I suppose it does,' conceded Morden unhappily.

The wind had picked up since Bartholomew and Michael had been inside the priory, and was now blowing hard. It made the voluminous folds of Michael's habit billow wildly, while Bartholomew struggled to stay upright. They began to trudge back towards the town.

'I am confused,' said Bartholomew. 'Blaston heard Lyng quarrel with a "black villain" – we assume Hopeman – in Maud's Hostel at dusk. But if Lyng had slapped Hopeman then, why would Hopeman risk another encounter with Lyng a few hours later?'

'The answer is obvious: it must have been someone else who Blaston heard – he admits that he did not see this other person. And we are learning a lot about Lyng. He was no gentle saint, as we all believed, but someone who issued ultimatums, engaged in vicious rows, and used threats and physical violence. What are you doing?'

Bartholomew had stopped, and was staring across the

flat expanse of the Barnwell Fields. As he watched, the rising gale whisked a piece of rubbish high into the air, where it was carried some distance before becoming entangled in an alder copse.

'The wind,' he said. 'It is blowing from the same direction as it was on Tuesday.'

'Yes,' agreed Michael, pulling his thick winter mantle more closely around him. 'And it is cutting right through me.'

'The killer's cloak was whipped from the tower and carried towards these fields.'

'I know,' said Michael drily. 'My beadles and I spent hours searching for the wretched thing, and our failure to produce it has fuelled the rumour that it was Satan.'

'Where did you look exactly?'

Michael spread his hands in a shrug. 'Every inch of ground between St Mary the Great and the Dominican Priory. Why?'

Bartholomew stared at the church tower, angles and distances running through his mind. When there was no reply, Michael repeated the question, then sighed in annoyance when it was ignored a second time. He began to walk away, loath to stand around while the physician ruminated in silence – it was far too cold for that. Bartholomew barely saw him go.

His calculations complete, Bartholomew stepped off the Hadstock Way and began to plod in a north-easterly direction, sure that Tuesday's gale had been strong enough to carry a garment such a distance – and equally sure that Michael had been looking in the wrong place.

The Barnwell Fields were pretty in the summer, when sun and showers created luxurious meadows of thick grass and wild flowers, but they were bleak in winter, when they tended to flood. Bartholomew squelched through knee-deep puddles, struggling to keep his balance on the uneven ground, a task made more difficult still by the buffeting wind. His feet soon turned to ice, while it was impossible to keep his hood from blowing back, so his head ached from the cold. He persisted anyway, determined to succeed where Michael had failed. Then the sun began to set.

'Good afternoon, Matthew,' came a familiar voice through the gloom. It was Thelnetham, snugly wrapped in a thick winter cloak and a scarlet liripipe – a long-tailed hood that also served as a scarf. He saw Bartholomew eyeing it in surprise, and shrugged. 'I did not expect to meet any voters all the way out here, so I decided to indulge my penchant for colour. I shall take it off before I arrive though, as it would be inappropriate for the occasion.'

'Before you arrive where?' asked Bartholomew, continuing to stare at it as he imagined its soft, warm folds wrapped around his frozen ears.

'At Widow Miller's house,' replied Thelnetham. 'Lord, it is bitter today! The sky had an ugly hue earlier, and there will be snow before long. Shall we walk the rest of the way together, and pray that it holds off until we have both finished and are safely home again?'

Bartholomew's mystification intensified. 'What is happening in Widow Miller's home?'

Thelnetham frowned his own bemusement. 'She is dying, and my prior sent me to sit with her. I assume you are going there, too – to see what can be done to ease her final hours.'

Bartholomew shook his head. 'She is Rougham's patient, not mine.'

Thelnetham regarded him askance. 'Then what on Earth are you doing out here? It is scarcely wise on such a foul day, and a lot of paupers rely on your continued good health for their free medical care. You, of all people, cannot afford to be reckless.'

Bartholomew gestured towards the sturdy bulk of St

Mary the Great. 'The killer's cloak blew off the roof when Tynkell was killed, and it came in this direction. I am trying to find it.'

'It was not a cloak,' averred Thelnetham firmly. 'It was the Devil – too many folk saw him for that not to be true. Nicholas was among them, and he is as honest a man as you could ever hope to meet. If he says it was Satan, then it was Satan.'

'Hopefully, he will revise his position when I show him the garment.'

'Or he will tell you that it is the one Satan wore when he flapped away,' countered Thelnetham. 'So if you do find the thing, poke it with a stick first, to make sure he is not still inside it. But I had better hurry, or poor Widow Miller will be dead before I arrive.'

He turned and trotted away, at which point Bartholomew became aware that the wind had shifted. When he reworked his calculations accordingly, they took him farther north. The ground was soggier there, and the icy puddles deeper. As the last vestiges of daylight faded and he was getting ready to concede defeat, he glimpsed something black lying in the grass.

He snatched it up eagerly. It was a cloak, too good a garment to have been discarded deliberately, even by someone wealthy. There was a tear near the collar, where the clasp that had kept the two edges together had been ripped out. It proved what Michael had suspected from the start: that it had come loose as its wearer and Tynkell had grappled, after which the wind had carried it off.

It was not much of a step forward, but Bartholomew hoped it would be enough to throw doubts on the tale that Tynkell had been unequal to besting Lucifer.

His mind full of questions and solutions, Bartholomew hurried to St Mary the Great, where he asked Nicholas to show him the Chest Room. The secretary narrowed his eyes in rank suspicion, making the physician feel as though he had asked for something untoward.

'I think I know how Tynkell's killer escaped from the tower,' he explained. 'I will show you if you let me up there – it will be easier than telling you down here.'

Nicholas remained wary. 'I cannot – I do not have the keys. Only Michael and Meadowman do. Besides, we do not let just anyone up there, you know. It contains all our most precious documents and most of our money.'

Michael heard their voices and came to find out what was going on. Bartholomew showed him the cloak and told him where he had found it.

'Can it be identified?' asked the monk, seizing it eagerly. 'Even soaked and muddy, it is obviously expensive. Someone might recognise it.'

'It is also black,' Bartholomew pointed out. 'Like the ones owned by virtually every scholar in the University, not to mention most priests. Many can afford decent cloth.'

'So can burgesses and merchants,' put in Nicholas. 'And black is by far the most popular colour. Clothiers sell it by the cartload, as Matthew's sister will attest.'

'But there are tears and marks on this one,' persisted Michael. 'It is unique.'

'Yes – from its spell out in the Barnwell Fields,' said Bartholomew. 'It is impossible to say what it looked like *before* flying off the roof and spending five days in the mud.'

Michael sagged in disappointment. 'So its discovery means nothing?'

'It proves that Satan was not involved,' said Bartholomew.

'It will take more than a discarded mantle to change people's minds about that,' predicted Nicholas. 'They love that tale.'

271

'I am afraid that is true, Matt,' said Michael, seeing the physician prepare to argue. 'More is the pity. But what do you want in the Chest Room?'

'I think I know how the killer hid from us that day.'

Michael raised questioning eyebrows at Nicholas. 'Then why did you refuse to let him in? You know where Meadowman keeps his keys, and we are desperate for answers.'

'It is against the rules,' replied the secretary indignantly. 'Which say that the tower should never be opened unless *two* University officers are in attendance.'

Michael rolled his eyes, and indicated with an irritable flick of his hand that Nicholas was to do as Bartholomew had requested. The secretary responded with an offended sniff intended to remind the monk of who had written the guidelines in the first place.

'He really is a pedantic fellow,' muttered Michael, as he and Bartholomew followed him up the nave. 'And I have an uncomfortable feeling that he thinks *I* am the killer – my motive being that I want to see Suttone safely installed before I leave for Rochester.'

'What did Godrich say about being on the jury that acquitted Moleyns of murder?' asked Bartholomew, hoping the secretary had more sense than to suspect the Senior Proctor.

'Nothing,' replied Michael sourly. 'Because he had stormed out of Michaelhouse in a rage by the time I arrived home. I went to King's Hall, but he was not there either. Warden Shropham has promised to let me know the moment he returns, and then he will be in for an uncomfortable interview.'

'Then did you speak to Hopeman about his arguments with Lyng?'

Michael nodded. 'He openly acknowledges that they were often at loggerheads, but says he cannot recall specifics. I suggested that he try, and he informed me that God speaks through him, so any threats he might have issued actually came from the Almighty.'

'So he might be stabbing people in the belief that he is doing God's will?'

'It is possible, although Godrich remains my chief suspect.'

He unlocked the tower door and began to ascend the stairs, Bartholomew following and Nicholas bringing up the rear. Bartholomew paused at the bell chamber, and looked at the three metal domes, remembering Stanmore as he did so. He wondered what his brother-in-law would have made of the decision to silence them until after the election, and was sure he would have disapproved. Oswald had always loved the noisy jangle of bells.

Michael had unfastened the two locks to the Chest Room by the time Bartholomew and Nicholas arrived, and was waiting inside, holding a lantern aloft. Bartholomew stepped across the threshold and looked around. The only thing that had changed since his last visit was that mice had been at the poison in the little dishes, because there was less of it than there had been.

'The killer did *not* hide in here, Matt,' averred Michael. 'Even if he had managed to lay hold of Meadowman's keys, the door cannot be locked from the inside.'

Bartholomew smiled. 'Assuming it *was* locked.'

'It was,' averred Michael. 'I rattled it on my way past, and so did you.'

'Go and stand on the stairs, then come back in when I call you.'

Puzzled, Michael went to do as he was told, although Nicholas declined to join him, clearly of the opinion that the physician might make off with the University's treasure if left unsupervised. Once the door was closed, Bartholomew took one of the plates of poison and jammed it underneath, kicking it hard to ensure it was securely lodged.

'Enter, Brother,' he shouted. 'If you can.'

There was a rattle as the monk seized the handle, followed by a determined series of thumps as he pushed at it with increasing vigour. The door held firm.

'You have locked it!' he shouted accusingly. 'How?'

Bartholomew removed the dish, and showed him what he had done. The monk was thoughtful.

'Then I submit that Tynkell came up here alone, unlocking the doors with Meadowman's keys. The killer followed, and they had some sort of confrontation. Or perhaps Tynkell saw him sneaking past, and hared after him to the roof, where they fought. Once Tynkell was dead, the villain started to descend . . .'

'But he heard us coming up,' said Bartholomew. 'Fortunately for him, you fell and twisted your knee. I went back to help you, which delayed us just long enough to let him duck in here – the door would have been left open when Tynkell gave chase. He jammed it shut . . . you can see scratches on the floor where the dish was lodged.'

'My word!' breathed Nicholas, peering at them.

'Tynkell almost certainly left Meadowman's keys behind when he went to the roof,' Bartholomew went on. 'So the killer calmly waited until we had gone on upwards, after which he came out, locked the door behind him, and returned the keys to their hiding place.'

Nicholas looked from one to the other. 'But that means the culprit is a University officer! We are the only ones who know where they are kept.'

'Not so,' said Michael. 'Most of the beadles have seen Meadowman "hide" them, and not all are discreet men. One may have let something slip in a tavern. Or sold the information.'

'No!' gulped Nicholas. 'They would never betray you – they are loyal men.'

'Generally,' agreed Michael. 'But none are very well paid, and all like a drink.'

Nicholas was thoughtful. 'Even the Sheriff was betrayed by a soldier he thought he could trust. Perhaps we all put too much faith in the vagaries of human nature.'

Bartholomew continued with his analysis. 'However, when we arrived at the church, the porch and the vestry doors were locked from the inside, and the building was empty because everyone had gone out to watch. That means those doors were secured *after* Tynkell had started to fight. It could not have been before, or people would not have been able to leave.'

'What are you saying?' demanded Michael. 'That he had an accomplice?'

'He must have done.'

Michael turned to Nicholas. 'So why *did* Tynkell come up here? You must have an inkling – you were his secretary after all.'

'He did not confide in me, Brother. I told you: he had grown withdrawn and secretive these last few weeks, and kept shutting himself in his office.'

'Look in the Chest,' suggested Bartholomew. 'Perhaps something will be out of place.'

Michael obliged, and he and Nicholas began a careful analysis of its contents, although it looked like a random jumble to Bartholomew.

'This,' said Michael eventually, pulling out a piece of vellum. He opened it and began to read. 'It is a deed of ownership for the chapel in Stoke Poges.'

'Thelnetham said that Tynkell hoped to get it for the University,' recalled Bartholomew. 'And that he visited Stoke Poges to such an end, determined to make sure he was favourably remembered when he retired. Well, it seems he did. And as that manor once belonged to Moleyns, the chances are that *he* was involved in helping Tynkell to acquire it for us.'

Michael's expression was dark with anger. 'Moleyns murdered his wife's uncle to get that manor – his ownership of it is tainted, which means we cannot possibly accept its chapel. No wonder Tynkell shut himself away! He knew I would stop him if I knew what he was doing.'

'Oh, Tynkell,' whispered Nicholas sadly. 'We would have remembered you fondly anyway. You did not have to stoop to such antics.'

Michael stared at the deed. 'So he came up here to deposit this for safekeeping – or perhaps to gloat over it – when his killer happened across him.'

'It seems likely,' agreed Nicholas. 'So how does it help us identify the culprit?'

Michael rubbed a weary hand across his face. 'I am damned if I know.'

Bartholomew went to bed early that night, but woke at midnight and could not go back to sleep. Eventually, he rose and went to the conclave, intending to work on a lecture he was to give on Galen's *De urinis* later that term. He arrived to find he was not the only one who was restless. Michael was there, too, so they fell to discussing the murders. The monk had questioned the other University clerks about the deed to Stoke Poges chapel, but Tynkell had mentioned it to none of them, and all professed themselves astonished that he had succeeded in getting it.

'Perhaps Moleyns helped him because of their shared interest in witchery,' suggested Bartholomew. 'Moleyns visited Marjory Starre, while we know that Lyng and Tynkell had horned serpents inked on their—'

He stopped in horror when he realised that he had just broken Tynkell's confidence.

Michael's jaw dropped. 'They had *what*? Did you say horned serpents? But that is a mark of Satan!'

Bartholomew began to speak in a gabble about Moleyns

and Lyng, in the desperate but futile hope that Michael would forget Tynkell had also been mentioned.

'Lyng and Moleyns had snakes on their feet. Or rather, Lyng did – Moleyns was buried before I knew what to look for, so I cannot be sure about him. However, one of your clerks claims to have seen them comparing these symbols in St Mary the Great. Of course, I have not questioned the man myself, because I do not know who he is . . .'

'And Tynkell?' asked Michael sharply, when the physician trailed off. 'He had one, too? Is *that* the mysterious secret you and he shared for so many years?'

Trapped, Bartholomew nodded wretchedly. 'But he made me promise never to tell anyone. I did not understand why he was so insistent until Marjory Starre explained their significance yesterday.'

'But *I* would have done, and you should have told me,' said Michael angrily. 'You have put the whole University at risk with your misguided principles. Do you not know what will happen if word seeps out that we had a Satanist at our helm?'

'Tynkell was not a Satanist, Brother! There is no reason to suppose that he was anything other than a devout Christian.'

'You are my Corpse Examiner,' said Michael heatedly. 'You have a responsibility to me, as well as to your patients, and your silence has done me a serious disservice. Not to mention damaging our investigation.'

'It was not my secret to share. Besides, Tynkell always said it was the result of a youthful prank, and I had no reason to disbelieve him. Unfortunately, Marjory thinks that is unlikely, given the number of serpents he had put on himself, and the time it takes to draw them . . .'

Michael gaped anew at the implications of that revelation. 'How many of these horrible things did he have?'

Bartholomew rubbed a hand through his hair,

wondering whether to answer. However, the cat was out of the bag now, so there was no point in refusing to cooperate, especially as Michael could just ask Marjory. Besides, Tynkell had lied to him, and loyalty went both ways.

'Lots,' he mumbled. 'Two dozen or more, of varying sizes. However, I never saw any indication that he attended covens or did . . . whatever it is that Satanists do. It is entirely possible that this so-called connection is completely irrelevant.'

'Not if Lyng and Moleyns showed each other these symbols in St Mary the Great, where we know they met Tynkell for sly discussions.' Michael continued to glare. 'I cannot believe you kept such vital information from me, Matt. I am stunned!'

'But I did not know it was vital,' objected Bartholomew. 'And perhaps we are overstating its importance anyway. It is not necessarily a sinister—'

'Anything to do with witchery is sinister, and all three men have been murdered. Of *course* it is important! Oh, Lord, here comes Cynric. Now what?'

'A brawl at the King's Head,' the book-bearer reported tersely to Bartholomew. 'Cook is there, tending the injured, but some are the Sheriff's men and he wants you to see to them instead. It will mean trouble, boy. Cook will not like being deprived of customers.'

'I will come at once,' said Bartholomew, relieved to be away from the monk's scolding tongue, even if it did mean another confrontation with the vicious barber.

Bartholomew gathered what he needed from his room, and set off at a brisk trot, Cynric loping at his side. The streets felt oddly uneasy for the small hours, and he was disconcerted to see lights in hostels that were normally in darkness with their occupants fast asleep. Lamps also burned in the Carmelite Friary, Bene't College, the Hall of Valence Marie and Peterhouse, while the Gilbertines' refectory was lit up like a bonfire. Scholars darted in and out of the shadows, visiting neighbours and friends in defiance of the curfew that should have kept them indoors.

'They are plotting,' surmised Cynric. 'About how to install their preferred candidate. But Suttone need not worry. I have bought several costly charms on his behalf, so he *will* win.'

'Bought them from Marjory Starre?' asked Bartholomew warily.

Cynric nodded. 'She is very good, and she is kindly disposed towards Michaelhouse at the moment – because of Suttone himself, as a matter of fact.'

Bartholomew regarded him in alarm. 'What do you mean by that?'

'People have not forgotten the terrors of the plague, and *he* claims it is on the brink of return. His beliefs – which he has been airing in his election speeches – have driven folk to take all the precautions they can. Scholars and townsmen alike have flocked to Marjory for warding spells, and she says business has never been so good.'

'Then we must tell him to stop,' said Bartholomew worriedly. 'Especially if he does win. We do not want half the University queuing up for her services.'

'No,' agreed Cynric. 'It would be a nuisance for us regulars. However, it is Suttone's intention to let scholars loose on townswomen that concerns me more. I do not want hordes of amorous academics after my wife – she may not like it. But Lord, it is bitter tonight! Marjory says we shall have snow the day after tomorrow.'

Bartholomew thought she might be right, as it was as cold as he could ever remember. It hurt to inhale; his nose, ears and fingers ached; and the frozen mud on the High Street made for treacherous walking. He began to wish he was back in the conclave, but then remembered that Michael would be there, and decided he was better off outside.

He and Cynric arrived at the King's Head to find the carnage was not as great as they had been led to believe. Most wounds were superficial, although Cook was busily sewing them up anyway, so he could claim a fee. One victim was a ditcher named Noll Verius, who never had any money, and would almost certainly have to resort to crime to pay what was demanded.

'That will heal on its own,' he said, feeling it would be unethical to look the other way while Cook embarked on a painful and wholly unnecessary procedure.

Predictably, Cook resented the interference. 'I was here first, so these injuries belong to me.' His hands were red to the wrists, like glistening gloves, and his needle was thick with gore from his previous customers. 'Now piss off.'

'Watch your mouth, you,' said Cynric dangerously. 'Or I will—'

'Good, you are here at last, Matt,' said Tulyet, bustling up and blithely oblivious of the fact that he had just prevented a second brawl. 'I want you to look at Robin. He has—'

'He will look at no one,' interrupted Cook angrily. 'Surgery is my prerogative, not his.'

'You may tend the patrons of this tavern, if they are reckless enough to let you near them,' said Tulyet coldly, 'but stay away from my men.'

'Where and when I practise is dictated by the Worshipful Company of Barbers,' flashed Cook. 'Not you.'

'How good are you at inserting stitches into yourself?' asked Tulyet malevolently. 'Because that is what you will need to do if you challenge me again.'

Even the combative barber knew better than to argue,

and he prudently slunk away, although not without a vicious glower that would have unnerved any lesser man. Bartholomew went to tend Robin, who was white with shock, because someone had pinned his hand to a table with a dagger. Fortunately, the blade had missed bone, tendons and arteries, and would heal well enough. Helbye stood with a comforting hand on his shoulder, looking old, grey and tired.

'Please do not leave,' begged Robin, as the sergeant turned to go. 'When that wretched barber sees Doctor Bartholomew with me, he will storm over and try to push him away. And I do not want Cook. Not when he killed Widow Miller and Mother Salter. You should never have sent for him.'

'Of course I had to send for him,' argued Helbye irritably. 'He is the town surgeon – and a good one, too.' He raised his sleeve to reveal a healing gash. 'Look at that – a lovely neat job! Not even a woman could have done better stitches.'

'You were lucky, then,' said Robin. 'Perhaps he likes you.'

'Most folk do,' quipped Helbye, although his grin did not touch his eyes, and Bartholomew saw he was shocked by the speed with which the trouble in the King's Head had erupted. 'But the hero of Poitiers can protect you from Cook, and I should hunt for Isnard before there is any more fighting.'

'Isnard,' sighed Robin. 'I was right, you know – we should not have come in here, demanding to see him. We should have waited for him to come out, like we usually do.'

'We have the authority to go wherever we please in the town we rule,' said Helbye indignantly. 'And that includes the King's Head.'

'Yes, but . . .' began Robin, then decided there was no point in arguing. He explained to Bartholomew. 'We wanted to ask Isnard about the new stuff that was stolen, you see – Wilson's lid, Trinity Hall's scaffolding, and some nails from Lakenham's shed.'

'Isnard is a rogue,' said Helbye grimly. 'And it cannot be coincidence that these things went missing at the exact moment that he and Gundrede returned from their mysterious excursion to God knows where.'

His voice was flat and strained, so that Bartholomew sensed he knew he had made a serious error of judgement by invading the King's Head, and was embarrassed by it. He muttered something about finding Isnard and hurried away, his shoulders slumped.

Bartholomew finished with Robin and went to the next patient, a lad who had fainted at the first splash of blood and was still feeling queasy. He refused to let Cook puncture the boy's eardrum to 'release the excess of bad humours', and instead settled him quietly in a corner with a cup of honeyed ale.

'I have been practising my trade since I was ten years old,' said Cook, eyeing Bartholomew with open hatred, 'while you wasted years by reading books. I am far more experienced than you, and you have no right to gainsay me.'

Bartholomew ignored him and moved on, gratified when this annoyed Cook far more than any retort. But the barber would not leave him alone, and was a constant presence at his side, braying that anyone who put his faith in physicians was courting Death.

'For God's sake, Cook!' snapped Tulyet eventually. 'I cannot hear myself think with all your carping. If you cannot hold your tongue, go home.'

Cook opened his mouth to object, but had second thoughts when he recalled the Sheriff's earlier threat. Wordlessly, he collected his implements and stalked out. It was easier for Bartholomew to work once he had gone, and he soon finished what needed to be done. He packed up his equipment and was about to leave when Cynric approached.

'Isnard needs you outside,' he whispered. 'But he is hiding from Helbye, so he wants you to come discreetly. He is waiting in the stable.'

Bartholomew arrived in the outbuilding to find Gundrede with Isnard, both showing signs of being in the thick of the trouble. The bargeman had cuts on his face, while Gundrede's nose was askew.

'Why could you not just answer the soldiers' questions?' Bartholomew asked them reproachfully. 'A spat was unwarranted, and you are lucky no one was killed.'

'It was the principle of the thing,' explained Isnard earnestly. 'They *know* the King's Head is a sanctuary for . . . hard-working folk, but they came storming in like Pontius Pilate after vestal virgins. It was an outrage that had to be challenged.'

'We would have gone outside, if they had asked nicely,' added Gundrede, while Bartholomew was still pondering the bargeman's curious analogy. 'There was no need for them to race in and start making accusations.'

'Besides, we never stole anything last night,' said Isnard. 'We were not even here.'

'Then where were you?' asked Bartholomew.

'Away,' replied Isnard airily. Then he regarded the physician with eyes that were full of hurt. 'They accused me of taking Master Wilson's lid, but he was once a member of Michaelhouse – the College I love with all my heart. I would *never* steal anything from you.'

'Of course not,' said Bartholomew, aware that Gundrede was studiously looking in the opposite direction.

'Michaelhouse is dearer to me than my own home,' Isnard went on tearfully. 'Indeed, I plan to live there when I take over the choir.'

'Oh,' said Bartholomew, startled. 'Do you?'

'Unless you can persuade Brother Michael that his future lies here,' said Isnard pleadingly. 'Remind him of all the good things he has – not just the biggest and best choir in the country, but friends who are devoted to him.'

'And who wants to be a bishop, anyway?' asked Gundrede. 'All they do is eat, drink and ponder about how to get one over on their colleagues.'

If that were true, then Michael would be in his element, thought Bartholomew. He worked in silence for a while, listening to Tulyet rounding up his soldiers in the street outside. Helbye was repeating the orders in a ringing voice, and Bartholomew supposed the sergeant was trying to claw back some of the authority he had lost with the ill-advised raid.

'Incidentally, we have been looking for the woman in the fancy cloak,' said Gundrede, breaking into his thoughts. 'Lots of people saw her run off after Moleyns was killed – including you – so she probably knows the killer. Unfortunately, the wretched lass has disappeared.'

'We want to take her to the Sheriff, see, so she can tell him that the Devil did it,' elaborated Isnard. 'And not us. We will keep searching. I am sure she will surface eventually.'

'Unless Satan has silenced *her* with a claw to the heart, of course,' said Gundrede darkly.

Bartholomew finished tending their injuries, and left them moaning about Michael's disloyalty to the choir. He collected Cynric and started to walk home.

'Blaston claims that fight was audible in Milne Street,' said the book-bearer. 'Helbye was a fool to march in and start throwing his weight around. It was deliberately provocative.'

'So it would seem,' sighed Bartholomew.

'He probably wanted to prove that he is not too old for a skirmish,' Cynric went on. 'But it did the opposite

'– it showed everyone that it is time he retired.'

'He should not bear all the blame for the brawl. It would not have happened if the patrons of the King's Head had shown some restraint.'

Cynric shot him a sour glance to show he disagreed. 'Speaking of restraint, Master Langelee should impose some on Kolvyle. That boy is a horror. In fact, it was probably him who killed Tynkell and the others.'

'Was it?' asked Bartholomew mildly. He was used to Cynric making outrageously unfounded remarks, and had learned to take them with a pinch of salt.

'He murdered Tynkell because *he* wanted to be Chancellor, and then he stabbed Lyng for being popular. He was jealous, see.'

'And why did Moleyns have to die?'

'Oh, that is simple. You remember Dallingridge, the man who was poisoned in Nottingham? Well, Moleyns killed him for Kolvyle's benefit. Dallingridge was a brilliant scholar, and Kolvyle was afraid that he would be seen as second-best.'

'Right,' said Bartholomew. 'And what did Moleyns gain from this arrangement?'

'Nothing,' replied Cynric promptly. 'Because the moment he asked for a favour, Kolvyle stabbed him. Now Kolvyle supports Godrich, who is the candidate least likely to do a good job, at which point he will demand another election and stand himself. There, I have solved the case. Now all you have to do is arrest the brat.'

At that moment, a familiar figure emerged from St Michael's Lane with a train of beadles at his heels.

'I am summoned to King's Hall,' said Michael worriedly. 'Godrich is missing, and they fear the killer has struck again.'

CHAPTER 12

'*Has* the killer struck again, Brother?' asked Langelee a little later that morning.

It was still early, but he and his Fellows had already attended their devotions, broken their fast, and repaired to the conclave, where they were busily preparing for the day ahead. Michael was fluttering around Suttone with a brush and scissors, struggling to render him a little more Chancellor-like; Langelee, William, Clippesby and Kolvyle were assembling their notes for the morning's lessons; Bartholomew was making a list of the texts he wanted his students to read; and Langelee himself was honing his letter-opener, originally an innocuous little implement but now a very deadly weapon. Clearly, he was of the opinion that only a fool would not take precautions to protect himself if Michael's answer was yes.

Michael stopped primping Suttone, his expression bleak. 'Well, Lyng went missing, and look what happened to him. However, I can tell you that Godrich is not on the banks of the King's Ditch, because we searched them very thoroughly – by torchlight.'

'Personally, I thought Godrich was the murderer,' said William. 'So perhaps he sensed the net closing in around him, and fled before he was arrested.'

'Nonsense,' declared Kolvyle. 'He would never—'

'He was my main suspect, too,' interrupted Michael, ignoring Kolvyle and addressing William. 'He is a despicable rogue. First, he was on the jury that acquitted Moleyns of poisoning Peter Poges. Second, Dallingridge was poisoned in Nottingham, and Godrich was there at the time, although he insists on denying it—'

'Dallingridge was not poisoned,' snapped Kolvyle irritably. 'He died of natural causes, as I have told you on countless occasions. And Godrich *is* telling the truth about Lammas Day – I would have noticed if he had been at the feast in the castle.'

'Dallingridge wrote a list of all the people he suspected of killing him,' Michael retorted. 'It included you, so forgive me if I do not accept your opinion on the matter.' He turned back to William. 'And third, Godrich stoops to buying votes to make himself Chancellor.'

'I heard that he turned to the Devil for help during the plague, too,' said William, cutting across the response Kolvyle started to make. 'He bought charms and spells from witches to keep himself safe.'

'Many people did,' said Clippesby, hugging a mangy dog. 'And we should not judge them too harshly for what happened during that terrible time.'

'We should if they want to be Chancellor,' retorted Suttone. 'Because they might do it again, when the disease sweeps through us a second time.' Rashly, he addressed Kolvyle. 'I trust this will make you rethink your allegiance to him?'

Kolvyle's face was hard and cold. 'And vote for you? Do not make me laugh!'

'I will make a good Chancellor,' protested Suttone, stung. 'I am a—'

'You will never be elected,' declared Kolvyle viciously. 'But if you are, I shall threaten to resign. And that means you will not keep your post for long, because no one will choose an old man over the University's brightest young mind.'

'Be careful what you promise,' warned Langelee, while the others blinked their astonishment at such brazen hubris. 'Thelnetham resigned in favour of a better offer, and he ended up with nothing.'

'And good riddance!' scoffed Kolvyle. 'But I am

different, because I am a rising star, whereas he is just another elderly has-been. Like the rest of you.'

'Now just a moment,' said William dangerously. 'I am in the prime of my—'

'You are all too old,' Kolvyle declared contemptuously. 'And it is time a clean sweep was made to rid the University of its deadwood.'

He turned and stalked away, but Michael raised his hand when William started after him. 'Leave him. He is not worth the effort.'

William scowled. 'Even Thelnetham was nicer than him, and that is saying something. I recommend we never hire any more Fellows. They are a menace!'

'Other than Aungel,' said Langelee. 'We shall enrol him when Bartholomew abandons us for matrimonial bliss. He has his failings, but better the devil you know.'

'I am not going anywhere,' said Bartholomew, disliking the way his future was being decided without him. 'At least, not yet. I shall see out the academic year, no matter what.'

'You will not need to go at all if Suttone is Chancellor,' said William. 'He will let you have your woman *and* keep your Fellowship.'

'I will,' agreed Suttone. 'And why not? It is stupid to lose a good teacher, just because he has normal manly appetites. However, I hope Godrich is *not* dead. He has powerful friends at Court, and I do not want the King accusing me of his murder.' Then a thought occurred to him, and he blanched. 'Lord! Do you think *I* am in danger? After all, we started with five candidates, but now we are four.'

'There is no harm in being careful,' replied Michael. 'So Cynric can stay with you today.'

'Tell us what you learned at King's Hall last night, Brother,' said Langelee, returning to his original question. 'Should we be concerned for Godrich's safety?'

'Unfortunately, I think we should,' replied the monk

unhappily. 'Especially as Whittlesey seems to be missing too.'

'Whittlesey?' echoed Langelee, shocked. 'God's teeth! The Church will be livid if anything happens to *him*. He is the Archbishop of Canterbury's favourite nephew, and an important cleric in his own right.'

'Godrich organised a feast at King's Hall in Whittlesey's honour,' Michael went on, 'but neither appeared for it and I am very worried. As I said, Godrich was my chief suspect, but now he has vanished . . . well, it just bodes ill.'

'This dog,' said Clippesby, indicating the creature in his arms. 'She is the one who was made to run across the road when Moleyns died – after a bone. A lamb shank, she says.'

'And?' demanded Michael eagerly. 'Is she going to tell us who threw it?'

'She does not know. However, she tells me that it was definitely not Godrich, because he loves dogs, and would never have put one in danger.'

Michael seized his arm urgently. 'Are you *sure*? Please, Clippesby – no madness now. This is important, because if Godrich can be eliminated as a suspect, then it means he probably *is* dead. And Whittlesey with him. They were rarely out of each other's company these last few days, so Whittlesey may have been dispatched just because he was in the killer's way.'

'I am sure. I happened to be watching Godrich when Moleyns fell off his horse – one of his hounds was limping, you see, and I was waiting for an opportunity to tell him so. He did run towards the mêlée, but he did not kill Moleyns. I would have noticed.'

'Damn it, Clippesby!' cried Michael, exasperated. 'Why did you not tell me this at once?'

'Because I did not know that Godrich was a suspect until you announced it just now.'

'I do not suppose you noticed Whittlesey in the scrum, did you?' asked Michael, fighting down his frustration. The other-worldly Dominican often closed his eyes to the sordid affairs of men; most of the time, Michael did not blame him.

'I did, actually,' replied Clippesby serenely. 'He was trailing after you and Matt, although I did not know then that he was an envoy from Rochester. When Moleyns fell, he raced forward with the rest, but I did not see what he did when he got there.'

'I never did like Whittlesey,' declared William. 'Too greasy by half. *He* killed Tynkell, Moleyns and Lyng. Then he dispatched Godrich, but realised it was one murder too many, so he fled while he was still able.'

'But they are cousins,' Suttone reminded him.

'Quite,' said William tartly. 'People are far more likely to kill their family than strangers – you can usually avoid the one, but you are stuck with the other until death.'

Not long after, when the debate about the killer's identity was still in full swing, the door opened to admit Thelnetham and Nicholas. The Gilbertine was wearing pink hose, shoes with shiny silver tassels, and his cloak was fastened by the gaudy purple-jewelled brooch. He opened his mouth to address the Fellows, but sneezed twice in quick succession instead. When he tried a second time to speak, he was convulsed by four more.

'It is the dog,' explained Nicholas. 'They always have this effect on him.'

'Take her outside, Clippesby,' ordered Langelee. 'Or we will never hear what Thelnetham has to tell us.'

'I should have known better than to visit when *he* was here,' wheezed Thelnetham, eyes streaming as he glared after the Dominican. 'It reminds me why I was so glad to leave.'

'You were not glad,' countered William spitefully. 'You begged to be reinstated.'

'Then thank the good Lord I was not,' snapped Thelnetham, dabbing at his nose with a piece of puce silk. 'Because it means I shall not have to wait until the end of term before I return to my Mother House in Lincolnshire.'

Suttone blinked. 'You are leaving Cambridge? But why?'

'Because Godrich is buying votes, Hopeman is bullying everyone with threats of divine vengeance, and you have the Senior Proctor behind you,' replied Thelnetham shortly. 'I cannot compete against such odds, and I was a fool to think the University might consider brains to be an important quality in a Chancellor.'

'They are overrated,' said William. 'Most officials manage perfectly well without them.'

'So I am withdrawing from the race,' Thelnetham went on. 'Nicholas will draft a suitable notice and post it on the Great West Door today. With your permission, Brother.'

Michael inclined his head. 'However, before you do anything rash, it is only fair to tell you that Godrich has disappeared. It may only be a three-way competition.'

Thelnetham smiled thinly. 'I appreciate your honesty, Brother – you could have mentioned it *after* you had accepted my decision to stand down. But it makes no difference. I have learned more than is pleasant about University politics these last few days, and I want no further part in it. I shall journey to Lincoln as soon as there is a break in the weather.'

'Besides, Godrich has spent a lot of money on his campaign,' added Nicholas, 'so I doubt he will stay away long. Indeed, his "disappearance" is probably a ploy to gain support.'

'Perhaps it is,' acknowledged Michael. 'But I shall be sorry to see you go, Thelnetham. You would have been my second choice.'

'That is what most people have told me,' said Thelnetham sourly. 'Although I do not consider it much of a compliment. However, until the weather breaks and I can safely ride north, I shall make myself useful by helping Suttone.'

'You will?' asked Suttone suspiciously. 'Why?'

'Because as long as you have Michael behind you, you are the best man for the post. I may be leaving the University, but that does not mean I want it in the hands of a fanatic or an opinionated ass like Godrich.'

'That is very decent of you,' said Michael approvingly. 'If you encourage your supporters to vote for Suttone, we shall win handily.'

'Not necessarily,' warned Thelnetham. 'Godrich has purchased a lot of "loyalty" over the last few days, while a great many priests have been persuaded to follow Hopeman. But we shall work together to see what might be done to thwart them.'

'You will not regret it,' promised Michael. 'I am thinking of establishing the post of *Vice*-Chancellor. I will offer it to you, should you change your mind and decide to stay.'

'What would such a position entail?' asked Nicholas curiously.

'Stepping in when the Chancellor is indisposed or travelling – and Suttone will be required to spend a certain amount of time in Rochester. He will need a reliable deputy.'

But Thelnetham shook his head. 'This deputy would make decisions, only to have them overturned when Suttone comes back. It would be a mere sinecure.'

'I disagree,' argued Michael. 'And Suttone would be delighted to have someone like you at his side – a strong man, who understands the University.'

'It is kind of you, Brother, but my mind is made up. Perhaps I shall return one day – or even chance my hand in Oxford – but for now, I hanker for the serenity of

Lincolnshire. It has been too long since I was there.' Then Thelnetham grinned impishly. 'But there is a bright side to my withdrawal: I can dress as I please once more. Black and white are dull colours, and do not suit my complexion at all.'

He bowed and took his leave, Nicholas limping at his heels.

'I have never understood him,' said Michael. 'He is arrogant, cruel and vain, yet also capable of great generosity. He slipped me a lot of money for the choir when he was a Fellow, although always anonymously. He thinks to this day that I never knew it was him.'

'He is a swine,' countered William. 'And I shall not be sorry when he goes.'

'Was his sneezing genuine?' asked Langelee. 'Because if so, he can be eliminated as a suspect – he could never have snagged the dog and held it until he was ready to lob a bone.'

'It was genuine,' replied Bartholomew. 'It is partly why he objected to Clippesby bringing animals in here when he was a member of Michaelhouse. And he was never a suspect as far as I was concerned.'

The first task that day was to find out what had happened to Godrich, so Bartholomew and Michael walked quickly to King's Hall, in the hope that there had been some news. The tale of his disappearance was already all over the town, and several scholars approached to say that they were now shifting their allegiance to Suttone.

'Even if Godrich is alive, we do not want a man who slopes off without explanation,' said Master Braunch of Trinity Hall. 'And there are nasty rumours about him anyway – that he acquitted Moleyns of murder, dabbled in witchery, and poisoned a man in Nottingham.'

'Let us hope you find the killer soon, Brother,' added the haughty Master Heltisle of Bene't College. 'Or people might start to wonder if *you* are responsible for all this slaughter. After all, the deaths of Tynkell, Lyng and possibly Godrich – and perhaps even Moleyns, too – have certainly benefited Suttone.'

'They have benefited Hopeman, too, Heltisle,' Braunch pointed out. 'And he is far more likely to kill than our Senior Proctor. He is a zealot, who thinks his nasty opinions reflect the will of God. There is no reasoning with that sort of person, and we must all pray that he does not win, or our University will become a very unpleasant place to live.'

'Braunch is right, Matt,' said Michael, when the pair had gone. 'So we shall have words with Hopeman later.'

They knocked at King's Hall's handsome gate, and were conducted to the conclave, where Warden Shropham and thirty or so of his Fellows had gathered. They were sitting around a long table, and in the middle of it was a piece of parchment: Godrich's will.

'You have found his body?' cried Michael in dismay. 'Why did you not send word?'

'There has been no news either way,' replied Shropham. He gestured sheepishly at the document. 'Assessing his estate is merely a precaution.'

'Godrich *is* dead,' stated Dodenho, an opinion that was evidently shared by the others, because a murmur of agreement went around the room. 'We have visited all his favourite haunts, and there is no sign of him. He would never have left the town willingly – not when he was poised to win the election – so there is only one explanation: he has gone the same way as Tynkell and Lyng.'

'Not necessarily,' countered Bartholomew. 'He might just be sitting quietly somewhere, waiting for certain rumours to die down.'

'The ones about his chequered past?' asked Shropham

with a grimace. 'That claim he bought charms from Marjory Starre, and did the King's bidding in Moleyns' trial for murder? You think he is lying low to avoid a scandal?'

'Well, it is certainly possible,' said Michael.

'No, it is not,' declared Dodenho, 'because he was a warrior, a man trained to stand and fight. His vanishing means one thing and one thing only: that he is murdered.'

'It is a pity he never saw his tomb started,' sighed Shropham. 'It will be such a glorious structure. All I hope is that we shall have a corpse to put in it.'

'Glorious indeed,' muttered Dodenho acidly, 'given that every penny he owned will be squandered on the thing. And King's Hall will get nothing. It is disgraceful!'

His remark – and his colleagues' angry agreement – explained why no one was overly distressed by the notion that Godrich might be dead. There was an unwritten but inviolate rule that anyone who accepted a University Fellowship would repay the honour with a legacy, and if Godrich had indeed stipulated that everything was to be spent on his monument, then he had committed a serious breach of trust.

'He took his cue from Dallingridge,' Dodenho went on crossly, 'who also wanted his entire estate spent on a tomb. What a wicked waste of money!'

'Speaking of Dallingridge,' said Shropham, 'there is no truth in the tale that Godrich poisoned him. First, Godrich was more of a sword man. But second, and perhaps more convincingly, he did not arrive in Nottingham until *after* Dallingridge was taken ill.'

'How do you know?' asked Michael. 'If it is because he told you so, I am not sure we can believe it.'

'I sent him north on King's Hall business over the summer,' explained Shropham. 'And just today, I unearthed three deeds signed and dated by several independent witnesses that prove he was in Derby on Lammas

Day. He did not arrive in Nottingham until the following week.'

'My mother always said that you cannot take your money with you to the grave,' muttered Dodenho bitterly, more interested in his colleague's last will and testament than his innocence. 'But obviously, she never had met Godrich and Dallingridge.'

'What have you done to find him?' asked Michael. 'Other than visit his favourite places?'

'We made a thorough search of our grounds, and traced his last known movements,' replied Shropham. 'After storming out of Michaelhouse, he went to the Dominicans, where he offered Morden a bribe of ten marks for forcing Hopeman to stand down. Morden refused.'

'Godrich took Whittlesey with him,' added Dodenho, 'although Whittlesey grumbled about it being too cold for a jaunt outside town. Afterwards, Whittlesey insisted on a warming drink in the Cardinal's Cap to recover, so Godrich accompanied him there.'

'Godrich had organised a feast in Whittlesey's honour,' said Shropham. 'But neither was around at dusk, so we started without them. Unfortunately, we all enjoyed the free-flowing wine so much that it was past midnight before we realised that neither had put in an appearance.'

'So no one saw them after they visited the Cardinal's Cap?' asked Michael.

'I *heard* them,' said Dodenho. 'I spilled some claret on myself during the revelries, so I went to change. As I passed Godrich's room – at roughly ten o'clock – I heard the pair of them quarrelling. I was not so ungentlemanly as to eavesdrop, but I can tell you that the conversation was heated.'

'So one might have done the other harm, then fled to avoid the consequences?'

'Of course not,' said Dodenho indignantly. 'This is King's Hall, not a hostel.'

'Right,' said Michael. 'But this row . . . surely you can remember *something* useful about it? It could be critical to finding out what happened to them.'

'Well, I cannot,' said Dodenho shortly. 'I told you: it would have been rude to listen.'

'Even though you must have been curious as to why both had missed the feast, especially as one had arranged it in the other's honour?'

'There was a *lot* of wine,' explained Dodenho sheepishly, while his cronies exchanged the kind of glances that suggested it had been quite an evening. 'And if I thought about Godrich and Whittlesey at all, it was just to assume that they would join us when they were ready. It is only now that we realise they never did.'

Michael plied them with more questions, but learned nothing else of use. He asked to see Godrich's room – prudently not confessing that he had searched it once already – and he and Bartholomew were conducted to the handsome chamber in the gatehouse. The bed was loaded with furs and silks, and the floor was thick with expensive rugs. What caught Bartholomew's attention, however – perhaps because Cynric had done something similar – were the charms that were dotted around the place, while in a chest by the window were several books on witchcraft that the University had banned. He picked one up at random, and opened it to see annotations in Godrich's writing, suggesting that the King's Hall Fellow had been more familiar with their contents than was appropriate for a God-fearing man.

'What happened here?' asked Michael, pointing to the shattered remains of what had been a pretty and probably expensive bowl.

'I thought I heard something smash,' mused Dodenho, gazing at it. 'I suppose it must have been knocked over by mistake.'

'There is blood on it,' said Bartholomew, inspecting

it closely. 'I think it is more likely that one lobbed it at the other.'

'Godrich was not given to hurling his belongings around,' averred Dodenho. 'Although I am not sure about Whittlesey. I did not take to him at all. Lord! I wish we had been more abstemious with the wine. Then Godrich might still be alive, and we could have persuaded him to make a more sensible will.'

'There was a letter,' blurted Shropham suddenly. 'I just remembered!'

'From Dallingridge?' asked Michael innocently, not about to confess that it was currently residing in his office at St Mary the Great.

'No, no – that would have been delivered months ago. I am talking about one that arrived more recently, although the messenger said it had been delayed because of the weather. Perhaps that will give us the clue we need to understand what has happened.'

There followed a concerted effort to find it. Eventually, it was located under a chest, where it had evidently been placed to keep it from prying eyes.

'It is from Bishop Sheppey,' said Michael, scanning it quickly. 'Written the day before he died – in a hand that is firm and strong, for which I am glad; I was afraid that he had been ill for so long that he might have . . . lost his reason.'

'You mean you feared that you might have been nominated by a madman,' surmised Shropham. 'Well, you need not be concerned: Whittlesey told me that Sheppey named you weeks ago. But what does the missive say? And why would Sheppey write to Godrich?'

Michael frowned. 'It is addressed to his "favoured son in Christ", and cautions Godrich to beware of black brethren arriving with false smiles and insincere offers of friendship.'

'It refers to Whittlesey!' breathed Dodenho. 'Now all

is clear. *Whittlesey* is the killer, and the Bishop predicted that there would be trouble when his envoy arrived in Cambridge.'

'Have you searched Whittlesey's quarters yet?' asked Michael urgently.

Shropham shook his head. 'We are not in the habit of invading the privacy of important guests. They tend not to like it.'

He led the way there, only to discover that all the envoy's belongings had gone.

'The sly dog!' cried Dodenho in dismay. 'I was right – *he* killed Godrich, packed up and left. How could he? We were on the brink of counting a Chancellor among our ranks, and he has struck us a grave blow.'

'So is that it?' asked Bartholomew when he and Michael were out on the street. He felt a strange sense of anti-climax. 'Whittlesey is the killer? The murders did start when he arrived, and I said from the start that he was a suspicious character. I am surprised it was not Cook, but . . .'

'I suppose he came to install his kinsman as Chancellor,' said Michael unhappily. 'He killed Tynkell to create a vacancy, Lyng to eliminate a rival, and Moleyns lest he revealed Godrich's dubious dealings in Stoke Poges. Then the relationship turned sour, as such alliances often do, so he brained Godrich with the bowl, hid the body and disappeared while he could.'

'Why would a powerful Benedictine be interested in who leads our University?'

'I told you before, Matt – we train the priests who work in dioceses all over the country. All high-ranking churchmen are interested in us.'

'And Sheppey feared that Whittlesey might turn violent, so decided to warn Godrich?'

Michael shrugged. 'Sheppey knew Whittlesey well,

because all bishops work closely with their envoys. And the warning certainly explains why Godrich was loath to let Whittlesey out of his sight – dragging him to Michaelhouse, taking him to see the Dominicans, accompanying him to the Cardinal's Cap . . .'

'I would have thought he would do the opposite – stay as far away from Whittlesey as possible.'

'By keeping him close, Godrich could watch what he was doing. I would have done the same. I shall tell my beadles to intensify the search for him. He cannot have gone far.'

They had not taken many steps towards St Mary the Great before they met Cynric. The book-bearer was guarding Suttone, who was strolling along the High Street, shaking hands with anyone who would stop to pass the time of day with him. Cynric's jaw dropped when Bartholomew told him what had happened.

'But I *saw* Whittlesey!' he cried. 'I returned to the King's Head after seeing you home last night, and we went through the Trumpington Gate together – me walking and him on horseback. I wished him God's speed, and he thanked me. Then, the moment I entered the tavern, he shot off south like an arrow. I should have known then that there was something amiss.'

'How did he seem?' demanded Michael. 'Anxious? Angry? Frightened? Gratified?'

'Tense and worried,' replied the book-bearer. 'I assumed he was just uneasy about riding in such icy weather. There was a full moon to light his way, but it was still dark.'

When they reached the church, Michael charged Meadowman to go after the envoy and bring him back. Delighted to be entrusted with such an important task, the beadle chose four cronies and set about commandeering ponies and the necessary supplies.

'Do not worry, Brother,' he said cheerfully. 'We will catch him, even if we have to travel to London to do it.'

And then he and his party were gone. Michael sketched a benediction after them, and his lips moved in a silent prayer for their well-being – and the success of their mission.

'Yet something about Whittlesey as the killer feels wrong,' said Bartholomew unhappily. 'I know he is a villainous character, but . . .'

Michael turned a haggard face towards him. 'I agree. I cannot escape the sense that we are missing something important, so I suggest we continue with our enquiries as though this had not happened. After all, even if Whittlesey *is* the culprit, we shall need more than a letter from a dead bishop to convict him.'

'Where first?' asked Bartholomew.

'We had better tell Dick Tulyet what has happened. Then I want another word with Egidia and Inge. I have never been comfortable with their role in this affair.'

They left St Mary the Great just as Nicholas was nailing the notice about Thelnetham's withdrawal to the Great West Door. Regent masters clustered around to read it.

'It means you must now choose between Suttone and Hopeman,' Nicholas explained, a remark that caused a ripple of consternation to run through them.

'And Godrich,' called someone at the back. 'He might have disappeared, but he has not withdrawn. Not officially. We can still vote for him.'

'Actually, you cannot,' said Nicholas apologetically. 'The statutes stipulate that all the candidates must "keep full term", which, as you know, means they must be resident here for a specific number of nights. By vanishing yesterday, Godrich cannot prove he has fulfilled this stipulation, and has thus rendered himself ineligible.'

'And I thought *I* lived by the statutes,' breathed Michael to Bartholomew. 'But he makes me look like an amateur. Perhaps I should promote him to Senior Proctor's Secretary instead.'

'We do not want a Chancellor who swans off without explanation anyway,' said Vicar Eyton of St Bene't's. 'It means he is unsteady, and not the sort of man to serve as our leader.'

'He might be dead,' called someone else. 'He may not have gone voluntarily.'

'If his body is found in Cambridge, I suppose it means he *will* have kept full term,' mused Nicholas, frowning thoughtfully. 'So we can still vote for him, as there is nothing in the statutes about excluding corpses from the running. However, it would not be wise for us to elect one – it would find fulfilling its duties very difficult.'

There was a startled silence at this proclamation, although it did not last long.

'A corpse could not be worse than Tynkell,' drawled Master Heltisle of Bene't College. '*He* might have been dead, for all the decisions he made.'

'It does not matter if Godrich is in the land of the living or lying in a ditch,' said Eyton impatiently, 'because he will not be Chancellor anyway. We must choose between Michaelhouse and Maud's.'

Those who had agreed to support Godrich in exchange for free books began to argue, unwilling to accept that the promised riches would not now be theirs. Then someone accused Hopeman's followers of engineering a situation where his only rival was Suttone, and a furious quarrel broke out.

'The tension might ease if we told them that Whittlesey is the killer,' said Bartholomew to Michael. 'Then there would be no grounds for charges of foul play, and the election could settle into a peaceful race between the two remaining candidates.'

'No event will be peaceful if Hopeman is involved,' remarked Michael wryly. 'Besides, neither of us is entirely sure that Whittlesey *is* the guilty party, so I recommend we wait to hear his side of the story before making public allegations.'

'Then let us hope Meadowman hurries,' said Bartholomew. 'He—'

He stopped when a gaggle of men from the hostels surged forward to surround them, clamouring to know why the Senior Proctor had not protected Godrich. They were led by Vicar Frisby, who was drunk.

'You should have known that his offer of free books for the poorest hostels would make him unpopular in some quarters,' Frisby slurred. 'You should have kept him safe.'

'You should,' agreed Master Thomas of Bridge Hostel tearfully. His cloak was pitifully thin, and he was shivering. 'We were so looking forward to having our own copy of Augustine's *Sermones.*'

'He might be alive,' said Michael with quiet reason. 'It is not—'

'He is dead,' interjected Frisby firmly. 'Or he would be here now, buying more votes. And I am furious about it.'

'You are?' asked Thomas, bemused. 'Why? You told us that Suttone would be your second choice, should Thelnetham become unavailable. Godrich is irrelevant to you.'

'He *was* irrelevant, but then Cew's brass was stolen from my church,' explained Frisby. 'He offered to pay for another if I switched my allegiance to him. Naturally, I agreed.'

'So will you revert back to Suttone now?' asked Thomas curiously.

Frisby nodded. 'The Senior Proctor's new puppet is infinitely preferable to Hopeman. I have never held with an overabundance of religion, and he is a bore with his pious sermons and conversations with the Almighty.'

He raised the wineskin in a sloppy salute and tottered away, leaving behind a number of baffled hostel men, all wondering why one priest should condemn another for talking to God.

Bartholomew and Michael were just passing St Clement's on their way to the castle when Vicar Milde emerged, his face unusually sombre.

'Have you heard, Brother?' he asked. 'All the pinnacles on the Holty tomb were stolen last night, probably shortly after I finished prayers at midnight. Personally, I like it better without them, but that is beside the point – which is that someone burgled a holy church. Do these people care nothing for their immortal souls?'

'Not as much as they care about their purses,' retorted Michael, and then frowned. 'Do I hear Hopeman's voice coming from your domain?'

'I am afraid so,' sighed Milde. 'He just marched in and began holding forth. I shall be glad when this election is over, as I am tired of all these aggravating speeches.'

Michael and Bartholomew went to listen. The building was full, and Hopeman's dark face burned with the power of his convictions as he informed his listeners that a vote for Suttone was an invitation for the Devil to rule the University. Michael was about to go and suggest he choose his words with more care when he was hailed by an urgent shout.

'Brother! Brother!' cried Nicholas, distraught. 'My little bell has gone! *Gone!*'

Michael frowned his bemusement. 'What little bell?'

'Someone sneaked up the tower and made off with her,' sobbed the secretary, wringing his hands in distress. 'We only have two left. My poor bell! What will become of her?'

'You mean one of the bells that Oswald bought?' asked Bartholomew, wondering if Nicholas had been at Frisby's claret. 'But that is impossible. They are heavy – hardly something that can be tossed over one's shoulder and toted away.'

'Nor were Master Wilson's ledger slab, Dallingridge's feet and Holty's pinnacles,' wailed Nicholas, 'but *they* were stolen. And now my little treble has suffered the same fate.'

'How do you know?' asked Michael, turning and beginning to hurry back to St Mary the Great. 'Did you take Meadowman's keys and go to look?'

'Of course not! I never go up the tower alone, as I have told you before.'

'Then how—'

'I was afraid they might get stiff if they were left unused for days on end,' sniffed the secretary. 'So I gave their ropes a bit of a tug.'

Michael raised admonishing eyebrows. 'But I issued an edict that they were not to be rung until after the election.'

'I was not *ringing* them, Brother. I was making sure they were in good working order. The bigger two sounded faintly when I pulled their ropes, but my treble . . . who could have done such a dreadful thing?'

They reached St Mary the Great, where Michael began the laborious process of unlocking the tower door. Then he climbed up the stairs, with Bartholomew behind and Nicholas bringing up the rear, still weeping. They reached the bell chamber to discover that one of the great metal domes was indeed missing. When he saw it, Nicholas dropped to his knees and sobbed so violently that Bartholomew was concerned for his health.

'Edith will buy you another,' he said kindly. He had no idea if it was true, but he had to say something to stem the frenzied outpouring of grief.

'But what will happen to her?' cried Nicholas, when he had controlled himself enough to speak. 'Will she be sold to another church or . . . *melted down?*' The last words were spoken in an appalled gulp that precipitated a fresh wave of tears.

'Neither,' said Michael, patting his shoulder comfortingly. 'As Matt said, bells are heavy, and cannot be toted about like sacks of grain. Someone will have seen the thieves, and we shall get her back. Matt – climb up to the frame and tell me how it was done.'

Bartholomew was tempted to tell the monk to do it himself, but Nicholas shot him a pleading look, so he put his foot in the stirrup formed by Michael's hands and hauled himself upwards. However, when he put his hand on the frame to steady himself, he felt it move in its moorings, and jumped back down again fast.

'Heavens!' he exclaimed, glancing up uneasily. 'It is loose.'

'It is supposed to be loose,' sniffled Nicholas. 'The tower will crack if the frame is too rigidly attached to the walls. Just ask any bell-hanger. It needs to be able to rock.'

'I see,' said Bartholomew, making a mental note never to stand beneath the bells when they were ringing. He turned to Michael. 'The thieves unfastened the bolts that secured the treble to its headstock. Then they lowered it to the floor, opened the trapdoor, and winched it down to the narthex.'

The trapdoor in question had been cut into the middle of the floor when the bells had been installed, as they had been too big to fit through the windows or up the stairs. It was a flimsy affair, which had worked to the thieves' advantage – a child could have lifted it up.

'There was all manner of filth on the narthex floor when I went to ring . . . I mean to *test* the bells this morning,' whispered Nicholas unsteadily. 'Dust, feathers, pigeon droppings . . . I assumed those filthy masons were responsible, getting ready to work on Tynkell's tomb.'

'When did you last see the treble?' asked Bartholomew.

'When you dragged me up here to demonstrate how the thief "locked" the Chest Room yesterday,' sniffed Nicholas. 'However, I know she was still here at three o'clock this morning, because I gave her a bit of a tug just before nocturns. I felt her swing.'

'The villains chose their time well,' mused Michael. 'The church is rarely empty, even in the small hours, but it was different last night. Too many scholars are angry about the election, so I told my beadles to oust everyone after each sacred office, to prevent spats.'

'And you gave the order that the bells are not to be rung until Wednesday,' said Bartholomew. 'The thieves assume that they will not be missed until the election, and probably aim to come back for another tonight and the last one tomorrow.'

Nicholas stopped crying and a vengeful expression suffused his face. 'Then I shall stand guard, and when they appear I shall run them through. Where can I get a sword, Brother? I want one with a *very* sharp point, because no one attacks *my* bells and lives to tell the tale.'

'I think we had better let the beadles do it,' said Michael kindly.

'This dust,' said Bartholomew, prodding a pile of wood shavings with his toe. 'Someone has been sawing. Are you *sure* the frame is safe, Nicholas? Because if you are wrong, the remaining bells – and perhaps the frame, too – will crash through this floor and land in the narthex. On you, if you happen to be ringing them.'

Nicholas gave him a pitying look. 'I see you know nothing about the technicalities of bell-hanging. The frame is designed to last a lifetime, and it will take more than a bit of sawing to render it unsound. The bells are quite safe, I assure you.'

They returned to the nave, where Michael detailed a

few beadles to monitor the tower, as well as questioning visitors to the church about the missing bell.

'The Sheriff will help us find it,' he said to Nicholas, who had started to sob again. 'A bell is bulkier and more distinctive than slabs of stone. We will catch the villains, never fear.'

'Good,' snuffled Nicholas. 'Because I have set my heart on ringing them when the next Chancellor is elected. *All* of them, not just two.'

CHAPTER 13

For the second time that morning, Bartholomew and Michael set out for the castle, now with even more reason to speak to the Sheriff, but were saved from climbing the hill when they met Tulyet on the Great Bridge. He was striding along briskly with a wet and very muddy Helbye at his heels. The older man was struggling to keep up with him.

'What have you been doing to get into such a state?' Bartholomew asked the sergeant, while Michael gave Tulyet a brief summary of all that had happened since they had last met.

'Hunting Yevele,' replied the old soldier curtly. 'I had a report that he was in Trumpington, but it was a lot of rubbish, because none of the villagers had seen him. Then, on the way back, I saw a barge that looked very heavy in the water. I gave chase, but it promptly cut off down a channel, where I could not follow. It was the thieves – I am sure of it.'

'What kind of barge?' asked Bartholomew uneasily, thinking of Isnard.

Helbye read his mind. 'Yes, it could have been his, although it was difficult to be sure.'

Bartholomew was puzzled. 'Yet if you saw this craft from the Trumpington road, it must have been travelling south. Why, when the sea and the Fens are north and east?'

'Because I suspect they have a base down there,' explained Helbye. 'They will take their loot a few miles by boat, then load it on to carts, to be transported to London by road.'

'I do not suppose you noticed a bell on board, did you?'

'A bell?' Helbye was thoughtful. 'There *was* something bulky, now you mention it. Why? Have you lost one?'

'The University Church has.' Bartholomew nodded at the sergeant's sodden clothes. 'I hope you did not try to swim after this boat.'

Helbye grimaced. 'I jumped across a ditch. I thought I could make it with room to spare, but there were roots and I stumbled . . . I landed with an awful thump. My arm is agony.'

'Would you like me to look at it?'

'Not in the street.' Helbye looked around quickly. 'I cannot have the lads seeing and thinking me feeble.' He nodded to a nearby tavern. 'But it will be nice and warm in there, and I would not mind a sip of hot ale. It is perishing out here.'

'We shall all come,' determined Michael, overhearing. 'We have much to discuss, and it will be more pleasant to do it indoors.'

The tavern was the Ship, a small, seedy establishment with an owner whose eyes bulged in alarm when the door opened to admit the Sheriff and Senior Proctor. His agitation did not diminish when Michael asked what victuals were available, making it clear that he intended to stay a while. The other patrons promptly melted away, ignoring his whispered pleas not to leave him alone with such a party. Oblivious of the fact that they were ruining his day, Michael and Tulyet began to discuss murder and theft, while Bartholomew examined Helbye.

The sergeant had fallen directly on his older wound, partly reopening it, and adding a deep cut that reached the bone. He had bound it to stem the bleeding, but the wound was filthy and would fester without proper care. Bartholomew began to clean it, a painful, laborious process that made Helbye groan and hiss between his

310

teeth. He had not been working long before there was a familiar and unwelcome voice at his elbow.

'What are you doing?'

Bartholomew could only suppose that one of the Ship's patrons had gone to tell Barber Cook what was happening, probably in the expectation of getting a coin for his trouble.

'He is tending one of my men,' said Tulyet coolly. 'Not that it is any of your business.'

'It *is* my business,' countered Cook, all haughty dignity. 'That is a laceration, and those are *mine* to treat, as stipulated in the charter of the Worshipful Company of Barbers. Helbye, come with me. I know how to heal injuries without making my patients swoon from the pain. Better yet, I will throw in a shave, gratis.'

Bartholomew doubted the barber could be more gentle than he had been, but Helbye seized the offer with relief.

'Thank God!' he gulped, standing at once. 'I can take a bit of discomfort, but no man enjoys having his wounds poked with sharp spikes.'

'No, Will,' snapped Tulyet. 'Stay with Matt.'

'Do not listen to him,' instructed Cook. 'He is—'

He backed away fast when Tulyet came to his feet with a dangerous light in his eyes: he had not forgotten the threat that had been issued the last time he had dared challenge the Sheriff's authority.

'It is all right, sir,' said Helbye. 'This small scratch is not worth any trouble. I will go with Cook, and he will soon set me right.'

'It is not a "small scratch",' argued Bartholomew. 'It is a serious injury that needs proper attention or it will turn bad.'

'I know how to treat wounds,' said Cook curtly. '*I* am a barber-surgeon. Helbye, if you value your life, follow me. If you want to die, then stay here with this *physician*.'

He spat the last word like an insult, before spinning

on his heel and stalking out. Bartholomew opened his mouth to appeal to Helbye's sense of self-preservation, but the sergeant raised a hand to stop him.

'Do not worry,' he said with a lop-sided grin. 'He did a lovely job sewing me up last time, and it barely hurt at all. You can do me a horoscope later, and then everyone will be happy.'

Bartholomew was not happy at all, and followed him to the door, where he watched Cook grin triumphantly as he took the sergeant's arm and escorted him into the Griffin Inn opposite. He was about to return to Michael and Tulyet when he saw his colleague Doctor Rougham of Gonville Hall. Rougham was wearing a handsome, fur-lined cloak against the chill, although it was too long for traipsing around Cambridge's mucky streets, and the bottom was sadly soiled with manure and something unpleasant picked up from walking past the slaughter-houses.

'Did I just see Helbye surrendering to Cook's tender mercies?' Rougham asked. 'I thought he had more sense. Still, when that lunatic kills him, at least he can have the satisfaction of lying in his grave with a beautiful haircut and a very close shave.'

'Helbye's life is not a matter for jests,' said Bartholomew sharply.

'Who is jesting? Cook is a menace, and should be banished from our town before he kills someone import-ant – or worse, someone rich. He almost deprived me of Inge the other day, and he has been one of my best clients.'

'Why did Inge need a *medicus*?'

'He accidentally swallowed some resin, so Cook brewed him an emetic, which made him vomit so violently that his stomach bled. The resin would have done him scant harm, but the emetic . . . well, suffice to say that he was lucky I was on hand to administer an antidote.'

'How does one "accidentally swallow" resin?' asked Bartholomew, bemused.

'According to Inge, he mistook it for honey, although it sounds a peculiar tale to me. But I cannot loiter here gossiping, Bartholomew. I have patients to tend.'

Bartholomew re-entered the Ship, hoping that Helbye would not take too long to come for his horoscope, so he could check Cook's handiwork before there was a problem.

'Why did you send him to Trumpington, Dick?' he asked, a little reproachfully. 'You must see that he is no longer up to that sort of jaunt.'

'I did not *send* him,' replied Tulyet. 'He volunteered. Besides, it was meant to be a short, easy ride, followed by putting a few questions in a tavern. How was I to know that he would take the opportunity to hare off in pursuit of barges?'

'Speaking of barges, how is your hunt for the thieves going?' asked Michael. 'I am afraid I have learned nothing to help, although my beadles have been told to keep their eyes open.'

'It is not "going" at all,' replied Tulyet sourly. 'And the rogues continue to outwit me at every turn. Your University has just lost a bell, while Holty is now missing his pinnacles.'

'But you have the tomb-makers under surveillance,' Bartholomew pointed out. 'Your men would have noticed the masons or the latteners slipping away to steal, which means they can be eliminated as suspects. Yes?'

'Not really,' sighed Tulyet. 'The nights are bitterly cold, and although my guards claim they stay at their posts every moment of their watch, I am not such a fool as to believe them. Of course they disappear for a quick walk to get their blood moving again, or even to find a warming drink. And who can blame them?'

'But what Helbye saw was valuable,' said Bartholomew encouragingly. 'I imagine you have been concentrating on craft travelling north and east – towards the Fens. But he saw one heading south, which will give you a new place to look for the thieves' base.'

'I monitor *all* the waterways and roads, regardless of direction, and that barge was not carrying your bell, no matter what Helbye thinks. No boat or cart that could have been toting such an item has left the town.'

'Then it is still here,' surmised Michael. 'Stashed away until you lower your guard.'

'Yes, but where? So much material has gone missing – all of it heavy or bulky – that a house or a large shed would be needed to store it all. I have searched all the likely places, but there is no sign of it.'

'Then perhaps it is cached in lots – a bit here and a bit there,' suggested Bartholomew. 'Or it has been moved piecemeal. Lead does not take up much room when it is rolled up, so perhaps it was hidden in a handcart or a travelling pack.'

Tulyet eyed him lugubriously. 'We would have found it, believe me.'

At that moment the door opened and Robin walked in. The young soldier looked around doubtfully as he approached their table, clearly of the opinion that the Sheriff had lost his wits by frequenting such an insalubrious establishment. Bartholomew was inclined to agree when the taverner began to bring the food that Michael had ordered – a plate of greasy fried pork and a pot of something that reeked powerfully of garlic.

'A letter has arrived for you, sir,' said Robin. 'I thought it might be important, so I decided to deliver it at once.'

Tulyet glanced at the seal, but tossed it on the table when it was one he did not recognise, more interested in what else Robin had to tell him.

'Well?' he demanded. 'What did you find out? Which

boats and carts left the town last night, and what were they carrying?'

'One barge and three carts,' reported Robin promptly. 'The men searched them all, as per your orders. The boat was empty, and the carts carried sacks of flour. Then there was the usual trickle of folk going to the King's Head, along with two horsemen. They frisked the drinkers but not the riders.'

'Why not?' asked Tulyet sharply. 'I said no exceptions.'

'Because one was that envoy from Rochester, who told them that he was on urgent University business and needed to hurry – which was true, as Cynric was there, and wished him God's speed. Once he was through the gate, the lads say he took off like lightning – he was riding Satan, you see.'

'Stephen,' corrected Tulyet automatically. He explained to the scholars. 'I could hardly keep the animal after what happened to Moleyns, but I could not bring myself to destroy him either, so I sold him to King's Hall.'

'Whittlesey,' said Michael through gritted teeth. 'Who used Cynric's chance presence to deceive your men, because he is *not* on any business of ours. And the lie certainly means we shall have questions to ask when Meadowman drags him back. Who was the other horseman?'

'Master Godrich of King's Hall,' replied Robin, 'who left a couple of hours earlier. It is a good thing there was a full moon, or riding would have been very treacherous for—'

'Godrich?' cried Michael. 'But we have been scouring the town for him for hours!'

'Have you?' said Robin, startled. 'Then it is a pity you did not ask our sentries – they could have told you not to bother.'

'I *did* ask them,' snapped Michael. 'They told me that they had not seen him.'

'They must have misunderstood your question,' said Robin, spreading his hands apologetically.

Michael knew that was unlikely, but was not surprised he had been misled. He and Tulyet worked well together, but the same was not true of their people – the soldiers struck sly blows at the University at every opportunity, while the beadles did the same to the castle. The guards had no doubt taken great delight in watching their rivals hunt for someone who was not there.

'When did Godrich go exactly?' he asked between gritted teeth.

'Before nocturns,' replied Robin. 'Perhaps two o'clock, or a little later. The lads say he also set off like greased lightning.'

'Did either mention where they were going?' asked Tulyet.

'The envoy did not, but Godrich thought the boys were taking too long to open the gate, and muttered that he would never reach Royston if they worked at the pace of snails. So *that* is where he was heading.'

'A journey of less than fifteen miles,' mused Bartholomew. 'But why there?'

'Because it has an inn where you can hire fresh horses,' explained Tulyet. 'It is not necessarily his final destination.'

'Did he seem frightened or uneasy?' asked Michael urgently of Robin. 'As if he was fleeing for his life?'

Robin shook his head. 'Apparently, he was just his usual self – arrogant, rude and nasty.'

'Well, at least he is not dead,' said Bartholomew. 'That is good news.'

'He was not dead at two o'clock last night,' corrected Michael. 'But that was hours ago, and Whittlesey is hot on his trail, riding a very fast horse. I had better send more beadles after them. Meadowman needs to know that he might be required to defend Godrich from attack.'

'He also needs to know that he must bring both of them back,' added Tulyet. 'I will send soldiers to help. If Whittlesey *is* the rogue who killed my prisoner, then the castle should play a role in his capture.'

'The Benedictine will not be caught,' predicted Robin. 'Not if he is riding Satan.'

'Even Stephen will need to rest at some point,' said Tulyet briskly. 'Now go and pick four of our best men—'

'Preferably ones who understand that we are all working to the same end,' put in Michael acidly.

'—and tell them to meet the beadles at the Trumpington Gate,' finished Tulyet. 'Hurry!'

'I am confused,' said Bartholomew, watching Robin stride away. 'Everything made sense – after a fashion – when we thought Whittlesey was the killer, who fled when he realised Godrich's murder was one too many. But now we learn that Godrich went first. Why? Could *he* be the culprit after all? In which case, why did Whittlesey go after him?'

'Perhaps Whittlesey aims to corner Godrich himself,' suggested Tulyet. 'Or he wants to help him escape – they are cousins, after all. Or maybe Godrich left on some unrelated mission, and has no idea that a ruthless killer is on his heels.'

'And Whittlesey *is* up to no good, or he would not have lied to the sentries,' said Michael worriedly. 'Moreover, Godrich spent a fortune on buying votes, and I strongly suspect that he did not intend to be gone for long. The fact that he has failed to return bodes very ill, as far as I am concerned.'

'Well, there is no use in speculating,' said Tulyet practically. 'We shall have answers when our people bring them back.'

'*If* they bring them back,' said Michael grimly. 'They have a significant lead.'

But Bartholomew was shaking his head. 'Tynkell and

Moleyns were murdered in front of dozens of witnesses, telling us that the killer is bold, confident and ruthless. He is not someone who runs at the first sign of trouble, and especially not from the paltry "evidence" that we have managed to put together. He would stay and brazen it out.'

Tulyet frowned. 'What are you saying? That Godrich and Whittlesey are innocent?'

'Not "innocent" – they are clearly up to something untoward, or they would not have raced off in the middle of the night, telling lies and riding King's Hall's fastest horses. But I am not sure that either killed Tynkell, Moleyns and Lyng.'

'So our culprit is still here?' asked Tulyet. 'Perhaps waiting to strike again?'

'It seems likely,' said Bartholomew.

While they waited for the beadles and soldiers to don travelling clothes, pack supplies into saddlebags, and ready horses, Bartholomew, Michael and Tulyet continued to discuss what they had reasoned. Michael was torn between despair that they still did not know the killer's identity, and relief that he might be spared the embarrassment of accusing one of the Archbishop's nephews of the crimes. Meanwhile, Bartholomew had continued to ponder the thefts.

'Pitch,' he said, suddenly and somewhat out of the blue. 'Lakenham lost a bucket of it to thieves, did he not?'

Tulyet regarded him warily. 'So he claims. Why?'

'Because Rougham told me that Inge had "accidentally swallowed" some resin.'

'And?' asked Tulyet, even more mystified. 'What of it?'

'Pitch is distilled from resin,' said Bartholomew. 'And Lakenham's was taken at night, when it is difficult to see. Burglary is a tense business, and anxious men are often clumsy . . .'

Tulyet blinked. 'You think *Inge* is the thief now? And he swallowed pitch in the process? I hardly think—'

'We know Moleyns escaped from the castle to steal,' interrupted Bartholomew, speaking urgently, because the more he thought about it, the more he was sure he was right. 'So why not Inge and Egidia as well?'

'Because I questioned them thoroughly, and I am satisfied that neither was involved. They knew what Moleyns was doing, certainly, but were not invited to take part. Which annoyed them, actually, as I suspect they would have welcomed a chance to earn some quick money.'

'Exactly! Being excluded must have been extremely galling, especially as Moleyns held the purse strings, and was not overly generous. I suspect they saw how easy it was for him to steal, so they decided to do the same.'

Tulyet made an impatient sound at the back of his throat. 'And you think they then elected to filch great lumps of stone and metal? That is ridiculous, Matt! Even if you are right about them taking a leaf from Moleyns' book – and I am not saying you are – they would have opted for coins, too. Cash, which is readily slipped into a purse and hidden.'

Bartholomew shook his head. 'First, they do not have "friends" to tell them about hidden hoards. Second, Moleyns was already targeting coins, and they would not have dared to compete with him. And third, his crimes won him only modest returns – he was careful never to take too much lest someone complained. The theft of stone and brass, however, is on a much grander scale – one that will allow them to break away from Moleyns once and for all.'

'I am not convinced, Matt,' warned Tulyet. 'Why would a lawyer and the wife of a friend of the King opt to take building supplies, of all things?'

'Because they knew the tomb-builders in Nottingham, where the cost of raw materials was almost certainly discussed. Inge is an intelligent man – he would have seen the enormous profit that could be made. Moreover, he hails from the Fens, and so will know how to spirit illicit goods away through the marshes. He may even have local contacts to help him.'

'Isnard and Gundrede,' spat Tulyet. 'I knew it!'

'Not them,' said Bartholomew quickly. 'They helped Moleyns to steal, not Inge and—'

He trailed off in horror, wondering what was wrong with him. First, he had blurted the secret of Tynkell's inked symbols to Michael, and now this. Tulyet eyed him balefully.

'So that is how you found out what Moleyns had been doing: *they* told you. Of course, I imagine their uncharacteristic attack of honesty only happened once he was dead, and they were no longer in a position to profit from him.'

'I still do not see Inge and Egidia stealing stone feet, pinnacles, bells and brasses,' said Michael, taking pity on Bartholomew and deftly steering the discussion away from the uncomfortable topic of Moleyns and his local helpmeets.

'Then how did Inge come to swallow resin?' persisted Bartholomew. 'It is not something that can happen under normal circumstances, which means it happened under *abnormal* ones – such as that he was out burgling and some splashed into his mouth.'

'This is arrant nonsense,' said Tulyet irritably. 'I cannot believe we are even discussing it when we have so much else to occupy our minds.'

Bartholomew raised his hands in a shrug. 'Can we question them anyway? It will cost us nothing, and what do we have to lose?'

'Nothing, I suppose,' conceded Tulyet reluctantly. 'But—'

He broke off as the landlord of the Ship approached.

'You forgot this, sir,' the man said obsequiously, handing over the missive that Robin had brought. 'You left it on the table.'

Tulyet nodded his thanks and opened it. He scanned it absently, then gaped his astonishment. 'It is from Godrich! Written in haste on his journey south. It says that—'

Michael grabbed it and read it himself. 'That when Moleyns was tried for the murder of Peter Poges, the evidence pointed to Inge and Egidia as the culprits, which is why he arranged for Moleyns to be acquitted. He claims there was nothing improper in the jury's verdict.'

Tulyet snatched it back again. 'He also says that he requested another trial, but powerful people intervened and the matter was quietly forgotten.' He looked up at Bartholomew. 'So, it seems you were right to suspect Inge and Egidia of something untoward. My apologies.'

'*If* Godrich is telling the truth,' cautioned Michael. 'It is difficult to know what to believe in this web of deceit and lies.'

'It is,' agreed Tulyet. 'But I am sure about one thing: it is time we had a word with Inge and Egidia. About the hapless Peter Poges *and* the thefts.'

Inge and Egidia had moved from the castle to the Griffin, the large tavern where Cook had taken Helbye for treatment. It was a pleasant, rambling affair that smelled of the fresh rushes that had been scattered on the floor and the half-sheep that was roasting on a spit over the fire. Bartholomew, Michael and Tulyet entered to see the pair by the window, although Cook and Helbye had chosen to sit in a different chamber, for which Bartholomew was grateful – he did not want another confrontation with the barber quite so soon after the last one.

'We have questions,' said Tulyet, addressing Inge and

Egidia without preamble. 'If you answer truthfully, I shall allow you to abjure the realm. Refuse, and you will hang.'

Bartholomew blinked his surprise at the Sheriff's opening gambit, but supposed a bombastic approach might serve to frighten them into a confession. Egidia was visibly alarmed, but Inge was made of sterner stuff, and regarded Tulyet in open disdain.

'Do not threaten me,' he sneered. ' I know my rights. You cannot charge in here and—'

'We can start with murder,' interrupted Tulyet, brandishing the letter. 'We have written testimony from a witness, who claims that *you*, not Moleyns, poisoned Peter Poges.'

'Lies!' declared Egidia, although the flash of fear in her eyes suggested otherwise.

'Is that from Godrich?' asked Inge, trying to examine the missive as Tulyet continued to wave it around. 'That appears to be his seal.' He laughed derisively. 'And you believe it? A man who is steeped in corruption, and who perverted the course of justice at Moleyns' trial?'

'Did he?' pounced Michael. 'I thought you said the outcome was the proper one – that Moleyns was innocent.'

'We did,' said Inge smoothly. 'But that was when Moleyns posed a danger to us. Now he is dead, we can tell the truth.'

'That is right,' nodded Egidia, licking her lips nervously, 'Of course my husband killed Uncle Peter, and Godrich *did* pervert the course of justice by bribing the jury. And if you want more evidence that Godrich is a rogue, ask him about all the gold that Inge and I paid him to—'

'Paid him to buy books for impoverished hostels,' interrupted Inge sharply, and from the way Egidia jumped, it was clear that he had kicked her under the table. He leaned back on the bench, feigning nonchalance.

'Well, that explains how Godrich was able to spend so

much on his election campaign,' murmured Michael to Bartholomew. 'He had a plentiful source of easy money.'

'You had better say your prayers,' said Tulyet to Egidia, instinctively targeting the weaker of the two. 'Because this letter is enough to see you on the scaffold.'

'It is a forgery,' said Inge with a shrug, although Egidia blanched. 'Why would Godrich make such a claim when he is about to be Chancellor? It damages him as much as it does us.'

'Yes – he *would* rather forget what happened in Stoke Poges all those years ago,' agreed Egidia. 'It shows him in a very poor light and—'

She jumped when Inge gave her another warning kick.

'Think about it,' Inge went on smoothly. 'If there was any truth in those allegations, he would have made them years ago.'

'Too right,' said Egidia, ignoring the lawyer's angry grimace for refusing to shut up. 'That letter is a piece of dirty mischief, and you should put it in the fire, where it belongs. Give it to me at once.'

She made a lunge for it, but Tulyet held it aloft.

'That reaction tells me all I need to know,' he said coldly. 'You *did* kill Peter Poges, and Moleyns' acquittal was not the miscarriage of justice we all thought. Did he ever guess that his wife and friend left him to stand trial for a crime that they committed?'

Their sullen silence suggested he had not, and Bartholomew supposed it was just as well Moleyns was dead, or they could have expected some serious retribution. Belatedly, Inge drew breath to deny the charge, but the physician spoke first.

'Tell us how you came to swallow resin,' he ordered, deciding to follow Tulyet's example and opt for a frontal attack.

'Rougham!' muttered Inge in disgust. 'So much for professional discretion.'

'Answer the question.' Tulyet waved the letter again. 'You are already accused of murder, so a charge of theft makes no odds now.'

'Theft?' echoed Inge, raising his eyebrows. 'What are you talking about?'

'And you will never prove murder anyway,' put in Egidia. 'Not now.'

'We had nothing to do with Moleyns' antics.' Inge spoke quickly, in an obvious effort to prevent Egidia from saying any more. 'We went through all this yesterday: we guessed what he was doing, but we were not involved.'

'No,' agreed Bartholomew. 'But when you saw how well his scheme worked, you decided to devise one of your own. He stole coins, but you opted for marble, lead, brasses, nails, pinnacles, pitch—'

'All valuable commodities that will fetch high prices in London,' said Tulyet, watching Inge in a way that suggested he had revised his opinion of Bartholomew's theory, and was now ready to accept it.

The lawyer sneered. 'And can you *prove* any of this? No? Then I suggest you desist with these slanderous allegations. I have already written to the King about our treatment here, and this will do nothing to help your case.'

'That is true.' Egidia nodded eagerly. 'Your accusations will look like what they are – a sly attempt to escape the blame for John's murder. No one will believe you, regardless of whether or not they are true.'

'That was a confession,' pounced Tulyet, while Inge shot her an irritable scowl. 'And I have heard enough. You are both under arrest. We shall resume this discussion in the castle.'

He stepped forward purposefully. Egidia immediately began to screech her outrage, while Inge leapt to his feet and grabbed a knife from the table. Unfortunately for him, it was a blunt one, used for smearing cheese on bread, and Tulyet regarded it contemptuously. Inge gulped his alarm when the Sheriff drew his sword, and promptly dived under the table.

The ensuing commotion, as Tulyet tried to lay hold of the lawyer without losing his own dignity by getting down on all fours, drew spectators from the other rooms, including Cook and Helbye. When one of Inge's wildly flailing fists caught Tulyet a glancing blow on the cheek, Helbye bellowed his fury and waded into the fray, trailing bandages. Unfortunately, he did more to hinder than help, particularly as his right arm was useless.

Michael managed to lay hold of Egidia, but she bit him, so he yelped and let her go, leaving Bartholomew to grab her. Then Inge scrambled from beneath the table and darted towards the door, but when Tulyet tried to follow, his feet became entangled in Helbye's dressings. He stumbled over them, and Helbye's scream of agony froze him in his tracks.

Bartholomew shoved Egidia at him, and hurtled after Inge, whom he would have caught with ease, if Cook had not decided that it was a good opportunity for some sly revenge. The barber launched himself at Bartholomew and managed to land several hefty thumps before the physician was able to turn and fend him off.

With no one to stop him, Inge shot through the door and dashed into the street. Michael set off in lumbering pursuit, but the lawyer had already disappeared, and the monk returned moments later, shaking his head to say Inge had escaped.

'Enough!' roared Tulyet, in a voice so full of anger that Egidia stopped struggling and Cook desisted in his efforts to hit Bartholomew. The physician used Cook's momentary inattention to land a punch that made him stagger; he was ashamed of how much pleasure it gave him.

'Go after Inge,' Tulyet ordered one of his men, who had rushed in to help when he had heard the sounds of a skirmish. 'And send me a couple of lads to escort Egidia to the castle. Matt, leave that butcher alone and help Helbye.'

'Barber,' corrected Cook, rubbing his jaw and glaring at Bartholomew. 'I am a *barber*.'

'Do not worry about me,' said Helbye, although he was clutching his elbow and his face was grey with pain. 'I shall be as right as rain when Cook has bound me up.'

'He has not had his shave yet either,' said Cook, and shot Bartholomew a glance that was full of malicious hostility. '*I* do not cheat my customers, unlike some I could mention. Come, Helbye. Let me finish mending your arm.'

Tulyet started to object, but Helbye raised a weary hand and made a feeble joke about his stubble. Then soldiers arrived to conduct Egidia to the gaol. She went with quiet dignity, her head held high, which suggested that she did not expect to be incarcerated for long before Inge rallied powerful forces to free her.

'She is going to be disappointed,' said Tulyet, watching her go. 'Her husband wielded a certain power, but no one will listen to Inge. Which is why he ran, of course – he knows there would have been no rescue for him.'

While Tulyet went to supervise the hunt for Inge, Bartholomew and Michael aimed for Maud's Hostel, to speak to Hopeman again.

'Inge will not get far,' predicted Bartholomew. 'He will be caught if he tries to hire a horse, and he does not seem like the kind of man who will fare well hiding in the marshes.'

'He might,' said Michael. 'He hails from this area, if you recall.'

'So do I,' said Bartholomew. 'But that does not mean I can survive the Fens in winter without the necessary clothes and equipment.'

Michael shook his head slowly, still thinking about the confrontation in the tavern. 'I am astonished, Matt – your wild theory was right. Who would have thought it?'

'They did not actually admit to stealing the supplies,' Bartholomew pointed out.

'They did not have to – their guilt was obvious from Egidia's reckless replies and Inge's flight. Unfortunately, while you have solved the thefts, we still have a killer at large, given that we both have reservations about Whittlesey or Godrich being the culprit. And we are running out of suspects.'

'It is Cook,' said Bartholomew. 'Hopeman would brag if he was the killer – claim that God told him to do it or some such nonsense.'

'He would not,' argued Michael. 'He may be a fanatic, but he is not stupid.'

'Then can we be sure that Inge and Egidia are innocent? It seems they killed Peter Poges, so how do we know they did not kill Tynkell, Lyng and Molcyns as well? They were near Moleyns when he died – which they later lied about – and they were in St Mary the Great when Tynkell was on the roof.'

'They had good reason to dispatch Moleyns,' mused Michael. 'His imprisonment was lasting a good deal longer than they had anticipated, and he was mean with the money he stole – as evidenced by the fact that he refused to buy them new cloaks when they were inspecting suitable cloth with Edith in the Market Square.'

'I sense a "but",' said Bartholomew, shooting him a sidelong glance.

Michael nodded. 'But in the conclave earlier, I quizzed Clippesby very closely about exactly what he saw when Moleyns fell off his horse. It took some doing – and he insisted the intelligence came from that mangy dog – but I managed to ascertain that Inge and Egidia could not have reached Moleyns' side in time to stab him. And that means they did not kill Tynkell and Lyng either.'

They walked the rest of the way in silence, aware again of the tension between those who supported one of the two remaining candidates, and those who felt they had been disenfranchised by the loss of their favourite. Quarrels were rife, and the beadles struggled to keep the peace, especially as the situation was exacerbated by the inflammatory taunts of townsfolk. When Bartholomew and Michael reached Maud's, they ran into Thelnetham, who was just coming out.

'There are five more votes for Suttone,' said the Gilbertine with a triumphant grin. 'I *knew* I could entice them to our side by pointing out the benefits of an alliance with Michaelhouse. This might be Hopeman's home, but they do not like him very much.'

'Who can blame them?' murmured Michael. 'I take it he is not inside then?'

'He is at his friary, pontificating about the Devil, apparently – about whom he knows rather more than is appropriate for a man in holy orders.'

Michael decided to visit Maud's anyway, to see what might be learned about the Dominican from his colleagues. He began by asking about the row that Blaston had overheard between Lyng and the "black villain", followed by the one that Almoner Byri had witnessed between Lyng and Hopeman in St Botolph's churchyard.

'We have already told you,' said Father Aidan, exasperated. 'We were not at home when Blaston was mending the table, and we were certainly not in St Botolph's churchyard after dark. And I do not believe Blaston's story, anyway. Lyng was not a violent man – he would never have hit anyone.'

'He threatened to kill me once,' said Richard sheepishly. 'But I probably deserved it, so I did not take it to heart. I am afraid I quite often irritated him into a bad mood.'

'Lyng?' asked Aidan in disbelief. 'But he was a gentle man. A saint!'

'Perhaps,' shrugged Richard. 'But he still had a bit of a tongue on him. He could be rather free with his fists, too, although he was old and slow, so I usually managed to duck.'

'*Lyng?*' breathed Aidan again, stunned. 'Are you sure?'

Richard pulled a rueful face. 'I might not be as intellectual as my brother the librarian, but I do know the difference between our teachers. Yes, Father – it was Lyng.'

'I am astonished, too,' confessed Michael. 'And it makes me wonder whether we can ever really know another person. However, Lyng's violent temper might explain why he was killed. Could Hopeman have witnessed it, and decided it meant he was possessed by the Devil?'

And dispatched him for it was the unspoken question.

'Hopeman sees Satan in everything,' said Aidan wryly. 'But perhaps he did spot something in Lyng that the rest of us missed, although I would be surprised – he is not a percipient man.'

'I hope you are wrong, Brother,' said Richard. 'It would be embarrassing for Maud's if Hopeman is the culprit. After all, no foundation likes its members slaughtering each other.'

Michael and Bartholomew hurried to the Dominican Priory. It was not a pleasant journey, as the road was treacherous with ice and the wind was getting up again.

'Marjory Starre says it will snow soon,' gasped Bartholomew as they staggered along.

'You should keep your friendship with her quiet,' advised Michael. 'Especially if our colleagues ever discover that Tynkell and Lyng were closet Satanists. There will be all manner of trouble, and you do not want to be part of it.'

'No,' agreed Bartholomew sincerely.

They reached the friary to discover Hopeman just leaving. He was being escorted out by Prior Morden and Almoner Byri, and through the open gate, a lot of Dominicans could be seen standing together in worried huddles.

'Hopeman has been telling us about Lucifer again,' explained Morden, casting a sour glance at the fanatical friar. 'We shall all have nightmares tonight. It was a terrifying discourse.'

'It was meant to be,' boomed Hopeman, who looked rather demonic himself, with his blazing eyes and hooded face. 'The Devil is not someone to be taken lightly, and there is too much complacency in this town. I shall put an end to it when I am Chancellor.'

'Lyng,' said Michael crisply. 'You were heard arguing with him – twice – on the evening when he disappeared and was probably murdered. What did—'

'Yes, all right, we argued,' hissed Hopeman. 'What of it?'

Michael narrowed his eyes at the abrupt capitulation. 'You denied it when I asked you before – you said you could not remember.'

Hopeman shrugged defiantly. 'I have since re-examined my memory. Lyng was Satan's spawn. He pretended to be good and saintly, but he was a Devil-lover, and he carried the mark of it on the sole of his foot.'

'How do you know?' asked Bartholomew suspiciously. 'I cannot imagined he showed you.'

'I saw it at Maud's, when he was soaking his aged toes after a day of marching around the town, telling people to vote for him,' replied Hopeman vengefully. 'Oh, he tried to hide it, but it was too late – I had seen. He told me it meant nothing, but I am no fool. So, yes, we quarrelled – in St Botolph's, where I tackled him about it, as your spy reported.'

'And you only "remember" this now?' asked Michael accusingly.

Hopeman met his gaze with a defiant stare. 'Yes. Why? Do you want to make something of it? However, the simple explanation is that I am busy with *important* matters, and I cannot be expected to recall every encounter with Satan's minions.'

In other words, thought Bartholomew, regarding him with dislike, he had been afraid that he would be accused of murder if he had admitted to quarrelling with one of the victims, but was less concerned about it now that he had convinced himself that God was on his side.

'What about the incident in Maud's?' he asked accusingly. 'When Lyng slapped you and called you a "black villain"? That cannot have been pleasant.'

Hopeman regarded him askance. 'He would not have dared to lay hands on the Lord's anointed. And I did not confront him at home anyway, because Richard Deynman was there.'

'Why should that make a difference?' asked Bartholomew, bemused.

Hopeman's eyes gleamed manically. 'I did not want witnesses to what I had to say to him – witnesses who might gossip, and put it about that the next Chancellor hails from a hostel that houses Satanists. However, once I had exposed Lyng's evil, God took matters in hand, and arranged for him to be eliminated.'

Michael raised his eyebrows. 'You accuse the Almighty of murder?'

'Of eradicating vermin,' corrected Hopeman. 'The Bible is full of such tales, so go away and read it, Brother. It might save your soul.'

'Have you heard that Godrich might not be in a position to stand for election on Wednesday?' asked Bartholomew, before the monk could take exception to the advice.

'Yes!' Hopeman grinned wildly. 'The race is between me and Suttone now: the agent of the Lord and the Senior Proctor's creature. I do not think there will be much of a contest. I shall win, and then I will revoke all the evil edicts you have passed, Brother.'

'Hopeman,' warned Prior Morden. 'I thought we had reached an understanding about these radical remarks. You agreed to moderate them in exchange for our support.'

'And we shall not vote for you unless you do,' added Byri. 'Just because you are a fellow Dominican does not mean—'

'I do as *God* commands,' flashed Hopeman. 'And you *will* vote for me, because to support Suttone is to invite Lucifer to rule.' He laughed suddenly, a harsh bray that grated on the ears. 'Oh, there will be changes when I am in power! For example, no one will study any subject but theology, so do not think that you will teach here, Bartholomew.'

'But we shall need physicians,' objected Morden worriedly. 'Or would you rather have someone like Cook come to tend you when you are ill?'

'God protects the righteous from sickness,' hissed Hopeman. 'And the sufferings of sinners will be good for their souls, and thus assure them a place in Heaven.'

Prior Morden tried to reason with him, but Hopeman flicked his fingers at his deacons, and they all marched away, singing one of the more warlike Psalms.

'He is deranged,' declared Michael in distaste. 'You should lock him away before he brings your Order into disrepute.'

'I am sure you would like that,' said Byri bitterly. 'It would leave Suttone free to win.'

'It would,' conceded Michael. 'But at least our University would not be in the hands of a lunatic – and one who lies about his interactions with murder victims into the bargain.'

None of the Dominicans had an answer for that particular charge, and Morden spared himself the chore of thinking one up by announcing that it was time for afternoon prayers. Relieved, the Black Friars hurried to their chapel, leaving a lay brother to shut the gate on the outside world. Bartholomew and Michael turned to trudge back to the town.

'Did you see Morden's face?' asked Michael. 'He thinks Hopeman might be guilty of these murders, even if his almoner is too stupid to see it. And if Hopeman's own Prior thinks he might be capable of such terrible deeds . . .'

CHAPTER 14

The next day – the last before the election – was bitingly cold, but clouds had rolled in, and Marjory Starre stood in the Market Square declaring to anyone who would listen that there would be snow before the day was out. Bartholomew thought she might be right, as the sky was a dirty yellowish grey and the wind so keen that it sliced right through his clothes.

'Heavens!' gasped Suttone, as he stepped into Michaelhouse's yard and was buffeted by an icy blast. 'I hope this will not prevent people from turning out to vote tomorrow.'

'It will not stop the young,' said Kolvyle archly. 'It is only the old who are bothered by inclement weather, and who cares what they think? The future lies with us, the fresh and vibrant – not tedious ancients who moan about their aching bones.'

'I am really beginning to dislike him,' muttered Suttone, as Kolvyle strutted away.

'I hate to admit it, Suttone,' said Michael, 'but it will be a close-run thing between you and Hopeman, so you must work hard today. '

Suttone groaned. 'Must I? I thought I might be able to relax, given how frantically I have laboured over the last few days.'

'Hopeman will not relax,' Michael pointed out shortly. 'And you should take *some* responsibility for winning. I am doing all I can, but it has been much harder than I anticipated.'

'Because you have been busy solving murders?' asked Suttone, removing a slice of cake from somewhere on his portly person and beginning to eat it. Some crumbs tumbled down the front of his habit, and others stuck to his lips.

'Yes, along with other things,' replied Michael, looking disapprovingly at the pastry and the mess Suttone was making with it. 'So shave, don a clean habit, and go out to persuade people that you are a credible alternative to Hopeman.'

Suttone shuffled into his place in the procession, still eating. He was wearing odd hose, one new and black, the other grey from repeated washing, and the hem of his habit had come unravelled. He yawned widely, then scrubbed at his face and hair with his hands, which did nothing to improve his appearance. Bartholomew wondered if the Carmelite had always been slovenly, or if it was just more apparent now that it mattered.

'Lord help us!' muttered Michael. 'No wonder people tell me they are unhappy with the choice they are being offered – a fanatical bigot or him. I confess I expected more when he offered me his services.'

As far as Bartholomew recalled, Suttone had just stated a desire to be Chancellor, and offering his services had never been part of the equation. He changed the subject by asking if there had been any news about the hunt for Whittlesey and Godrich.

'Yes,' replied the monk. 'A message arrived from Meadowman in the small hours. Whittlesey passed through a village called Walden yesterday, but no one remembers Godrich. Meadowman thinks that Whittlesey caught up with him – Satan is by far the faster horse – dispatched him, hid the body and galloped on.'

Bartholomew frowned. 'Then he is wrong, because we decided that Whittlesey was not the killer. Besides, what is not to say that Godrich turned off the road before Walden, blithely oblivious that his cousin was hot on his heels? And "no one remembers Godrich" does not mean that Godrich was never there. Perhaps he rode through this village without being noticed.'

'True.' Michael shook his head slowly. 'Their flight bothers me profoundly. Even if it is unrelated to what happened to Tynkell and the others, it is still suspicious, particularly given its timing. Godrich might well have won the election had he stayed, and I do not understand why he has thrown all that away.'

'Unless they have hatched a plot that will see him installed anyway,' suggested Bartholomew. 'I know Godrich has rendered himself ineligible by not keeping term, but I do not see him allowing a technicality to stand between him and his ambitions.'

'Nor do I,' acknowledged Michael. He rubbed his chin thoughtfully. 'We know he and Whittlesey quarrelled, but what does that mean? That Whittlesey objected to his cousin's machinations and ordered him to desist, or that they just disagreed on tactics?'

'And why has Whittlesey told so many lies?' Bartholomew was more suspicious of the slippery envoy than the belligerent scholar. 'Not just to the soldiers on the gate, but about his knee – I am sure he made up the tale about falling down the stairs. *And* there was the whispered discussion with Lyng on the night that Lyng died – the one Richard Deynman witnessed.'

'I had not forgotten that – or the fact that we do not know whether to believe his claim about not being in Nottingham when Dallingridge was poisoned.' Michael sighed dispiritedly. 'All I can say is that the behaviour of both is odd and worrisome.'

'Of course, we still have two other good suspects for the murders. Namely Hopeman, who is tipped to win the election now that Godrich is no longer eligible. And Cook.'

'Yes,' said Michael tiredly. 'But we have no evidence against either. So today, I shall speak to everyone who

336

saw Tynkell and Moleyns die. Again. Perhaps time will have altered their perspective, and something has occurred to them that will lead us forward.'

They attended church, but Bartholomew found it difficult to concentrate, his thoughts bouncing between the murders and Matilde – because if Meadowman had made such good time on the roads, then perhaps she had, too, and would arrive sooner than expected. And then what? He still had reached no decision about what to say to her. Wryly, it occurred to him that if he dithered long enough, he might not have to make one – she would grow tired of waiting and abandon Cambridge a second time.

He was equally distracted at breakfast, although it was a paltry affair, over in record time when Langelee decided that the victuals did not warrant a moment longer than was absolutely necessary to swallow what was offered.

'I shall not be teaching today,' announced Kolvyle, as the Fellows stood to leave the hall. 'I have business of a personal nature to conduct.'

'Then it can wait,' said Langelee tartly. 'Because we are too busy to—'

'Bartholomew or Michael can take my classes,' interrupted Kolvyle. 'I have minded theirs often enough these last few days, and it is time they returned the favour.'

'That is not how it works,' said Langelee irritably. 'You cannot pick and choose when you deign to work, and your students are expecting what you promised them today – three lectures on Gratian, and a good debate on primogeniture.'

'Then they will just have to live with their disappointment,' retorted Kolvyle carelessly. 'Because I shall not be here. And do not threaten to dismiss me, because we all know that if you do, you will never recruit another scholar of my intellectual calibre. I am here to stay, so I suggest you get used to it, *Master.*'

The last word was injected with such sneering contempt that Bartholomew was sure Kolvyle was going to lose teeth for it. Fortunately for Kolvyle – and for Langelee, as Masters punching Fellows was frowned upon in the University – Michael stepped forward to intervene.

'What is the nature of this personal business, Kolvyle?' he asked briskly. 'If it is urgent, I am sure some accommodation can be reached.'

'It is private,' replied Kolvyle loftily. 'Now, get out of my way.'

'Come back!' roared Langelee furiously, as the youngster began to flounce off. 'Or keep walking and never return, because this is the last time you will defy me.'

Kolvyle turned, gave a provocative little wave, and aimed for the gate.

'Right, that does it,' snarled Langelee, clenching his fists. 'I shall clear out his room and toss his belongings into the street. I refuse to endure another moment of his odious company.'

'Please wait until tomorrow afternoon,' begged Michael. 'We cannot afford a scandal in Michaelhouse right before the election, as it might adversely affect my . . . I mean *Suttone's* chances of winning.'

Langelee inclined his head stiffly. 'Very well. But keep Kolvyle out of my way, or there may be another murder for you to solve.'

'Speaking of murder,' said Suttone uneasily, 'may I have Cynric again, Matt? It would be a pity if I were dispatched on the very eve of my victory.'

Bartholomew nodded absently. 'I wonder what manner of "personal business" draws Kolvyle away from his duties. It must be important, as he has never refused to teach before.'

'It does not matter, because he is no longer a member of Michaelhouse,' declared Langelee. 'But enough of him. Suttone, why are you still here? Smarten yourself up, then go and win some more votes. The honour of the College is at stake here, man.' He turned to Michael. 'And you should be out hunting the killer if you aim to leave us on Thursday.'

'And leave you must,' added Suttone. 'Because we do not want the grasping Bishop of Bangor to get there first, and lay sticky fingers on your mitre.'

'No,' agreed Michael fervently. 'We do not.'

There was a long list of patients wanting Bartholomew's attention, and Aungel grinned his delight when informed that he was to mind the physician's classes yet again. He produced a sheaf of notes that suggested he had anticipated as much, and had probably spent much of the night preparing. Bartholomew called for Islaye and Mallet, aiming to take them with him on his rounds, and was taken aback when they informed him that they had other plans.

'There is a two-mark reward for recovering the University's missing bell, sir,' explained Mallet. 'And Master Langelee says that we can keep a shilling each if we find it, with the rest going to the College coffers.'

'But it is a weekday in term time,' objected Bartholomew. 'You are here to study, not go hunting stolen property. Besides, Egidia will tell Dick Tulyet where to find it now she is charged with its theft.'

'She cannot, because she does not know,' said Islaye. 'She was questioned thoroughly last night, and the Sheriff is satisfied that, while she definitely helped to organise the thefts, Inge never trusted her enough to tell her where he stashed what they stole.'

'And he was right to be wary,' put in Islaye. 'Because I hear it was her incautious tongue that betrayed them in the Griffin yesterday. If she had kept her mouth shut, they would have got away with it.'

'So the only way you will ever see the bell again,' said

Mallet, 'is if someone like us finds it before it is spirited out of the town, into the Fens, and around the coast to London.'

'Kolvyle will be looking for it,' added Islaye. 'That is why he abandoned his classes today – he aims to have that two marks for himself. Well, we do not want him to get them. We will never hear the end of it if he does, and his gloating will be unbearable.'

'Besides, your sister would be glad if we got the bell back,' said Mallet. 'She must be distraught that her beloved husband's donation is in the hands of greedy thieves.'

'All right!' Bartholomew threw up his hands in defeat at the onslaught. 'But only until noon. I want you back in the hall with Maimonides after the midday meal.'

Grinning their delight, the two students hurried away before he could change his mind. Bartholomew visited his patients alone, and met Edith on his way home.

'The Sheriff has promised to catch the culprits,' she said unhappily. 'But why should I believe him? He has had no luck so far, and so many things have been taken – Dallingridge's feet, Wilson's lid, Holty's pinnacles, Gonville's lead, Cew's brass . . .'

'But he *has* caught them,' said Bartholomew. 'Well, Inge is still on the run, I suppose, but Dick has sent patrols to hunt him down, so it is only a matter of time before he is caught.'

'Oh, Inge and Egidia were involved certainly,' said Edith bitterly. 'But they cannot have done it alone, and whoever helped them is cunning in the extreme.'

'Yes, they had helpmeets,' acknowledged Bartholomew. 'But it was Inge who masterminded the scheme. And when he is arrested, he will give Dick the names of his accomplices.'

'But he may be as ignorant as Egidia. He might hail from the Fens, but he is not a local, and no stranger could have outfoxed the Sheriff and his men all this time. Of course, there are rumours about who is the *real* brain behind this operation . . .'

'And who do these tales accuse?' Bartholomew had already guessed what was coming.

Edith grimaced. 'You know who: Isnard. I appreciate that you are fond of him, Matt, but Gundrede is bad news, and Isnard should have kept his distance.'

'It is not Isnard,' said Bartholomew firmly. 'He would never have taken Wilson's lid or struck at St Mary the Great, because he loves Michael and the choir.'

'Does he? Or does he feel betrayed, because Michael is going to Rochester? And even if you are right about him, Gundrede owns no such allegiance and Isnard is clay in his hands.'

'Is there evidence to prove these allegations?' asked Bartholomew, a little coolly, knowing there was not, or Tulyet would have acted on it.

'Well, first, there is only one way to transport heavy goods over long distances: the waterways, which Isnard knows like the back of his hand. Second, he owns suitable craft. Third, Gundrede was a metalsmith, who knows how to sell such goods illegally. And fourth, both he and Isnard have been gone a lot recently.'

'That is not evidence, it is supposition. Besides, *why* can't the goods be moved by road?'

'Because Tulyet watches them like a hawk – no cart gets past him without an inspection. Moreover, horses or oxen can pull heavy wagons short distances, but not all the way to London.'

Bartholomew was not sure what to think, but sincerely hoped she was wrong.

He hurried from patient to patient through streets that buzzed with excitement as news of the reward began to spread. Any number of folk – students and townsmen

– were determined to have it, and skirmishes broke out when searchers invaded the property of those who objected.

Most Regent masters, however, were more interested in the election, and were beginning to form factions. Unfortunately, the largest ones comprised not supporters of Suttone and Hopeman, but those of Lyng, Godrich and Thelnetham, who felt that events had conspired to deprive them of a voice. Emotions were running high and altercations were frequent, although so far confined to words and the occasional jabbing finger.

'Psst! Doctor!'

Bartholomew knew without looking that it was Isnard who hailed him so slyly. He hesitated, not sure whether to respond given what Edith had just said, but then he relented. Isnard was a patient, and might need medical help. The bargeman was beckoning frantically from a nearby alehouse, an establishment that sold cheap ale to those with undiscerning palates. He and Gundrede were in the shadows of the porch, both looking tired, unshaven and furtive.

'We are hiding,' said Isnard, somewhat unnecessarily. 'From the Sheriff, who thinks we stole the University's bell.'

'Can you prove you did not?' asked Bartholomew, speaking frostily, because Edith had been right about one thing: Isnard had not made a good choice of friends in Gundrede.

'No,' replied Gundrede gloomily. 'Because I was spying on Lakenham – from shortly after you fixed my nose, right up until dawn. Obviously, he had no idea I was there, which means he cannot give me an alibi.'

'And the same goes for me,' said Isnard. 'Except that I was minding Petit. We are tired of being accused of *their* crimes, so we decided to monitor them ourselves – to catch them in the act and prove our innocence.'

'That was unnecessary,' said Bartholomew. 'The Sheriff is doing it.'

'Yes, but his men slip away for quick drinks or to stretch their legs,' explained Isnard. 'Whereas we do not leave our posts for an instant. Our good reputations are at stake here, so we are much more careful than guards with no vested interest.'

'We minded them most of Sunday and all Monday night,' Gundrede went on, yawning. 'Which is why we are so tired now. However, our exhaustion will not stop us from starting again, once we have had a bit of bread and cheese to fortify us.'

'Unfortunately, the rogues decided to take those particular times off,' said Isnard glumly, 'and they both stayed in. Indeed, I think they were asleep.'

He sounded indignant that they should dare do such a thing when he had been waiting to witness something criminal.

Bartholomew was thoughtful. 'The bell went missing between nocturns and dawn. If you were watching Lakenham and Petit at those times, then it means that neither of them can have taken it.'

'Damn it, Gundrede!' cried Isnard in alarm. 'We have proved their innocence, but put nooses around our own necks! I told you it was a stupid idea.'

'Then maybe they sent one of their apprentices to do it,' said Gundrede, thinking fast. 'Or a wife – that Cristine would have no problem lifting a bell.'

'Aye,' agreed Isnard in relief. 'That must be what happened – she is a strong lass. But speaking of lasses, that is why we hailed you: to ask you to visit Yolande. She usually sees me on a Tuesday, as you know, but today she refused to open her door. Something is wrong.'

'Perhaps she is busy with someone else,' suggested Bartholomew, unwilling to be drawn into a dispute between a man and his prostitute.

'She would never give my spot to another client,' declared Isnard, affronted. 'And I am afraid that Barber Cook has got at her, because I saw him leave her house. He should not be allowed to physick a goat, let alone a person.'

'I cannot abide Cook,' spat Gundrede. 'He was sewing up a cut on my leg when the Chancellor fought the Devil on the tower, and he would not let me outside to watch.'

'Cook was with you when Tynkell was stabbed?' asked Bartholomew urgently. 'Are you sure? Because if you are, then it means that Cook is not the killer.'

'You had him on your list, did you?' asked Gundrede. 'Well, I do not blame you, because he is a devious bastard. However, he did not kill the Chancellor. He was with me and half a dozen others when Tynkell was up on the roof.'

'I watched that fight,' said Isnard, while Bartholomew struggled to mask his disappointment. It was unworthy of him, he knew, but it would have been so very satisfying to see the loathsome barber charged with murder. 'I was so shocked to see Chancellor Tynkell challenge Satan that I sat down hard and hurt my back, if you recall. But by the time Gundrede came to carry me home, the excitement was over. He had missed it all.'

'Then, a bit later, we were among those who saw Moleyns fall off his horse,' Gundrede went on. 'Unfortunately, so was Cook, and he spent the whole time demanding to be paid for tending my leg. So he did not kill Moleyns either.'

'I wish you had mentioned this sooner,' groaned Bartholomew. 'It would have saved a lot of wasted time.'

'Why would we want that?' asked Gundrede artlessly. 'The longer Tulyet takes to solve the murders, the less time he has to persecute me and Isnard.'

The two townsmen led Bartholomew on a circuitous route to the Blaston house, partly because they were keen to avoid meeting the Sheriff, but also because Milne Street was still blocked by Trinity Hall's rubble, and there was a lot of irritable jostling from those who wanted to squeeze down the narrow opening that had been punched through the middle of it.

They arrived at the Blastons' home to hear loud sobbing emanating from within. Isnard and Gundrede exchanged uneasy glances, wished Bartholomew luck, and melted away before they were seen.

Bartholomew knocked on the door, and was admitted by a child with frightened eyes. He touched her shoulder reassuringly, and followed her to the bedchamber, where Yolande lay surrounded by her family. There were so many of them, all grave-faced, that he was uncomfortably reminded of the deathbed of a monarch or a high-ranking churchman.

'Do not waste your time here,' whispered Yolande. 'I shall be dead in a week.'

Blaston's face was as white as snow. 'She cut her hand last night. Barber Cook heard about it, and came to do her a horoscope. But the news is not good.'

Bartholomew sat on the bed and unwrapped the bandages that swathed Yolande's arm to the elbow. The wound was deep but clean, while the skin around it was pink and healthy, so there was no reason to think it would not heal. He looked at her in mystification.

'My stars,' whispered Yolande, her expression haunted. 'They say that I shall be in my grave within seven days. Show him Barber Cook's workings, Robert.'

Bartholomew did not believe in the predictive power of horoscopes, and for many years had refused to calculate them at all, considering them a waste of his time and the patient's money. Such a stance had earned him a good deal of condemnation, and had contributed to his reputation as a maverick. However, age and experience had taught him that some patients recovered more quickly if they believed their stars were favourable, so he had come to accept that astrology had its place in a physician's arsenal.

Yet the one Blaston handed him was like nothing he had ever produced – or seen devised by anyone else. It had a few Latin words, but they were in no particular order, and were interspersed with meaningless symbols and squiggles. All around the edges were drawings of horned serpents.

'What does it say?' he asked.

Blaston blinked his surprise at the question. 'You are the one who can read Greek, Doctor. Barber Cook says that particular language is the best for matters pertaining to stars.'

'This is not Greek,' said Bartholomew, feeling anger stir within him as he pushed the parchment in his bag, intending to confront the surgeon with it later. 'It is gibberish. And he is not qualified to produce horoscopes anyway. That is the domain of physicians.'

Yolande gazed at him, hope lighting her eyes. 'So I will not die?'

'Not yet, certainly,' replied Bartholomew. 'And to prove it, *I* will read your stars. Then I will give my calculations to Rougham and Lawrence, who will check them for you.'

'Three University men,' breathed Blaston, impressed. 'They will know a lot more than Barber Cook.'

'Of course they will,' said Bartholomew briskly, and set to work at once, while parents and children watched in taut silence, even the babies. When he had finished, he informed Yolande that there was no reason she should not live to be a hundred. She grasped his hand tearfully, but he could not hear her whispered thanks over the delighted whoops of her family.

He walked outside and looked around rather wildly, hoping to see Cook there and then. Instead, he spotted Rougham, who was just emerging from Trinity Hall.

'Look,' he said, all righteous indignation as he pulled the barber's augury from his bag. 'And Cook accuses me of trespassing on *his* domain! He gave this to Yolande.'

'Heavens!' Rougham took it from him gingerly. 'It is a long time since I have seen one of these. They were sold during the plague, to those who thought the Church had deserted them. Do you see these horned serpents? They are the Devil's mark.'

'How do you know?' asked Bartholomew, startled.

'Desperate times called for desperate measures,' replied Rougham evasively. 'But I am told that witchery is becoming popular again – probably thanks to Suttone, who keeps announcing that the plague is about to return.'

Bartholomew frowned. 'So Cook is a proponent of witchcraft?'

'It would seem so. Give that document to me, and I shall include it with the letter I am writing to Tulyet, asking him to banish Cook from our town. We do not want that sort of person practising medicine in Cambridge. He will give us all a bad name.'

By noon, the hunt for the missing bell had reached fever point. Unfortunately, it was causing friction, not only between the searchers and those people who owned the places they aimed to ransack, but between students and the town. On the High Street, Bartholomew witnessed a furious fracas over who should have first dibs on exploring St Edward's crypt.

'We do,' one of Hopeman's deacons was snarling. 'Because that bell is *University* property, and it will be desecrated if secular hands maul it.'

'But this church belongs to the town,' retorted a butcher's boy. 'And *that* will be sullied if the likes of you is allowed inside. So sod off and—'

He stopped speaking abruptly when he saw Tulyet striding towards them. Under the Sheriff's gimlet eye, both sides had the sense to break off their quarrel and slink away without further ado.

'Who offered this reward, Dick?' asked Bartholomew disapprovingly. 'It cannot have been the University. Michael would know better.'

'Unfortunately, the same cannot be said of Secretary Nicholas,' replied Tulyet. 'It was his idea, and he announced it before Michael could stop him. The money is his own, apparently.'

'Well, he does love the bells.'

'I like them myself, but it was stupidity itself to offer such an enormous sum to get one back again. But I am glad to have caught you, Matt. I have been looking everywhere for you. Will you come to examine Helbye? I think Cook did something terrible to his arm yesterday, because he is ill.'

He turned and set a cracking pace towards the castle before the physician could reply. He spoke in short, agitated bursts as they went, and Bartholomew saw the strain the last few days had brought, with the King's favourite dead and thieves running circles around him.

'Egidia knows nothing,' Tulyet confided bitterly. 'Her role in the affair was to distract Moleyns while Inge sneaked out. They did not want Moleyns to know what they were doing, you see, because he would have ordered them to stop, lest it interfered with his own antics.'

'What will you do about Moleyns' crimes against his wealthy "friends"?' asked Bartholomew uneasily, afraid of what such an investigation might mean for Isnard.

Tulyet's expression was wry. 'Nothing, so you can tell Isnard not to worry. Moleyns' victims do not want the King to know they are fools easily parted from their money, lest he tries to get some of it for himself – the royal coffers are always empty. I have been told to let it drop.'

'Good,' said Bartholomew in relief. 'Not just for Isnard, but because Moleyns' plan to humiliate you will fail. Now the King will never know that he escaped your custody to steal.'

'True,' acknowledged Tulyet, although his youthful face remained troubled. 'We found no sign of Inge, by the way. I have soldiers scouring the marshes in ever-widening circles.'

'Are you sure he is out there? He did not move those heavy items by himself, which means he has accomplices in the town. Perhaps one of them is sheltering him.'

'You mean Isnard and Gundrede? I searched their houses – he is not there.'

'No, I do not mean them! *They* were watching the tomb-makers when the bell was stolen – far more carefully than your guards, as it happens, because they are determined to prove their innocence. Besides, thanks to my incautious tongue, you know that they helped Moleyns. They could not have obliged Inge and Egidia as well.'

'Oh, yes, they could,' countered Tulyet. 'But I shall give them the benefit of the doubt. However, I still want to know where they go when they disappear so slyly – such as on Saturday, when no one saw them for hours.'

Bartholomew recalled Isnard's suspicious demeanour when he himself had asked where they had been, and was sure Tulyet was right to smell a rat. He said nothing, though, unwilling to betray Isnard a second time.

'I suspect Inge fled the town under cover of darkness,' Tulyet went on, more concerned with the missing lawyer. 'We watch the gates, but he could have waded across the river or the King's Ditch. Still, the marshes are bleak at this time of year, so he will not get far.'

Bartholomew glanced up at the lowering sky and shivered, thinking he would not want to brave the Fens in such weather.

Helbye was indeed unwell. His injured arm was hot and swollen, and Bartholomew was appalled to see that Cook

349

had applied a poultice comprising what appeared to be mud and strands of riverweed to the wound. He did his best to wash it off, but some of the smaller fragments were difficult to see in the swollen tissue, and he was far from certain that he had removed them all.

'Cook sewed me up once before with no ill effects,' said Helbye defensively, when Bartholomew had finished, 'so I do not know what happened this time.'

'Wounds are often unpredictable,' said Bartholomew non-committally.

At that moment, there was a commotion in the bailey. Tulyet had received Rougham's letter of complaint about Cook in the interim, and had sent Robin to bring the barber to the castle. Cook was livid, screeching his outrage so stridently that his guards were wincing.

'You *medici* should have made your concerns official weeks ago,' said Tulyet, looking out of the window at the spectacle. 'But better late than never, I suppose. That charlatan will leave my town by nightfall or I shall arrest him for murder.'

Helbye blinked his astonishment. 'Murder? You mean it was Cook who killed all those people – Moleyns, Tynkell, Lyng and the tomb-builders' apprentices?'

'No, I mean Mother Salter and Widow Miller,' replied Tulyet. 'His patients.'

There was a clatter of footsteps on the stairs and Cook appeared, his face as black as thunder. He threw off the guards who held his arms and stalked towards the Sheriff – until he saw Bartholomew with Helbye, at which point he stopped dead in his tracks.

'You trespass on my professional domain *again*?' he snarled. 'How dare you!'

Tulyet stepped in front of him. 'Here is the "horoscope" you calculated for Yolande de Blaston. Perhaps you would care to explain why it is covered in demonic symbols.'

Cook's eyes took on a sly cant. 'I did not give her that

– she must have bought it from some other practitioner. Rougham or Bartholomew, for example.'

'Do not lie,' warned Tulyet. 'You will only make matters worse for yourself.'

'How could you do such a terrible thing?' asked Bartholomew reproachfully. 'Telling her she was going to die! It was cruel, and it frightened her children.'

'It serves her right for going around telling everyone that I killed Mother Salter,' flashed Cook viciously. '*I* was not the last *medicus* to see her before she died. *You* were.'

'But it was you who provided the "care" that caused her demise,' countered Tulyet. He waved the horoscope again. 'And here is the evidence that you wilfully defrauded a townsperson – you know Yolande cannot read, so had no way to tell that she was being fobbed off with rubbish. Now, you have two choices: leave Cambridge and never return; or spend the next few months in my gaol, awaiting trial. Which will it be?'

'Neither,' snapped Cook. 'I have complaints pending with the Worshipful Company of—'

'Arrest, is it?' interrupted Tulyet. 'As you wish.'

'Wait!' Cook backed away hastily. 'I will go, but I need time to pack. I own a lot of valuable equipment, and I am damned if I am going to leave it for the physicians to steal.'

'You have nothing we want,' retorted Bartholomew, unable to help himself.

Furious, Cook started forward with the clear intention of delivering a punch, but Tulyet deftly intervened by enveloping him in a grip that he often used on awkward customers. It involved one arm around the neck, which was tight enough to restrict the barber's airflow. Panicked, Cook began to claw at it, and as he did, one sleeve fell back to reveal the skin of his forearm.

'What is that?' demanded Bartholomew, pointing at the symbol that was inked there.

'A horned serpent,' mused Tulyet. 'Well, well, well! Our barber is a Satanist.'

'No!' gasped Cook, once the Sheriff had loosened his hold enough to let him explain. 'It is a symbol to ward off evil. Lots of folk have them.'

'So that is why you met Lyng, Moleyns and Tynkell in St Mary the Great,' said Bartholomew. 'To plot with like-minded—'

'You are mistaken!' gulped Cook. 'If you must know, Lyng, Tynkell and I went there to *grovel* to Moleyns – he liked to feel himself important, and he was a friend of the King. But there was no harm in it, and he had to have some pleasure in life.'

'He did have some pleasure,' said Tulyet acidly. 'Sneaking out of the castle and depriving his wealthy friends of their money.'

Cook managed to twist around and gape at him. 'Wait a moment! *Moleyns* broke into my house and took my purse? And Lyng's charity box and the money Tynkell had saved for the Michaelhouse Choir? We did note that he was the only other person who knew about them, but we assumed he was innocent, because they disappeared at night, when he was locked up.'

There was a curious plausibility to Cook's explanations, and Bartholomew found he was inclined to believe them. So was that all there was to the secretive meetings in St Mary the Great? A man who liked to be the centre of attention, and acquaintances who aimed to exploit his weakness to win themselves a good word at Court? Tulyet was obviously convinced, because he released the barber with a grimace of disgust.

'You have an hour to pack,' he said coldly. 'You are finished here, and if I ever see your face again, I will clap you in gaol. Is that clear?'

Cook glowered, but could see that arguing would be futile. He stalked out without another word, the soldiers at his heels to make sure he did as he was ordered. They almost collided with Robin at the door. The young soldier was muddy, breathless and triumphant.

'We have had a report of Inge,' he told the Sheriff excitedly. 'Five miles to the east.'

Helbye struggled to his feet. 'Half a dozen men should be enough to run him down. Do not worry, sir. I will bring him back.'

'Not this time, Will.' Tulyet indicated a rough-looking soldier with short, greasy hair and a scar down one cheek. 'Norys can go. You stay here and rest.'

A short while later, Bartholomew and Tulyet walked down the hill together, aiming for St Mary the Great, where Tulyet had agreed to meet Michael. Bartholomew was surprised to hear one of its bells clanging in the distance – he had thought they were to remain silent until the University had a new Chancellor. They had just crossed the Great Bridge when Bartholomew saw Edith again. She was talking to Rougham and he could tell just by looking that something was wrong. He hurried over to her, Tulyet at his heels.

'Perhaps you should offer a reward for its safe return,' Rougham was saying. 'Like Nicholas has done for his bell. However, I wish he had advanced a more modest sum. Every student in the University is out looking for the thing, and lectures have ground to a halt.'

'What have you lost, Edith?' asked Bartholomew anxiously.

'Oswald's tomb-chest,' replied Edith tearfully. 'The whole thing – top, base *and* sides. Lakenham says that Petit failed to cement it to the floor properly, which rendered it easy to pick up and tote away. Petit denies it, of course.'

'Inge,' muttered Tulyet between gritted teeth, while Bartholomew gaped his astonishment at the scale of the undertaking. 'He lingered here to wreak his revenge on us for exposing his schemes, and only then did he vanish into the Fens.'

'Stanmore's grave is not his only victim,' said Rougham. 'Do you remember our old colleague Linton, Bartholomew? Well, his monument was stolen last night, too. Admittedly, it was smaller than Stanmore's, but it was an audacious act, even so. It makes me think that Lyng had the right idea – a modest burial in the churchyard, with a simple wooden cross.'

Bartholomew was reluctant to leave Edith while she was upset, but Tulyet's wife arrived at that moment, and whisked her away for mulled wine and sympathy. Satisfied that she was in kindly hands, he and Tulyet continued on their way, and reached St Mary the Great to find a large gathering of scholars outside, all of whom were shouting. The horde included Michael, Suttone, Hopeman, Thelnetham and Nicholas.

'I swear it!' the little secretary was insisting. 'I was in my office at the time, as a dozen colleagues will confirm. I did *not* ring the tenor – she sounded of her own accord. Unless the Devil . . .'

'*Yes!*' thundered Hopeman. 'Satan chimed her, because Thelnetham persuaded Bene't College to vote for Suttone. Lucifer is delighted with that outcome, because he feels it brings him closer to taking over the University. He rang the bell to celebrate.'

'Satan keeps away from St Mary the Great these days,' said Thelnetham with considerable authority. 'Ever since he was obliged to make an undignified getaway from the tower roof. So if anyone rang the bell, it was God – because He is pleased that Suttone is winning.'

'Suttone is *not* winning!' yelled Hopeman. 'I have secured far more votes, and tomorrow will see me installed as Chancellor.'

'We shall see,' said Suttone with quiet dignity. He was wearing his best habit and was freshly shaved. For the first time since he had put himself forward, he looked like Chancellor material. 'I trust our colleagues to make the right decision.'

'It is *God* who will decide, not them,' countered Hopeman. 'And anyone who votes against me will be damned for all eternity.' He glowered around, causing several scholars to cross themselves as protection against his malign gaze. 'Hah! Listen! The bell sounds yet again. That is the Almighty saying that I am right.'

'It is a *person* up there,' stated Michael firmly. 'Not Satan or God.'

'Heresy!' shrieked Hopeman. 'He is—'

'It cannot be a person, Brother,' interrupted Vicar Milde from St Clement's. 'Because I was in the narthex when it donged earlier, and I saw the rope move of its own volition. No one was anywhere near it.'

'And the tower is locked,' added Nicholas. 'I checked before I came out. No one is up there pushing the bells around.'

'Then the wind did it,' shrugged Michael. 'The louvres are open and—'

'What wind?' asked Thelnetham. 'There is not so much as a breath of it.'

'But that will change tonight,' brayed Hopeman. 'Because God will send a blizzard, as a warning to all those who plan to vote for a man who wants to turn the University into a brothel. He told me so Himself.'

'You do not need to commune with God to know that there will be snow soon,' countered Michael scathingly. 'There are all manner of signs – the dirty yellow colour of the sky, the way the clouds are moving, the behaviour of the birds—'

'You have been talking to Mad Clippesby!' spat Hopeman in disgust. 'That is the kind of inane remark he might make. I shall petition for him to be defrocked when I am Chancellor.'

There was a roar of agreement from his acolytes, followed by a bellow of anger from those who valued Clippesby's quiet goodness.

'You scholars!' muttered Tulyet in disgust. 'Any excuse for a spat.'

'Right,' said Michael purposefully, removing the tower keys from his scrip as the tenor sounded yet again. 'I have had enough of this nonsense. Hopeman, Suttone – come with me. You can help me nab this prankster – a rogue, who has the credulous all a-flutter.'

Hopeman surged forward determinedly, although his acolytes held back, preferring to let him tackle whatever was inside. Suttone turned a little pale, but gamely fell in at Michael's heels. No one else was inclined to follow, and there was a buzz of excited anticipation as the onlookers waited to see what would happen next.

'Should we offer to help, Matt?' asked Tulyet. 'Or can Michael handle the mischief-maker on his own?'

'He can manage.' Bartholomew nodded to where a pack of beadles had assembled nearby. 'They will take the culprit off his hands when he comes down. I imagine a student is up there, having a bit of fun at our expense.'

'In that case, shall we go to St John Zachary? I hate wasting time, and Michael will be busy for a while yet. Rather than twiddle our thumbs, I suggest we find out what Frisby has to say about the tomb that was stolen from his church.'

They arrived to find the vicar in the graveyard, his back resting against a tomb, while his legs were splayed in front of him. He was drinking from a very large jug. It looked dissipated, and Bartholomew wondered why the Bishop did not oust him and appoint someone more suitable to the post.

'Another theft from my poor chancel,' Frisby slurred,

his eyes red-rimmed and angry. 'And from right under my nose, as well.'

'What do you mean?' asked Tulyet.

'I mean that I guessed it was only a matter of time before something else was swiped, given that those wretched tomb-makers have been using my church as their personal battleground, so I decided to stay here all night and keep watch.'

'And what did you see?' asked Tulyet eagerly.

'Nothing, because I fell asleep. It was dark and quiet, and I was very tired.'

'But you must have heard something,' pressed Tulyet irritably. 'Moving an entire tomb cannot be a silent task.'

'It is if you know what you are doing,' averred Frisby. 'I could hardly believe my eyes when I woke up an hour ago to discover the whole thing missing.'

'An *hour* ago?' echoed Bartholomew in disbelief. 'You slept all night and half the day?'

'I was tired,' repeated Frisby, although his dissipated appearance suggested that he had not been overcome by healthy sleep, but a drunken stupor. He sighed self-pityingly. 'Monuments might look pretty in a church, but between you and me, they are more trouble than they are worth.'

Sensing that questioning him further would be a waste of time, Bartholomew opened the door to the church, and was immediately assailed by the sound of voices raised in fury. They belonged to Lakenham and Petit, who were in the chancel, quarrelling heatedly. The mason had his apprentices to back him, but Lakenham had Cristine, and when her stabbing finger connected with a rival's chest, it hurt. Several lads were rubbing places where bruises would appear by the morning.

But it was the empty spot where Stanmore's tomb had been that caught Bartholomew's eye. All that remained were gouges in the floor, where it had stood. He glanced across at the vault, noting with relief that the thieves had left that alone at least, perhaps because the sealing slab was now suspended on its hoist, so moving it would be tricky.

'I think I am beginning to understand at last,' he said to Tulyet, who was at his side, watching the argument wearily. 'We know the tomb-builders are innocent of the thefts, because they have alibis in Isnard and Gundrede.'

Tulyet eyed him lugubriously. 'I accepted your reasoning about that when you explained it the first time. There is no need to repeat it – I realise I was wrong.'

'It must be a lucrative business,' Bartholomew went on, thoughts racing. 'Or Inge would not have bothered. People happily kill where large amounts of money are concerned – and *that* is why Lucas, Reames and Peres were murdered. Not because of the tomb-makers' feud.'

Tulyet lost his resigned expression and regarded him intently. 'Go on.'

'Lucas was first, stabbed with a chisel while he was waiting to sell us information. He talked about knowing "people and places", and we assumed he referred to the killer. But he misled us.'

'I disagree. Michael offered him threepence for the culprit's name, and his response suggested that he knew it.'

'He wanted the money,' corrected Bartholomew. 'So he said what was necessary to get us into the churchyard at midnight. However, I suspect what he had to sell was information about the thefts, not the murders. The thieves guessed that he was going to betray them, so they stabbed him, doing so messily and without finesse.'

Tulyet nodded slowly. 'Very well. And Reames?'

'Everyone thought his death was revenge for Lucas. However, he was killed – brained with a stone – not long after being questioned by you about the disappearance of lead from Gonville's chapel. Did you notice his hands?'

'Yes, they were filthy. He told me it is an occupational hazard for latteners, although I confess I was suspicious of the fact that he kept hiding them behind his back.'

'You should have been – lead leaves black marks, but brass does not. I suspect he *was* involved in the thefts, and his accomplices grew nervous when he was summoned to the castle.'

'They need not have been,' said Tulyet bitterly. 'He told me nothing.'

'Not that time, but you would have tried again, and they are unwilling to take chances – especially with a man who strutted about with incriminating stains on his hands. They killed him to protect themselves.'

Tulyet was thoughtful. 'You may be right. Lakenham and Cristine are poor, but Reames was always very well dressed, so he must have had an additional source of income. However, it cannot have been another job, as that is forbidden to apprentices. Could it have come from an inheritance? Lakenham did mention that he was an orphan.'

'I suspect that was a lie on Reames' part, to explain the sudden windfall that allowed him to indulge his penchant for new clothes.'

'So his money came from helping Inge,' surmised Tulyet. 'What about Peres? Lakenham and Cristine are convinced that Reames was killed by the masons, regardless of whether or not it is true, so I am inclined to think that they killed Peres for simple revenge.'

'The aqua-coloured thread snagged in Peres' fingernail proves they did not.'

Tulyet frowned. 'It does? How?'

'Because you did not find such a garment in their house – if you had, you would have arrested them on the spot.'

'I would,' acknowledged Tulyet. 'But they could have got rid of it before I arrived.'

'That is unlikely for two reasons. First, we did not make the discovery of the thread public, so how could they have known what to do? And second, when Cristine's cloak was stolen from St Mary the Great, she complained about being too poor to buy another – they cannot afford to throw good clothes away.'

'Fair enough. Continue.'

'Peres was sent to buy a chisel, but used the opportunity to come here instead, probably to grind the horned serpent off Oswald's tomb – he was the one who carved it, but Edith complained, so Marjory probably asked him to remove it. I think he was labouring away quietly when the thieves came for Cew's brass. Peres saw them, and was stabbed to ensure his silence.'

'Stabbed messily,' mused Tulyet. 'Like Lucas. Very well. I accept your reasoning – it fits with the facts as we know them. So who are these thieves?'

'Now *that* I cannot tell you,' replied Bartholomew. 'I can only say that they are not Petit, Lakenham, Isnard or Gundrede.'

CHAPTER 15

Bartholomew and Tulyet left St John Zachary, noting with alarm the increasing number of scholars who gathered in groups, muttering. Some were Regent masters, vexed over the fact that their new Chancellor would be one of two men they did not much like, but most were students from the hostels, who always took to the streets when trouble was brewing.

'They will settle down after noon tomorrow, when we have a new leader,' predicted Master Braunch, who was standing near the rubble that comprised his fallen building. The path that had been cleared was in great demand, and he was there to prevent spats over precedence.

'I hope you are right,' said Tulyet worriedly. 'Because I sense mischief in the air – and you do not need me to tell you that there are townsfolk who will join in any brawls.'

'It is the uncertainty that bothers our scholars,' said Braunch. 'Even Michael's detractors admit that he represents stability, and we are all fearful of what will happen when he leaves. The hunt for that bell is not helping either. It has turned into a contest between us and the town.'

They saw what he meant when a trio of lads from Physick Hostel engaged in a furious altercation with three villainous characters from the Swan. Tulyet quelled it with a few sharp words, after which he and Bartholomew hurried on to St Mary the Great.

They arrived to find that Michael had completed his mission to the belfry, and had prevented further debate on the self-ringing bell by sending Hopeman and Suttone off in different directions. Their supporters had gone with them, while the remaining spectators, deprived of entertainment, eventually drifted away.

'Well?' asked Tulyet. 'Who was in the tower? Kolvyle? He strikes me as a lad to cause trouble, just for the delight of annoying you and seeing gullible colleagues jabber about Satan.'

'No one was up there,' replied Michael. 'I can only assume that the wind set them clanging.'

'There is no wind,' said Bartholomew. 'And it would take quite a gust to make those bells chime anyway – they are heavy.'

'Then some mischievous student found a way to tug the ropes with no one seeing,' said Michael irritably. 'God knows, most are resourceful enough. But never mind them. Where have you two been?'

Bartholomew gave him a brief summary of their conclusions regarding the thefts.

'So while Inge is probably the mastermind behind the scheme,' he finished, 'we do not know who helped him. And he *did* have help, given that the missing items are too bulky for him to have carried alone.'

'We are rapidly running out of suspects for the murders as well,' added Michael gloomily. 'The only ones left on my original list are Hopeman, Kolvyle—'

He broke off as an urgent clatter of hoofs heralded the arrival of one of the beadles who had gone with Meadowman in pursuit of Godrich and Whittlesey. The man flung himself from the saddle and dashed towards Michael, leaving his horse lathered and trembling from the speed with which it had been ridden.

'We found Godrich,' he gasped. 'In a tavern just south of Royston. He told us that Whittlesey had hurtled past on Satan a few hours earlier, going like the wind.'

'Going where?' asked Michael. 'After Godrich, without realising that his cousin had stopped?'

The beadle shook his head. 'Whittlesey believes that Godrich went north, because that is what he told him to do – slip away to live quietly in York or Chester. He does not know that Godrich ignored the advice and was aiming for France instead. You see, Whittlesey promised that if Godrich did as he was ordered, no charges would ever be brought against him.'

'Charges?' demanded Michael sharply. 'What charges?'

'Devilry,' replied the beadle grimly. 'Whittlesey burst in on Godrich while he was changing for the feast, and saw a horned serpent inked into his skin. He was horrified, and declared that someone bearing that sort of mark could never be Chancellor.'

'No,' agreed Michael, while Bartholomew recalled the number that had covered Tynkell, and wondered what the envoy would have said about those. 'And Godrich meekly agreed?'

'They had a blazing row, during which hot words were exchanged and a bowl was lobbed – it cut Whittlesey's hand. But then they calmed themselves, and Whittlesey issued his ultimatum: that Godrich leave or be exposed.'

'That explains the broken pot and the argument Dodenho heard,' said Michael. 'But why did Godrich bide by it? He spent a fortune on his campaign, and he is not the sort of man to shrug and walk away, just because a meddling kinsman threatened to tell tales – he would just have denied the allegations.'

'Because of the Archbishop of Canterbury,' explained the beadle. 'It was *him* who Whittlesey threatened to tell, not our scholars.'

'A shrewd move,' said Michael grudgingly, and explained to Bartholomew and Tulyet. 'The Archbishop would demand to see Godrich's mark, and the truth would be out. Then, as no prelate can be seen condoning witchery, he would have to disown Godrich. The rest of the family would inevitably follow suit, cutting Godrich off without a penny.'

'Right,' said the beadle. 'So Godrich had no choice but to do as Whittlesey ordered – unless he wanted to live in penury for the rest of his life, shunned by his kin.'

'Godrich confided all this willingly?' asked Bartholomew sceptically.

The beadle grinned. 'Of course not! We told him that we had orders to hang him for Chancellor Tynkell's murder, and Meadowman posed as a priest to hear his last confession. Godrich was livid when he realised he had been deceived, but it could not be helped. We did not have time to devise a different plan.'

'But he did not admit to murder?' asked Michael, smirking at the thought of the haughty Godrich quailing in terror at the prospect of summary execution.

'He assured "Father" Meadowman that he was innocent of those. He owned up to a lot of other nasty things, though – including not pressing for justice when he found out that Inge and Egidia had murdered Peter Poges. Oh, and he also said that he was with Whittlesey when Tynkell died, so if he is not the culprit, Whittlesey is not either. It pained him to say it, though.'

'Because he wanted Whittlesey in trouble, I suppose,' surmised Michael. 'And resented being the one who would prove his innocence.'

The beadle nodded. 'And because he thought Whittlesey *might* be guilty of dispatching Moleyns. He received a letter, you see, from Bishop Sheppey, warning him that Whittlesey was dangerous. He kept a careful eye on him afterwards, lest Whittlesey did something to lose him votes.'

'Which explains why he tried to keep Whittlesey close,' sighed Michael. 'It was not for the kudos of having an influential churchman at his side, as Whittlesey believed. But we can ask him all this when he comes back. I assume Meadowman is bringing him?'

The beadle shook his head. 'We locked him in the tavern's cellar, and I will fetch him tomorrow. Meadowman and the others have gone after Whittlesey.'

'Why?' asked Bartholomew. 'You just told us that he is not the killer.'

'Because once Godrich learned that his cousin had also raced off in the middle of the night, he kept saying that it was suspicious. We agreed: that envoy *is* up to something untoward. So we decided we had better try to find out what . . .'

'Good,' said Michael. 'But let us hope it does not take them too long. I need them here.'

'Kolvyle and Hopeman,' said Bartholomew a short while later, when Tulyet had gone to supervise the increasingly fraught search for the woman in the cloak with the fancy hem, who he thought represented their best chance of answers. 'We should speak to them again – and soon. I have a bad feeling that unless we do something quickly, the killer will strike again.'

'Yes, with Suttone likely to be the next victim,' said Michael. 'Cynric will do his best, but . . . Do you really think the culprit is one of those two?'

Bartholomew shrugged. 'Neither has given us a reason to think otherwise.'

They began to hurry to the Market Square, where they could hear Hopeman making another speech. The Dominican had a powerful voice, and Bartholomew hoped he would not win the election, if for no other reason that it would be taxing to hear it at every turn.

'I hate to admit that I was wrong,' said Michael as they went, 'but I wish I had nailed my colours to Thelnetham's mast. He is by far the most able candidate, and I am sure I could have devised a way to keep him in line. It is a pity he withdrew.'

'Can you persuade him to re-enter the race? Most of

our colleagues would welcome a third option now that Lyng and Godrich are unavailable. And it might serve to calm the trouble that is brewing – the Regent masters feel cheated as matters stand.'

'The statutes forbid it.'

'Then perhaps Hopeman is right to suggest they be scrapped. They are meant to serve us, not the other way around.'

Michael did not bother to argue. They reached the Market Square, where the Dominican had attracted a small but fervent gathering of like-minded zealots.

'Suttone does not care what happens to the University,' he was bawling, 'because he thinks we will all be dead of the plague in a few months. But before he goes, he intends to sample every woman in Cambridge, and encourages us to do likewise.'

Michael marched towards him, and Hopeman evidently knew he would not win a public battle of words with the monk, because he jumped down from the trough on which he had been standing, and indicated that one of his acolytes was to take his place.

'What do you want, Brother?' he demanded. 'Hurry up! I am busy with God's work, and cannot afford to squander time with you.'

'Did God tell you to murder Tynkell in order to force an election?' asked Michael baldly. 'And then dispatch Lyng, because he was the candidate most likely to win?'

'My conversations with the Lord are private,' declared the friar, then gave a grin that verged on the malevolent. 'You will never convict me of those crimes, so go to Rochester and forget about them. Your time here is done.'

'Was that a confession?' asked Michael, as the priest strutted away, bristling defiance in every step. 'It sounded like one.'

'It was a challenge, certainly,' replied Bartholomew. 'But you need *evidence*. Accusing him without it will achieve nothing – the Dominicans will defend him, just because he is one of them, regardless of what they really think. And then he will claim that you arrested him just to make sure your candidate was the only one left.'

'Lord!' muttered Michael. 'That will be difficult to deny, even though it would be a lie.'

Bartholomew nodded. 'So you cannot arrest him until you have real evidence of his guilt – hard facts or material proof.'

'Then go and find me some,' ordered Michael. 'Try the King's Head. It is a good place for gossip, and the patrons will talk to their *medicus* more readily than me.'

'What will you do?' asked Bartholomew, thinking the monk must be desperate indeed if he was resorting to that sort of tactic.

'Tackle Kolvyle. And let us hope that one of us succeeds in shaking something loose, or the election will be upon us, and then it will be time for me to go to Rochester. I said I would not leave until the killer was caught, but I am beginning to think it is a promise I may not be able to keep.'

Dusk would come early that night, because clouds had rolled in from the north, and lamps were already lit in those houses that could afford fuel. In the rest, the residents shivered in the gloom, waiting for the daylight to fade completely so they could go to bed. The bitter cold had driven most of the bell-hunters indoors, too, although a hardy few were still out and about. Mallet and Islaye were among them.

'I thought I told you to return to Michaelhouse at noon,' Bartholomew said coolly.

'We did,' replied Islaye blithely, 'where we ate dinner, read a bit of Maimonides, and then went out again. Two marks is a lot of money, sir, and we do not want Kolvyle to get it.'

'Honour is at stake here,' added Mallet. 'Us versus him. You must understand why we are determined to win.'

Bartholomew did not have the energy to argue. He listed several texts he wanted them to learn that evening, ignoring their insistence that studying by candlelight hurt their eyes, and they parted ways. He passed the little church of St Mary the Less, where the scholars of Peterhouse were emerging from a special service at which prayers had been said for a break in the icy weather. Their petitions had evidently gone unheard, because snow was in the air.

He reached the King's Head, and heard the rumble of conversation emanating from within. Beyond, the road curved south like a brown ribbon through the empty countryside, fringed by winter-bare trees and scrubby hedges. The Gilbertine Priory had lamps lit outside its gates, which shed a warm yellow halo, welcoming and cosy. Reluctantly, Bartholomew turned to the King's Head, which was neither.

He was just reaching for the handle when the door opened and Isnard hobbled out, Gundrede and several scruffy cronies at his heels. All were dressed for a long journey. Those who did not own cloaks were wrapped in oiled sacks, boots had been given a liberal layer of grease to repel water, and there was a fine variety of snow-proof headgear.

'Who blabbed to him?' demanded the bargeman angrily, turning to glare at his friends. 'I told you to keep your mouths shut, and now he is here to stop us from going.'

'Going where?' asked Bartholomew, cutting across the indignant chorus of denials.

'To attack the thieves' lair,' replied Gundrede. 'Miller here has found it.'

'He has?' asked Bartholomew, looking at the man in question, a puny individual who eked a meagre living from the river. 'How?'

'He happened across it when he was out poaching fish,' explained Isnard, then flushed scarlet at the weary groans that followed. 'I mean visiting his mother.'

'His mother is dead,' said Bartholomew, recalling that Widow Miller had been one of Cook's victims. 'And their lair is not by her cottage, because I searched that area when I was looking for the killer's cloak – the one that blew off the tower when he stabbed Tynkell.'

'His *other* mother,' said Isnard, blithely oblivious to the absurdity of this claim. 'Who lives by the manor of Quy, in the Fens. We are going there now, to confront the villains, and prove our innocence once and for all.'

'No,' said Bartholomew firmly. 'That is the Sheriff's responsibility.'

'But he will think we are part of their operation if we do not catch the villains ourselves,' objected Isnard. 'He does not believe us when we say we are not.'

'It is too dangerous,' argued Bartholomew. 'They have already killed Lucas, Reames and Peres. Please – just go to the castle and report what Miller has learned. The soldiers are trained in this sort of thing. You are not.'

Isnard considered carefully. 'All right, then, but only if you come with us. Perhaps the Sheriff will agree to a joint venture – us and him, standing shoulder to shoulder against villainy.'

Bartholomew could not see it, but dared not say so, lest Isnard changed his mind.

It was a strange procession. Bartholomew walked at the front with the bargeman and Gundrede, while the remaining King's Head's regulars streamed at their heels. While they went, Isnard confided his plans for the choir when Michael left, speaking in bursts, because Bartholomew had set a brisk pace for a man with one leg and crutches to manage.

'Brother Michael will be sorry,' he vowed. 'We shall be better than ever . . . and when he comes back . . . to tell Suttone how to be Chancellor . . . he will regret abandoning us.'

'Look at them!' sniggered Gundrede, as they passed a group of students who were exploring the Brazen George's outhouses. '*We* will be the ones to get the two marks, because the bell is not in the town – it will be in the thieves' lair.'

They refused to enter the castle – understandably enough, given that the previous times they had visited had been when they were under arrest – so Tulyet came out, where he listened carefully to what Miller had to say. It was a faltering, disjointed report, interspersed with a lot of asides and unhelpful details from Isnard.

'How do you know it was the thieves you saw?' Tulyet asked. 'Not Fenland fishermen?'

'Because fishermen do not use cargo barges for their trade,' replied Miller promptly. 'It was the felons, right enough. And besides, they *looked* untrustworthy.'

'Then they must be ruffians indeed,' murmured Tulyet, eyeing the scruffy horde that was ranged in front of him. 'And this happened by the canal outside Quy?'

Miller nodded. 'I watched them for ages. They have a shed full of stolen goods, although it will not be full now – I heard them say they were going to start loading everything on a boat.'

'A sea-going vessel,' put in Isnard. 'Which will hug the coast to London, where you can always get higher prices for such items. Not that we know from experience, of course.'

'Of course,' said Tulyet. 'How many of these thieves were there?'

'Just two – a captain and his mate,' replied Miller. 'However, they talked about being joined by "others" soon.'

'Then we had better mount a raid,' said Tulyet, and called for Helbye.

When the sergeant arrived, Bartholomew was concerned. He was clearly ill, with sweat beading his face, despite the chill of the fading day, and his eyes were fever bright.

'Not tonight, sir,' he said tiredly, when he heard what Tulyet intended to do. 'It will be dark soon, and the Fens are no place to be on a cold winter night. Look – it is starting to snow.'

'We have torches and good cloaks,' said Tulyet briskly. 'And we cannot wait until morning. We do not want to arrive and find the villains have sailed.'

'But the weather,' objected Helbye. 'And the track – it will be hard and treacherous . . .'

'Norys?' bellowed Tulyet, and when the soldier stepped forward, he asked, 'You travelled that road when you went to hunt Inge earlier. How was it?'

Norys drew his cloak more closely around him. 'Miserable, sir. The wind from the Fens is like no other – a knife scything through you. I am still chilled to the bone.'

'But the going was reasonable?'

Norys nodded, albeit reluctantly, so Tulyet issued an order for horses to be saddled.

'I had better fetch a thicker jerkin, then,' said Helbye without enthusiasm. 'It is—'

'I need you here, Will,' interrupted Tulyet. 'The scholars are in a feisty mood, and I do not want them embroiling the townsfolk in one of their spats.'

'Quite right,' agreed Isnard. 'Those academics are a rough crowd.'

'You can stay, too,' said Tulyet shortly. 'Go back to the King's Head and leave this to us. Here is a shilling for ale.'

It was a generous sum, and an excellent way to keep Isnard's companions where they belonged. Eyes lit up, although the bargeman was dismayed.

'But we want to watch them caught! We deserve it after all we have been through.'

'If Miller's report is accurate, you will see them when we bring them back in chains. If he is sending us on a fool's mission, it will be you lot in my gaol. So, I ask you once more, Miller: are you *sure* about what you saw?'

'Yes,' replied Miller firmly. 'Go to Quy manor, then take the track that runs by the lode. Shortly before the lode meets the river, you will find a great big warehouse. *That* is where the villains keep their loot.'

'A *warehouse?*' asked Tulyet, sceptical again. 'All the way out there?'

'It is a convenient spot for smugglers,' said Miller, with the authority of one who knew. 'There is a good road to Quy, and canals that run north and east.'

'Let me lead the raid, sir,' begged Helbye plaintively. 'I know the area better than you. I was born up there.'

'You are not well enough,' said Bartholomew quickly, lest Tulyet weakened. 'Let me see your arm. You seem to be—'

'It itches,' interrupted Helbye shortly, waving away his concern, 'which means it is getting better. Cook said so.'

'I hardly think we can trust *his* opinion,' spat Tulyet in disgust. 'Now go and pick me six good men, Will. We leave as soon as they are ready.'

Helbye limped away, shoulders slumped. However, when more snow floated down, Bartholomew suspected he was secretly glad to stay at home.

'If we cannot come, we want *him* to represent our interests out there,' said Isnard, pointing at Bartholomew. 'To make sure everything is done properly.'

'Very well,' said Tulyet, although Bartholomew opened his mouth to protest. 'There is always room for the hero of Poitiers.'

Bartholomew shot him an unpleasant look. 'Take Cynric. He will be far more useful.'

'He is needed to guard Suttone. God's blood, man – do not give him that one!' Tulyet's last remark was directed at Robin, who was in the process of presenting Bartholomew with the reins of an enormous black stallion. 'It will have him off before we leave the Barbican.'

With considerable trepidation, Bartholomew climbed atop a brown mare instead, hoping she would not buck and prance, as horses invariably did when he was on their backs. He winced when the wind whipped a flurry of snow into his face, and was grateful when Isnard removed his own cloak and handed it up to him – it was thick and warm, and far more suitable for a jaunt to the Fens than his threadbare academic one – along with a leather hat and a pair of fur-lined gloves.

'Stay back if there is any skirmishing,' instructed Isnard in a low voice. 'I know what Cynric says about you, but you do not have the temperament to be a good warrior. Let the Sheriff do the killing.'

'Hopefully, there will not be any,' said Bartholomew, more unhappy than ever about being included in the venture.

'I am afraid there will,' said Isnard, 'because Helbye has picked the castle's fiercest warriors to go with you – men who would far rather fight than take prisoners.'

Bartholomew glanced towards them and saw what Isnard meant. Their leader was the loutish Norys, while the other five were hard-bitten soldiers in functional armour, all of whom sported a terrifying arsenal of well-honed weapons. Then he noticed there was a seventh – a young lad with an eager grin and a brand-new jerkin.

'Not you, Harold,' snapped Helbye. 'Get off that horse at once.'

'Let him come,' countered Tulyet, when Harold's face fell in dismay. 'He needs the experience.'

And with that, he wheeled his mount around and set off, his troops streaming at his heels.

* * *

It was a miserable journey. Tulyet rode harder than Bartholomew thought was safe in the failing light, especially as the track was slick with ice. The occasional flurry of snow soon became a regular fall that drilled directly into their faces, making it even more difficult to see where they were going. Bartholomew was obliged to cling hard to the pommel of his saddle, and not for the first time wished he had paid more heed to the riding lessons he had been given as a child.

'You do realise this is a waste of time?' said Tulyet, coming to trot next to him. He was able to speak only because that part of the road was heavily rutted, forcing them to slow down. 'There will be nothing to find at Quy.'

Bartholomew frowned in confusion. 'I thought you believed Miller's story.'

'I am sure he saw thieves, but I doubt they are the ones who took Stanmore's tomb, Dallingridge's feet, the University's bell, and the rest of it. And Miller's rogues will not be at Quy now anyway. Not in this weather.'

'Then why are we going?' demanded Bartholomew crossly.

'*I* am going because Helbye would not have countenanced me giving the command to anyone else. And *you* are going because you put me in that position by telling me that I can no longer use him as my second.'

'I had not taken you for a petty man.'

Tulyet laughed. 'The excursion will do you no harm, and will give you a fine tale to tell your colleagues at the election tomorrow. Besides, your inclusion placated Isnard – I suspect he would have followed if I had refused to let you come, and I do not want his "help".'

'But the weather . . .'

'A bit of snow should not bother a seasoned old campaigner like you. It will not settle anyway – the wind will whisk it away.'

'The wind will whisk it into drifts,' argued Bartholomew.

'We will be home long before then,' said Tulyet dismissively. 'I have reached Quy in less than an hour in the past. Granted, it was not in the dark . . .'

Eager to be done with the foolish mission as soon as possible, Bartholomew jabbed his heels into the mare's sides. She snickered angrily, warning him not to do it again.

'We must hurry,' he said, when Tulyet regarded him enquiringly. 'You saw for yourself that the University is uneasy tonight, and I may be needed. Moreover, Michael is expecting me to provide him with information about the murders – which *have* to be solved by the day after tomorrow, as that is when he leaves for Rochester.'

'I imagine the killer is Kolvyle. Langelee locked him in a cellar earlier, to keep him out of mischief, but just before you came to the castle, I had word that he had escaped.'

Bartholomew regarded Tulyet in alarm. 'Running is not the act of an innocent man.'

'Quite.'

Bartholomew reined in. 'Then I should go back and help Michael to—'

'His beadles are more than capable of laying hold of that silly youth.' Tulyet grabbed Bartholomew's bridle and urged the mare into a trot. 'Did I tell you that I am closing in on the woman in the cloak with the embroidered hem, by the way?'

'No – that is good news.'

'She was seen taking it off in a tavern shortly afterwards. The witness who saw her is away today, but will be back tomorrow, and I am confident that he can take us to her. Then she can tell us who murdered Moleyns – Kolvyle, in all probability.'

'Surely you want to be there when all that happens – not chasing about in the Fens?'

'I can do both. We will be home long before dawn.'

'We had better be,' muttered Bartholomew. 'I have to vote for Suttone at noon, because my colleagues will never forgive me if I miss it, and he loses by one.'

Tulyet spurred his horse on when the track became firmer, and then it was all Bartholomew could do to keep up with him.

After what felt like an age, the physician bumping and lurching uncomfortably in the saddle, they reached Quy, which comprised a church surrounded by a few cottages, and a winding track that led to the manor. Lights gleamed in some houses, but no one came out to see why travellers should be passing at such an hour.

'They have been paid to look the other way,' surmised Tulyet. 'Well, well! Perhaps these thieves of Miller's will be worth catching after all.'

The lode lay to the east of the village, a long, arrow-straight canal cut centuries earlier to connect with the River Cam. A towpath ran along its side, just as Miller had said. It was too narrow for horses, so Tulyet ordered them tethered to a tree. He detailed one soldier to guard them, and ordered the rest to continue on foot.

The track was fringed by a line of scrubby trees, intended to act as a windbreak from the flat, boggy Fens on the other side. Unfortunately, it was badly positioned for when the wind blew from the north, and Bartholomew grumbled under his breath about the Sheriff's reckless assumptions regarding drifts – snow was already beginning to pile up against the hedge, and he hoped they would not reach the end of the path, only to find they could not get back again.

They walked for some time, and just when he was beginning to fear that Miller had spun them a yarn after all, a building loomed out of the darkness. Tulyet squeezed through the hedge, and led his troops through the marshes, so as to approach it from behind. They edged closer cautiously.

The 'warehouse' was huge for the middle of nowhere, and had been carefully constructed so that its roof was lower than the surrounding trees, thus ensuring that it could not be seen from the road. It was unusually sturdy, and had clearly been built for one purpose and one purpose only: to store goods ready for smuggling through the Fens.

'It has clearly been here for years,' whispered Tulyet, peering at it through the swirling snow. 'Inge must have remembered it from his youth, and decided to put it to good use.'

'Regardless, it is abandoned now,' said Norys, his voice shockingly loud in the silence of the night. 'Miller was lying, just like we thought. We should leave and go home before—'

He flinched when Tulyet whipped around with a glare, warning him to keep quiet. Then the Sheriff indicated that everyone was to stay hidden while he crept forward to reconnoitre by himself. He was gone for a long time, and Bartholomew grew increasingly concerned. Eventually, he could stand it no longer.

'Something is wrong,' he whispered. 'He should have been back by—'

He stopped speaking abruptly when Norys removed a cudgel from his belt. The last thing he heard before all went black was a shriek of pain from Harold.

CHAPTER 16

Bartholomew opened his eyes to darkness, and for a moment, he could not remember where he was or why he was so cold. His head pounded, but he could not raise a hand to rub it because both were tied behind his back. Gradually, his wits and his memory returned. He blinked to clear his vision, and saw the faint outline of the warehouse to his left.

No one was with him except Harold, whose hands were also bound. Unfortunately, either by design or accident, the lad was lying with his face in a half-frozen puddle. Bartholomew struggled frantically against his bonds, surprised when they came loose almost immediately – he could only assume that whoever had tied him up had not had the benefit of fur-lined gloves.

He crawled to Harold and hauled him over, but the young soldier was already dead. He sat back on his heels, shock and confusion washing over him. What was going on? Where was Tulyet? He stood on unsteady legs and began to search. Then he heard voices. He lurched into the undergrowth, to hide until he could determine whether they belonged to friend or foe, but no one appeared, and he realised the sound had come from inside the shed. Norys and the others were laughing together.

He rubbed his aching head, trying to marshal his thoughts. What should he do? Run back to the horses and ride to Cambridge for help? But the guard Tulyet had left with the animals might be in cahoots with Norys, and even if Bartholomew could overpower a professional warrior, how was he to gallop all the way home, on his own and in the dark?

Then what about the manor? He slumped in defeat. That was no good either. Tulyet had drawn attention to the fact that no one had come to investigate the sound of travellers in the middle of the night, meaning they were either involved in whatever was happening, or had been paid to ignore anything suspicious.

Norys laughed again, and there came the sound of metal goblets clinking together. Bartholomew took a deep, unsteady breath and began to inch forward, to see what might be learned from eavesdropping.

He crept all the way around the warehouse, expecting at any moment to meet a guard, but everyone was inside. Other than the door, there was only one opening – a tiny window at the back, presumably for ventilation. His medical bag was gone – lost somewhere behind the hedge – but he still had the small knife he carried on his belt. Working with infinite care, and aware that even a tiny scrape might give him away, he bored a hole in a place where the wood was rotten, twisting the blade this way and that until he had created a gap big enough to look through.

The first thing he saw was Tulyet, bound hand and foot, and with a sack over his head; his sword lay on a pile of oiled sheets nearby. There were seven men with him – the six surviving soldiers, including the one who had been left to mind the horses. And Inge.

With resignation, Bartholomew recalled Norys's previous foray to the Fens – to investigate a sighting of the lawyer *five miles east*. At Quy, in other words. Bartholomew was disgusted, both with himself and with Tulyet, for failing to make the connection.

Other than people and the heap of tarpaulins, the building was empty except for a few sticks of furniture, presumably for the use of those guarding whatever was stored there, and a pair of elegantly sculpted feet. Bartholomew immediately recognised them as from the Dallingridge tomb.

He stared at the men as answers began to flood into his mind. No wonder the thieves had evaded capture for so long – they were soldiers on the very patrols that Tulyet had sent to snag them! And as the likes of Norys would be unequal to organising such an audacious scheme, Inge *was* the sly mastermind behind it, just as he had surmised.

The pile of oiled sheets told their own story, too: they were the kind that were thrown over carts, to protect their cargoes from inclement weather – clearly, these had covered the stolen goods during the first stage of their journey from the town, discarded now they were no longer needed. The size of the heap revealed that any number of wagons had rolled into the Fens, laden down with wares that would fetch high prices in London's illicit markets, every one of them waved through the town gates with a nod and a wink from Norys and his associates.

He froze in alarm at a sudden rattle of footsteps on the towpath, then sagged in relief. It was Helbye. The old warrior had not been content to sit at home while his Sheriff led a potentially dangerous expedition, and had come to help. Bartholomew was about to run forward and warn him when alarm bells jangled in his mind. He sank back into the shadows, heart pounding.

Helbye had chosen the six soldiers himself, after insisting that *he* should lead the raid. He had also objected to Harold, who now lay dead. Then there were the patrols to catch the thieves – all unsuccessful, and all briefed by the sergeant. And who claimed to have chased a boat travelling south – a totally different direction from the one the *real* thieves would have taken, not to mention a different mode of transport?

Bartholomew closed his eyes in disgust as more evidence of Helbye's perfidy crashed into his mind. First, there was Inge's escape from the Griffin – the lawyer would have been caught with ease if Helbye had not waded into the fray, trailing bandages. Second, Helbye had mounted a foolish and noisy raid on the King's Head at the exact time that Holty's pinnacles had gone missing – clearly, it had been a diversion. And third, Helbye had been at pains to accuse Isnard and Gundrede of the crimes: of course he had – it took eyes away from the real culprits.

But why had Helbye turned traitor? Bartholomew knew the answer to that question, too: for money, because retirement on half-pay would be bleak, and it was clear that the sergeant was about to be put out to pasture. Bartholomew also knew *how* Helbye had been recruited: he had escorted Moleyns – and Inge – to Cambridge from Nottingham, which had allowed the lawyer plenty of time to befriend a bitter and anxious old man.

Voices drew Bartholomew back to the hole he had drilled. Helbye had entered the hut and was stamping snow from his boots. A second man was with him, but he was so deeply huddled inside his cloak that Bartholomew could not see his face.

'I offered to come out here instead,' Helbye told Inge; Tulyet's head snapped around at the sound of his sergeant's voice. 'But he would not let me. Where are Harold and Bartholomew?'

'Out back,' replied Norys. 'They know enough to hang us, so they will have to die. So will he.' He nodded towards Tulyet.

'Good,' muttered the man in the cloak. There was something familiar about his voice, but Bartholomew needed more than a single word to place it. The fellow went to sit near the window, in a place where nothing could be seen of him but his legs.

Helbye's face was cold and hard, and Bartholomew saw the battle-honed warrior who had claimed countless lives during his long military career. There was no kindness in it, and no remorse that he had betrayed a man who had offered him friendship and trust. Then he swayed slightly, one hand to his arm, and Bartholomew noticed again the signs of fever. Unless he had medical help soon, he would not live long to enjoy the fruits of his deceit.

Bartholomew moved away from the warehouse and took cover in the undergrowth, his mind racing with questions, solutions and worries. The snow was falling in earnest now, a thin white veil that was blown almost horizontal by the wind. He peered along the towpath, and saw that Helbye had brought two more soldiers with him – they were standing a short distance away, blocking the route to the horses.

Bartholomew was close to despair. How could he rescue Tulyet from eight soldiers, Helbye, Inge and the man in the cloak? The only good thing about his situation was that he had not tried to make his way back to Cambridge, and so had avoided running directly into Helbye – he had the strong sense that he would not have survived such an encounter.

That thought gave him an idea. The Quy side of the towpath was obstructed by Helbye's guards, but what about the side that ran deeper into the Fens? He knew that the Roman engineers, who had constructed the many canals and dykes in the region, had arranged them in a grid pattern to facilitate ease of transport. Many had paths running along them, so perhaps he would be able to take three right turns, and rejoin the main road.

But what about Tulyet? He could hardly leave him, knowing what the thieves planned to do. He put his eye to the hole again. Helbye was dozing fitfully in a corner, the soldiers were dicing, and the cloaked man was still invisible except for his legs. Tulyet sat motionless with the sack over his head, although his tense posture suggested he was awake and alert.

Bartholomew leaned his forehead against the wall,

struggling to think. He hated the notion of abandoning his friend, but challenging eleven men would help no one. Nor would continuing to lurk uselessly behind the building. There was only one real option open to him – he had to run home as fast as he could, and fetch help in the form of Michael and his beadles.

With a heavy heart, he left the warehouse, and eased through the undergrowth until he was sure he would not be seen. Then he scrambled up to the towpath and began to trot along it, heading deeper into the Fens. There were already footsteps in the snow, which told him two things: first, that the ones he was leaving would not give him away; and second, that someone had had a good reason to walk in that direction, which gave him hope that there might be something there that he could use to his advantage.

He did not have far to go before the lode met a much wider waterway, which stretched away to his left and right until it disappeared into the darkness. Reeds grew at its ice-encrusted edges, but he knew instinctively that its middle was deep. A sturdy pier ran along the bank, and tethered to it was a barge – a sea-going one, as Isnard had predicted. It had two masts and its deck was covered in oilskins. It was low in the water, suggesting a heavy cargo.

Bartholomew crept towards it, glad of the light cast by the lamp hanging from the foremast, which allowed him to see that no one was outside on watch. The only sounds were the wind hissing in the reeds and snoring – the crew were fast asleep in the cabin at the stern. With infinite care, Bartholomew climbed aboard, and lifted the nearest tarpaulin, although he already knew from the domed shape what lay beneath it. The bell gave a muffled ding as he covered it again.

He lifted another sheet to see a slab of pink stone. There was a partially obliterated horned serpent in one corner, which told him that it was part of Oswald's tomb.

He stared at it, recalling Edith's distress when it had gone. Gradually, the numb despair that had dogged him since he had woken next to Harold's body began to give way to a dark, cold anger. Perhaps the thieves *would* escape with their ill-gotten gains, but he was damned if he was going to make it easy for them.

But what could he do? The boat was clearly ready to leave at first light, and that would be that. Then he had an idea.

He jumped back on the pier, glad the crew was slovenly and had only used one mooring rope. He struggled to unhitch it with fingers that were clumsy with tension. For a moment, nothing happened, but then a slit of black water appeared between boat and wharf. The gap grew larger as the current caught the barge and tugged it away from the bank. Yes, the crew could sail it back again, but not without inconvenience. It was revenge of sorts.

Unfortunately, Bartholomew's hopes of finding an alternative route home were quickly dashed. There was no towpath to his right, and he was on the wrong side of the lode to take the one to his left. The only way to reach it would be to swim, which would be suicide in such weather – he would freeze to death long before he reached the road.

Reluctantly, he returned to the warehouse. Perhaps the two guards would have gone inside with their cronies, and he could sneak past them unseen. But both were still out, vigilant and with weapons at the ready. Cursing softly, he ducked back into the undergrowth and crawled through it until he reached the window again.

Helbye was awake, shivering and clearly in pain. Inge was watching the soldiers dice, while Tulyet was as he had been earlier – stiff, alert and angry, but alive. Bartholomew shifted positions to look at the last man, and saw that the fellow had made himself comfortable by loosening his cloak. Underneath, he wore an aqua tunic – the same colour as the thread from the murdered Peres' fingernail.

'Tulyet has never afforded me the respect I deserved,' Inge was saying sourly to no one in particular. 'He forgets that I am a lawyer, not a criminal.'

'I thought they were one and the same,' quipped Norys. His cronies guffawed.

Inge ignored them. 'And he failed to protect Moleyns. It is *his* fault that my only client is dead. Moleyns would have repaid my loyalty tenfold when the King pardoned him, and Tulyet's incompetence has deprived me of a comfortable future.'

Helbye frowned. 'I thought *you* killed him. You were right next to him when he died, and you had good reason – you dutifully shared his imprisonment, but he treated you like dirt. Besides, I thought our business here was to earn you enough money to ditch the man.'

'It was so I would not have to rely on him for life's little luxuries,' corrected Inge. 'But leaving him was never part of the plan – not after investing three years of my life in him. We would have done great things together once he was free.'

'So who did kill him then?' pressed Helbye. 'Egidia? There was no love lost between them, and I was under the impression that she preferred you.'

'She does,' said Inge smugly, 'but neither of us wanted him dead. I suppose the culprit was one of the crowd that gathered when he fell.'

'Aye, but which?' mused Helbye. Then his expression hardened. 'You should have told me that Yevele let him out to steal. Not knowing made me look stupid – got the lads thinking that I am too old for my duties.'

Norys and his ruffians exchanged the kind of glances that suggested they still did.

'You do understand why he did it, do you not?' asked Inge. 'To punish Tulyet for denying him his rights and privileges when we first arrived. When he was back at Court, he was going to tell everyone that Cambridge Castle's security is a joke.'

Bartholomew could see Tulyet's hands clenched tightly behind his back.

'The witness in the embroidered cloak will tell me who killed Moleyns,' said Helbye. 'Then I will stick a knife in the bastard's gizzard for you.'

'Speaking of killing, when shall I dispatch the prisoners?' asked the man in the aqua tunic, strolling towards the pile of sheets and picking up Tulyet's sword.

Bartholomew did not know whether to be gratified, angry or sorry when he saw it was Cook, although he was certainly not surprised. With hindsight, evidence of the barber's involvement shone out like a beacon. First, Helbye had almost certainly injured his arm doing something criminal – not chasing a suspicious barge, as he had claimed – and Cook had rushed to tend him lest he blurted something incriminating. And second, Cook had also joined the fray at the Griffin, which had allowed Inge to escape. As if on cue, the barber began to brag.

'You would all be hanged by now, were it not for me,' he said, swishing the sword from side to side, although so clumsily that Bartholomew could tell he was no warrior. 'Lucas had guessed the truth, and was going to sell it to the Senior Proctor, while that ridiculous Reames would certainly have betrayed us if the Sheriff had questioned him a second time.'

'He nearly betrayed us the first,' said Inge with a shudder, and ran his fingers lightly over Dallingridge's feet, no doubt anticipating the price they would fetch. 'The fool went to the castle with lead stains all over his hands! I was sure Tulyet would put two and two together.'

'I dashed out Reames' brains to keep you safe,' boasted

Cook. 'And I stabbed Peres, because he caught me prising Cew's brass off the wall. Do you hear that, Sheriff? *I* killed them, and you had no idea! You are stupid, and I shall be *glad* to leave your nasty little town. I am only sorry that you and Bartholomew will not be alive to tell everyone how I bested you.'

'You do not like Cambridge?' asked Helbye, surprised. 'I would have thought it was the perfect place for you, with no other barber-surgeon to compete for business.'

Cook grimaced. 'I like cutting hair, but what I really wanted was another patient like Dallingridge. Unfortunately, Bartholomew watched me like a hawk, so I dared not risk it.'

'Dared not risk what?' asked Inge, frowning. Then his jaw dropped. 'You mean Dallingridge's claims were true? He really was poisoned?'

'I slipped a little something into his drink on Lammas Day,' replied Cook airily. 'And then I earned a fortune by providing the necessary medical care afterwards, although I was disappointed when he failed to remember my devotion in his will.'

'That resin you swallowed,' said Helbye to Inge, shooting Cook a wary glance. 'How did it splash in your mouth, exactly? Was it when *he* happened to be holding the bucket?'

'Poor Helbye has a fever,' said Cook quickly to the lawyer. 'But I have a potion that will quell these wild delusions. Of *course* I did not splash the resin in your face on purpose.'

'I bet he did,' countered Helbye sullenly. '*And* I bet he did something bad to my arm. There must be some reason why it hurts so much.'

There was, thought Bartholomew bleakly, and the reason was that Cook aimed to have the sergeant's share of the profits as well as his own. Perhaps he intended to have Inge's, too.

'It hurts because it is mending,' said Cook shortly, and held out a small phial. 'Here, drink this. It will soon make you well again.'

Wisely, Helbye declined. Inge had been quaffing wine, but he set down his cup quickly, giving Cook a suspicious glance as he did so. Then he became businesslike, clearly unwilling to challenge the barber when their association was almost at an end anyway.

'We will all travel to London on the barge at first light,' he determined. 'Except Helbye, who must direct any patrols away from this part of the Fens until we are clear. When the hue and cry has died down, he can join us in the city.'

'What about Egidia?' asked Helbye. 'You cannot leave her in gaol.'

'She confessed, so she must live with the consequences,' said Inge, showing that Cook was not the only one with a ruthless streak when dealing with accomplices. He pointed at Dallingridge's feet. 'We shall load these now, and be ready to sail at dawn. You had better start back to the castle, Helbye, before you are missed and have awkward questions to answer.'

'And I shall dispatch the prisoners,' declared Cook, grinning his delight. 'What a coup – Bartholomew and Tulyet on the same night! That will teach them to annoy me.'

Bartholomew ducked back into the undergrowth as the thieves emerged from the warehouse. Inge turned towards the barge, holding aloft a lantern that illuminated all eight soldiers toting Dallingridge's feet. Helbye started back towards Quy, while Cook remained inside with Tulyet. Bartholomew tensed in an agony of indecision. Was there any point in running after the sergeant, to remind him of Tulyet's affection and trust in the hope of winning an ally?

But when he peered back through the hole, he saw he would not have time. Cook was testing the edge of Tulyet's sword for sharpness. Frantically, Bartholomew stumbled towards the door, slowed by drifting snow and the bitter cold that had numbed his legs. He drew his little knife with frozen fingers. It was not much of a weapon, but it might be enough to save Tulyet's life. He flung open the door, holding the blade ready to lob.

And lowered it in astonishment.

Tulyet was free. The ropes that had bound him lay on the floor, along with the sack from his head. He held the sword, and Cook was pressed against the wall with its tip at his throat.

'It seems no one ever taught Norys how to tie proper knots,' he explained, when he saw Bartholomew. 'Even you seem to have slipped them. Where is Harold? He will not be part of this unsavoury affair.'

'Drowned,' whispered Bartholomew, glaring at Cook.

'He cannot be!' cried Cook. 'But if he is, it had nothing to do with me.'

'He will be avenged,' declared Tulyet hotly.

Bartholomew closed the door quickly. Cook and Tulyet were all but yelling, and sounds carried at night. Still, with luck, there would be some consternation when the others discovered that their boat was not where they had left it. It might keep them occupied for a while.

'You cannot believe anything you just heard,' bleated Cook. 'I lied, to gain their confidence, so that I could save you.'

'Do not treat me like a fool,' snarled Tulyet. 'Or I will kill you where you stand.'

Cook could see he meant it. 'Please! I will tell you everything. It was all Inge's idea. His and Helbye's.'

'Helbye,' said Tulyet coldly. 'You have murdered him, because even I can see his wound has turned bad. You did it deliberately.'

'Yes, but he betrayed you. I have done you a favour.'

'Keep him quiet, Dick,' begged Bartholomew. 'His cronies will come back if—'

'*We* did not stab Moleyns, Tynkell and Lyng,' interrupted Cook loudly, clearly aiming to make as much noise as possible. 'But I know who did. I will tell you, but only if—'

'Do not listen to him,' interrupted Bartholomew, then cocked his head in alarm. Had he heard voices outside?

'Who killed them?' demanded Tulyet, all his attention on Cook.

'Stoke Poges,' replied Cook tauntingly. 'That is the key to the mystery.'

'No, it is not,' snapped Bartholomew, aiming to bring an end to the discussion before it alerted Cook's accomplices. 'Stoke Poges is irrelevant, although the killer has been happy for us to think otherwise.'

'It is *not* irrelevant,' argued Cook, shooting Bartholomew a furious glance. 'One of the jurors was Godrich, who is now murdered himself.'

'You see?' asked Bartholomew, exasperated. 'He knows nothing – Godrich is alive.'

'The killer is a scholar,' said Cook, ignoring him and continuing to address Tulyet. 'I heard him bragging about his evil deeds to Inge.'

'You *heard* him?' echoed Tulyet sceptically.

Cook nodded earnestly. 'At four o'clock on Monday morning, in St Mary the Great. We were getting ready to remove the bell, and I heard him boast that he had stabbed his victims in full view of you, the Senior Proctor and half the town.'

Bartholomew went to the door and peered out. The path appeared to be deserted, but for how much longer? Seeing it open, Cook began to speak in a bellow, causing Bartholomew to shut it again hastily.

'Inge believed this man was telling the truth, because

he eased away – he was obviously afraid the same would happen to him. I could tell he was dangerous, just by looking, so I kept to the shadows.'

'So you *did* see him,' pounced Tulyet. 'Describe him to me.'

'I cannot. The lamps were turned low for obvious reasons – we did not want them spotted by passing beadles, who would have come to investigate. All I saw was a man in a cloak.'

'Dick!' hissed Bartholomew. 'We are wasting time. Come away, before—'

'Then what did he sound like?' Tulyet was unwilling to give up.

'Educated, clever and confident. He made sneering remarks that put Inge in his place, and a bit later, he bludgeoned Helbye into diffidence. He said there will be trouble at the election – trouble that will result in the deaths of the new Chancellor and the Senior Proctor.'

Bartholomew stared at him. Was this another lie, to keep their attention until he could be rescued? Or was Cook telling the truth, and he and Tulyet needed to learn as much as they could before racing back to Cambridge to intervene?

'What sort of trouble?' he demanded.

'He did not say, but it was to the effect that he had organised a "special surprise" that would change everything, and that the University could look forward to a future without Michael and Suttone. Oh, and he mentioned a ring.'

'A piece of jewellery?'

'I imagine he meant a seal. Perhaps he has impregnated it with poison.' Cook smirked. 'What a pity you were not nicer to me, *Matthew*. Then I might have told you all this sooner, and you could have saved Michael. Now he will die without ever wearing his bishop's mitre.'

'You bastard,' snarled Tulyet, and the sword began to bite.

'There is one more thing,' squeaked Cook, gloating turning quickly to panic. 'Moleyns had an inkling that he might die, and said that if he did, I was to ask the secret air.'

Tulyet's eyes narrowed. 'What does that mean?'

'It was two days before he was killed, and we were in the castle. He leaned towards me, and said just that: that if anything were to happen to him, I should ask the secret air.'

A sudden crack made Tulyet glance around quickly, and Cook seized his momentary inattention to push him away and lob a knife. Bartholomew gaped in horror as it thudded into Tulyet's chest. The Sheriff stumbled, and then Bartholomew himself was thrown backwards as Cook sprang at him.

The skirmish did not last long. Bartholomew stunned Cook with a punch, and turned quickly to see what could be done for Tulyet. But a sound from behind made him whip around again. Cook was on his feet and he held another dagger. Appalled, Bartholomew watched him take aim, cursing himself for not hitting the man harder. Then there was a thump, and Cook toppled backwards with a sword through his throat. The knife slid from his nerveless fingers.

'Christ God, Matt!' swore Tulyet crossly. '*Never* turn your back on an enemy until you are sure he is dead. Did you learn nothing at Poitiers? He almost killed you!'

'I thought he *had* killed you,' replied Bartholomew shakily.

'Armour,' explained Tulyet, pulling aside his tunic to reveal a breastplate. 'Standard practice when the town is uneasy.'

Bartholomew took a deep, steadying breath. 'I heard a crack before Cook attacked . . .'

'Just the building creaking in the cold. I should not have let it distract me.'

Tulyet went to the door and peered out, while Bartholomew knelt next to the barber. Unlike his victims, Cook had died quickly and cleanly. Tulyet came to retrieve his sword, then looked at Bartholomew with haunted eyes.

'Helbye has been my right-hand man for years. I would never have imagined . . .'

Bartholomew knew no words of comfort. 'Mourn him later. We need to go.'

Tulyet nodded once, then became businesslike. 'We must stop the barge from leaving, or the villains will escape and never face justice.'

'I do not care about them. We have to rescue Michael.'

'Not tonight,' said Tulyet. 'We must wait for daylight and an easing of the blizzard, or we will get lost. And you know what happens to those who lose their way in the Fens.'

'It is a risk I must take. Michael is my friend.'

'And mine, but we will be of no use to him dead. We *must* wait, Matt. To do anything else would be certain suicide, and that will help no one. The election is not until noon, anyway – there is plenty of time yet.'

'Even so, we still cannot tackle the thieves. Not alone.'

'We have the element of surprise. And do not underestimate my soldiering skills.'

'Then do not *over*estimate mine. I am a physician, not a warrior.'

'Oh, I know,' said Tulyet drily. 'Believe me.'

Bartholomew was far from happy as he followed Tulyet along the towpath towards the barge, although it soon became clear that the Sheriff was right about waiting for the blizzard to ease before setting off for Cambridge – even struggling the short distance to the pier took an age, with snow now blowing directly into their faces. Following a track by the side of a lode was one thing, but crossing the Fens was another, and they would get lost for certain.

They slowed when they heard voices, and approached more cautiously, alert for guards. The barge had been sailed back to the wharf, and was moored again. This time it had been secured with three ropes, each tied with care. Everyone was on board, and the boisterous nature of the conversation suggested that they were celebrating their imminent departure with a drink.

'I thought it would be more difficult to manoeuvre the thing back,' muttered Bartholomew bitterly. 'I should not have bothered.'

'On the contrary,' Tulyet whispered back. 'It kept them busy while we spoke to Cook.'

They inched forward again, then climbed aboard. There was more light this time, as lamps were lit in the cabin. A crack in the door revealed the soldiers lounging in an attitude of ease, legs stretched in front of them and beakers in their hands. Inge was perched uncomfortably on a pile of rope near two sailors, one of whom wore a cap and was obviously in charge. Then Norys began to sing. The others joined in the chorus, although Inge remained silent.

'It is lower in the water than it was earlier,' whispered Bartholomew.

'Of course it is,' Tulyet murmured back. 'They have loaded it with more stolen goods.'

'I doubt Dallingridge's feet made that much difference, which means they have miscalculated what it can carry. I believe it is sinking!'

'That is wishful thinking, Matt. The crew will know their business. Now stay here and keep watch while I reconnoitre. We need something to give us an edge when we attack.'

'Attack?' gulped Bartholomew. 'I hardly think—'

But Tulyet had gone. Bartholomew glanced along the barge in agitation. Then he narrowed his eyes. Just moments ago, the deck had been the same height as the pier, but now it was a finger's width lower. He was right – it *was* going down!

'The villains!' muttered Tulyet when he returned. 'Wilson's lid, Stanmore's tomb, lead from Gonville, Holty's pinnacles, bits of scaffolding, brass plates, boxes of nails . . . I cannot believe how much they have filched. Perhaps you are right to wonder if the boat is overloaded.'

'It *is* overloaded,' Bartholomew whispered back fiercely. 'Now help me.'

He hurried to the nearest bollard, and began the tortuous business of unshipping a rope that was tight, frozen hard and slippery with snow. It was far more difficult than it had been earlier, and Tulyet swore under his breath as he wrestled with the second. Both stopped in alarm when the singing ceased abruptly, but there was a hoot of laughter from Norys, and the racket started up again.

Bartholomew and Tulyet exchanged an agonised glance and returned to their labours. Tulyet's rope came free first, and Bartholomew's plopped into the water shortly after. They worked together on the third. Then Inge opened the cabin door and peered out into the swirling flakes. Bartholomew and Tulyet crouched down in alarm, waiting for the howl that would tell them they had been spotted. But there was a click, and they looked up to see the door closed again. Frantically now, they wrestled with the last rope. There was a splash as it fell.

They retreated to the shadows to watch. At first, nothing happened. Was it too heavy to drift now it was loaded with Dallingridge's feet and nine passengers? Or grounded, perhaps? But then it began to move, slowly at first, then faster as it was caught by the current. The singing faltered into silence, after which came voices raised in fright. It was difficult to make out words, but it seemed that water was seeping into the cabin.

'We are unshipped *again*,' howled the captain, hurtling out of the cabin to peer over the side in horror. 'It must have been your barber – I *told* you to go and find out what was taking him so long. Now we are going down, and I cannot swim!'

'These manmade channels are not very deep,' said Inge. 'Do not worry. We shall wade—'

'This is *not* a manmade channel,' shrieked the captain, his voice shrill with terror. 'It is a natural one. And it *is* deep – four fathoms at least.'

'Then hoist the sails,' snapped Inge, alarmed at last. 'Take us back towards the pier, like you did the first time.'

All was a whirl of activity, but fright turned the captain and his crewman clumsy, and the soldiers made matters worse by trying to help. They got in the way, and hauled too roughly on the wrong ropes. The barge eased ever further from the shore, and then the lamps winked out in the cabin as they were doused by inrushing water. Three soldiers promptly leapt overboard in panic. Only one bobbed to the surface.

'This is your fault,' screamed the captain at Inge. 'I told you that she could not take the last few pieces. But, oh, no, you had to have the lot. Well, your greed has killed us all!'

'We risked our lives to get those things,' snarled Inge. 'They are too valuable to—'

He broke off with a yelp as the vessel listed violently, hurling him against a rail. Tulyet emerged from the trees and went to stand on the pier, sword in his hand.

'Surrender, and we will help you to safety,' he bellowed. 'Or stay where you are and die.'

'We surrender!' howled Norys. 'Please, Sheriff, sir! Help us!'

Inge released a petrified shriek as the barge began to roll. Two more soldiers toppled into the water, along with the crewman. Inge was left clinging to the foremast.

'Here!' Bartholomew had found a coil of a rope on the pier, and he threw it towards the stricken vessel. 'Catch it and—'

But the barge tilted even further, and the captain disappeared with a wail of terror. There was a faint white splash where he hit the water, and then he was gone. Bartholomew reeled the empty rope back quickly, and tossed it out again.

'Grab it!' hollered Tulyet. 'Hurry, or the boat will take you with it when it goes.'

It was not the right thing to say to panicky men. Frantically, Inge seized the rope and began to wrap it around himself, but Norys leapt forward with a roar of rage and wrested it from him. There was a brief tussle, which Norys appeared to win. But the rope was caught under the bell, and he could not pull it free. There was a muffled rumble as the cargo shifted, and the barge jerked savagely to port. Water fountained up all around it, and then it slid out of sight. The rope tore through Bartholomew's hands.

He could see heads bobbing in the black, ice-frosted water, and looked around desperately for something else to throw. There was nothing, but a coracle was tethered nearby, an unwieldy craft that threatened to tip him into the river when he jumped into it.

He paddled out as fast as he could, and reached a half-submerged body. It was the captain, eyes closed in death. Bartholomew grabbed the crewman next, but the fellow kicked and thrashed so frantically that it was impossible to haul him aboard. He was lost when one of his flailing feet struck the coracle and sent it spinning away – by the time Bartholomew had sculled back again, there was no sign of him.

Meanwhile, two soldiers had reached him. They clung to the side, so determined to be rescued first that they began to punch each other away. The resulting fracas saw them both disappear, and although Bartholomew fished about with his paddle for several minutes in the hope that one would grasp it, neither did. He looked around wildly, wondering if they had been caught by the current and pulled downstream, but the water there was black, glassy and empty.

'Come to *this* bank,' Tulyet was yelling, and Bartholomew glanced around to see three soldiers staggering unsteadily up the opposite one. 'You will die over there – there is no shelter.'

Then Bartholomew heard a muffled groan, and turned to see Norys floating nearby. He managed to pull him halfway into the little craft, and rowed for all he was worth to the dock, where Tulyet was waiting to help. But Norys had been knifed, probably by Inge during the tussle for the rope, and he did not live long, despite Bartholomew's best efforts.

'No,' said Tulyet, gripping Bartholomew's arm as he aimed for the coracle again. 'It is too late. You will only be retrieving corpses, and it is not worth the risk.'

'The men who swam to the other shore,' said Bartholomew hoarsely, appalled by what had happened. 'What about them?'

'They are soaking wet in a raging blizzard,' replied Tulyet sombrely. 'And there is nothing over there but bogs. They will be dead long before morning.'

CHAPTER 17

Dawn was still some way off, but there was a perceptible lightening of the sky in the east. The wind had dropped, and the snow no longer swirled quite so thickly. Bartholomew peered into the gloom for the towpath. It was hidden under a billowy whiteness. It would not be easy to fight their way along it, and the going would be harder still in the open.

'Come on,' he said urgently. 'It will be light by the time we reach the horses, and then we can ride the rest of the way.'

They stopped at the warehouse, where Bartholomew quickly exchanged his wet clothes for some left by the soldiers – they stank and were full of fleas, but at least they were dry. Then he and Tulyet began to plough along the path towards Quy. To take his mind off their agonisingly slow progress, he considered Cook's claims about the killer. There were only two suspects left on the original list, and try as he might, Bartholomew could not imagine young Kolvyle intimidating the likes of Inge and Helbye. Which left Hopeman.

Did the Dominican know that Michael might try to usher Suttone in by cheating, so had devised a contingency plan by poisoning the official ring-seal? After all, if the winner died at the election, the stunned University would simply invite the runner-up to take the post instead. And Michael would be killed, too, because the Senior Proctor always wore the ring-seal during the ceremony, until it was presented to the victor.

'Ask the secret air,' muttered Tulyet behind him. 'What does that mean?'

Bartholomew was panting so hard that he could barely hear, and there was an instant when he thought Tulyet had said something else. He stopped walking abruptly and whipped around. 'Not ask the secret air – ask the *secretary*! That is what Moleyns mumbled. Cook misheard him – as I misheard you just then.'

'What secretary? Moleyns did not have one.'

'But Tynkell did – and he was the first victim.'

'You think Nicholas is the killer?' asked Tulyet doubtfully. 'But he is lame.'

'A bad leg will not prevent him from sliding a spike into someone's heart. And although he has no tower keys of his own, he knows where Meadowman's are kept.'

'I did not see him among the crowd that clustered around Moleyns,' mused Tulyet. 'Although that does not mean he was not there – I could not identify everyone, because most folk had their hoods up. But he cannot be the culprit, Matt. He is such a mouse.'

'Even mice have teeth. And if it was he who fought Tynkell on the roof, it explains why the spectacle went on for so long – neither were natural warriors.'

'But why would he do such a thing?'

'So his lover Thelnetham could be Chancellor. Which is why he killed Lyng, too – the most popular candidate.'

'Thelnetham is involved, too?'

Bartholomew shook his head. 'If he were, he would not have withdrawn – he would have battled on, to make the crimes worthwhile.'

'Then why would Nicholas stab Moleyns?'

'Because Moleyns knew who killed Tynkell,' replied Bartholomew triumphantly. Aware that he was wasting time, he began to plod forward again, more determined than ever to reach Cambridge before it was too late. 'At least, he said he did.'

'But Moleyns told Cook to "ask the secret air" two days

before he was killed. Or are you suggesting he knew in advance that someone would murder him?'

'Why not? Perhaps the threat to their safety is what he, Tynkell and Lyng discussed in St Mary the Great.'

'Where Cook met them, too,' said Tulyet, then added quietly, 'and where Moleyns was being "guarded" by Helbye.'

It was all beginning to make sense to Bartholomew, and he spoke excitedly. 'So Nicholas unlocked the tower with Meadowman's keys, went to the roof to fight Tynkell, then hid in the Chest Room until Michael and I had gone past on the stairs. When the coast was clear, he descended to the church, but he could not leave openly, lest he was seen. So he donned a disguise – a cloak with an embroidered hem.'

'How do you—' began Tulyet uncertainly.

'Cristine had removed *her* cloak to ring the bells – at Nicholas's invitation – after which it was stolen. I wager anything you like that it has an embroidered hem, and that Nicholas wore it when he went to ensure that Moleyns kept his silence.'

'I did not see this "woman" but you did. Could it have been Nicholas?'

Bartholomew nodded. 'Which means "she" was not a witness running terrified from a murder, but a man fleeing the scene of his crime. I assumed it was female, because it was wearing a lady's cloak. It was a stupid mistake.'

'If all this is true, then it means that Nicholas is involved in the thefts – why else would he have talked to Inge and Helbye in the church while the bell was being stolen? Yet he was distraught by its disappearance.' Tulyet sighed as the answer became clear. 'What better way to avoid suspicion than pretending to be a victim?'

Bartholomew stopped walking a second time as a terrible thought occurred to him. 'What do you do to a bell? You *ring* it! Cook heard the killer say "ring" to

Helbye and Inge, and drew his own conclusions, but he was wrong!'

Tulyet frowned. 'I do not understand—'

'The killer was not referring to jewellery, but to bells, which will be *rung* when the new Chancellor is elected. The thieves sawed through the frame to get the treble out, and I thought then that the whole thing looked precarious. Moreover, the trapdoor beneath is flimsy. And who assured us that there is no problem and that everything is safe? Nicholas!'

'You think that is what he intends to do? Crush his opponents with falling bells?'

'Yes! When the new Chancellor gives them a tug, they will crash through the ceiling and kill everyone below – him, Michael, Hopeman and all the University's most senior officials. Then Nicholas will step forward and recommend Thelnetham as the next Chancellor.'

'But Thelnetham withdrew. He is no longer eligible.'

'Nicholas will find a way around it – he knows how to manipulate the statutes, especially if Michael is not there to contradict him. And Thelnetham will be the only candidate left of the original five – Hopeman, Suttone and Lyng will be dead, and Godrich has run away.'

Tulyet was still unconvinced. 'If the bells were that unstable someone would have noticed.'

'We *did* notice!' shouted Bartholomew, beginning to surge forward again. 'Yesterday, when one slipped, and rang of its own accord. Nicholas cleverly blamed the Devil, and the fanatical Hopeman was quick to agree.'

'Which explains why Michael did not find anyone when he took Hopeman and Suttone up the tower,' mused Tulyet. 'Yet if the frame is so precarious, surely they would have mentioned it yesterday?'

'They were looking for pranksters, not structural problems. Of course it escaped their attention. Now *run*! We

402

must warn Michael, because I am not letting Nicholas kill him.'

They battled along, desperately struggling to see against the swirling flakes. The wind was bitter, and made their heads ache, while the muscles in their legs burned from their exertions.

'Matt!' yelled Tulyet suddenly, dropping to his knees and beginning to scoop away handfuls of snow from one drift. 'Help me.'

'What are you doing?' cried Bartholomew in agitation. 'We do not have time—'

He faltered when he saw the frozen face that Tulyet had exposed.

'Helbye,' said Tulyet in a choked voice.

Bartholomew swept away more snow. The sergeant had dispensed with his cloak and jerkin, and his shirt was awry, as if he had tried to remove that, too.

'Cook's handiwork,' said Bartholomew softly. 'Helbye was burning with fever from his festering wound, so he loosened his clothes to cool off. Then he sat down, thinking to rest for a moment, but closed his eyes and fell asleep. The cold did the rest.'

'At least he will be spared the shame of . . .' Tulyet could not finish.

They continued again, every step an agony of effort, which meant neither had the breath to talk. Bartholomew was acutely aware that it was now fully light, and that time was ticking past far too quickly. Then the path ended, and he saw with horror that the horses had gone.

'We will walk,' said Tulyet with quiet determination. 'If we keep up a steady pace—'

He grabbed Bartholomew's arm suddenly, and hauled him into the undergrowth. There were voices, some very near. With despair, they heard the sounds of people searching, converging on them from at least three separate directions.

'The villagers,' said Tulyet tightly. 'The ones who are almost certainly in league with the thieves, and who will fight us if we are found.'

'Then spin them a yarn,' urged Bartholomew, heart pounding with tension. 'Convince them that we are involved, too.'

'That will not work – they know me. We must hide until they have gone. I am not sure we would have reached Cambridge in time now anyway, not in this weather. But if we are alive, we can at least ensure that Nicholas pays for what he has done.'

'No!' hissed Bartholomew fiercely. 'I am not giving up. I will distract them while you run for the town. I will keep them busy for as long as I can. Go!'

He leapt up and began to plough towards the road before Tulyet could stop him. There was an immediate chorus of yells as he was spotted. The searchers howled for him to stop, but he ignored them, wading through ever deeper drifts and sincerely hoping that he was managing to draw their pursuers after him so that Tulyet could escape. Then he heard a familiar voice.

'Doctor, wait! You are going the wrong way.'

It was Isnard. Bartholomew whipped around in confusion, then sagged with relief when he saw who was with him.

'Cynric!'

CHAPTER 18

'I told you he would be more than a match for thieves,' said the book-bearer proudly, coming to grip the physician's shoulder in a comradely gesture of affection. He turned to the men who were with him – Isnard and Gundrede, along with Robin and several soldiers from the castle. 'He has killed every last one of them, and was coming to tell us what happened.'

'Then why was he running towards the Fens?' asked Gundrede doubtfully.

'He got disoriented at the last moment,' explained Cynric, and gestured at the uniform whiteness around him. 'You can see why – it is a different world out here today.'

'Is it true, Doctor?' Isnard was agog. '*All* the thieves are dead?'

'Probably – by now,' replied Bartholomew shakily. 'But we did not—'

'The hero of Poitiers,' interrupted Cynric with satisfaction. 'Where is the Sheriff, boy? Did he help or did you manage alone?'

'I helped,' drawled Tulyet, ploughing forward to join them. 'But only a little.'

'Please,' begged Bartholomew. 'Where are the horses? We need to get to Cambridge.'

'Horses are no good,' said Cynric disdainfully. 'The drifts are too high. Yours are safe though. We took them to—'

'Michael is in danger,' blurted Bartholomew. 'We *have* to warn him.'

'What sort of danger?' demanded Isnard, protective of the man who ran his choir.

Tulyet explained in a few terse words, then asked, 'How did you get here if the roads are blocked?'

'By the only *proper* mode of transport,' replied Isnard grandly. 'Barge. Now come with me. I do not know if we can reach the town by noon, but we shall certainly try.'

He swung off down a track, remarkably surefooted on the treacherous surface. It was not far to the river, where several vessels were moored. He chose the smallest. Bartholomew, Tulyet and Cynric scrambled in after him, but he raised a hand to stop the others.

'The lighter we are, the faster we shall move.'

'We will put our time here to good use by rooting out the guilty villagers,' said Robin, helping the bargeman to cast off. 'Two have already confessed to turning a blind eye to mysterious comings and goings.'

The boat eased away from the bank, slowly at first, then faster as Isnard deployed a combination of pole and sail. He adapted constantly to the shifting wind and currents, and for the first time, Bartholomew began to appreciate the true extent of his skill.

'You should have taken me with you last night, boy,' said Cynric accusingly. 'You know I like an adventure, and it was cruel to leave me out.'

'You were guarding Suttone.' Bartholomew glanced at him in alarm. 'Is he—'

'Mallet and Islaye are with him,' replied the book-bearer. 'Do not worry.'

Isnard explained how they had come to be there, taking a respite from his exertions when a lucky breeze set them skimming along a wide stretch of open water.

'I was uneasy from the start about being sent home, and I said as much to Cynric. So we decided on a foray of our own. Then we met Robin. He insisted on coming with us, because Helbye was missing and he was worried.'

'Then thank God for your suspicious minds,' murmured Tulyet.

It was an agonising journey for the occupants of the little boat, through a landscape that was unrecognisable under a thick blanket of white. Isnard was soon scarlet-faced with effort – the others had been allowed one turn at the pole, but he had snatched it back furiously when they had failed to reach what he considered an acceptable speed.

'I will not see Brother Michael dead, just because you cannot punt,' he gasped. 'How much longer do we have before the ceremony?'

Bartholomew squinted up at the sky. 'More than three hours, but less than four. Probably.'

'Then it will be tight,' panted Isnard, and turned all his attention to his labours.

Sitting immobile in a wind that still carried the occasional icy flurry was unpleasant, and Bartholomew wondered if he, Tulyet and Cynric would be capable of movement when they arrived. The boat slid silently across the glassy water, and the whole country seemed dead and still. Trees were weighted down with great clods of snow, while bushes and shrubs were mere humps in an undulating white sea. No birds sang, and the only sounds were the rhythmic splash of Isnard's pole and his ragged breathing.

'So tell me, Isnard,' said Tulyet, during a spell in which the bargeman was able to use the sails again, 'where did you go when you disappeared with your barge? I know it was not to help Inge with his stolen goods.'

'It is all right, boy,' said Cynric, when Isnard looked as if he would refuse to answer. 'These two can keep a secret.'

Isnard sighed. 'Very well, but they had better not blab, or I shall be cross, because it will ruin the surprise.'

'What have you done?' asked Bartholomew with considerable unease, knowing from experience that not all the bargeman's surprises were pleasant ones.

'We have been collecting supplies to mend Michaelhouse's damaged pier,' explained Isnard. 'We know Master Langelee does not have the money to fix it up again, although he would sooner die than admit it, so the choir decided to help. It will be our gift, to thank the College for all that free bread and ale.'

'But they had to sail a long way south to find a place where the odd bit of wood would not be missed,' explained Cynric. 'So it took them a lot of time.'

'That Benedictine envoy followed us once,' said Isnard, pursing his lips. 'He automatically assumed we were up to no good, which was not very nice.'

Bartholomew refrained from pointing out that they *had* been up to no good – stealing was a crime, no matter what the culprits' motive.

'He aimed to embarrass you, Sheriff, by presenting you with the "thieves" himself,' Isnard went on indignantly. 'But he fell over and cut his leg, and had to beg us for help. We picked him up and offered to ferry him home – on condition that he did not tell.'

Bartholomew smiled wanly. 'He kept his promise – he never breathed a word, even though he knew I did not believe his tale about falling down the stairs.'

'Master Lyng was party to the secret as well,' Isnard went on. 'Because Gundrede let it slip during a confession. I think he and the envoy talked about it.'

They had, thought Bartholomew – a whispered conversation on which Richard Deynman had tried, unsuccessfully, to eavesdrop.

'It is a pity you did not confide in me,' said Tulyet tiredly. 'It would have saved us all a lot of bother. I might even have given you supplies from the castle.'

Isnard grinned as he took hold of his pole again. 'I

shall come for them later then. If we work fast, we might have finished it before Brother Michael leaves, and then who knows? Perhaps he will stay when he sees what we have done for him.'

Tulyet started to say that it had been a hypothetical offer, but Isnard was not listening, concentrating instead on navigating the boat down a series of narrow, reed-infested channels. Then they emerged into a stretch of water that was too deep for punting and the wrong direction for wind.

'Row,' ordered Isnard. 'One oar between two, and pull on my orders. Now!'

Soon, they were skimming along at an impressive lick, although it was impossible to maintain such a pace for long, and it soon slackened off. Seeing it, Bartholomew pulled harder, but the boat slewed to the left, and Isnard barked at him to match his speed to the other paddle.

'There!' shouted Tulyet, glancing behind him to where familiar towers and turrets loomed on the horizon. 'We are nearly home. Heave!'

The barge veered to the right, forcing Bartholomew and Cynric to tug hard to correct it.

'I can hear the Franciscans' bells!' cried Isnard in dismay. 'They are chiming for sext, which means it is noon. We are too late!'

'No!' yelled Bartholomew, as the bargeman slumped in defeat. 'They will hold the rite earlier today, because of the election. We still have a chance. Come on – hurry!'

Encouraged, the others bent to the task, and they raced towards the Great Bridge. It was strange to see it from water level, and Bartholomew disliked the sense of it looming over him as they scudded underneath. He adjusted his stroke, aiming to land at the nearest quay.

'No – we want the Michaelhouse wharf,' panted Isnard. 'It will be quicker than battling through the town on foot, believe me.'

They rowed quickly past the backs of St John's Hospital, Michaelhouse and Trinity Hall, until the little craft bumped alongside the pier's blackened remains. Bartholomew almost took a dip when he trod on a plank that crumbled under his weight, and was only saved by a timely lunge from Cynric. Exhausted by his herculean efforts, Isnard collapsed backwards, indicating with a weak flap of his hand that the others were to go on without him.

Bartholomew, Tulyet and Cynric clambered ashore, and began to struggle towards Milne Street, quickly learning that Isnard had been right to keep them on the river for as long as possible – the snow was thigh-deep in places. There was not another scholar in sight, despite the fact that Water Lane was home to seven or eight hostels.

'Oh, God!' groaned Tulyet. 'Have the bells already fallen, and everyone has gone to gawp? They must have done! Students cannot vote, so you would think some would be here.'

'They will have gone to watch the election,' predicted Bartholomew. 'It is not every day that a new Chancellor is voted in – they will want to watch history in the making.'

Then Cynric grabbed his arm. 'There is Nicholas!'

The secretary was limping through St John Zachary's churchyard with Vicar Frisby at his side. They were an odd pair – one small, neat and prim, the other hulking and dissipated.

'He does not look like a man who has just committed murder,' remarked Tulyet, watching him intently. 'Perhaps he has yet to strike.'

Bartholomew wanted to believe it, but could not help recalling that Nicholas had stabbed the Chancellor and Moleyns while half the town looked on. He was a man with iron nerves.

'Cynric and I will tackle him,' determined Tulyet. 'You go to St Mary the Great, Matt. If the bells are still in the tower, clear the building. If they are down . . . well, you will be of more use there than us.'

He and Cynric clambered over the churchyard wall – the gate was too deep in snow to be opened – and plodded towards the porch. Bartholomew turned left and began to plough along Milne Street, the wind buffeting his back. It was snowing again, a thick swirl that made it impossible to see very far ahead. However, when he reached Trinity Hall, he encountered a major problem.

Snow had drifted against the rubble, and the clearing through the middle was obliterated – all that remained was a solid cliff of white. Stomach churning, he lurched forward to see if he could scale it, but it quickly became obvious that such a feat was impossible. Cursing himself for not remembering it was there, he turned and retraced his steps. He would have to go back past St John Zachary and up Piron Lane instead.

It was difficult to move with snow beating into his face, and he felt sick with tension at the time he had lost. He reached St John Zachary, hoping to see Cynric and Tulyet emerge with prisoners, but there was only Nicholas, standing in the porch as he gazed idly up at the swirling flakes.

Bartholomew gaped at him. Why was he still free? Surely Cynric and Tulyet could defeat a little clerk, even if Frisby had lurched to his kinsman's assistance with a weapon? Or was he wrong to underestimate the man who had murdered Tynkell, Moleyns and Lyng, and the Sheriff and book-bearer were lying inside with spikes in their hearts?

He hesitated, full of panicky indecision. Should he go to St Mary the Great, or see what had happened to Cynric and Tulyet? Then Nicholas turned and strolled confidently back inside, at which point Bartholomew thought he heard Tulyet cry out. Without conscious thought, he was over the churchyard wall and aiming for the door.

411

He stepped into the porch and listened intently. Nicholas and Frisby were talking in the chancel. He eased forward, stopping en route to grab a heavy pewter jug – the only thing lying around that would be of remote use as a weapon.

Nicholas was by Stanmore's vault, talking in an undertone. Bartholomew advanced stealthily, aiming to disable him with a tap to the head before looking for Cynric and Tulyet. He was just raising the jug when he heard a sound from behind him. It was Frisby, who was not listening to his kinsman, but lying in ambush, while Nicholas only pretended to engage him in conversation. Bartholomew ducked in time to avoid the crossbow bolt that whipped past his ear, but fell heavily. Frisby tossed the weapon aside, grabbed a cudgel, and advanced with murder in his eyes.

CHAPTER 19

'I told you I could lure him in, Frisby,' said Nicholas smugly. 'Now kill him.'

Frisby stepped forward to oblige, but he was unsteady with drink, so Bartholomew was able to roll away before the cudgel landed. The force of the blow chipped a flagstone, and caused the vicar to stumble. While he staggered, Bartholomew scrambled to his feet.

'Matt!' It was Tulyet's voice, muffled and indistinct. 'Be watchful!'

Bartholomew looked around wildly. It sounded as though the Sheriff had spoken from below him. Then he noticed that Stanmore's vault was sealed. Or almost sealed – the granite slab had been positioned badly, so that one side was higher than the other and there was a gap all along one edge. His stomach lurched: Cynric's hat was caught in it. The book-bearer and Tulyet were inside.

Frisby swiped with the cudgel again, dragging Bartholomew's attention back to the fight. Bartholomew darted behind a pillar, dodging first one way and then the other as the vicar tried to reach him. At the same time, Nicholas surged forward and jumped on the lopsided stone. There was an immediate grating sound, and Cynric released a wail of terror.

'Petit is an indifferent craftsman,' called Nicholas tauntingly. 'This slab is too small, and it will not take much to send it crashing down on those below. Surrender, or they die.'

Bartholomew felt despair begin to overwhelm him. Was he to lose all his friends that day? He tried to force his shock-numbed mind to work – to devise a plan to defeat Nicholas and Frisby, while staying alive to rescue Michael. Or was it already too late?

'The bells,' he said in a choked voice. 'You arranged for them to fall . . .'

Nicholas smiled coldly. 'I expect to hear them plummet any time now.'

So it had not happened yet. Bartholomew glanced towards the door. Could he reach it without Frisby braining him? It would condemn Cynric and Tulyet to certain death, but he might be able to avert a massacre in St Mary the Great. Or would the journey take too long in the snow – in which case, should he try to save Tulyet and Cynric? He experienced a futile surge of anger with Nicholas, for forcing him to make such a terrible choice.

The secretary seemed to read his mind. 'Your friends stormed in here, expecting to catch me with ease, but Frisby shot Tulyet, while I knocked Cynric senseless with a slingshot.'

'You *shot* Tulyet?' asked Bartholomew in horror.

'In the leg – we guessed he would be wearing armour,' said Frisby. 'But it immobilised him enough to let us shove him and the book-bearer down the vault. They will die when the slab falls on them – unless you desist this lurching about and give yourself up.'

'Please,' begged Bartholomew, knowing perfectly well that Nicholas would then just dispatch all three of them. 'There has been enough killing.'

'On the contrary, it has only just started.' Nicholas shifted slightly, and the stone scraped against the edge of the hole; Cynric whimpered. 'But the end is in sight. The bells will fall and we shall be rid of Michael, Suttone, Hopeman and everyone else who stands in our way. Then we can install a better Chancellor.'

'Thelnetham will not do it,' warned Bartholomew. 'He will never accept a post that has been won by such foul means.'

'Of course he will,' slurred Frisby, lunging again. 'And he will reward me with a nice easy living somewhere. Stoke Poges, perhaps.'

'I doubt that is in the University's gift.' Bartholomew pointed at Nicholas. 'I imagine *he* fabricated the deed of ownership, to make us think that manor held the key to the murders. But the connections between it and the victims are spurious.'

Nicholas could not resist a smirk. 'They are, although you followed the crumbs I left like hungry birds. Lyng did not hail from the next village, Tynkell never tried to get its chapel, and neither ever visited the place.'

'You will not have an easy living, Frisby,' said Bartholomew, aiming to drive a wedge between the pair. 'Because when you are of no further use, he will kill you as well.'

'Nonsense,' said Nicholas, so quickly that Bartholomew was sure the vicar's fate was already sealed. 'He is my kinsman: I would never harm him.'

'He is angry with you for telling us about the dog,' lied Bartholomew. Had he heard shouting in the distance? Did it mean the voting was over and the procession was on the move? 'The clue that explained how he made Moleyns fall off his horse.'

Frisby frowned. 'Yes, I mentioned the dog, but only because others must have done the same, and it would have looked suspicious to keep it quiet.'

'It gave you away,' persisted Bartholomew. 'Along with telling us that the bone was a lamb shank – a detail no one else knew. There is a warrant for your arrest—'

'Ignore him, Frisby,' instructed Nicholas. 'He is making it up.'

'Nicholas is *much* cleverer than you,' sneered the vicar. 'He laid not one false trail, but two: Stoke Poges and witchery. Tynkell and Lyng made some youthful mistakes, but were good sons of the Church most of their adult lives. Moleyns was not, but Satanism is not what they discussed in St Mary the Great.'

'I know,' said Bartholomew. 'We had the truth from Cook. Tynkell and Lyng went to grovel to Moleyns, in the hope of winning favourable mentions at Court.'

He glanced at the vault. Cynric and Tulyet were resourceful. Were they devising an escape plan while he kept Nicholas and Frisby talking? But the hole was deep and the stone too heavy to move from the inside, especially if both were incapacitated. He raised a hand to his head. It shook with tension.

'But not for themselves,' explained Nicholas. 'For the University. You see, Tynkell *did* confide his plans to me. He aimed to use Moleyns to promote the University to royal ears – his parting gift before he retired. Lyng agreed to help.'

'Why would Lyng do that?' asked Bartholomew suspiciously. 'His colleagues told us that he despised Moleyns.'

'Oh, he did, but he was willing to swallow his distaste for the benefit of the University he had served for so many years. Poor Tynkell devoted his every waking moment to the scheme – at the expense of all his other duties. And when Moleyns invited Tynkell to discuss "certain business", he referred to his power to expedite royal patronage.'

Bartholomew knew he needed to forget about Nicholas and get to St Mary the Great. He could not help Tulyet and Cynric, and it was time to be pragmatic, unpleasant though that was. He forced himself to take a step towards the door, but Frisby blocked him.

'You told Michael that Tynkell was quiet and withdrawn,' he said, in an effort to distract them with more words before making a dash for freedom. 'And that he had developed a habit of muttering about Satan.'

Nicholas laughed and the stone wobbled. 'I lied.'

Bartholomew was aware of a creeping sense of defeat

416

as he recalled all the 'clues' that had led him astray: Marjory's claim that Moleyns had spoken to Lyng before he died – perhaps he had, but it was irrelevant; Kolvyle's association with Moleyns, which was just a continuation of a harmless friendship started in Nottingham; the curious antics of Whittlesey and Godrich; and the arguments between Hopeman and Lyng. None were pertinent to the murders.

'You will not profit from helping Cook and Inge,' he said desperately. 'They are dead, and your beloved bell lies at the bottom of the river.'

'I already have what I wanted from the thieves,' smiled Nicholas. 'Namely adjustments made to the remaining two bells and their frame. A share of their profits was never part of the agreement.'

Bartholomew took a step to his left, and this time Frisby did not notice, because he had retrieved his crossbow and was fiddling with it. Fortunately for Bartholomew, its rough treatment had smashed the winding mechanism. He spoke to Nicholas again.

'You offered two marks for its return, an enormous sum designed to cause trouble.'

'It worked. The resulting fuss distracted the Sheriff and Senior Proctor very nicely. Of course, they are not the only nuisances we saw off . . .'

'Whittlesey,' surmised Bartholomew. 'He is an intelligent, observant man, and you feared he might realise what was happening, so you sent a letter to Godrich, purporting to be from Bishop Sheppey, warning him to watch his cousin.'

Nicholas inclined his head. 'Godrich did not let Whittlesey out of his sight, which made it impossible for the man to pry. How did you guess?'

'Because Sheppey would never have written such a thing about a man he considered to be a friend. Because it was dated the day before Sheppey's death, but the signature was too strong and firm for a dying man. And because it was addressed to a "favoured son in Christ".

'Which Godrich was not,' chuckled Nicholas. 'A small joke on my part.'

'You wrote other letters, too,' said Bartholomew, shifting another inch to his left. 'To Whittlesey, telling him about Godrich's predilection for witchery, knowing that a Benedictine would never countenance such a man in charge of a university. And to Lyng, which you had to retrieve by breaking into Maud's.'

'The handwriting,' explained Nicholas. 'Michael would have recognised it as mine.'

Bartholomew rubbed his aching head. 'But why go to all this trouble when Tynkell was on the verge of retiring anyway? Why not wait?'

'And give the wealthy all that time to *buy* the post? You saw how many scholars Godrich bribed in a few days – imagine what he would have managed over a period of months. Hah! More cheers. It will not be long now.'

'You cannot murder people in a church.' Bartholomew's voice cracked with despair. 'You will be damned for all eternity.'

Nicholas laughed. 'You think that worries me?' He pulled back his sleeve to reveal the horned serpent that was inked there.

Bartholomew gazed at it in despair, and tried another tack. 'Are you skulking in here because you cannot bear to watch the results of your despicable crime? You are cowards, who dare not look on the faces of their victims?'

'No,' replied Nicholas. 'We are hiding here so that no one can accuse us of having a hand in the disaster later.' He glanced at Frisby, and his muscles bunched as he prepared for the jump that would send the granite crashing downwards. 'Do you have a knife, Frisby? Good. Then stop messing about with that useless crossbow, and stab him.'

* * *

Even the drunken Frisby was unlikely to miss from such close range, so with nothing to lose, Bartholomew hurled himself at Nicholas, aiming to knock him off the slab in the desperate, if unrealistic, hope that Cynric and Tulyet might be able to use the respite to save themselves.

Nicholas was in the act of jumping down hard when Bartholomew slammed into him, but the physician misjudged the distance. Instead of knocking Nicholas clean away, he only spun him around, and the secretary landed on one corner of the stone. Bartholomew's own momentum sent him tumbling across the floor to fetch up against the far wall. Cynric howled his terror as there was an unpleasant grating sound, and the stone juddered disturbingly.

At the same time, Frisby released a bellow of frustration: his wild swipe had missed Bartholomew, but the blade had flown from his fingers and was clattering away from him over the flagstones towards the vault.

Bartholomew struggled to his feet and gazed at the slab in alarm, expecting to see it in the process of crashing downwards. But it was wedged at an angle, and he saw it was held there by Nicholas's leg, which was trapped in the space between it and the lip of the vault. The secretary was silent for a moment, then he screamed in pain.

'Behind you, Matt!' yelled Tulyet.

Bartholomew turned to see Frisby, ham-sized fists ready to deliver a pummelling. But the physician was faster and lighter, and was able to deliver two brisk clouts to the dissipated face before snatching up the jug he had brought from the porch. Meanwhile, despite his agony, Nicholas had managed to grab the dagger his kinsman had dropped.

'Drive him towards me, Frisby,' the secretary rasped in a voice that was thick with pain. 'I will stab him, and then you can help me out. Hurry – it hurts!'

Frisby started to oblige, but Bartholomew swung the jug with all his might, and knocked him backwards. It was another misjudgement on Bartholomew's part, because the blow sent the vicar staggering towards the vault. He could hardly bear to watch as Frisby's foot caught on the edge of the granite and over he went. The vicar landed on top of Nicholas, who released another shriek of anguish.

But by some miracle, the granite slab still did not fall, although Frisby lay unmoving across his howling cousin.

'He came down on the dagger,' shouted Tulyet to Bartholomew, his eyes just visible through the slit between the stone and the lip of the vault – he was standing on Cynric's shoulders. 'Did it kill him?'

Bartholomew felt for a life-beat, then hauled the dead vicar away before his weight could drive the slab downwards anyway. 'Yes. Can you push—'

'Stop!' cried Tulyet, as Bartholomew put his fingers under the enormous stone and prepared to heave. 'You will bring it down on us for certain if you try to lift it on your own. Examine Nicholas. Is he still alive?'

Bartholomew winced when he saw the state of the secretary's leg. Even if Nicholas survived the shock of such a terrible injury, the limb would have to come off in its entirety. 'He has fainted.'

'Here,' said Tulyet, shoving a piece of rope through the gap. 'Fasten that to the hoist – it will keep us safe until help arrives.'

'How badly are you hurt? Frisby said he shot you?'

'I will survive. Now go to St Mary the Great. Quickly!'

Outside, snow had started to fall again. Bartholomew began to wade through it, cursing the unsteadiness of his legs. Then he heard a round of applause, although not a particularly enthusiastic one. It told him that someone had been declared the University's new Chancellor, which meant it would not be long before the procession moved towards the narthex.

He tried to move faster, legs burning with exhaustion

and breath coming in ragged gasps. There came the sound of singing as the choir began the final anthem. He skidded on ice, twisting his knee, which made him limp for a few steps. His uneven gait reminded him of the way Nicholas walked. And then he stopped in horror.

The secretary was not the killer! How could he be? A lame man could never have done battle with the Chancellor on the roof, then scampered down the stairs to hide in the Chest Room. There was also the 'woman' in the cloak with the embroidered hem – 'she' had not been limping. And scrambling down the ivy at Maud's would have been an impossible feat.

Bartholomew stumbled on again. Nicholas had taken credit for the killings, but it was a lie. However, he knew so much about the crimes that he had obviously discussed them with the real culprit – which meant that the two of them were friends. Very close friends.

Bartholomew felt sick with horror. Thelnetham! *He* was the clever mind behind all the plots and misinformation. And with that, answers tumbled into Bartholomew's mind so fast that it was difficult to analyse them all.

Thelnetham stood to gain the most from the plan, and was doubtless waiting impatiently for the bells to fall, so he could offer to step into the breach afforded by the death or disappearance of the other four candidates. And his colleagues would accept him without demur. He had demonstrated himself to be eloquent, decent and intelligent, a man who had stood aside and graciously lent his support to a rival.

Then there was Stoke Poges. Who had claimed that Lyng hailed from the next village, that Tynkell wanted its chapel for the University, and that both men had visited the manor? The story about a horseman bearing the Stoke Poges insignia had been Thelnetham's, too – another falsehood probably, given that no one else had seen it. Then there was Yevele, who had left Stoke Poges and begged for work at the castle on the Gilbertine's recommendation. And what had Yevele done? Let Moleyns out at night!

It was not only false trails that Thelnetham had left – he had contributed to the confusion about witchery, too. *He* had told the tale about Lyng, Moleyns and Tynkell comparing horned serpents in St Mary the Great, but it was something that would never have happened – Tynkell had gone to considerable trouble to keep his symbols hidden, and would never have risked baring them in a public place.

Bartholomew reached Piron Lane to find the drifts even deeper. His legs ached so badly that he longed to stop, but the thought of Michael and the others who were about to be slaughtered kept him slogging on. To take his mind off the agony, he thought again about Thelnetham.

Why had the Gilbertine 'discovered' Lyng's body, when it would have been better to leave it for someone else? Bartholomew closed his eyes. Thelnetham was devious indeed! He had known exactly what everyone would conclude – that he would not have raised the alarm if he had been the killer. The ploy had worked – they *had* taken it into account when they had dismissed him as a suspect, especially as it came with a confession about his illicit relationship with Nicholas. It had lost him votes, of course, but what did that matter, when he had other plans to see himself in power?

Bartholomew reached the High Street, relieved beyond measure to find it clearer, allowing him to make better time. As he stumbled along this final leg, he pondered Cook's testimony.

The barber had overheard the killer talking to Inge – someone 'educated, clever and confident', who had put the lawyer in his place. Nicholas was incapable of such a feat, but Thelnetham's caustic tongue made him formidable. And when Moleyns had charged Cook to 'ask the secret air', he had not been suggesting that the secretary was the killer, but that Cook should question Nicholas about the culprit.

St Mary the Great was closer now, and the singing was much louder. Bartholomew groaned. He might have been able to yell a warning if it had been any other group of singers, but the monk had contrived to use the Michaelhouse Choir, which meant the noise inside would be deafening. He could bawl all he liked, but no one would hear him.

Answers continued to pour into his mind as he struggled along the last few steps. Lyng had quarrelled with two people the night he died: Hopeman and someone he had called a 'black villain' – not a Dominican, but a Gilbertine, who had 'howled like a girl' when he had been slapped. And finally, there was the dog. They made Thelnetham sneeze, so it was doubtless Frisby who had obliged with the lamb shank, while the Gilbertine lurked in the cloak he had stolen from Cristine, ready to ply his deadly spike.

Bartholomew reached the church at last, and stumbled inside with relief. It was packed with scholars and awash with noise. He scrambled on to the base of a pillar, and peered over the sea of heads towards the chancel. Suttone stood triumphantly next to the Senior Proctor, while Hopeman glowered ungraciously from the sidelines.

Bartholomew looked around wildly. Where was Thelnetham? Hiding, like Nicholas and Frisby, so he could claim to have been elsewhere when the disaster occurred? Then he glanced towards the tower. No! Thelnetham was meticulous, and would not risk his plan failing at the last hurdle. He would be with the bells, to ensure that they fell on cue.

He began to shove through the massed scholars,

earning himself retaliatory pokes and shoves in the process. He tried to shout to them, to beg their help, but the choir was bellowing at the top of its collective lungs, and the few words he could make heard were greeted with incredulous gazes. His appearance did not help – he was wearing Isnard's leather hat and the clothes he had taken from the warehouse, while every other Regent master was in his ceremonial best.

He reached the narthex just as the procession began to move down the nave. He would have a little time, because Suttone would walk slowly, thanking those who had voted for him, and accepting the sheepish congratulations of those who had not.

Beadles stood ready to throw open the Great West Door when Suttone reached it, but there was a problem: it was unexpectedly locked, and no one could find the key. Bartholomew watched their rising agitation helplessly. Thelnetham was thorough indeed – those at the back of the procession would push forward when those at the front stopped, creating a crush that would see a veritable massacre when the bells and their frame crashed through the ceiling.

Bartholomew managed to reach the tower door, and was startled when a frantic shove saw it swing inwards. But of course it was open – Thelnetham would want to be on hand as soon as possible after the tragedy, to take command with a show of calm competence. Locked doors would slow him down.

'Help me!' he howled at the top of his voice, grabbing Master Heltisle of Bene't College by the arm and giving him a vigorous shake. 'Please!'

He could not hear what Heltisle said in return, but the expression on the man's haughty face made it clear that no assistance would be coming from that quarter – and also told him that trying to recruit anyone else would likely be a waste of valuable seconds. He was on his own.

Taking a deep breath to steady himself, he turned to the spiral staircase and began to climb.

Thelnetham was in the bell chamber, perched on a narrow ledge behind the frame and holding a crowbar. He jumped in surprise when Bartholomew stumbled in, and stood slowly. He had left his cloak in the doorway, folded neatly with the large purple brooch laid on top of it. For the first time, Bartholomew saw the back of the brooch – it had a long, thin pin.

'So that is how you killed them,' he said, watching the Gilbertine inch around the wall towards him. 'I should have guessed.'

'You should.' Thelnetham was too intelligent to bother with denials. 'I never made an attempt to hide it, and a brooch that large will inevitably have a big fastener.'

'Come down,' ordered Bartholomew. 'Nicholas and Frisby are caught. It is over.'

'Do not take me for a fool, Matthew. If it was over, there would be pandemonium. Instead, the choir is happily singing.' He lunged suddenly, and kicked the door closed. There was a snap as the latch clicked down on the outside. 'There. You cannot escape now. You will go down with the bells. I, of course, will be safe up here.'

'But you will be locked in – and no one will come to let you out.'

'I do not need anyone's help to escape. I shall merely prise the door open with this crowbar when it is time for me to save the day.'

Bartholomew looked around quickly. Thelnetham had inserted his lever between the wall and the frame – one good heave would see the whole thing pop out, especially if Suttone set the bells swinging at the same time. The frame was already listing badly, pulled down by the great weight of the tenor. But a plan was beginning to take shape in Bartholomew's mind, although it was a desperate one, and he was not sure it would work.

'Why did you kill Tynkell on the roof?' he asked, aiming to keep Thelnetham talking while angles, weights and measurements flashed through his mind.

Thelnetham smiled. 'It suited my penchant for the dramatic, although I did not expect him to put up quite such a fight – he almost throttled me at one point. I was tempted to do something similar for Lyng, but Nicholas advised me against it.'

'You were sorry about Lyng, though,' said Bartholomew, walking cautiously across the trapdoor, which flexed alarmingly under his weight. He glanced up; the bells hung directly above him. 'You arranged his body with care.'

Thelnetham shrugged. 'I asked him nicely to withdraw, but he refused. Slapped me, in fact. Even so, I had no wish to kill an old man . . .'

The choir was singing even louder. Did it mean they were nearly at the narthex? Bartholomew was seized by a sudden panic. If his plan failed, the carnage would be terrible!

'Moleyns knew you were dangerous,' he gabbled, afraid that Thelnetham would read his mind if he remained silent. 'He told Cook. How did he guess?'

'Because of Yevele – the soldier who let him out at night. Rashly, I confided my ambitions to the lad, but he betrayed me to Moleyns for a shilling.'

'So you killed him,' surmised Bartholomew. 'The tale about helping Yevele escape was pure fabrication.'

'Not entirely. I did give him money. I also gave him a flask of poisoned wine.'

'You lied about the horseman who rode away after Moleyns was killed too.'

'Yes, and about my alibis – neither Nicholas nor my Gilbertine brethren were with me at the time, although you did not bother to check.' Thelnetham shook his head in disgust. 'It has been so easy to fool you that I am glad I shall soon be in charge. The University deserves better.'

'I cannot believe that you have stooped to such evil,' said Bartholomew, taking a small step to his right. 'You! A monk and a friend.'

'A "friend" who was ousted from Michaelhouse,' countered Thelnetham bitterly. 'And what better way to avenge myself than winning the chancellorship? When I am in post, Mad Clippesby will be locked away, and William and Langelee will be sent packing. I need not bother with you, Suttone and Michael: you will be dead.'

'And Kolvyle?'

'He can stay. He reminds me of myself at that age – ambitious, clever and undervalued.'

Bartholomew took another step. 'If you are so clever, why did you not find the cloak that blew away from the top of the tower? I know that is why you were out in the Barnwell Fields that day – it was nothing to do with the dying Widow Miller. Your poor grasp of geometry meant you could not predict where it had landed.'

'Well, you did not find it either,' retorted Thelnetham, nettled.

'Yes, I did – it is in Michaelhouse. Langelee will show it to Agatha, and she will identify it as yours. Laundresses are well acquainted with the garments they look after. You will be exposed as "the Devil" who fought Tynkell on the roof.'

Thelnetham shrugged. 'Then I shall deny it, and who will doubt the Chancellor? But I am afraid our little chat must end now. The bell ropes are beginning to move, which means that someone is preparing to ring.'

Bartholomew had also been watching the ropes. He grabbed the one that was twitching and hauled it upwards as fast as he could, then did the same to the other. Below, the anthem petered out as the peculiar phenomenon was observed. Thelnetham laughed derisively.

'The frame will fall regardless of whether the bells are pulled, because it will—'

He faltered when Bartholomew reached up, and swung the clapper hard against the side of the nearest bell – the self-chiming tenor had caused considerable consternation the day before, and he prayed it would do so again. The frame gave an almighty groan, and dust poured from one wall as it shifted in its moorings, but the bell sounded loud and clear. The singing stopped altogether, which was Bartholomew's chance.

'Satan is in the tower!' he hollered. 'Run for your lives!'

Thelnetham snatched up his crowbar. 'It is too late, Matthew. The Great West Door will not open, and everyone will mill around in confusion, trapping those in front. Nothing you do can make any difference now.'

'Lucifer is here!' howled Bartholomew at the top of his voice, giving the bell another belt and then stamping hard on the trapdoor, so it gave a hollow and sinister boom. 'Run!'

Thelnetham released an almighty bellow of effort as he heaved on his lever, and Bartholomew dived towards the window as the frame began to tip. There was a groaning roar as the great mass of wood and metal slid to the floor, accompanied by the distraught clanging of bells. There was a moment when it held, but then the floorboards began to buckle.

'Goodbye, Matthew,' called Thelnetham tauntingly.

'Geometry,' Bartholomew shouted back from the windowsill, watching the Gilbertine's gloat turn to alarm as his ledge began to crumble. 'Your grasp of it *is* poor, or you would have chosen somewhere else to stand.'

And then the frame and bells were gone in a tearing rumble. There was a split second of silence, followed by a crash and a massive billow of dust and plaster. Before he was enveloped in a dense cloud of it, Bartholomew saw two things: Thelnetham clinging frantically to the ledge with his fingertips before tumbling downwards, and – through the window – Michael, Suttone and the choir racing away to safety.

EPILOGUE

Two weeks later

'I think Suttone will make a very good Chancellor,' said Michael, as he stood with Bartholomew, William, Langelee and Cynric in St Mary the Great, where the Carmelite had just been installed. 'I thought he lacked gravitas, but he has a lot more of it than poor Tynkell.'

The Carmelite was radiant in his new robes of office, and had addressed the University in a clear, authoritative voice that carried even to Hopeman and his resentful deacons at the back. The speech had been a masterpiece of conciliation and optimism, and every word of it had been written by Michael.

'When do you leave, Brother?' asked Cynric. 'I thought you needed to be in Rochester days ago, lest the Bishop of Bangor arranged to have himself consecrated in your place.'

Michael smiled serenely. 'I heard a rumour that he stands accused of misappropriating diocesan funds, so I felt duty bound to pass the information to Canterbury. The charge will have to be investigated, so he will not be usurping anyone's See for the foreseeable future.'

'So when are you going?' pressed Cynric.

'Tomorrow, but I shall be back after Easter. After all, I cannot leave Suttone too long.'

'No,' agreed Langelee. 'Thelnetham's machinations proved yet again just how much we need you. It was a close thing with those bells.'

'It was a despicable thing to have attempted,' said Michael, still angry. 'Had it succeeded, it would have

431

been indiscriminate slaughter – not just of Suttone, me and the other officials, but of my choir. And all for Thelnetham's personal gain.'

'I spoke to Cristine Lakenham yesterday,' said Bartholomew. 'Her stolen cloak did have an embroidered hem.'

Michael nodded. 'I found it in Thelnetham's room at the Gilbertine Priory, which is yet more proof of his guilt. But speaking of the tomb-makers, did you know they left this morning?'

'What, all of them?' asked Langelee, startled. 'Masons *and* latteners?'

'Petit and his people have gone to London, while the Lakenhams head west to Hereford. They will feud no longer.'

'But Lakenham cut Oswald's brass before he left,' said Bartholomew. 'A plain one with a simple cross – very tasteful. And the tomb-chest was the first thing we retrieved from Quy, so it is back in its place at St John Zachary. Oswald's monument is now officially finished, and Edith is delighted.'

'But what about Wilson?' asked Langelee worriedly. 'Who will trim his lid – assuming it is ever found, of course?'

'Perhaps we should fill his chest with soil and grow vegetables in it,' suggested Cynric irreverently. He had not liked Wilson.

Bartholomew laughed. 'Do not worry, Master. Dick's engineers are confident that they will find everything that was lost. They plan to fish out the treble bell today.'

'And Dallingridge's executors have offered to pay for it to be rehung,' added Michael, 'in exchange for his mortal remains. They will take them to Sussex next month, and his monument here will be dismantled.'

Cynric frowned. 'That is a peculiar thing to do. And why Sussex?'

'It is the Dallingridge family seat,' explained Michael. 'And his executors live there – which means they can keep an eye on the new tomb's progress. The builder will not be Petit, though: they are suing him for breach of promise, and have hired a new mason instead. Dallingridge is fortunate to have such devoted friends.'

'Especially given that he suspected them of poisoning him,' said Bartholomew. 'But that was Cook, to gain himself a wealthy patient.'

'Cook was a rogue,' said Michael in distaste. 'He killed Lucas, Reames and Peres in cold blood.'

'Not to mention the harm he did to his patients,' put in Bartholomew. 'He would have let Isnard and Gundrede hang for his crimes, too – Dick was sure they were guilty.'

'Isnard and the choir will miss you when you go, Brother,' said Cynric. 'He told me only last night that Cambridge will not be the same without you.'

'Of course not,' agreed Michael. 'I am indispensable, as Rochester will also discover.'

'Dallingridge is where all this started, of course,' sighed Langelee. 'He waxed so lyrical about Cambridge that Moleyns, Cook and the tomb-makers decided to make it their new home as well.'

'Bringing with them their criminal ways,' said Cynric disapprovingly. 'Did you ever find out why he chose to write to Godrich, of all people, informing him that he *had* been fed a toxin, and appending a list of all the folk he thought might have done it?'

'Dallingridge wrote to lots of people,' explained Langelee. 'Including Tynkell, the vicar of St Mary the Great and the Mayor. The poison took weeks to work, and all he could do as he lay there was try to work out who had killed him. He never did though.'

Michael's thoughts returned to Thelnetham. 'Perhaps we should have let him back into Michaelhouse – then he might not have felt the need to prove himself by becoming Chancellor. After all, he was an excellent teacher, and his death is a waste of a brilliant mind.'

'Where is Kolvyle?' asked Bartholomew, thinking of another brilliant mind.

'Gone to Avignon,' replied Langelee with a sudden grin. 'Some weeks ago I wrote to our Bishop and told him that Kolvyle was the wiliest scholar I had ever met. Well, you know de Lisle – ever eager for sly minds to further his own ambitions – so Kolvyle has been offered a post in his retinue. Our Junior Fellow will be gloating over his good fortune as we speak.'

'But?' asked Bartholomew. 'I sense a caveat.'

'Oh, yes. De Lisle is a fading star, beleaguered by scandal and accusation. His fall from grace has already begun, and it will not be long before he hits the bottom, taking his followers with him. Afterwards, Kolvyle will be lucky to find a village school that will employ him.'

'My own appointment came just in time then,' said Michael comfortably. 'I do not need de Lisle any longer.'

'I feel sorry for Tulyet, though,' said Langelee, nodding to where the Sheriff stood with the other town worthies, leaning heavily on a stick. 'He remains distressed by Helbye's betrayal. I can scarce believe it myself. Helbye always seemed such a solid man.'

'He liked to give that impression,' sniffed Cynric. 'But you should have heard him when he was in his cups, moaning and complaining. The Sheriff should have asked *me* about his loyalty. I would have given him the truth.'

'But Tulyet had some good news this morning,' Langelee went on. 'The King is satisfied that Moleyns' killer met his just deserts, and wrote to say that the matter is closed. The messenger is a friend of mine, and he told me that His Majesty is actually rather relieved that Moleyns is dead. They were friends, but . . .'

'But what?' asked Michael curiously.

'But his captivity meant he was no longer as rich as

he was, so he was unable to make such generous donations – at which point, he became more embarrassment
than boon. Tulyet has been told to raise no monument
to his memory, and to ensure he is quietly forgotten.'

'What about Egidia?' asked Bartholomew. 'Is she still
under arrest?'

Langelee shook his head. 'Stoke Poges has been
returned to her, and she will live out her life there in
quiet obscurity. Inge is dead, so she is unlikely to resume
a life of crime on her own. At least, not successfully.'

'Before she left, Dick asked her if Moleyns had a horned
serpent inked on his foot,' said Michael. 'He did not –
Thelnetham lied about that, as he lied about so much
else.'

Cynric was more interested in the thieves. 'Greed killed
Inge and his cronies,' he said. 'If they had stolen less, their
barge would not have sunk and they might have lived. It
was divine justice at its best. The same is true of Nicholas
– if he had not tried to kill me and the Sheriff, his leg
would not have been crushed, maiming him for life.'

'He died last night,' said Bartholomew soberly. 'I did
my best, but he lost the will to live once he heard that
Thelnetham was dead and all their plans lay in tatters.'

'I have arranged for him to be buried next to
Thelnetham and Frisby,' added Michael. 'Behind the
Gilbertine Priory.'

'In a muddy spot near the latrine,' smirked Cynric.
'Which is popular with slugs. Thelnetham would have
been mortified – and it serves him right.'

A short while later, when the celebrations were over, the
four Michaelhouse men were walking home when they
heard the clatter of hoofs. It was Meadowman, back at
last from his hunt for Whittlesey.

'Which was a waste of time,' muttered Cynric sourly.
'Given that Whittlesey was innocent. Indeed, he was

actually on our side, and gave Isnard a list of excellent places for begging, borrowing and stealing the supplies necessary for mending our pier.'

'You took your time,' said Michael, looking the exhausted beadle up and down. 'I was worried. I sent another patrol after you, but they lost you in London.'

'Because I went on to Canterbury,' explained Meadowman. 'I am not sure how to tell you this, Brother, and I have been thinking about the words every step of the way back . . .'

'Oh, Lord!' gulped Michael. 'Now what?'

'Whittlesey,' began Meadowman wretchedly. 'He rode straight to the Archbishop and told him that you would not make a very good prelate after all. He said that *he* should be Bishop of Rochester instead.'

Michael blinked. 'Then I had better ride there at once! Whittlesey will *not* snatch my mitre from under my nose.'

'I am afraid he already has,' whispered Meadowman. 'He was consecrated last Sunday. I tried to come back and warn you, but he kept me in prison until the rite was over.'

Michael regarded him in dismay. 'But Sheppey nominated *me* as his successor, a decision that was approved by the King. And the Archbishop, for that matter.'

'Whittlesey has a silver tongue, and he is the Archbishop's favourite nephew. Moreover, he is under the impression that you paid Godrich to spy on him. He believes it is because you have nasty secrets.'

'Godrich was monitoring Whittlesey on the grounds of a forged letter from Thelnetham and Nicholas,' objected Michael. 'It had nothing to do with me.'

'I told Whittlesey you were innocent, but he refused to listen.'

'But why did he not *ask* me about it?' cried Michael in bitter frustration. 'It was hardly cause to gallop off and steal my See.'

'To be honest, I suspect it was something he had been planning for some time,' said Meadowman. 'Claiming that you have "nasty secrets" is just a convenient excuse.'

'Which was why he followed you so slyly, of course,' said Bartholomew, tempted to point out that he had been wary of the envoy from the first time he had set eyes on him. 'He was not watching you to see if you were worthy to fill Sheppey's shoes, but to find a pretext for stealing them from you.'

Meadowman reached in his scrip and produced a piece of parchment. 'I have a message for you from someone else – a monk who came to Canterbury for the installation. He visited me in prison.'

Michael took the missive with hands that shook and scanned it quickly. 'It is from Prior Robert, head of the Rochester Benedictines, and an old friend. He informs me that Whittlesey will not rule for long, because the Bishop of Bangor is already contesting the appointment. There have been several unseemly spats, and he advises me to keep my distance.'

Bartholomew took the letter and read it himself. 'Perhaps this is a blessing in disguise, Brother. Robert says that both men are much diminished by this quarrel, and you do not want to be involved in that sort of thing.'

'You may be right,' sighed Michael. 'And I *was* worried about leaving my University so soon after Thelnetham's machinations. It will not hurt to oversee matters here a while longer.'

'It will not hurt at all,' agreed Langelee. 'And there will be other dioceses.'

'Not if the Bishop of Ely falls from grace,' said Michael unhappily. 'Because no one else at Avignon will remind the Pope that there is an eager and competent candidate for the next available bishopric.'

'Whittlesey will,' said Langelee. 'Write and congratulate him on his good fortune, and claim that you bear him no grudge. He will be so relieved that he is not to fight you as well as Bangor, that you will turn him into an ally. And if Ely does fall, who will be on hand here to step into the breach?'

Michael brightened. 'Ely would be much more convenient than Kent.'

'It would,' agreed Langelee. 'And once you are installed there, you can devise a plan to pay him back for this monstrous betrayal. It is—'

He stopped speaking as Clippesby arrived. The Dominican had Ethel the chicken under one arm and the College cat under the other. Neither looked particularly happy with the arrangement.

'A carriage has just arrived,' he reported, and smiled at Bartholomew. 'Matilde is in it.'

'So,' sighed Langelee ruefully. 'We keep Michael but lose Bartholomew. What a pity. Aungel is able, but hardly of the same calibre.'

'You had better go and meet her, Matt,' said Michael, when the physician made no effort to move. 'It is time to make your decision. And just be grateful that you have a choice – unlike me, presented with a *fait accompli*.'

'Well, go on, then, boy,' urged Cynric. 'See what terms she offers. You can always refuse.'

'You can,' agreed Langelee. 'And if you need help negotiating a better deal, then call on me. I will not let her cheat you.'

'Follow your heart, Matt,' said Michael softly. 'It will not let you down.'

HISTORICAL NOTE

Grand funerary monuments were popular among the medieval rich, and grieving kin had a choice of ways to commemorate their loved ones. The more expensive option was a tomb topped with a sculpted effigy, while the cheaper one was a brass. One of the most famous fourteenth-century latteners was Richard Lakenham, who had a wife named Cristine and an apprentice named James Reames.

A paper in *Historical Research* by Nigel Saul, Jonathan Mackman and Christopher Whittick relates the curious case of a mason named John Petit (he had an apprentice named Peter Lucas), who was taken to court for producing inferior work in 1421 by the executors of Sir John Dallingridge. One of these executors was Henry Cook the barber. A fragment of Dallingridge's tomb still survives in Bodiam Castle, but it is an alabaster effigy, not the marble tomb that was specified in the contract. This suggests that Petit's services were dispensed with, and someone else was hired to provide the finished product. Dallingridge was a Sussex man, and never made arrangements to join the University in Cambridge.

Other characters in *A Grave Concern* were also real. Michaelhouse scholars included Master Ralph de Langelee, Michael (de Causton), William (de Gotham), John Clippesby, Thomas Suttone, William Thelnetham and William Kolvyle (Colville). John Aungel, Francis Mallet and John Islaye were later members of the College.

Thomas Hopeman was a Dominican friar who got into trouble in 1355 for going overseas (probably to Avignon) without a licence; he wrote several commentaries on the

Bible. William Morden was Prior of the Cambridge Black Friars, and Byri (or Bury) was one of his priests. James Nicholas was a University clerk in the 1360s, while John Godrich was a Fellow of King's Hall. He was the son of the King's cook, and later became keeper of various royal forests.

Roger Frisby was a Franciscan priest who attended the University but later embroiled himself in politics and was hanged for treason in 1402. Richard Milde was vicar of St Clement's in the 1350s, and Hugh de Gundrede was a thief who spent time in Cambridge Gaol in the 1330s.

There was indeed an election for the post of Chancellor around 1360. This position had been held by Richard Lyng in 1339, 1345–1346 and 1351–1352. Lyng actually died in 1355. By March 1359, William Tynkell had stopped being Chancellor, and went on to an ecclesiastical career before his death in 1370. Thomas Suttone became Chancellor in March 1359, and was heavily involved in expanding Michaelhouse's holdings. He died in 1384.

John Sheppey, Bishop of Rochester, died in 1360. He was succeeded by the Benedictine William Whittlesey, who had been Master of Peterhouse. Whittlesey was related to Archbishop Islip, which may explain his meteoric rise. He stayed at Rochester for two years before becoming Bishop of Worcester, and eventually succeeded his uncle as Archbishop of Canterbury in 1368. He died six years later, and left his law books to Peterhouse.

Sir John Moleyns was a flamboyant character, who rose from obscure beginnings to embroil himself in all manner of trouble; his entry in the *Oxford New Dictionary of National Biography* lists him as 'administrator and criminal'. He married Egidia in the 1320s, and promptly murdered her uncle Peter Poges, so that she would inherit his estates. The manor of Stoke Poges then became the centre of Moleyns' power. He was a lawyer, and avoided a murder conviction by picking his own jury. His partner in crime was fellow Justice of the Common Bench, John Inge.

Moleyns was later accused of treason, and was obliged to flee to France. He returned to favour in 1346 by joining the Crécy campaign, but it was not long before he was in trouble again. He had been appointed Queen's Steward but by 1357 he had blotted his copy book by indulging in robbery, cattle rustling, horse theft, burglary and harbouring felons. He was found guilty and imprisoned in Windsor Castle. He was later taken to Nottingham, and then Cambridge, where he probably died in 1360. Egidia was pardoned shortly afterwards, and the estates that had been confiscated were returned to her. She died seven years later.